Starcrossed

A Starstruck Novel

BRENDA HIATT

ISBN: 1940618045
ISBN-13: 978-1-940618-04-3

DEDICATION

For everyone who has wished upon a star.

1

Rigel (RY-jel): *a star in the constellation Orion*

"Here, boy, hang this up." Allister Adair tosses his cashmere coat at me and continues talking on his cell while my parents just stand politely by.

My expression has to show what I think of the jerk, but since he's not looking, it doesn't much matter. Still, my mom gives me a tiny frown and shake of her head. I turn away and take the stupid coat to the hall closet.

This is Allister's third visit since September, when he found out about M—Princess Emileia to Allister and his cronies, Marsha Truitt to all the regular humans in town.

Of course, *I'm* the one who found her in the first place, but Allister never gives me any credit for that. No, it's clear he'd rather anyone but me had met her first. Like that would have kept M and me from forming our soul-deep bond. The bond Allister claims he doesn't believe in . . . but still blames me for.

"—better not to, just yet. We don't want to bias anything," he's saying into his phone when I come back. "Yes. Later, then." He hangs up and finally turns to greet my parents, who are just, you know, letting him stay in our *house*. For free. Whenever he wants.

"Council business," he tells them without apologizing. "I hope I haven't kept dinner waiting?"

"Not at all." My mom sounds perfectly pleasant, though I can tell by the way she holds her mouth that she's a little pissed. "Why don't you and Van go into the dining room and I'll have it on the table in a couple of minutes. Rigel, suppose you help me in the kitchen?"

I follow her, just as glad not to spend any extra time around Allister.

"Why do you let him—?" I whisper as soon as he seems out of earshot, but she immediately shushes me.

"Not now, Rigel. Here. Take these into the dining room." She

1

hands me a basket of dinner rolls and the butter dish.

Allister glances up when I come in, the first time today he's looked directly at me.

"I presume the Princess is well, or you would have told me immediately. Have you seen her recently?"

"M—er, the Princess is fine. I saw her in school yesterday." And this afternoon, after her Saturday Taekwondo class, but Allister doesn't need to know that. He's already glowering at my slip.

"I've told you before, boy, not to use that vulgar nickname. It's disrespectful."

My dad opens his mouth and for a second I think he's going to defend me, but then he closes it again.

"Sorry," I say. "It's what everyone calls her at school. Since, y'know, nobody there knows she's a princess."

Allister keeps frowning at me for a second, like he doesn't believe me or something—which is just nuts, since he has to know what I said is true. Then Dad finally speaks up.

"It's true, Allister, that all of her friends call her that. It's not a pet name of Rigel's, as you seem to think."

"Hm. Well." Allister pulls his gaze away from me and looks a little more cheerful. "Soon it won't matter anyway."

"What do you mean?" I demand. "What won't matter?"

"This little infatuation of yours," he says, "which I've warned you all along is ill-fated."

"Why? If you're going to try sending her away again—"

He looks almost genuinely startled. "No, no, of course not. She made her wishes on that point quite clear. Never mind, boy. Forget I said anything."

"Go see if your mother needs more help in the kitchen," Dad tells me before I can ask more questions. "She won't want these rolls to get cold before everything else is ready."

I leave them, but not before catching the smug expression on Allister's face. An expression I suspect doesn't bode well for me—or for M.

2

Emileia (em-i-LAY-ah): *current Banfriansa
(Princess); sole heir to the Nuathan monarchy*

For early November in north-central Indiana, it was a glorious day—
bright sunshine, an impossibly blue sky and just chilly enough for a
light jacket. Of course, it was even more glorious for me because I
was walking hand in hand with the most wonderful guy in the world.
Even after two months together, I still couldn't believe Rigel Stuart
—Jewel High's star quarterback and the most gorgeous guy I'd ever
met—was my boyfriend. No, not just my boyfriend. My soulmate.

"What do you think, M? Too cool for ice cream today?" Rigel
asked, slowing in front of Dream Cream, one of our favorite places
in tiny downtown Jewel.

I gazed up at him, savoring his flawless profile and rich,
mesmerizing voice. "Ice cream sounds good. We may not have many
more days like this before winter."

"Good point." He opened the screen door for me, then the solid
one with the store's name etched on the glass.

We headed for the counter, already perusing the hand-painted sign
on the wall above, when I heard a gasp off to my right and
simultaneously felt a familiar twinge. I instinctively glanced that way,
to find two middle-aged women I'd never seen before staring at me,
their mouths twin Os of amazement.

"Is it?" one whispered to the other, who nodded furiously.

"It is! Get your camera!"

Rigel and I both froze, then turned quickly back to the door.

"I just remembered, I left my bag at Glitterby's," I said, for the
benefit of old Mrs. Posner at the counter, who was watching us all
with a distinctly curious gleam in her eyes.

We left the shop and turned back up Diamond Street toward the
artisan jewelry store I'd mentioned, only to hear rapid footsteps

3

behind us.

"Wait!" one of the women called. "We just wanted to—"

Rigel rounded on them so quickly it startled me nearly as much as it did them. "Quiet! Are you crazy?" he demanded in a fierce whisper.

Rocking back on their heels, they gaped at him, then glanced at each other, their faces reddening.

"We're sorry," said the woman with the camera. "We didn't mean to cause a stir. But please, if I could just get one photo of the Princess?"

"Nobody is looking," the other woman said, peering up and down the street with such exaggerated caution, she was likely to draw attention just from that.

"Fine," I muttered. "Just be quick, okay?"

They exchanged ecstatic smiles, then took turns with the camera, each taking the other's picture as she stood next to me.

"Do you suppose—?" one asked then, holding the camera out to Rigel.

"No," he snapped. "That's enough. People are starting to stare. What are your names?"

They both reddened again. "Gladys and Orana Pickerell," one of them practically gasped in answer. "But please don't report us or . . . or anything. We didn't mean—"

"It's fine," I said with a quick frown at Rigel. "But please, don't do anything else to attract attention. And, uh, have a nice day."

Nodding and thanking me profusely, they backed away, then turned and hurried off down the street, whispering excitedly to each other.

"Well, that was awkward," I murmured.

Rigel took my hand again, which helped to ground me after that brush with the bizarre. "Yeah. And they should know better. They all should. You okay?"

I nodded, though I was still slightly freaked. About three weeks ago, word had gone out to all the transplanted Martian colonists here on Earth that their long-lost Princess—me—had been found alive. Since then, some had started making pilgrimages to Jewel to gawk at me. I didn't think I'd ever get used to it.

As recently as September, I was a complete nobody, possibly the most average, boring high school sophomore ever. So imagine my shock to learn that I'd been born in an underground colony on Mars, smuggled to Earth as a baby, then orphaned—twice—to be raised by people who still had no clue about my origins.

I hadn't yet come to terms with the idea that I was some kind of secret celebrity to thousands of people I hadn't even known existed until all those stunning revelations. Plus, I still felt kind of skittish around Martians other than Rigel and his family, since a bunch of them had tried to kill me just last month.

Even though it had now been two months since I'd learned my true identity, I still didn't feel anything like a princess. Probably because nobody in Jewel, apart from Rigel and his family, had the first inkling of the truth. My own family—my Aunt Theresa and Uncle Louie, that is—definitely didn't treat me like royalty. Quite the opposite.

Which reminded me.

"I won't be able to stay out very long this afternoon," I told Rigel. "I have laundry duty now that Aunt Theresa is working some evenings at the florist shop. I meant to get to it over the weekend, but . . ." I shrugged.

Now that football season had ended, leaving Rigel's afternoons free, we spent that extra time together in town more days than not. He wasn't allowed to come to my house unless my aunt or uncle were home, and I felt weird going to his place all the time—plus my aunt didn't like it.

"That's okay." He gave my hand a delicious squeeze. "I have to get home early, too. Allister is visiting again."

I grimaced. "This is, like, his third visit, isn't it?"

"Yeah." Rigel looked disgusted, too. "At least he's hasn't asked to see you again—yet."

"Thank goodness for small favors." I'd seen Allister Adair twice over the last month and both times had left a definite bad taste in my mouth.

For one thing, it was creepy the way he always *watched* me, like he was just waiting for me to screw up. He was the head dude on Earth of the Martian Royals—which, as far as I'd been able to figure out, was like their conservative party—so he seemed to think it was his job to make sure I acted like a Sovereign. Which I clearly didn't, not having been trained up to it. Like I cared.

For another thing, he'd once tried to force me to leave Jewel, Indiana—and Rigel—so he and his cronies could "keep me safe," which meant hiding me away in some Martian compound in Montana. I'd avoided that, but I didn't trust him not to come up with some other excuse to spirit me away in the dead of night.

Worst of all, he always made it crystal clear he *totally* did not approve of Rigel and me dating. I hoped he wouldn't still be around for Rigel's sixteenth birthday party, a week from Saturday.

"So, you still want that ice cream?" I asked, refusing to worry about it when I could be enjoying Rigel and one of the last nice days of the year.

"How was laundry duty?" Rigel asked on the way to our first class the next morning.

I wrinkled my nose. "Don't remind me. Four loads—and my aunt still got pissed because I put jeans and towels in together. How was your evening with Allister?"

He shrugged. "He's a pain, but Grandfather gets in tomorrow night. That usually helps a little."

Shim, Rigel's grandfather, seemed to be the only person Allister Adair ever deferred to, even though Shim wasn't a Royal like Allister. Maybe because Shim was the oldest Martian on Earth. Shim intimidated the heck out of me, too, but I liked him a lot and trusted him completely. The fact that he'd saved my life last month had something to do with that, along with him running interference with Allister.

A minute later I took my seat in Geometry next to Debbi Andrews.

"Hey, did you hear there's a new transfer?" she asked.

Petite and blond, Deb was my second-best friend after Brianna Morrison, though lately it seemed like the two of them were closer to each other than to me. Not that I could blame them, between the time I spent with Rigel and all the secrets I couldn't tell them.

"Really? Two in one semester must be a record." I grinned over at Rigel, who'd been the new kid at the start of the school year. "Boy or girl?"

"Boy. I haven't seen him yet. I think he's a junior or senior. Natalie said—"

The teacher cleared his throat then and Deb had to shut up. I was sure I'd hear more later, from Bri if not from Deb. New students were a huge deal at our little rural school.

Sure enough, the new guy was the first thing Bri talked about when we met up with her in the lunchroom a couple hours later.

"Hey, Rigel, looks like you're off the hook for the basketball team." Bri had been pestering Rigel for days to try out, egged on by her father, who was on the coaching staff. "This new guy, Sean, is just what our sucky team needs, according to my dad."

"Sean?" Deb asked eagerly. "So that's his name?"

I glanced at Rigel, who looked more relieved than curious. I, meanwhile, was having a mild *deja vu* moment, remembering when Bri had been all excited about the wonderful new quarterback we were getting—Rigel.

"Yeah, Sean O'Gara," Bri told Deb.

"So, is it true he's from Ireland? That's what Natalie told me this morning."

Bri nodded, her long, dark curls bouncing. "That's what Dad said, too. I didn't even know they played basketball in Ireland! But apparently it's huge there."

"Ireland? Really?" I glanced at Rigel again, remembering something he'd told me a while back, and saw he looked a little more interested.

"Yeah, he and his family just moved here last— Ooh, that must be him!" Bri broke off to point.

Of course, we all looked. The new guy was definitely tall enough to play basketball, maybe three or four inches taller than Rigel. He was fair bordering on pale, with bright, copper-colored hair. Very good looking, though of course he couldn't compete with Rigel in that department. Who could?

"Let's go say hi," Bri suggested, already heading his way. "You know, welcome him to Jewel."

It looked to me like plenty of people—mainly girls—were already doing just that. Again I was reminded of Rigel's first day, especially when I saw Trina Squires—cheerleader, flirt and bitch extraordinaire —saunter up to to the newcomer. Rigel and I followed Bri and Deb, since it seemed the nice thing to do. We were maybe halfway across the lunchroom when both of us stopped cold to stare at each other.

"Do you—?" Rigel asked.

I nodded. "I feel it, too." It was the *brath*—the weird, almost electric vibe Martians sense when other Martians are nearby. Like what I'd felt from those two tourist women yesterday.

Sean O'Gara was one of us.

3

brath: *Martian "vibe" detectable by other Martians*

By unspoken agreement (Rigel and I were getting better and better at that as our special bond strengthened), both of us slowed our approach to this new Martian in our midst. I was trying not to panic, but couldn't help remembering that the last Martian who'd shown up unannounced at our school had wanted to kill me.

Who *was* this guy, really, and why was he here?

We were close enough now that I could see the scattering of freckles across his nose and cheeks. His smile seemed open and friendly and he didn't *look* more than seventeen or eighteen. According to Rigel and his parents, even though Martians typically lived at least twice as long as "normal" humans, aging didn't slow until full adulthood. So maybe he really was just a teenager. Or maybe—

"Come on," Rigel murmured, cutting into my mental babbling. "Might as well make nice since it's too late to hide."

It didn't help to know he was worried, too.

Even as a sophomore, Rigel had enough social status as quarterback to make the crowd part before him. As Rigel's girlfriend, I had enough that people grudgingly let me through, too. A moment later Rigel was face to face with the newcomer, oh-so-casually shielding me as he stuck out his hand.

"Hey, welcome to Jewel."

"Thanks," Sean replied. He seemed even taller up close, at least six-six.

Maybe it was the press of people or maybe he just hadn't been concentrating the way we were, but not until they gripped hands did the newcomer realize Rigel was another Martian. Sean's eyes widened, then narrowed, and then he released Rigel's hand like it had burned him.

"Let me guess. Stuart?" Sean's voice had a slight Irish lilt, not as

9

strong as I'd've expected from someone who grew up there. I wondered if he really had—or if he was just good with accents.

"Rigel Stuart. That's right." Rigel's voice didn't give anything away.

Sean's gaze slid past him to me and his eyes widened again. "Then this must be—"

"Marsha Truitt," I said quickly before he could say something he shouldn't in front of all these witnesses. Those tourists yesterday weren't the first to get stupidly obvious in town and I definitely didn't want it to happen right here in the lunchroom. "Everyone calls me M."

"M," he repeated, his surprise giving way to a perfectly charming smile. "It's really great to meet you." He extended his hand.

I hesitated for just a fraction of a second before doing the same, hoping I didn't look as nervous as I felt. He seemed harmless enough, so far.

But the moment our hands touched, I nearly jerked away and had to clamp my teeth together to keep from exclaiming aloud. Sean's hand gave me a zap nearly as intense as the one I'd felt the first time Rigel touched me!

That first jolt, back on the second day of school, had totally freaked both of us out. We still felt an echo of it every time we touched, though now it was exciting instead of scary. Later I'd discovered all Martians gave me a slight tingle, but Sean's was more than that—more like the half-electric, half-adrenaline zing I got from Rigel. *No* other Martian had ever done that.

Sean's hand—his very big hand—trapped mine for what seemed like minutes but was probably only seconds, while I struggled to control my shock. I glanced up, expecting him to be as startled as I was, but instead found him watching me intently, an almost expectant look in his brilliantly blue eyes. Then, finally, he let go.

Frowning, I immediately stepped back, closer to Rigel, but Sean gave me a knowing smile and the ghost of a wink.

Before I could think of anything to say, Trina stepped in. For once, I was actually grateful. "So, Sean, why don't I introduce you around to some of the people you should know?" Her dismissive glance making it clear I wasn't in that category, she turned to Rigel with a smile. She still hadn't given up trying to steal him back from me. I hoped Sean might give her another focus.

"Looks like you've already met Rigel Stuart, the guy responsible for taking Jewel's football team to its first Regional championship in twenty years," she said.

Sean nodded, though it looked like he dragged his eyes away from me with an effort. "Yeah. Quarterback, right?"

"Right." Rigel took my hand again. "C'mon, M, let's go eat."

I was too surprised to argue, since Rigel was almost never rude. But now I could feel his uneasiness, maybe mixed with some irritation. Unfortunately, thoughts didn't come through as clearly as emotions. Had he been able to sense that jolt I'd gotten from Sean?

"What was that about?" I asked once we were out of even Martian earshot. "Should I be worried about this guy?"

He didn't answer until we were back at our table—alone, since Bri and Deb were still in the circle around Sean. "I don't know. There was something about the way he looked at you— And no, I'm not just being jealous," he added with a crooked grin.

"I wasn't going to ask." Though the thought *did* cross my mind. "You should know by now you never need to be."

Because Rigel and I were bonded by the *graell*, a powerful link so rare that most Martians regarded it as folklore instead of fact. So much so, I wasn't sure even his family had totally accepted it.

Our bond enhanced us to the point that I no longer needed the glasses I'd worn all my life, and Rigel's football skills had attracted national attention. We could also sense each other's moods and sometimes, if we focused hard enough, each other's thoughts.

The downside of our bond was that it really sucked to be apart. In September, when we broke up for a couple of weeks, we both became physically ill. So even if I hadn't been totally, irrevocably in love with Rigel, the very idea of wanting to be with another guy was ludicrous. Already, I was wondering if I'd imagined that unexpectedly strong zing from Sean.

"I guess we'd better find out what he's really doing here, huh?" I finally said when Rigel remained silent.

"Yeah. I'll see if my folks know anything."

"Or we could just ask him," I suggested. "Privately, I mean."

Rigel frowned again. "Only if it's both of us. Don't be alone with him until we know more, okay? And it's *not* jealousy! I just want you safe, especially after—"

"I know."

We'd come way too close to losing each other last month before we defeated those Martians who wanted to invade Earth and exterminate me, the last of the monarchy. At one point during that battle I'd thought Rigel was dead and I never, ever wanted to experience *that* again. So I understood how he felt.

"Maybe after school we can—" I began, but Bri and Deb rejoined us before I could finish.

"Wow, he's a hottie," Deb said, slipping into her chair across from me. "Kinda tall for me, but I could adapt." Deb was barely five feet tall, but blond, cute and curvy enough that guys noticed her anyway.

"No fair—you can date anyone without looking silly, unlike me. Leave the tall guys for us tall girls." Bri, who had long, dark, curly hair, was only an inch or so taller than me, about five-seven, so hardly a giant. But a cute new guy was a cute new guy, as far as she was concerned. I'd worry about her if she wasn't interested.

Though knowing what little I did already about Sean, I'd also be worried if he returned her interest.

"You guys did notice he's totally swamped by cheerleaders, right?" I said, trying to inject a shred of reality into the conversation. It was true that since I'd been dating Rigel, Bri's and Deb's social status had climbed a few rungs along with mine, but we were still basically sophomore geeks.

Bri gave me a sly grin. "That didn't stop you from going after Rigel, did it?"

"Well, no," I admitted. There were extenuating circumstances in my case—like us being the only two Martians in the school and having this amazing, soul-deep bond. But to anyone who didn't know that, it was like the geekiest girl in our class had just lucked into having the hottest guy in school fall for her. Who was I to stomp on anybody's dreams when mine had come so incredibly true?

"He has the dreamiest eyes," Deb was saying, glancing over her shoulder at Sean. I wondered if the poor guy was going to have a chance to eat lunch. "Hey, did you know he has a sister here, too? She's younger—a sophomore, like us. She was in my English class."

"And you're just now telling us this?" I exclaimed, exchanging a quick look with Rigel, wondering if this news would make him worry more or less.

Deb shrugged. "I was a little distracted," she confessed, with another look at Sean.

"So what's she like?" I prodded. "Is she here in the cafeteria?"

Deb dragged her eyes away from Sean to scan the lunchroom. "I don't see— Oh, there she is, over in the corner, by herself."

"Poor thing," I said instinctively, remembering way too many times last year when Bri and Deb were busy with chorus and nobody else would sit with me. "I'm going to go say hi to her."

Rigel came with me, though I suspected his motive was less social than mine. Still, it would be nice for both of us to have other Martian friends our own age. Wouldn't it?

The girl looked up as the two of us approached. She was as pale as her brother, but with dark hair—nearly as dark as Rigel's. She was also very pretty. Judging by the glances from several guys at nearby tables, she wouldn't be sitting alone tomorrow.

I felt a teensy twinge of something like envy or even jealousy. Yeah, it was true that my skin had cleared up since bonding with Rigel. My mousy brown hair had even developed waves and highlights. But I'd spent so many years being brutally plain that I still tended to think of myself that way—and to envy those who obviously weren't.

The stranger's long-lashed, blue-gray eyes widened as we got close enough to feel her *brath* and, presumably, for her to feel ours. This time I spoke before Rigel could.

"Hi, welcome to Jewel. I'm Marsha Truitt, but you can call me M. What's your name?"

Her eyes got even bigger. "You're— You mean— I didn't— Um, Molly. Molly O'Gara. Hi."

She was so flustered I felt sorry for her, no matter how pretty she was. She glanced over at Rigel and he smiled, an apparently genuine smile.

"Hi, Molly. I'm Rigel Stuart. It's great to have you guys here. We'll uh, talk later, okay?"

Her expression showed clearly that she knew what he meant—that what we needed to talk about couldn't be said in a crowded cafeteria. But her expression showed just as clearly that she was noticing how gorgeous Rigel was, and I wasn't sure how I felt about that.

"Sure, that'll be grand." Her smile seemed to be for both of us.

13

Like her brother, she had only a slight Irish accent.

"Later, then." I returned her smile. "I hope you have a good first day."

She nodded, still looking a little stunned.

We went back to our table to wolf down our lunches before the bell rang, then headed to History class with Bri and Deb.

"So, does she seem nice?" Bri asked.

I shrugged. "We only talked for a sec, but yeah, I guess."

Rigel didn't answer, which left me wondering what he thought of her. I'd ask him later.

As it turned out, Molly and Sean were both in our U.S. History class. They arrived together just before class started and looked around for empty seats after checking in with the teacher. Again I took pity on Molly and motioned her over to a desk near mine. Her face brightened, making her even prettier, and she hurried to join us, while Sean sat with a couple of jocks near the door.

"Thanks," she whispered.

I quickly introduced Bri and Deb and we all promised to hang out together soon. Rigel and I would have to find a way to talk privately with Molly and Sean before everybody got too chummy, just in case there was some reason not to.

I hoped there wouldn't be, though, and not only for my own safety. Because, it occurred to me, it would be really nice to have a girlfriend I didn't have to lie to.

4

Echtran (EK-tran): *person of Martian birth or descent living on Earth; expatriate*

Rigel and I didn't get the chance we'd—well, I'd—hoped for until after school. Molly had been in my French class, too, but hadn't been able to sit near me, so all we'd managed to do was smile at each other. But after my final class (during which Trina and her pals went on and on . . . and on . . . about Sean), I saw not only Rigel, but Sean and Molly waiting by my locker.

"Hey." Rigel greeted me with a quick kiss on the cheek that inexplicably made both Sean and Molly frown. "We ran into each other a couple minutes ago and Sean says he doesn't have practice today."

Sean quickly switched to a charming smile, though his sister's frown was slower to fade. "Yeah, Coach said I could have a day or two to settle in before starting. Mum's picking us up, but she's running late, so this seemed like a good chance to talk. She can drop you both off after."

"Sounds good," I said. "Where's a good place? It'll be chilly outside, but probably more private."

"Courtyard?" Rigel suggested. "No wind and we'll see anyone coming before they can hear us."

Still weirded out by that zing Sean had given me, I kept my distance as we walked—but tried not to be obvious about it. We all talked about everyday school stuff until we were in the courtyard with the door closed.

"So, what's the sitch?" Rigel asked without preamble. "What are you guys doing here, really?"

Sean and Molly exchanged a look that I thought wasn't so much confused as trying to *look* confused.

"Um, going to school?" Sean suggested.

15

"Right." I didn't try to hide my skepticism. "But why here and why now? You're not really going to tell us it's pure coincidence that four Martians from three different families just happened to end up in Jewel, Indiana, of all places?"

Sean looked back and forth between us. "But it *is* coincidence that both of *you* just happen to be here?"

"Not exactly," Rigel allowed, "but we can talk about that later. So?"

There was a brief, tense silence. To my surprise, it was Molly who broke it.

"It's not like we can keep it a secret, Sean," she said to her brother. Then, looking directly at me, "We're here because of you, of course. Our parents have been heading up the resistance for years, trying to get rid of that *unbaen*, uh, dictator, Faxon. It's why we had to leave Mars. But now you've been found . . ."

"How long ago did you leave Mars?" I interrupted. "And why, exactly?" It still felt strange to talk about this sci-fi stuff so matter-of-factly.

"Over a year ago," Sean answered. "Faxon's thugs raided a resistance meeting and got their hands on files incriminating our family. We—most of us—were lucky to escape." Both of their faces turned bleak.

I was almost afraid to ask. "What happened?"

"Our sister Elana." Sean's voice held anger as well as sorrow. "She was captured, maybe even killed. We still don't know, though we've been trying to find out ever since."

Molly nodded mutely, her beautiful blue-gray eyes tragic.

"So Faxon's thugs even drag off kids now?" Rigel was clearly aghast.

"I wouldn't put it past them," Sean said, "but Elana was—is—nearly forty."

"I'm sorry." I meant it, though the huge spread in ages between some Martian siblings still boggled me a little. I'd recently learned Rigel's father had a brother *forty-five* years older than he was.

"That doesn't explain why you're *here*," Rigel pointed out. "How is M supposed to help? Or is that even what you have in mind?"

Molly found her voice again. "Of course she can help—eventually. Meanwhile, our . . . family wanted to be here, where we can help

16

protect her and make sure she gets the instruction she'll need to eventually take her place as our leader. It's really important that everyone—*Echtrans* and especially Nuathans back on Mars—know that's happening."

I wasn't sure I liked the direction this conversation was taking. "Why?" I asked. "How can it make a difference now, when I'm only fifteen?"

"Faxon's grip is slipping." Sean's intensity was understandable, considering what had happened to his family. "Even before we left, some of his original supporters were joining the resistance—sick of the corruption and how he was screwing up a system that's worked for centuries. Now that word's got back to Mars about you, our dad says the resistance has exploded—more than quadrupled in size. But some still aren't sure a return to the monarchy is the way to go, even if they hate Faxon. They need convincing. Hearing that you're getting the training and forming the alliances that everyone expects of a Sovereign will help do that."

"Alliances?" Rigel echoed. "What does that mean, exactly?"

Sean's ears reddened but he shrugged. "Political stuff. My folks can explain it better than I can."

"But I thought—" Molly began. Her brother shook his head and she broke off, frowning at him suspiciously.

"So, is it true Faxon actually sent people here to try to kill you?" Sean's abrupt question was a blatant attempt to change the subject but I played along.

"Yeah, this guy Boyne Morven, Faxon's head nasty on Earth, was controlling a bunch of *Echtrans* with an Ossian Sphere. He brought a couple dozen of them to Jewel, along with the sphere, to get rid of me. But Rigel's grandfather, Shim, called in his own people and we, um, won," I ended lamely, realizing that the whole story would take way too long. Especially since I wanted more answers.

They both nodded. "That's about what MARSTAR reported, but we wondered if they told us everything," Sean said. "How did—"

He broke off to reach into his pocket and pull out a cell phone. Something I *still* didn't have. Not that I was bitter.

"Hey, Mum, yeah. Be right there. Um, do you mind a couple of extra passengers? (pause) Rigel Stuart and . . . Princess Emileia." There was a long pause and I heard a suddenly high-pitched voice talking very fast. "Yeah."

He turned to us. "Mum's out front. We can talk more in the car."

We all left the courtyard, my mind still teeming with questions. I couldn't quite wrap my head around the fact that these two had actually grown up in Nuath, the colony on Mars, and had lived there until so recently. What was it like now? Did I maybe have relatives there? There was so much I didn't know, so much they might be able to tell me.

So much I couldn't ask inside the school, where we might be overheard.

I settled for a question I could ask. "Where did you live in Ireland?"

"Where all the—I mean, a little village on the coast, nowhere near anything else," Sean said. "Bailerealta."

The Martian village I'd heard about. Cool.

"How many people live there? Is it as big as Jewel?"

They both laughed. "Hardly," Molly said. "I think at last count there were not quite four hundred people living there full time. Four less, now we've left."

"A whole town the size of this school?" I marveled. "And I thought Jewel was the middle of nowhere."

Sean chuckled and shook his head. "You have no idea. Oh, there's our mum."

We'd reached the front doors and he pointed at a rather battered maroon minivan with rust spots along the wheel wells. A far cry from the shiny Audi and SUV Rigel's parents drove. But then, Rigel's parents had been on Earth for seventy-five years, plus his mom was a doctor and his dad a computer consultant.

The O'Garas might have had to leave Mars with nothing, for all I knew. I felt a surge of sympathy since I knew what it was like to be one of the have-nots in school.

Sean opened the front passenger door for me. "Mum, this is . . . M. That's what people call her here."

Their mom looked about the same age as Rigel's folks—meaning not old enough to have teenaged kids. Not to mention a forty-year old daughter! She was a little on the plump side, but very pretty, with red hair bordering on orange and eyes as bright blue as Sean's.

"Hi," I said cautiously. Careful not to touch Sean, I climbed in next to her.

"Oh, my," she almost squeaked. "I mean, it's such an honor, Excellency. I hope these two scamps haven't taken any liberties."

"Um, liberties?" Confused, I glanced into the back seat, where the other three were buckling their seatbelts.

"I mean, I hope they've shown you the proper respect," she clarified.

"Oh, um, yeah, they've been fine. Er, I should tell you, Mrs. O'Gara, that nobody around here knows who I am except Rigel and his folks. So I'm not used to being treated special or anything. I'm just M, and that's fine."

Clearly startled, she stared at me for a long moment before suddenly relaxing into a smile. "Of course. How silly of me. You didn't even know who you were until quite recently did you, luv?"

"Not till a couple months ago, no. But Sean and Molly said you guys moved here because of me? I'm still a little confused about why." Maybe she'd be more forthcoming with reasons than they'd been.

She put the car in drive and pulled her gaze away to watch the road. "It was . . . thought that we could be of the most use here."

So she was going to be evasive, too. I started getting nervous again, though it was hard to imagine this warm, motherly woman having a sinister motive.

"Thought by who?" I prodded, hoping to shake loose more information.

"It was the consensus of quite a few people, actually. And, of course, we felt it would be good for Sean—and Molly—to get to know you, given our political connections. No doubt you can learn from them, as well."

Again with the politics. "Was there anyone *specific* who asked you to come here?" I was getting tired of the runaround.

She hesitated so long I thought she wasn't going to answer. Several fields of corn stubble went by my window before she finally said, "Well, yes. In fact, I believe you've met him once or twice. Allister is pleased that you're adjusting so well to your new status, but wants to be sure nothing, er, interferes with your continued progress."

"Allister?" Rigel asked sharply from behind me. "Allister Adair?"

"Aye, that's right, dear," Mrs. O'Gara replied, never taking her eyes from the road. I thought her expression looked a little tense.

"But . . . he's staying at our house right now. And he never mentioned anything about another Martian family moving to Jewel." Suspicion rang in his voice.

I gauged how fast the car was going, wondering how much it would hurt if I jumped out at this speed. If these people were all lying, there was no knowing what they really intended. They could even be another group sent to kill me. What if—

"Our house is a bit small for guests, you see, especially with all the boxes and clutter, as we're just moving in. I'm sure he felt he'd be more comfortable with you. As for not mentioning us, he, er, implied he isn't precisely your favorite person, Excellency. He may have wanted you to meet us without any preconceptions."

I relaxed slightly. Much as I disliked Allister, I was pretty sure he didn't want me dead. Just practically in prison.

"In fact," she continued, "I probably shouldn't have mentioned the connection at all just yet. I do hope he won't be put out with me."

"What connection, exactly?" If Allister had specifically sent for them—

She turned onto my street, making me wonder how she knew where I lived. Or did all the Martians know that now? I hoped not, but she pulled right into my driveway without me giving her any directions. She stopped the car and turned to face me, her expression anxious, which lessened my own fear a little.

"Allister Adair is my brother, Princess. Uncle to Sean and Molly."

5

Duchas (doo-kas): *normal Earth humans*

A whole different fear assailed me. "Wait. You mean, he moved you all to Jewel to . . . indoctrinate me or something?" I demanded.

"It's not like that," Sean said from behind me.

I turned around to glare at him and noticed Rigel wasn't looking happy, either. "So what *is* it like?"

Molly answered me. "He—we—thought you should get to know other Martians. Besides the Stuarts, I mean. You haven't had a chance to meet many, especially our age. And it will be important later for you to have . . . friends." I could tell she'd almost used a different word.

Still, her explanation did remind me of my earlier thought, how it might be nice to be friends. "I . . . *guess* that makes sense," I said slowly. I wanted to talk privately with Rigel before deciding how I really felt about all this, but now obviously wasn't the time.

"Thanks for the ride, Mrs. O'Gara. I'll see you guys at school tomorrow," I added to Sean and Molly. Then, in the half second when nobody else was looking, I mouthed "Call me" to Rigel.

Without a backward look, I went up the steps, across the wide porch and into the house—a supposedly historic two story, two bedroom, one bath house that had seen much better days. After pouring myself a glass of milk, I spread out my books on the kitchen table and started on my homework while waiting impatiently for the phone to ring.

I hoped Rigel would get a chance to call before my aunt got home, since the only phone in this creaky old house was the one in the kitchen, hardwired to the wall. It wasn't even a cordless. Which meant no private phone calls. Ever. I hated that.

I made my distracted way through Geometry, History and French, glancing at the clock every five minutes, before the phone finally, blessedly rang.

"Sorry," Rigel said as soon as I picked up. "The O'Garas came inside and only left a minute ago."

Just the sound of his voice calmed me. "That's okay. But my aunt will be home any time now. What's the deal? Did you find out?"

"Some, but I'm sure there's more they're not telling. It's pretty much what they said—Allister getting all proactive about preparing you for your role and stuff. According to them, more *Echtrans* will be moving to Jewel soon. Sounds like Allister wants to turn it into a kind of headquarters."

I wasn't sure how I felt about that. On the one hand, it was appealing to think I might meet more Martians who didn't want to kill me, maybe even make some friends. On the other hand, they'd probably gawk at me, the way the few who'd come through town so far had done. That wasn't appealing at all.

"What, since he can't convince me to go to Montana, he's going to bring everyone here? Turn Jewel into a new compound?"

I thought maybe he'd laugh, but he didn't. "Something like that. He probably thinks if you meet lots of other Martians you won't spend so much time with me. He's never been exactly happy about, you know, us."

Yeah, I knew. He'd made that pretty obvious. "Hasn't Shim convinced him we're really bonded by now? He said he was going to try."

Rigel's sigh came through the line. "He *has* tried. I've heard him. But Allister doesn't believe in the *graell*. Says it's just myth and wishful thinking and teenage hormones, and that Grandfather is only seeing what he wants to see."

"Sounds like Allister is only seeing what *he*— Oops, Aunt Theresa is home. Talk to you later. Arboretum after dinner?"

"I'll be there. Love you, M." He hung up before I could say it back.

"Talking to that boy again?" Aunt Theresa asked before even saying hello. Then, before I could answer, "Take your homework upstairs. I need the table to grade papers."

She knew Rigel's name perfectly well, but she never used it—to me, anyway. She was more than willing to say it when bragging to her friends that her niece was dating the champion quarterback. I'd overheard her a few times. To me, she acted like he was a budding sexual deviant or something.

"Nice to see you, too," I muttered under my breath as I gathered up my books so she could savage her poor third graders' assignments with her red pen. If she heard me, she pretended not to.

As usual, Uncle Louie didn't get home from work until after seven and, also as usual, dinner conversation consisted mostly of stories about the car lot where he worked as a salesman.

"So I told him, sure, I'd call him if we get a Porsche in," Uncle Louie was saying. "Like anybody in this town has one to trade in?" He laughed loudly.

I forced out a chuckle along with Aunt Theresa, who didn't pay much more attention to Uncle Louie's stories than I did. Not that he seemed to notice.

"You'd think someone who can afford a Porsche would be able to read the big 'All-American Auto Sales' sign, wouldn't you?" he continued. "I told him if he really wanted a foreign car, I could give him a great deal on one of the Toyotas in the back lot. We can't give those suckers away in this town. But no, he said he'd just go to Indy for a Porsche. More than an hour away, but it's his time and money." He laughed again.

It really wasn't funny, since I knew the dealership was struggling. If it closed, Uncle Louie would have to look for a job in Kokomo or even Indianapolis. Already, Aunt Theresa was working a couple evenings a week at Regina's Flowers For All Occasions, and once I turned sixteen I'd probably try to get an after school job to help out, too.

Uncle Louie launched into the next story—something about one of the guys in the service department forgetting his lunch—and my thoughts drifted to everything that had happened today, and about my planned meeting with Rigel. I hoped Aunt Theresa wouldn't figure out why I'd started jogging after dinner most nights.

I also wondered how Allister could be so willfully blind to Rigel's and my bond. He'd heard about the bolt of lightning we'd generated to knock Boyne Morven's sphere thingy out of the sky before it could kill us. According to Shim, that *proved* we had a *graell* bond. And what else could explain the miraculous cure of my nearsightedness, or even my acne? Or how sick Rigel and I both got when we tried to stay apart for a couple of weeks?

Oh, wait. We hadn't really told anybody about that, though his parents *had* to notice. Still, there was plenty of other evidence, if Allister weren't too stubborn to see it. Just because Rigel was from the wrong clan or party or whatever . . .

The second I finished eating, I jumped up to do the dishes so I'd be able to meet Rigel. Aunt Theresa didn't like me going out alone after eight-thirty, now that the days were getting shorter.

After standing the last glass upside down in the drying rack, I bolted upstairs to change into my sweats and running shoes, then hurried back down. "Going running," I yelled toward the kitchen as I headed for the front door.

"Wait, Marsha," Uncle Louie called from the other side of the hall. "There are some people here I want you to meet."

Irritated at the delay but curious, I went through the rounded archway into our little formal living room and stopped dead. The whole O'Gara family was sitting there—Sean, Molly, their mother, and a sandy-haired man I assumed was their father, chatting with Uncle Louie and Aunt Theresa like they were old friends.

"Um, hi," I said, and they all looked up—the three I'd already met smiling and Mr. O'Gara with the slightly awed expression his wife had when I first got into her car today.

Uncle Louie, oblivious as always, stood up to make introductions. "Marsha, these are the O'Garas—Lili, Quinn, Sean and Molly. This is our niece, Marsha." I guess they hadn't had time to tell him we'd mostly already met.

He continued before any of us could speak. "They bought a minivan from me yesterday and when we did the paperwork, I saw they'd moved in just around the corner, on Opal. So I told them to stop by, especially since their kids are about your age." He beamed around at all of us.

Right around the corner? No wonder Mrs. O'Gara had known where I lived. Or—a niggling suspicion arose—did they move into that house *because* it was right around the corner?

"That's great," I said, and hoped my cheerfulness didn't sound forced. "So we'll be riding the same bus and everything?"

"I guess," Sean said. "At least until I get my Indiana driver's license. And, er, a car."

Mrs. O'Gara raised an eyebrow, then turned back to me. "Marsha,

I have a favor to ask. I understand you take the same U. S. History class that Molly and Sean do, and it's a subject neither of them has ever studied. Would you be willing to tutor them a bit, since they're coming in mid term?"

"Sure." My smile was genuine now, which seemed to reassure Molly, who'd been looking embarrassed. "It'll be fun. And a good review for me, before finals."

"That's very kind of you, your, er, Marsha," said Mr. O'Gara, who still looked a little nervous. "I'm sure Sean and Molly will appreciate your help enormously."

They both nodded, Molly eagerly and Sean looking a little sheepish.

"Marsha is a very good student," Aunt Theresa informed them, managing to sound pompous instead of complimentary.

There was an awkward silence, then Sean asked, "So, you like to run?"

I glanced down at my sweats and running shoes. "Um, yeah. It's an easy way to keep in shape." I wondered how soon I'd be able to get away. The clock over the fireplace showed it was almost eight-thirty now, which meant Rigel was probably already waiting in the arboretum.

"Marsha, why don't you bring out coffee and some of those cookies I baked yesterday," Aunt Theresa said, dashing my hopes. "You can run any time," she added, which meant my disappointment must have shown. Oops.

"Sure, no problem." I headed to the kitchen, wishing for the umpteenth time that I had a cell phone, so I could send Rigel a quick text or something to let him know what was going on. I got out coffee cups and a plate for the cookies, then glanced at the phone on the wall. Maybe, if I was *really* quiet—

"Need any help?" I turned to see Sean standing in the kitchen doorway wearing an apologetic smile. "Sorry to descend on you in force like this," he whispered, coming over to pour coffee into the cups. "It was Dad's idea to take your uncle up on his invite tonight."

"That's okay," I lied, edging away from him. "Like Aunt Theresa said, I can run anytime. You're new neighbors, and this is just standard Indiana hospitality. You might as well get used to it." I gave him my best smile—the best one I ever gave to anyone who wasn't

Rigel—to gloss over my earlier reluctance, which he most have noticed.

I wondered if he also noticed how I avoided touching him as we put the filled coffee cups, cream and sugar on Aunt Theresa's antique black and gold tray. Sean carried out the tray while I followed with a plate of oatmeal-cranberry-walnut cookies.

As the next half hour ticked past, Aunt Theresa and Uncle Louie made small talk with the O'Garas about mundane things like grocery stores and churches and dentists' offices. Everything seemed so . . . so *normal*, it was hard for even me to believe our new neighbors had come to Earth from Mars barely over a year ago.

Finally, after receiving *way* too many details on what little Jewel had to offer, the O'Garas stood to go.

"Once we're all unpacked, we'll have to have you over for dinner," Mrs. O'Gara said to Aunt Theresa as everyone headed slowly toward the front door.

"Why, how kind. We'd be delighted." Aunt Theresa seemed to genuinely like these people, which was seemed unfair considering how stand-offish she'd always been toward the Stuarts. I'd assumed it was because they weren't third generation Jewelites, like she and Uncle Louie were, but apparently not.

By the time all the goodbyes were said and the O'Garas gone, it was a quarter past nine.

"So, um, can I go running now?" I asked without much hope.

Of course, Aunt Theresa shook her head. "Not this late, on a school night. You can get your exercise in taekwondo class tomorrow."

"But the reason I've started running is so I'll have more stamina for taekwondo," I explained in a last-ditch effort.

"I said no, Marsha. Not tonight. Now take all these cups into the kitchen and wash them so they can dry overnight."

With a sigh, I complied. Rigel had probably given up and gone back home by now anyway. I dawdled around the kitchen, drying and putting away dishes, hoping for a few moments alone so I could call him. But Aunt Theresa and Uncle Louie stayed within earshot, mostly talking about how nice the O'Garas were, until it was too late to call. I'd just have to explain to him tomorrow.

6

Rigel (RY-jel): *the 7th brightest star visible from Earth*

I check my cell phone again. 9:37pm. No effing way M is coming tonight. Her gorgon of an aunt never lets her out of the house this late.

Without her here, "our" metal bench in the arboretum is freezing my butt off, so I stand up.

I'm dying to talk to M. Shoot, just to be with her, since it's been a while since we've had real alone time. Long enough that I'm feeling a little off. And grouchy.

But if I'm not home by ten I'll catch hell from my parents. When Asshole Allister stays at our house, they're suddenly strict about stuff like me staying out late on school nights. Like it's a point of honor to prove to him they can control me.

I grab my bike from the rack by the arboretum entrance and take one last look down Diamond toward M's house, just in case. Nope, no sign of her. Feeling like my skin is too tight, I start home. Wasted evening.

I'm not blaming M, since she doesn't have a cell or even a private landline to let me know what's going on. Another one of her aunt's archaic rules. She's probably as pissed as I am that she can't get out of the house.

I go three blocks before I realize I'm pedaling way faster than a normal *Duchas*, even a jock. Luckily hardly anybody is around this late, since Jewel rolls up the sidewalks after dark. If it weren't for M, this town would suck.

'Course, if it weren't for M, we never would have come here at all. I'd probably have spent the last six years in California, going to the same school with the same kids, having actual friends—

I cut off that thought with a shudder. Because my life started, in every way that matters, when I met M in August. I can't think of a single thing I'd trade for what she and I have now.

Too keyed up to slow down, I make it home in about ten minutes. Unfortunately, Mom and Dad are in the kitchen when I come in through the garage, so there's no fudging how late I am.

"It's a school night, Rigel," my dad says. Duh.

"I know. Sorry." I try to sound it, even though I'm not. "I finished all my homework before I went out."

He frowns anyway, but Mom is more understanding. "Wasn't it awfully late for M to be out? How is she?"

I shrug. "She couldn't get away, so I waited. Longer than I should have, I guess."

They both know where I go on my evening bike rides. And they were fine with it until Allister got here. Which reminds me.

"Is our *guest* in bed?" They nod. "So, you don't think it's weird that he never mentioned he had family moving here—that he even had any family on Earth—until they were already in Jewel?" I couldn't ask before, since was within earshot from the moment the O'Garas left until I escaped on my bike after dinner.

They look at each other for several seconds before answering. I used to hate when they did that—communicating telepathically so I can't hear. But now that M and I are starting to be able to do it, I don't mind so much.

"Maybe he didn't want to name drop," Dad suggests. "Though of course it's no real secret what his sister's family has done, since he used it to his advantage when petitioning to be on the *Echtran* Council. I understand why you don't like Allister, Rigel, but I hope you won't allow that to influence your opinion of the O'Garas. They're true heroes."

I manage to nod, trying not to show how his attitude irritates me. Okay, so Quinn and Lili O'Gara were like these legendary resistance fighters back on Mars. So my folks—especially my dad—practically idolize them. That doesn't mean their kids are anything special.

"It was pretty obvious you and Sean didn't start off on the right foot," my mom points out gently. "But your father's right. You shouldn't let your feelings—justified feelings—about Allister keep you from making friends with Sean. I'm sure he could use a friend right now. You remember what it was like, always being the new boy, and he's had to make a much bigger adjustment than you ever did."

"I guess."

Knowing they're right doesn't improve my mood. Besides, it's not just his relationship to Allister that makes me not trust Sean. He pissed me off before I knew anything about that, the way he looked at M when he met her at lunch today. Sure, any Martian would be blown away by meeting the Princess everyone thought was dead. It *is* a big deal.

But there was more in his expression than that. Something . . . possessive. I didn't like it. Still don't.

My folks going all fan-club over his family doesn't help. Or Allister treating Sean like the son he never had, when he always treats me like some nobody trying to worm my way into the Sovereign's affections. Like what's between M and me is all in my head.

"I'm going to bed," I say, not wanting to talk about it any more.

"Do the dishes first," Dad says.

I blink at him. I do the dishes at least half the time, but I always volunteer. I can't remember ever being *told* to do them.

"You promised you would when you left," he reminds me.

Oh, yeah. "Because Allister was giving you guys that *look* about letting me go out after dinner. Why do you let him tell you what to do in your own house?"

"He's a powerful man, Rigel," my mother murmurs. "There's nothing to be gained by antagonizing him."

"He was powerful back on Mars, in the old days. What power does he have here? Really? What can he do to you—to any of us—if we don't listen to him?"

I really want to know. But instead of answering, my dad says, "Just do the dishes, Rigel."

"Fine."

I go into the dining room—we never eat in the kitchen when we have company—and gather up the dinner dishes. It takes me like two minutes to put the dishes in the cupboard that doubles as an ionic sterilizer and push the button. Presto. Dishes are washed and put away in one easy step. Allister must not know about this little remodel, or he'd have suggested I do some other chore instead. I almost find it amusing.

Almost.

Because I know these extra chores are just one more way for him to put me in my place. A place that's miles beneath the Sovereign. One more reminder that I'm nowhere near her class. That if Faxon had never overthrown the monarchy and we were all back on Mars, I'd never be allowed anywhere near her. That I'm not good enough to speak to her, let alone be her boyfriend. Her soulmate.

The worst of it is, sometimes I worry he's right.

I'm still in a lousy mood the next morning. I haven't had any serious alone time with M since Friday and being apart from her sucks. And she'll have taekwondo this afternoon, so we won't get a chance today, either. At least we have four classes together.

Feeling a serious need to see her, I walk a little faster to Geometry. Before I even reach the classroom, I sense her *brath* and the knot inside me starts to relax. I turn in the direction of her vibe and see her hurrying toward me, a worried expression on her adorable face.

"I'm so sorry!" she whispers the moment she reaches me. "I couldn't get out of the house last night. Would you believe—"

"Hey, M!" It's Sean, striding down the hall like he owns it, a big grin on his face. "It was great meeting your family last night. Hope we can all get together again soon. Oh, hey, Rigel." He totally says it as an afterthought, like he didn't even notice me standing here. Jerk.

I barely nod. "Sean."

"Well, catch you later, M." With another smile and a wave—completely for M—he continues on his way.

"He met your family last night?" I ask. "Why didn't you tell me that?" It sounds way more like an accusation than I mean it to. Insecure, much?

And it makes M look worried again. Maybe I'm the jerk.

"I was just about to. It's why I couldn't get out to meet you. The O'Garas—all of them—dropped by right when I was about to leave. And get this: they bought a house right around the corner from me, *and* bought their van from Uncle Louie! All those *Echtran* paparazzi are bad enough, but this is taking stalking to a whole new level."

No kidding! "Last night was totally not your fault, M," I say, trying not to frown so she won't think I'm mad at her. Because I'm definitely not. But this Sean thing is even worse than I thought. "I'll bet Allister's behind this. He probably found that house for them, maybe even convinced the previous owners to sell."

"Now that you mention it, I don't remember a house that close to ours with a "For Sale" sign. So . . . you really think he brought them here to spy on me?"

I can tell she doesn't want to believe that. I don't blame her, after those evil *Echtrans* almost killed her last month. We both assumed—hoped—the threat was over for good after that. And maybe *that* threat is. I have a growing suspicion that this is a completely different one. Not to her life, maybe, but to her happiness. And definitely to mine.

"To spy . . . or maybe to influence you," I say carefully. "Allister knows you don't like him much, which means it'll be hard for him to do that himself. Maybe he figures people your own age—"

The bell rings and we have to sprint for our seats. "We'll talk more at lunch," she whispers.

I just nod. Because I'm not sure I want to tell M what I really suspect—that Sean was brought to Jewel to steal her away from me.

7

Bailerealta (bay-luh-ree-AL-tuh): an *all-Martian village on the west coast of Ireland*

I was antsy during my next few classes, anxious for lunchtime so I could hear the rest of Rigel's theory about the O'Garas. But when we got to the cafeteria, Molly was already sitting at our usual table along with Bri, Deb, and a few guys from the football team. At least Sean wasn't there. I could see him at another table with most of the basketball team.

I paused for a second before Molly saw me, then decided I might as well give her the benefit of the doubt—for now. She'd seemed nice enough so far.

"Hey, Molly," I greeted her cheerfully. Then, to Bri and Deb, "Thanks for inviting her to sit with us, guys." I sat down next to her, across from my friends, and Rigel sat on my other side.

"She was just starting to tell us about Ireland," Deb said. "Doesn't she have the coolest accent?"

Molly laughed. "I told them it's nothing special—this is how everyone sounds in Ireland." Her accent was noticeably stronger than it had been yesterday.

"I guess you'd know," I said, amused. Could I put on accents that easily if I tried? "It's special to us, since we've never met anyone from Ireland before."

Molly echoed my amusement with a glance, and I felt a little glow of pleasure at sharing a secret with her. Of course, I'd been sharing the same secret with Rigel since learning the truth in September, but somehow it was different with a girlfriend.

Prompted by questions from everyone at the table, Molly talked about the tiny village of Bailerealta, things like always having to wait for sheep to cross the road, and being in a school so small that two or three whole grades shared a room and teacher.

I was at least as interested as the others but the stuff I really wanted to know, like whether everybody in the village used Martian technology and how often new people arrived there from Mars, were things I couldn't exactly ask about at lunch.

Twenty minutes later, just as we were gathering up our trays, Trina approached our table—something she almost never did. Even when she flirted with Rigel, she didn't do it here.

"Hi, Molly—it's Molly, right?"

Molly nodded.

"I'm Trina Squires and I wanted to officially welcome you to Jewel."

Bri and I rolled our eyes at each other. So Trina was the "official" voice of the whole town now? We weren't being subtle, but she ignored us.

"I also wanted to say you should totally try out for cheerleading before basketball season starts. You look like you'd be perfect, and you could cheer for your brother. Have you ever done any cheerleading?"

"Um, no." Molly was looking more confused than flattered by Trina's attention.

"Any gymnastics?" Trina prodded.

"A little, when I was younger."

Trina beamed at her. "Perfect! Come by the gym after school and I can introduce you to the squad." Without giving Molly a chance to reply, she gave her a last smile that pointedly did not include anyone else at the table and sashayed off to join her friends, who were waiting by the door.

Molly turned to me, still looking confused. "I don't really have to go, do I?"

"Of course not," Bri answered before I could. "Trina only *thinks* she's the queen of the school."

"But she can make things sticky for you if you piss her off," I felt obliged to admit. "Believe me, I know."

"Don't do anything you don't want to, though," Deb said. I thought she looked just a little bit envious.

"Maybe I can stop by and make up a good excuse why I can't try out?" Molly suggested. "I don't want to make any enemies my very first week." She sent a quick look Rigel's way—or maybe I imagined it.

As we all headed to History together, I managed to hang back a little with Rigel. "You were really quiet at lunch," I said. "What's going on?"

"Still not sure," he muttered. "How about I walk you to your taekwondo class today so we can talk?"

"Sounds good." We were way overdue for some alone time—plus I was dying to know what he really thought about the O'Garas.

Neither Sean nor Molly were on the bus that afternoon. I assumed he had basketball practice and Molly must have gone to talk to Trina —who maybe convinced her to try out for cheerleading after all. I tried not to mind.

I spent the half hour before I had to leave for taekwondo doing a little bit of homework and listening for Rigel's bike—not that he made any noise before ringing the doorbell. I bounced up and raced to the door.

"Hey!" I greeted him. "Come on in while I get my bag."

"I'd better not," he said, cocking his head. "Your neighbor's watching."

I looked over his shoulder and saw Mrs. Crabtree across the street spreading mulch under her front hedge and peering nosily at us. She'd definitely tell Aunt Theresa if she saw Rigel come into the house—in fact, she'd already done it once and I'd caught holy hell for it. I suspected my aunt had enlisted every neighbor who was home during the day to spy on me when she couldn't be here.

"Fine." I gave Mrs. Crabtree a pointed glare that at least made her glance away. "Be right back."

Leaving him standing on the porch, I ran up to my room, grabbed my gear bag and ran back down, not wanting to waste a moment I could be spending with Rigel.

"That was quick," he said with a grin when I rejoined him, then took my bag to carry it for me.

I locked the door and we headed into town, all of a block and a half away. "So, tell me what you think the deal is with the O'Garas," I said, once I was sure Mrs. Crabtree couldn't hear.

"I really don't know any more than I already told you," he said— evasively, I thought.

I looked sharply at him, trying to decipher the mix of emotions I sensed. Uneasiness and irritation definitely, and maybe something else.

"I didn't ask what you know, I asked what you think," I pointed out. "This morning, you sounded like you had a theory."

"I have several theories," he said after just a slight hesitation, "but they mostly involve wildly improbable political and military scenarios. I've probably been playing too much Starcraft lately. Until we actually know something, there's no point assuming there's more going on than they've told us."

He transferred my gear bag to his left hand so he could hold mine with his right. Though his touch gave me the same thrill as always, it also let his emotions come though more strongly and I was sure now that he was keeping something from me.

"So you don't think they're conspiring with Allister to ship me off to Montana or Ireland or something?" Those were the two main Martian settlements on Earth—and that was the possibility that worried me most.

Rigel gave my hand a squeeze. "I don't think so, no. If they are, we definitely won't let them get away with it."

"Promise?" I stopped walking to make him look at me. He did.

"Promise," he said, holding my gaze until I was sure he was telling me the truth. "Haven't I sworn I won't let anything happen to you, M?"

I relaxed enough to start walking again, but said, "There's more you're not telling me. Can't you at least share *one* theory? What did you start to say this morning?"

"You're a little too perceptive sometimes, you know that? Okay, probably the most likely thing I can think of is that Allister's hoping you'll spend more time with Molly . . . and Sean . . . and less with me. That they'll have an easier time getting you on board with the whole Sovereign thing than he's had. Get you invested in it."

"And that worries you." It was a statement, since I could feel it from him.

He just shrugged, and I let it drop. For now. I'd get more out of him eventually. But as long as nobody was trying to take me away from Rigel, I could face whatever political machinations they might be planning.

"So, want to try meeting at the arboretum tonight, since last night didn't work out?" I asked after we'd walked a little way in silence.

Rigel grimaced and I could feel a new frustration emanating from him. "I don't think I can. My grandfather arrives tonight so they'll expect me to stick around."

"Oh, that's right. But . . . I thought you were looking forward to seeing him?"

He shrugged. "I am. But I'd much rather spend time with you. It feels like we never get any time alone lately."

It did feel that way. I mostly blamed Aunt Theresa and all her stupid rules, but Rigel's folks didn't seem quite as eager to have us spend time together as they used to, either. Or maybe I was just being paranoid.

"Once Allister leaves it'll be better," I said, willing it to be true.

"Yeah." But he sounded less than positive about it.

The past month had been hands-down the happiest of my life. By, like, several orders of magnitude. Which meant I was both terrified it couldn't last, and determined to fight tooth and nail if anyone tried to take it away from me.

That line of thinking—not to mention the energy boost from Rigel's goodbye kiss at the door of the do jang—put me in an interesting mood for taekwondo class. I'd been steadily improving ever since Rigel and I had first touched in late August, but today it was like I was supercharged.

Master Parker came over to me after class ended. "Marsha, your sparring today was spectacular. I'd really like you to consider entering the regional tournament coming up in February. I think you'd do the school proud."

"Thank you, sir. I'll, um, ask my aunt."

"Do that. If she isn't keen on the idea, let me know and I can speak to her."

I nodded without committing. Though I was flattered, I wasn't sure competing in an actual tournament, with lots of people watching, was a great idea. I was feeling visible enough these days.

I changed out of my do bok and headed home, wishing now that Rigel and I had walked faster earlier so we could have had time for more than one kiss. Not that we'd progressed *beyond* kissing—we were both a little afraid of what could happen, considering what just kissing did to us—but we hadn't had a good make out session for over a week. It always seemed like someone was watching us or one of us had to be somewhere.

With a sigh, I trudged past the half dozen jewelry and craft shops on Diamond and turned up Opal toward Garnet Street, remembering our first secret meeting in the cornfield by the school. It had been such a magical afternoon. I'd only learned the truth about Rigel—and myself—a few days earlier and I'd been full of questions. He'd told me all about the *graell*—our bond—and about some of the Martian political stuff I still needed to learn so much about.

But what I mostly remembered about that day was the kissing, and how I'd felt when Rigel made it clear he liked me as much as I liked him.

Of course, my *last* memory of that clearing in the cornfield wasn't warm and fuzzy at all, since that's where the big showdown between Faxon's forces and my defenders had taken place. If Shim hadn't been so convincing—and if Rigel and I hadn't amazed everyone (including ourselves) by creating the lightning bolt that destroyed that awful Ossian Sphere—we'd probably all be dead now and Faxon's forces would be well on their way to conquering Earth.

"There you are," Aunt Theresa greeted me the second I opened the front door. "What took you so long getting home? I hear thunder in the distance."

"Sorry." It never paid to argue with Aunt Theresa.

"Well, go shower, then come down and snap the beans for me. Then you can do your homework."

Something in her voice caught my attention. "Is something wrong?"

"Wrong? Of course not." She hmphed. "But I did tell Lili O'Gara that you'd go over there after dinner to tutor Molly and Sean. So we're eating at seven, whether Louie is home or not."

I couldn't squelch a spurt of resentment. "You told her without asking me? What if I'd had plans?" Not that I did, but still.

"Plans you haven't cleared with me?" She arched one iron gray brow in that way that always made me feel like I'd screwed up. "Do you?" she prompted when I didn't respond.

"No," I grudgingly admitted. "I just wish you'd asked me first, that's all."

Now she frowned. "You seemed willing enough when Lili asked you last night."

"I am. It's just . . . Never mind. It's fine. I'll go shower."

By the time we sat down to dinner—Uncle Louie made it with two minutes to spare—I was over my snit. In fact, I was looking forward to a chance to learn more about the O'Garas, and the village in Ireland, and Mars, and maybe even their actual reason for being here, if there really was more going on than they'd admitted. I ate quickly, then did the dishes in record time.

"The O'Garas are on Opal, right? What's the house number?" I asked as I stuffed my history book into my backpack.

Uncle Louie told me and I headed out. It was starting to drizzle, but the thunder had moved off and I was only going around the corner, so I didn't bother with an umbrella. Less than five minutes later, I rang the doorbell of a house very similar to ours—a little Victorian with gingerbread trim, a deep front porch and slightly peeling paint.

I hoped I wasn't walking into the dragon's den.

8

omni: *a small, multifunctional device developed on Mars*

The doorbell had barely sounded when Sean opened the door and greeted me with a big smile. "Hullo, M, come in, do. Don't mind the mess."

He held the door and I stepped past him into the foyer, noticing again how tall he was. I was careful not to brush against him.

"Thanks. Is Molly home, too?"

"Sure look it, in here." He motioned with his head for me to follow him and we went into a small living room similar to ours. In fact, the house seemed to be laid out almost the same, except in reverse, with the kitchen off to the left, the living room to the right and the stairs straight ahead.

"Hi, M," Molly said, looking up from a desk in the corner with a smile. "Thanks for coming."

There were a few big moving boxes in the corners, but otherwise it looked like they were nearly settled in already.

"No problem. Though I can't imagine you guys really need much help." Considering how fast Rigel (and now I) could read, I figured they could finish the whole textbook in a day or two.

Molly shrugged. "It's not like we've ever studied the United States, since we never expected to come here until—"

"Yeah, I know. Until everybody found out about me." I crossed the room to join her at the desk and she shoved some books off a chair to make room for me. Sean dragged another chair over and sat on my other side.

"All we got back home was general Earth History," he explained, flipping open the textbook on the desk, "so we really could use some help—especially with the stuff that's not in books, stuff everyone just knows. Afterwards, our folks thought you might, um, have some questions we could answer?"

I drew in a quick, eager breath. "Now that you mention it—" I began, but just then their mother poked her head around the corner.

"Ah, welcome, Excellency! Er, M, rather. Can I get you a cup of tea?" Then, before I could answer, she blushed and exclaimed, "Oh, how silly of me! You've been raised in America. Of course you don't want tea. Perhaps a soft drink?"

Mrs. O'Gara was so embarrassed and eager to please that it made *me* embarrassed. I hoped she'd stop acting weird around me soon, or I'd start avoiding her—even though it was kind of nice to be fussed over.

"Actually, tea would be great, thanks," I said. "I drink tea all the time."

"Oh! Oh, that's lovely." She seemed way more relieved than the situation called for. "Perhaps something herbal? What do you like?"

"Oh, uh, anything's fine. Peppermint, chamomile, whatever you have. Thanks!"

She nodded and disappeared. In the awkward silence that followed, it felt inappropriate to start peppering them with questions about Mars. Plus, I suddenly felt a little too aware of Sean sitting next to me. Clearing my throat, I turned to Molly.

"So, did you go to cheerleading practice today?"

She nodded. "Trina talked me into trying out and . . . I think I may join. It would be a way to meet people. You should do it, too, M."

I laughed. "You've got to be kidding! I'm positive Trina didn't suggest that."

"Well, no, but—"

"Trust me, even if I tried out I'd never make the squad. I'm kind of a klutz"—well, I used to be, anyway—"and Trina hates me."

Sean made a disbelieving sound. "How could anyone—? Well, her loss, if so."

But Molly's eyebrows drew together worriedly. "I, um, could tell you aren't exactly friends."

"That's putting it mildly. I doubt there's anyone in the school she likes less than me. We've had a kind of feud going since third grade." A mostly one-sided feud, with Trina embarrassing me every chance she got. But lately I'd gotten better at defending myself against her —mostly thanks to Rigel, I reminded myself.

Molly looked alarmed. "In that case, maybe I shouldn't spend time with her."

"What? No! If they want you on the squad, you should totally join."

"Um, ladies? History?" Sean prompted, clearly tired of our girl talk.

But Molly just grimaced at him. "You really think I should?" she asked me.

"Sure. It's like an express lane to popularity and you'll probably have fun, too. And, uh, get to cheer for Sean at basketball games." I glanced at him as I said that and caught him watching me with a strange, quizzical smile. Flustered, I quickly turned back to Molly.

"You're sure?" Her brow had unfurrowed and I could tell she really wanted to.

"Absolutely. Though I can't promise Trina won't give you a hard time for being friends with me. That is, if you still—"

"Of course I want to be friends with you!" Her vehemence was flattering. "It's what we—" She glanced past me to Sean, then said, "I mean, even if you weren't . . . who you are, you're the only other *Echtran* girl in Jewel. And besides, I think you're really nice."

I couldn't help smiling, though I wondered what she'd almost said —and whether Sean had stopped her. "Thanks. And ditto."

Mrs. O'Gara bustled in with peppermint tea for all of us, made sure I had a napkin and enough sugar, then left us alone again.

"So, are there any classes besides history you guys need help with?" I asked as soon as their mother was gone, though I really wanted to ask about Mars stuff. Maybe there'd be time later.

"Not really," Sean said. "The rest is rather, uh—"

"Simplistic?" I said when he hesitated. "I guess coming from Mars, our math and science seems pretty primitive, huh?"

He shrugged, looking sheepish. "Kind of, yeah."

"Sean!" Molly protested. "That's not—"

"It's okay," I reassured her. "I'm not insulted or anything. It just makes sense."

She watched my face for a moment, then seemed satisfied I wasn't upset and nodded.

"So, history?" I pulled out my own book and started going over what we'd covered so far this year, pointing out the stuff Mrs.

George had spent the most time on, which was most likely to be on the next test. Sean seemed especially interested in the U.S. Constitution and branches of government.

"It's weird how similar our Nuathan government is in some things and how different in others," he remarked. "Like, we both have two-house legislatures and a separate judicial system, but we have hereditary Sovereigns instead of elected presidents."

"Until Faxon," I said, and they both grimaced. "Maybe not so strange, though, when you think about it," I suggested. "I mean, Martians have been on Earth for what, five hundred years now? And communicating with folks back on Mars that whole time. So it makes sense they'd copy anything that seemed to work well here, just like we copied some things from England. Honestly, I'm surprised the monarchy lasted as long in Nuath as it did."

"What?" they both exclaimed, looking positively shocked.

"Oh, no," Molly protested. "The monarchy has been wonderful for our people. I mean, I don't really remember it, since I was born around the time Faxon took over, but *everybody* says how much better it was under the Sovereigns."

"Everybody?" I couldn't help being skeptical, since I knew for a fact at least *some* Martians hated the monarchy enough to want me dead.

"Everybody except Faxon's people." Sean spoke with conviction. "And I expect most of them are deserting him now, or will soon. Not even the ultra-progressives ever wanted to do away with the monarchy, you know. At least not until Faxon started spreading his lies and buying people off. They just wanted to move more power to the legislature and make the houses more equal."

"So, make the Sovereign more of a figurehead, like in England?" I was a *lot* more interested in Nuathan government and history than the stuff in our textbook.

"Not at all." He seemed startled again. "I didn't realize you never even— Anyway, the Sovereigns have always been wise, compassionate, intuitive, fair—in other words, great leaders and the final word in resolving all kinds of disputes. Nobody wanted to change that. Some just thought more of the day-to-day governing should devolve to the legislature."

"So . . . how did the Sovereigns get to be so wise and intuitive and all?"

"Genetics, mostly. And, uh, training, I guess. Like Molly said—"

"This was all before your time. I know." I didn't think any amount of training would make me the kind of leader they were talking about, not even if I lived to be two hundred years old. Which I might. It was just as well I was on Earth and not Mars, completely apart from the threat Faxon posed. Nobody would expect as much from me here. Would they?

I was suddenly ready to change the subject. "So, that village where you lived in Ireland—" I began, when Mrs. O'Gara stuck her head around the corner again.

"Sorry to interrupt, but M's aunt just called. It's nine-thirty and she wants her home, as it's a school night."

"Wow, already?" Molly and I said at the same time. Then we looked at each other and giggled. I felt like we were already friends— maybe better friends than I could be with Bri or Deb nowadays.

"Can you come over again soon?" Molly asked as I zipped up my backpack.

"I hope so," I said automatically before remembering Rigel's theory—and that I wanted to hang out with *him* as many evenings as I could. If he could. "I'll ask my aunt."

"Did you bring an umbrella, dear?" Mrs. O'Gara asked then. "It's pouring outside."

Oops. "No, but I'll be okay. It's not far, and I can run."

"Don't be silly. Sean can walk you."

I frowned. "I hate to be so much trouble. I could just borrow an umbrella and give it back tomorrow."

"Oh, Sean doesn't mind, trust me," Molly said, her eyes twinkling.

"What do you—?"

"No, it's fine," he assured me with a quelling glance at Molly. "My pleasure. Really."

"Um, then thanks. Bye, Molly. See you at school tomorrow."

"Bye, M. And thanks!" She sounded genuinely appreciative, even though I'd learned a lot more from them than they'd learned from me.

It was only as Sean opened the front door that I noticed he didn't have an umbrella.

"Um, there's really no point in both of us getting wet," I said, peering out at the rain falling in sheets just past the porch overhang.

"No worries. We'll stay dry as dust. Come on."

Puzzled, I walked with him to the top of the porch stairs. A gust of wind blew a flurry of drops into our faces. "Dry as dust?"

"One sec." He pulled something about the size of a pack of gum —or a flash drive—out of his pocket. Suddenly a glowing screen, about six inches square, appeared in midair. It looked like some kind of control panel.

"Is that a hologram?" I gasped.

"Basically." He flashed me a mischievous grin, then touched a spot on the screen, which made a different screen appear. He made his selection on that one, then stuck the device back in his pocket. The screen disappeared.

"Okay, let's go," he said, taking my backpack from me.

I was briefly reminded of Rigel taking my gear bag this afternoon, but then my attention went back to the rain, which was coming down harder than ever.

"Seriously?"

"Seriously." He grinned again and held out the crook of his arm for me to take.

I hesitated but decided it would be rude to refuse. When I touched his arm I felt that jolt again, though his coat muted it somewhat. He escorted me down the first step and I squinted against the onslaught of wet on my face—except my face stayed dry. All of me stayed dry. I took another step down and so did he. Still dry.

"How—?"

"Call it an invisible umbrella," he said, watching my face with undisguised amusement. "It's a sort of force shield that keeps the rain off us."

I stuck my hand out and watched as the rain sheered away from my skin about an inch before it touched me.

"Cool! And it's generated by that thing in your pocket?"

He nodded. "My omni, yeah."

"Omni," I repeated. "So it does other stuff, too?"

"Loads of other stuff. I'll show you sometime."

Though I was dying for a demonstration right now, I just said, "Okay."

"Let's get you home. I got the impression last night your aunt isn't someone to mess with."

I laughed. "You got that right. But she seems to like you guys, so I probably won't get in trouble. This time."

"Glad to hear it."

He smiled down at me so warmly I was reminded again of Rigel's suspicions. I dropped my hand from his arm—and got a face full of rain.

"Watch out," Sean said, holding his arm back out to me. He was laughing! "It only works if we're touching. Sorry, I should have told you."

I wiped my face with my sleeve and put my hand back on his arm. "Yeah, that might have been nice."

"I really am sorry." But I thought he still looked amused. "I'm so used to everyone knowing this stuff, I didn't think to explain it."

"That's okay." I was starting to feel kind of silly now. "A little water won't kill me."

"Maybe not, but we can't take chances with our Princess, now, can we? Here." He pulled out his omni again, the screen appeared, he pushed a couple more holographic buttons, too quickly for me to see what he was doing, and suddenly I was totally dry.

"Holy crap! How did you do that?" I asked, the last of my irritation swallowed by amazement.

Again he was laughing at me, but not maliciously. "Just another function, the instavap."

"But how does it work? How does it dry just the water on the surface—and in my clothes—but not suck it out of my body?"

His eyebrows rose. "I guess your science education isn't as primitive as I thought. It works from the outside in. Because it only lasts a second, it doesn't have time to dessicate you, though your mouth might feel a little dry."

I checked and it did. But only a little, and only for a few seconds. Very cool.

"So what other, um, apps do you have in there?" I asked, even more curious than before.

He shook his head. "If I tell you now, how do I know you'll let me walk you home again? Anyway, we're here." He walked up the porch steps with me and handed me my backpack. I took my hand off his arm the moment we were under the overhang and the tingling stopped, making me realize I'd felt it this whole time without noticing.

"Thanks," I said, ignoring his question and being very careful not to touch his hand as I took the bag from him. "Guess I'll see you at school tomorrow."

"And at our house next time you, um, tutor us?"

"That, too. G'night."

He smiled down at me but didn't try to get too close—to my relief. "Good night . . . Emileia," he said softly, then turned and left.

I frowned after him for a moment, not sure what to think, then shook my head as I opened the front door. There was no point imagining motives where none might exist. And though I knew Rigel wouldn't approve, I couldn't help liking the O'Garas. Already, I found myself looking forward to my next visit to their house.

9

graell (grayl): *an emotional and physical bond believed mythical by most Martians*

"Didn't your aunt tell you I called when you got home last night?" Rigel asked when he met me at my locker the next morning.

"Good morning to you, too," I said, going up on my tiptoes for a quick kiss—quick enough that no passing teacher would yell at us. "She did tell me, but she also said it was too late to call you back, even though it was barely past nine-thirty. I hung around in the kitchen hoping they'd go upstairs early enough that I could call you anyway, but they didn't. I didn't want to risk calling after ten-thirty."

"You can call my cell anytime, M, you know that. So where were you, anyway? She wouldn't tell me."

I was startled he didn't know. Hadn't I told him I'd agreed to tutor Molly and Sean? Maybe not.

Watching his expression carefully, I said, "I was over at the O'Garas' house. My aunt promised Mrs. O'Gara I'd help Molly and Sean catch up in History, but she didn't tell *me* that until I got home from taekwondo."

As expected, he didn't look happy. "You were at their *house?* All evening? After everything I—"

"Not all evening, just for a couple hours after dinner. And you didn't tell me much of anything, remember?" I noticed people looking at us and dropped my voice to a whisper. "If you really know something, Rigel, some reason I should avoid them, then tell me. Please!"

He opened his mouth, then closed it, then opened it again, but only to ask, "So, it wasn't just Molly, but Sean, too? I can't imagine he needs any help with his classes."

Suddenly I saw where this was going and felt stupid I hadn't realized it sooner. Unfortunately, the truth would only make things

47

worse, but I had no intention of lying to him. Ever.

"Both of them, yeah. They had a lot of questions about U.S. History, since neither of them ever studied it before. And they told me some stuff about politics on . . . er, where they come from," I amended, since we were walking down the hall now and might possibly be overheard. "It was interesting."

I paused, bracing myself for his reaction, then confessed in a rush, "And then Sean walked me home because I forgot to bring an umbrella."

"Because you— Gee, wasn't that nice of him?" Rigel's jaw was tight and I could feel waves of anger rolling off of him. Which wasn't fair at all.

"I didn't ask him to. And it was like a three minute walk." I knew I sounded defensive. "Anyway, it was his mom's idea, not his. She's . . . really sweet."

The anger I felt from him ebbed slightly but became tinged with something else—sadness? But why? That's what I seemed to see in his eyes, too, when he looked down at me again.

"Sorry, M. It wasn't your fault, so I shouldn't take it out on you. It's just . . . There's something about Sean that rubs me the wrong way."

I knew better than to suggest jealousy again, even if it sure felt like that to me. "It was pouring, so it would have looked weird for me to refuse. And it *was* my fault I forgot my umbrella. But, Rigel, he has the coolest device!" I dropped my voice to something lower than a whisper but that Rigel, with his enhanced Martian senses, could easily hear. "This little thing he called an omni. It does all kinds of stuff, including generating a sort of rain shield, like an invisible umbrella. It was amazing."

Now he looked—and felt—alarmed. "An omni? And he actually used it out on the street?"

"So you already knew about them? How come you never told me? It was so cool!"

We reached the classroom but lingered just outside the door, still speaking so low no one else could possibly hear.

"I've never seen one, just heard about them. And yeah, they sound great. I used to beg my folks for one. But they said they're not allowed on Earth—along with a bunch of other stuff that would be too hard to explain if it was found. So if he—" The bell rang, cutting him off. "We'll talk more later," he said.

This was starting to feel like a pattern, but I was determined this time he really would tell me more. A couple of periods later, walking together from English to Science, I maneuvered him toward the edge of the hallway, holding tightly to his arm.

"If you think the O'Garas are some kind of threat you *have* to tell me," I whispered. "They expect me to come over again soon. If there's some reason I shouldn't, I need to know."

He slanted a glance my way but looked away before I could decipher it. I concentrated on his emotions instead and thought he felt nervous. Nervous?

"Rigel?" I prompted.

"Okay," he finally murmured. "I think Molly's probably fine. Maybe they all are—though they shouldn't go waving technology around like that. But I'm pretty sure Sean is . . . after you."

Flashing back to the scene in the cornfield last month, my heart leaped into my throat. "You mean he might—"

"No." I could tell he was responding to the fear he felt from me more than my words. "Not that way. I mean . . . romantically," he finally finished, with obvious reluctance.

I actually laughed out loud, right there in the hallway, before remembering to drop my voice again—not that we were exactly talking Martian stuff now. "No way. He knows I'm with you—it's not exactly a secret. And even if he is . . . *interested* in me, it doesn't matter. You know that. I won't ever think of anybody else that way. I can't."

Then I remembered that weird tingle I got from Sean—surely just some random Martian anomaly? Whatever it was, I definitely wasn't about to mention it to Rigel now!

He stopped and turned me toward him so he could look into my eyes. "I know, M. I trust you completely—with my life and my heart." I could tell beyond doubt that he meant it. "It's *his* motives I don't trust. His and Allister's. So . . . be careful, okay?"

"Okay. But they can't possibly change the way I feel, so their motives don't really matter, do they? I mean, I promise not to lead him on or anything."

Now he laughed. "That's *not* something I was worried about."

I was relieved to see him smiling again. "What, you don't think I can flirt with the best of them?" I joked.

He threw an arm around my shoulders and gave me a delicious squeeze. "You don't have to, believe me. You're already completely irresistible."

"To you, maybe. But thanks. And ditto."

During class, while filling in my water cycle chart, I occasionally focused my attention on Rigel behind me, gauging his emotions. Except for occasional spurts of irritation with Trina—his lab partner—he mostly stayed upbeat, though toward the end of class a darker edge crept back in.

"Want to grab something we can eat in the courtyard?" I suggested on the way to lunch.

As usual, Rigel saw right through me. "I'm fine, M." He gave me a smile to prove it. "Besides, it's drizzling and about forty degrees. But I appreciate the offer."

"Think you can get away tonight after dinner, then?" I asked as we got into the lunch line.

But he shook his head. "Dad, Grandfather and Allister have me helping them with a project. They say it's to get a young person's input, but I think it's really to keep me home at night. How about this afternoon?"

"It's a date," I promised, already tingling at the thought of some uninterrupted alone time with Rigel.

We sat down with our lunches and a moment later I saw Molly heading for our table. But she'd barely left the lunch line when Trina intercepted her. "Hey, Molly, you don't have to sit with the losers anymore. You can sit with us now." She gestured toward the cheerleaders' table.

Though no one else at our table could possibly hear the exchange, Rigel and I both could. We glanced at each other, waiting to see what Molly would say.

"Thanks, Trina, but I like M and her friends. They're really nice."

I could see Trina's lip curl from halfway across the room. "Nice? Trust me, you don't know Marsha like I do. I'll admit Rigel Stuart is easy on the eyes, even if he is a total player. But the others—?" She rolled her eyes. "Come on over if you change your mind."

Molly walked away from her without replying. "Hey, M," she

greeted me when joined us. "Do you think you can come over again soon?"

I wished she'd waited to ask when Rigel wasn't right there—not that I'd have hidden it from him, of course. But I wanted to preserve his good mood and I could feel it souring the moment she spoke.

Still, I nodded. "Probably. My aunt seems to be fine with it."

"Great! I was afraid you might have gotten in trouble after staying so late last night."

Honestly, was she *trying* to get me in trouble with Rigel? There was nothing calculating in her expression. but now Bri and Deb were interested.

"So what are you guys up to?" Bri asked, a little tinge of jealousy in her voice. Which was totally uncool, considering how much more time she'd been spending with Deb than me lately—and it wasn't *all* my fault.

"I'm just helping Molly and Sean get caught up in History—not that they need a lot of help." I smiled at Molly and she smiled back.

"It was my mom's idea," she explained to Bri, who was still frowning a little. "But M's being a really good sport about it."

"So, Molly, are you joining the cheerleading squad?" Deb said to change the subject. Deb hated anything like conflict.

Molly nodded. "I thought it might be fun to cheer at Sean's games. You guys will come, won't you?"

"Are you kidding?" Bri was instantly distracted. "I never miss a game. I especially won't now. Let's all go to the scrimmage against Alexandria week after next! Show our support."

She spent the rest of lunch talking basketball and I was surprised that Molly seemed to know as much about it as she did. Rigel made an occasional comment, too, but I stayed quiet, not wanting to display my ignorance. I was just happy Rigel was relatively cheerful again, despite the frequent mentions of Sean's name. I hoped that meant I'd successfully reassured him.

It was still drizzling when I got off the bus that afternoon. I worried it might keep Rigel from coming over but less than half an hour later he showed up wearing a rain poncho that covered most of his bike as well as his body.

"Nice!" I said, grinning at his attire when I opened the door.

He shrugged, grinning back. "It's not a force field, but it gets the job done. You want to go for a walk? I brought an umbrella—a real one."

"Let me grab my coat." No neighbors were out in their yards on a day like this, but I wouldn't put it past Mrs. Crabtree to be spying out her window.

A minute later we were walking toward Diamond hand in hand, Rigel holding the big black umbrella over both of us. Very romantic, in spite of the puddles. But then, pretty much everything was romantic when I was with Rigel.

"It sucks there's no place we can be alone without getting rained on," I commented after a moment.

"Yeah. Maybe after Allister and Grandfather leave you can come to my house again."

Aunt Theresa had made it clear that neither Rigel nor I were allowed in each other's houses without supervision. She'd even mentioned it to his parents after church a few weeks ago, so they now felt obligated to play by her rules. Fortunately, Rigel's dad worked out of their house about half the time, since he did a lot of his computer consulting over the internet. Rigel's mom was an OB/Gyn, so she was gone a lot during the day.

"We can go to the arboretum," I suggested. "It ought to be deserted."

He nodded and we headed that way.

"So what's this project you're working on?" I asked as we walked.

"Allister and Grandfather are writing up guidelines for new *Echtrans* on how to blend in without drawing attention. I mean, there have always been generally understood dos and don'ts, but with more coming in and others leaving the compounds, they want something standardized. Something bipartisan, I guess you could say."

"So where do you come in on this?" It sounded very governmental and official to me. I tried to ignore the fact that I really should be learning about this stuff myself.

"They want to include stuff for kids—all ages. Used to be, folks with young kids almost always stayed in one of the Martian compounds or villages until they were older but now, not so much. I'm supposed to come up with ideas for that part." He didn't sound happy about it.

"But you think it's really to keep you home? Away from me?" I could definitely see Allister doing that, but Shim? He'd seemed to like me, and even approve of us as a couple.

The arboretum was as empty as I'd predicted, so we went in and wandered slowly along the wet gravel path. It had been pretty when the roses were in bloom and the trees still had leaves a month ago, but now it was drab and gray in the cold drizzle.

"Maybe I'm wrong about that." He shrugged. "Anyway, it can't last forever—though starting next week, after my birthday, I'll have Driver's Ed most evenings for a while. But hey, we're together now, right?"

I smiled up at him, my heart beating faster. "We are. And I think we should make the most of that."

He lowered his lips to mine and for a while nothing else in the world—nothing else in the universe—mattered. Kissing Rigel always felt so right, so perfect. So intense. I sometimes worried I'd get used to this, that each kiss couldn't go on being better than the last one indefinitely. But so far, that worry hadn't materialized. Not even close.

After a blissful half hour or so, Rigel noticed I was shivering, even though I hadn't noticed myself.

"Come on," he said. "We need to get you warmed up."

We walked down the block to Dream Cream for hot chocolate, then it was time for me to get home, since it was my night to make dinner. Cold rain and all, I wished the afternoon didn't have to end.

On my front porch, Rigel gave me one last kiss, then handed me the umbrella. "Here, you keep this. You can take it with you next time you go to the O'Garas' house."

"Subtle," I said, giving him a grin and another quick kiss. "But I'll bring it."

I watched him ride off, still smiling, savoring the glow of our time together. But then I looked up at the darkening sky and sighed. Winter was nearly here, which meant fewer and fewer afternoons like this one. Aunt Theresa's rules, Allister's visits, new evening commitments, the worsening weather—sometimes it seemed like the world was conspiring to keep Rigel and me apart.

But that was silly. Soon Allister would leave again and everything would go back to normal. Why shouldn't it?

10

Nuath (NOO-ath): *the underground human colony on Mars*

"I feel like I understand the American perspective a lot better now," Molly said several nights later, when we finally finished going everything we'd covered so far in U.S. History.

"You're a good teacher, M." Sean grinned at me as he flipped his book closed. "Thanks."

"I'm glad I could help." I was almost sorry we were done. I'd enjoyed my visits to their house more than I'd expected to, especially the parts where I learned more about Mars. I was also becoming better friends with Molly . . . and with Sean.

As though he'd read my thoughts, Sean said, "You know, you don't have to tell your aunt we're caught up. There must be more *you* want to know, plus there's still lots of stuff you can tell us about America —and Earth. Stuff that everyone takes for granted."

My eagerness at learning more Martian stuff battled with wariness, in case Rigel was right about Sean. Even after Rigel and I spent that magical Thursday afternoon together, then another hour Saturday, he was definitely still jealous. I'd even sensed it in church, when the O'Garas showed up and sat with us and the Stuarts—and Sean didn't even try to sit next to me.

"Worth a try," I said after only the briefest hesitation. "So, what else can you tell me about Mars?"

Sean laughed. "That's like asking, 'What else can you tell us about Earth?' Where would you start?"

"Good point." I relaxed, laughing along with him. "Let's see. You've already told me some political stuff and your parents gave me a little Nuathan history when I was here Sunday night. But what it was like to actually *live* there? I still can't quite imagine it."

"You'll, um, you'd love it there, M." Sean spoke with conviction.

"Of course, things got a little crazy the year before we left, but most of our time growing up was great. I really miss it sometimes."

Molly nodded eagerly. "Me, too. And he's right, you'd love it! Everybody's super friendly. And . . . you never have to hide what you really are."

"That must get old, huh?" Sean asked.

It was cool that he understood. "Sometimes. But . . . what is it *like* there? I mean, the entire colony is underground, right? Isn't it weird living your whole life in . . . in caves?" How could anyone *miss* that?

They started laughing again. "It's really not like that at all," Molly assured me. "Actually, it looks a little like Ireland—we were surprised how much when we moved there last year."

"But isn't there a . . . a ceiling?"

"There is," Sean admitted. "I mean, we all know it's there, but it's about a mile up, and disguised to look exactly like the sky on Earth, with clouds, and stars at night and everything."

"Disguised?"

"Holographically," Sean clarified.

I'd seen the omni's little holographic screen, so I guessed that made sense. "So . . . like being inside a really, really big domed stadium with video screens on the ceiling?"

"Maybe, but it doesn't feel like that," Molly said. "It just feels like being . . . outside. Where we lived, there's even grass and sheep and stuff."

"*Sheep?*" Okay, maybe *not* like a huge cavern or an underground spaceship, which is what I'd been imagining. "You have sheep?"

"Well, not us, personally," Molly admitted, "but people do."

"So Nuath isn't just one big city?"

She shook her head, smiling at my confusion. "There are two big towns—well, not so big by Earth standards—plus a couple dozen villages, spread out over nearly a four hundred square miles."

"Four hundred—!" These new images were completely shattering my preconceptions.

"That's only twenty miles in each direction," Sean pointed out. "She means area, not diameter. You're taking Geometry, right?"

His tone was teasing and I gave him a mock glare. "Yeah, okay. But still, twenty miles . . . underground . . ." I shook my head again. "Are there, like, pillars or something, holding up the roof?"

"Antigravity supports," Sean said. "There are physical supports, too, but not many. They're not necessary."

It sounded kind of dangerous to me. "But what if the, uh, power died or something? Wouldn't the ceiling collapse?"

"It's worked for almost three thousand years," Molly pointed out. "Plus there's a lot of redundancy built in, just to be safe. Really, it's not something we even think about."

"Besides," Sean said, "it seems safer to me than having a sky that goes all the way out into space, where anything could just fall on you." He gave an almost imperceptible shudder.

I started to laugh, but stopped when I saw he looked embarrassed. "The only thing that's ever fallen out of the sky here has been rain, sleet and snow. Okay, and sometimes hail."

He didn't seem particularly reassured. "Even that . . . Guess I'm still not used to the idea. Hey, do you want to see some pictures?"

That distracted me immediately, as he'd probably intended. "Pictures? Definitely!"

Sean grinned at my enthusiasm. "Just a sec." He pulled his omni out of his pocket and pulled up the screen, touched a button or two and a photo—or maybe a video—popped up. I could swear it was three-dimensional.

"Wow," I murmured, examining what looked like a village street with reddish stone houses on either side. There were glimpses of green countryside in the background. In the foreground, a red-haired young woman and a dark-haired girl stood waving—literally waving —next to one of the houses. I realized with a start that the girl was Molly.

"That's me with Elana," she told me. "Just a few weeks before she . . . disappeared. And that's our house. Or, well, it was." She looked away from the picture.

I put a hand on her arm. "I'm sorry. I didn't mean to bring up sad memories."

"It's not your fault, M." Sean sounded a little choked up, too. "I'm the one who pulled up that pic. Sorry, Moll. Here, I'll—"

"Sean?" Mrs. O'Gara came into the room, looking apologetic. "I'm sorry to pull you away, but one of your teammates is on the phone and he said it was important."

Sean stood, putting the omni back in his pocket, to my

disappointment. "Coming, Mum, thanks. Back in a minute," he added to Molly and me as he left the room.

"Oh, I should have asked him to leave the omni," Molly said the moment he was gone. "I could have shown you more pictures of Glenamuir, our village."

"Not if it makes you sad. I can tell you—and Sean—miss it."

She shrugged. "But we really do like it here. And it's nice to know we have pictures of Elana, at least. It just caught me by surprise, is all."

"So, your whole family is redheads except for you, huh?" I asked, mainly to change the subject.

"Oh! I guess you wouldn't know. Um, I'm adopted." She shot me an uncertain look, like she wasn't sure how I'd react.

"Really? I had no idea." Then I smiled. "Something else we have in common."

She nodded, looking both pleased and relieved. "It seemed weird to just blurt it out earlier, like I was, I don't know, trying to make us seem the same or anything. Besides, I get the impression your aunt and uncle aren't as—I mean—" she broke off, looking embarrassed.

"Not as nice as your folks, no. But it's been fine. Mostly." I was ready to change the subject back to Mars. Now that I'd had a taste, I was burning with curiosity to learn more about the colony there and its people—even if that was the O'Garas' plan.

I was about to ask about the food when, out of the blue, Molly blurted out, "So, what's the deal with you and Rigel? How long have you two been together?"

I blinked, caught totally off guard. "Um, since the second or third week of school, I guess."

"Off and on," she amended, startling me even more.

"What? That's totally not true! Where did you hear that?" Even as I asked, I realized that must be the impression the whole school had.

"Trina," she admitted, a little sheepishly. "But the other cheerleaders backed her up. She said he'd gone back and forth between you and her since the beginning of school. That he's a real player and I should be careful. Not that that was why I was asking!" she added hastily.

"So, uh, why are you asking?"

Her gaze slid away from mine. "I was just curious. I mean, it

57

makes total sense that you two would get together, since you were the only *Echtrans* in the school."

"It's not just—" I began, but she rushed on.

"And I *totally* should have asked you instead of Trina. But she . . . made it sound like things have been kind of rocky between you two?"

Despite her denial, I couldn't help wondering if she was asking because she was interested in Rigel herself. I mean, what girl wouldn't be? Especially a Martian girl? Or—it suddenly occurred to me—if Rigel's suspicion about Sean was right, was it possible he'd put her up to this, to test the waters? Either way, the absolute best thing I could do was to tell the truth.

"Other than that first week we met, things have never been rocky between Rigel and me—even if it looked that way from the outside."

"But Trina said—"

"I know. And it probably *did* look that way, but that's not how it really was. When we found out Faxon's people were after me and might be watching Rigel, he decided being together was putting me in danger. So we *pretended* to break up. And, yeah, Rigel even paid attention to Trina to throw them off the scent. It worked, too, when one of Faxon's spies pretended to be a teacher."

I explained how we'd figured out Faxon's forces were planning to invade and conquer Earth—and how when they couldn't find me, they'd decided they could safely go ahead with it. Which made me convince Rigel to get back together, to let them know I did exist, to force them to change their plans.

"So it was because they were watching Rigel they found you?" she asked. "Why would he risk you like that?"

"It was risk me or risk everybody on Earth. And it was *my* decision, not Rigel's." I spoke a little sharply, but I didn't like her criticizing Rigel.

She didn't look convinced. "Wouldn't it have been safer for you to just hide somewhere and let the *Echtran* Council and their people take care of Faxon's thugs?"

"You sound like your uncle. That's *exactly* what he wanted me to do. But that would have left my aunt and uncle—who don't know about any of this—plus Rigel and his family in danger. And . . . it would have meant me leaving Rigel." That last reason had been the most important to me, even if it didn't sound as noble.

Molly waved it aside. "You'd only known him for a few weeks. What was the big deal?"

I hesitated for a long moment. Then, tentatively, "Molly, have you heard of the *graell?*"

She shocked me by laughing. "Of course! Who hasn't? It's the basis of, like, every romantic Nuathan fairy tale that exists."

That sidetracked me. "There are Nuathan fairy tales?"

"Sure, lots of them. Let's see . . ." She turned around to rummage through a box of books waiting to be put on an empty set of shelves. "Ah, here. *Hannahan's Fables.* This copy is in Martian, not English, but it's got stories like "The Gardener's Daughter" and "Isobail's Last Chance" and "The Engineer Prince"—those are the rough translations, anyway. They're all about unlikely romances because of the *graell,* overcoming impossible odds to be together, stuff like that."

I stared at the leather-bound volume with unfamiliar lettering on the cover, fascinated. "Fairy tales," I repeated, shaking my head. Then, "I'm surprised they still use regular books on Mars!"

"Oh, we don't. We got these in Bailerealta. I'd never even seen a paper-bound book before we got there. But back to you and Rigel . . . You weren't really about to tell me you think you're bonded with the *graell,* were you?"

I felt my face reddening at her amused expression. "Well, uh, actually—"

"It's okay, I don't blame you. Just about every girl I know—well, knew, back in Nuath, plus a few in Ireland—wanted to believe she had the *graell* with some boy she had a crush on. We all go through that. Then there are the boys who go along with it, just so they can get a girl to have sex." She grimaced. "As smart as we're supposed to be, you wouldn't think any girls would be that gullible, but some are."

"No," I protested, "that's not at *all* what—"

Her eyes went wide with horror. "Oh! I wasn't implying that Rigel — That you— It's not like *you'd* know any better, anyway."

Again she seemed to be implying that Rigel was at fault and I couldn't let her think that.

"Rigel did tell me it's incredibly rare—so rare that most people don't even believe in it. It's not like he tried to convince me or anything. In fact, it really freaked him out when he first suspected it. He didn't want to tell me anything about it at all, but it was the weird connection between us that first made me think something strange was going on—before I'd ever heard of the *graell* or Martians or anything."

She still looked skeptical. "So no other boy has ever given you a zing? Because it's really not that uncommon with someone your own age. Though I guess he was the very first *Echtran* boy you ever met, huh?"

I shook my head, willing myself not to blush. No way was I going to admit to that jolt I sometimes got from Sean. Not now. Besides, it *wasn't* the same thing I felt with Rigel. Not at all.

"Hey, just because I've never actually *known* anyone *graell*-bonded doesn't mean it's impossible. The stories had to come from somewhere." I could tell she didn't want to argue with me any more, but I could also tell she still didn't believe it.

"Really, Molly, I was completely—" I began, then broke off abruptly as Sean came back into the room. I wondered how much he'd overheard.

"Sorry about that," he said. "Pete Griffin had a bad practice yesterday and wanted some tips, so I— Oops, it's getting late again, M. We don't want your aunt to decide we're a bad influence. She might not let you come back."

Molly and I both looked at the clock and just like my last two times here, I was surprised at how quickly the time had gone. I'd told Aunt Theresa I'd be home by nine and it was five till.

"Thanks. I'd better head." I stuck my history book into my backpack.

"No prob. Walk you home?" He never said it like a come-on. In fact, last time both he and Molly had walked with me. But tonight I felt weird about it because of my conversation with Molly just now.

"Thanks, but I brought an umbrella." I still had Rigel's and held it up as both evidence and talisman.

He shrugged, his smile still casual. "I think the rain's stopped anyway, but I don't mind. You shouldn't be out this late by yourself, rain or not."

Maybe he hadn't meant it that way, but I bristled a little. "I *can* take care of myself, Sean. Besides, it's only around the corner and this is

Jewel, Indiana. Nothing ever happens here."

Not strictly true, since I had almost been killed here just last month, but those guys were long gone. I headed for the door, figuring that would be the end of it, but Sean's jaw jutted out, his smile becoming stubborn.

"C'mon, M, you don't want *me* to get in trouble, do you? My folks will get on my case if I let you walk home by yourself. What's the big deal?"

I let out my breath with a little huff. "No big deal. Sorry. You can walk with me if you want. I just think it's silly."

"Thanks for humoring me," he said, opening the front door with a wide grin. "See you in a few, Moll," he called over his shoulder to his sister.

"Yeah, bye, Molly. See you tomorrow."

It was colder than it had been when I arrived, but, as Sean had said, no longer raining. Which reminded me. "Hey, you promised to show me more of the stuff your omni does, remember?"

Sean chuckled—he did have a very pleasant chuckle. "So that's why you agreed to let me walk you home, even though I insulted your warrior-woman abilities?"

"Funny. Although I'll have you know I *am* a green belt in taekwondo."

He grinned down at me. "I consider myself warned. Okay, let's see." He pulled out the tiny device Rigel had said he wasn't even supposed to have here. Remembering that, I felt slightly guilty for asking to see more tricks. But my curiosity was stronger than my guilt, so I kept my mouth shut.

"It does anything your basic iPhone will do—music, video, communication. But I'm guessing you're more interested in its, ah, less mundane apps?"

I nodded, watching intently as he handled the thing.

"Okay, here." He pressed it and the holgraphic screen popped up like it had before. "Are you cold?"

"Um, maybe a little," I admitted. The temperature had dropped at least ten degrees since I'd put on my rain coat earlier.

He reached for my shoulder, then paused. "May I? Sorry—you act so much like a regular person, it's easy to forget you're the Sovereign."

"I *am* a regular person. But, um, sure." I resolutely ignored that annoying tingle when he put his hand on my shoulder, watching as he pushed a button on a sub-menu. Suddenly it was like I had my own personal space heater. In seconds, I was even tempted to take off my rain coat.

"Wow," I marveled. "So you never get uncomfortable with this thing, huh?"

Clearly enjoying my reaction, he shook his head. "Personal climate control. Oh, and that vid you saw earlier? Watch this."

He had to take his hand off my shoulder to bring up the new menu. I immediately felt the cold again, but I didn't want to say anything that might sound like I *wanted* him to touch me. A second later I forgot the cold when a screen several sizes larger than the earlier picture of Mars appeared in mid air.

"I can adjust the screen size pretty much as big as I want, though of course I'd only do that indoors. It'll pick up satellite TV signals, internet video, you name it."

As I watched, a scene from a movie currently playing in theaters flashed across the screen.

"That can't be legal," I commented.

Sean gave a little snort. "If your authorities knew about the omni, do you think movie piracy would be what they'd worry about?"

"Good point." We were already approaching my house and, like that first time, I'd have liked the walk to last longer—though not for any reason Rigel needed to worry about.

"Thanks, Sean," I said the second we reached my driveway, so he wouldn't walk me all the way to the door. "Guess I'll see you at school."

"I'm looking forward to it." There was an odd edge to his voice, but before I could analyze it, he gave a little nod and headed quickly back down the street toward his house.

Rigel's suspicions had me imagining things, I told myself as I went inside. Sean had never done anything that could be remotely construed as making a pass at me—though he probably knew I'd shut him down immediately if he did.

Lying in bed later, I thought back over my conversation with Molly tonight. It still rattled me to learn that the *graell* was literally the stuff of fairy tales. I'd made up a lot of stories over the years, with my overactive imagination—to include that I was a Martian Princess. While that one turned out to be true, the others, like my invisible pet cheetah and the elaborate plots acted out by my toys, had been completely in my head.

But my bond with Rigel wasn't. Even Shim believed it. Because there was lots of proof, no matter how skeptical Molly was, or how confusing that tingle from Sean might be. Rigel and I both knew for a fact our *graell* bond was real and that was all that mattered.

Wasn't it?

11

Rigel (RY-jel): *an extremely hot, rapidly-burning star*

Allister is still on my folks for not making me do more around the house, so I clear the table and start doing the dinner dishes before anyone asks. Anyway, I'd rather do dishes—even by hand—than talk *Echtran* guidelines. Especially with Allister.

I take an extra couple minutes to wipe down the sink and straighten some stuff on the counter, but finally I run out of excuses not to join my dad, my grandfather and Allister in the living room.

"So are we agreed that it's pointless to try to cover every conceivable situation?" my father is saying. He's the youngest and doesn't hold any kind of leadership position, so he tends to defer to them. Not that he's a wimp. He proved that during the big battle in the cornfield.

"I suppose so." Allister sounds reluctant. He's middle-aged for a Martian, maybe a hundred and fifty, and definitely has control issues. The type who'd rather legislate every detail of people's lives than risk them doing anything "wrong." Meaning, "not his way."

Grandfather agrees with my dad. "Our people have done remarkably well avoiding detection or even suspicion for over five hundred years without canonized regulations. I believe we can trust they will continue to do so. This can simply be a handbook to ease their transition into terran life."

I admire Shim more than anybody I've ever known, though when I was a kid I was so in awe I was practically scared of him. To be honest, he still intimidates me a little, but he probably intimidates most people. He gives off a sort of aura of power, like you might expect from a president or a king or something. Maybe because he's the oldest Martian on Earth—which makes him the oldest *person* on Earth—at two hundred seventy-eight.

64

"Should we at least include a list of proscribed technologies?" my dad asks, making notes on his handheld computer. It's just a souped-up tablet, though, not anything Martian. Not like Sean O'Gara's omni.

"I'd prefer to let our people use their own judgment," Grandfather says, "unless you think such a list would be helpful to them?"

Allister's frowning again. "We can't overstate the importance of secrecy, at least for the next few decades. Now that all rational people are agreed we should pursue peaceful integration with Earth culture, we must be careful not to jeopardize that by premature discovery. Any technology likely to be noticed—or abused—should be avoided."

"Of course," Shim agrees. "And some must obviously be banned entirely, such as the Ossian Spheres that Boyne Morven smuggled to Earth."

They all nod, and so do I—emphatically. That vicious thing nearly killed M and my mother last month, not to mention that he'd planned to use it to enslave humans by the thousands. Talk about abuse of technology!

"That goes without saying," Dad says. "Though perhaps we should note it anyway, just to be clear. But what about the gray areas? Most Martian households have at least a few, ah, improvements that would be difficult to explain to the average *Duchas*. Should we craft any guidelines for those?"

"What our people use in the privacy of their own homes doesn't concern me so much as things they might be tempted to use in more public settings," Allister says. "Not everyone has impeccable judgment, after all." He glances at me.

I totally know what he's thinking. Not only does he hate my relationship with M, he hasn't forgiven any of us for going against his advice when we let all the other Martians on Earth know about her. If he'd had his way, she'd have spent the last two months in that compound in Montana, well away from me. Which would probably mean she and I would both be dead by now, without any help from Faxon's goon squad.

"I think it might be wise to include more stringent and specific rules in the portion of this, ah, handbook intended for young people," Allister continues, "as they constitute our greatest risk of discovery."

I have to practically glue my mouth shut, I'm so tempted to tell Allister his precious nephew is carrying an omni around in his pocket. Should I? For the good of our people?

No. That's not my real reason and I know it. My real reason is petty. And stupid, because there's no way Sean can come between M and me, no matter how much Allister wants him to.

"It, uh, might not be a bad idea to say somewhere that kids can't take any kind of Martian technology to school," I suggest instead, proud of my restraint. "That way they won't be tempted to show something off to impress the other kids."

"An excellent point, Rigel. Of course, that goes for abilities as well as technology." Shim looks from me to Allister, and I know he's thinking of me on the football field and Sean on the basketball court.

Last year at Center North High School, near Indy, I was a good player for a freshman, but not any kind of phenom. Since coming to Jewel, though—since bonding with M—I've improved so much it sometimes does feel like cheating. My parents finally made me promise to hold back so I wouldn't attract *too* much attention, though I don't think they'd mind if I landed a football scholarship.

I haven't seen Sean play basketball yet but I know he's good, from what M's friend Bri said. As more and more Martians come to Earth, will we eventually dominate most sports? And if we do, how will the *Duchas*—native Earthers—feel about that, if the truth comes out? I guess I can see Grandfather's point.

"Most *Echtran* kids have grown up in compounds and villages so far, right?" I ask, though I was an exception. "Will that be changing?"

I watch Allister, hoping he'll admit why he brought the O'Garas here to Jewel. He doesn't say anything, but my grandfather does.

"That's always been the suggested course, as it seems unrealistic to expect children—especially young children—to maintain strict secrecy."

"It's why we didn't tell you the truth until you were older," Dad explains, though I'd already figured that out. Duh.

Shim nods. "However, if we are to truly integrate into terran society, it makes sense to allow our youngsters to interact with the

Duchas once they reach an age of reason."

"Particularly those who may eventually have a hand in guiding our people here on Earth," Allister says, not looking at me now.

He can't mean M, since she's lived like an Earther all her life. Does he mean Sean? Is he being groomed as Allister's successor or something? I can't ask without giving away how I feel about the jerk, so I keep my mouth shut. I'll just watch and listen and figure it out.

With barely any more input from me, the others hammer out the main points for their handbook or guidelines or whatever the hell it's going to be. It's nearly eleven when they finally call it a night—way too late for me to call M.

I can't help wondering if that's intentional.

I'm barely off the bus Wednesday morning when Sean O'Gara waylays me outside the school.

"Hey, Stuart! Got a minute?" He walks over and stops so close I'd have to crane my neck to look him in the eye. Not that I give him that satisfaction.

"What's up?" I glance past him toward the school, keeping my voice casual. No point turning this into a pissing contest. Yet.

"Molly and M had a real interesting conversation at our house last night." He says it too low to be overheard. "But you know how girls can be, all starry-eyed over nothing, so I figured I should get the scoop from you before jumping to conclusions."

His tone makes my fists want to clench but I force myself not to react. "I have no clue what you're talking about," I point out when he pauses like he expects me to say something.

"Glad to hear it. I guess that means you didn't really give M some stupid come-on line about the *graell* being real and try to convince her you guys are bonded?"

Now I do glance up at him. He's bigger than me, yeah, but I'm pretty sure I can wipe that smirk off his face. "How is that any of your business?"

His fake smile gets wider. "Oh, c'mon, Stuart, I thought better of you than that." *Not.* "You wouldn't really take advantage of her ignorance that way, would you? I mean, that line's so old, no *other* girl would ever fall for it. Guys back home have been using it for a few hundred years now."

That's news to me, but I'm not about to admit it. "Maybe it's not a line," I manage through clenched teeth. Asshole.

Now his eyebrows go up and he gives me this exaggeratedly sympathetic look that makes me want to punch him even more. "Oh, *sorry*, man. I guess, born on Earth and all, you're as naive as she is. But tell me this. If she were really bonded to you, would she keep asking me to walk her home at night? Think about it."

With a last obnoxious grin, he turns and walks into the school.

I glare after him, getting my anger under control. The icy wind helps a little. Then the warning bell rings and I curse out loud. I'd planned to meet M at her locker to ask her about last night and now I'll barely have time to drop my coat and backpack at my own locker before class.

It's tempting to sprint full speed through the school, but I don't dare draw that kind of attention, not now. Not when I might have to take down Sean O'Gara in the very near future.

Forcing myself to just a fast walk, I dump my stuff, grab my Geometry book and get to class right as the final bell rings. M is already in her seat, watching the door for me. "Sorry," I whisper as I slide into the desk next to hers.

"What—?" she starts to ask. I can tell from her expression she's sensing I'm pissed. But the teacher clears his throat and looks at us, so she has to shut up.

I'm hyper aware of M all through class. Even more than usual. For one thing, she looks totally hot in that green sweater. But mostly I'm trying to figure out if there's anything off about her expression when she looks at me. She catches me staring and frowns a question at me that I can't answer. Not yet.

When class finally ends, I turn to M to explain—or maybe to ask her to explain—but her friend Deb immediately starts talking to her about Mark Lennox, a guy on the football team, asking stuff like if M thinks he likes her. M sends me a little nonverbal apology but keeps listening.

It ticks me off, but not exactly at M. I mean, Deb is one of her best friends and M isn't the kind of girl to blow off a friend needing advice. But I *really* want to talk to her and we're in different classes next period.

Deb finally winds down and M says something encouraging to her and then it's just the two of us together in the hallway. Surrounded by a whole lot of other people on their way to second period.

But instead of telling her what Sean said, like I planned, I hear myself asking, "So, how did it go last night?"

She gives a cute little shrug and a smile that makes me want to kiss her. "It was fine, I guess. I finished catching them up on U.S. History, then we talked some more about, um, Ireland." That's our code for Mars these days.

"Learn anything interesting?" I want to ask about Sean, ask if he really walked her home again, but I don't. I'm not sure why.

"I did, actually. I'll tell you about it later when we can be, uh, private." We're already at the door of her Computer classroom. How did that happen?

"Yeah, we'll talk later." Then just before running off to Spanish, I blurt out, "I'm just glad you made it home okay."

She stares at me and opens her mouth like she's going to say something, but I just shoot her a tight smile and walk away, feeling like an even bigger jerk than Sean.

I trust M. I absolutely trust her. So why am I letting Sean make me act like a jealous idiot?

Maybe because I really am a jealous idiot? Crap.

12

efrin (EF-rin): *Hell; used as a mild curse*

I stared after Rigel, wondering what he'd meant by that last comment. It sounded like he already knew Sean walked me home again last night, even though I hadn't had a chance to tell him. Had Molly said something? He'd been late getting to Geometry, so he must have been talking to somebody.

Great. Just great.

I was so distracted when I sat down at my computer, I nearly forgot to ground myself on the table leg before touching it. I'd already fried one computer this semester and I knew Mr. Morrison—who was Bri's dad and really nice (for a teacher)—would be upset if I broke another one.

I hurried off when the bell rang, so I could explain to Rigel before English. Surely he wouldn't be mad once I explained how Sean had insisted because of some dumb idea that the "Princess" shouldn't be walking alone at night. And that he hadn't made any kind of pass at me or anything.

Maybe if I could convince Rigel that Sean wasn't at all interested in me romantically, the two of them could actually be friends. That would sure make *my* life easier, plus it would be fun if the four of us could do stuff together.

I imagined us all going to Dream Cream or over to Rigel's or the O'Garas' house. Rigel and I could both learn about life on Mars and we could tell Sean and Molly stuff about Jewel, and Indiana—and Earth. With that hopeful picture in mind, I started rehearsing my explanation for Rigel when I saw him coming toward me.

"Rigel, I really was going to—" I began, when he cut me off.

"No, M, it's okay. I'm sorry I was such an ass, saying that and then leaving." He held my gaze and took my hand so I'd know he meant it. "It's just, well, Sean made a crack this morning about you asking him to walk you home and it pissed me off. At *him*, I mean, so I was

70

a real jerk to take it out on you."

He said it in a rush, his eyes pleading for forgiveness—not that there was anything to forgive. But then I realized exactly what he'd said.

"Wait. Sean said I *asked* him to walk me? That is so not true! He insisted, even after I told him not to."

Rigel started to glower, so I kept talking before my rosy vision of the future crumbled completely.

"It's just because the O'Garas are all about me having to be protected and stuff. Really. It wasn't like, 'walk a girl home,' or anything like that."

I believed that, didn't I? I willed Rigel to believe it, too—and his frown eased a little bit.

"Okay. I didn't really think you'd asked him. I should have known he just said it to needle me. But . . . why would he do that if he doesn't like you?"

I shrugged. "I don't know what's going on in his head. But honestly, he hasn't come on to me at *all,* I swear."

Finally, Rigel smiled. "I guess I can let him live, then. Though sometimes I wonder if you'd notice if a guy *did* come on to you."

I smiled back, my insides finally warming the way they normally did when I was with Rigel. "If I don't notice, does it really matter?"

He gave my hand a squeeze and I reveled in the wonderful rush it gave me—*so* much better than that stupid tingle I got from Sean.

"I guess not. C'mon," he said, still smiling, "let's get to class."

Now that I'd smoothed things over, I was able to relax and enjoy Rigel's nearness during my next two classes. It was clear Rigel still didn't like Sean, but maybe my fantasy of us eventually hanging out with him and Molly wasn't *completely* impossible. It would just take a little more peacemaking on my part. Maybe I could get Molly to help, too.

I headed to lunch hand in hand with Rigel with that goal in mind, but we hadn't even entered the lunch line when Sean came up to us, a tense look on his face. Molly was hovering nervously behind him.

"Hey. Rigel," he said. "I've been thinking about what you said this morning and I think we need to talk. Any chance we go someplace more private?"

Rigel shot me a quick, concerned frown then nodded. "Sure. Courtyard?"

"That'll be fine. See you there in five." Sean stalked off toward an empty table but Molly, trailing behind him, gave us a backward, worried glance. Which of course started *me* worrying.

"What was that about?" I demanded. "What *did* you and Sean talk about this morning? Is this just about him walking me home or is something else going on?"

"I'm not sure." Rigel sent a glare Sean's way. "But it's probably time we settled things."

"What, like, 'let's settle this outside?' No way. You two are *not* going to—"

Rigel patted my arm reassuringly, which didn't reassure me at all. "Don't worry, M. I'm sure we can keep things . . . civilized. I just need to make it clear to him how things stand, that's all."

He grabbed a tuna sandwich and a carton of chocolate milk and I did the same, except skim milk instead of chocolate. I kept glancing over to where Sean and Molly were sitting, just the two of them, trying to hear what she was saying to him. She looked really earnest about whatever it was, but they were speaking too softly for me to pick their words out of the rest of the cafeteria noise.

Rigel and I went to our usual table, but he barely nodded at the others, just wolfed down his lunch and stood back up less than two minutes later.

"I'll let you know how it goes," he said to me.

Ignoring Bri and Deb's questioning looks, I watched him head for the door, then saw Sean get up a second later to follow him out. Molly immediately came over to our table, still looking worried.

"What's going on with Rigel?" Bri asked just as Molly got there.

I was trying to decipher the same thing from Molly's expression, since I couldn't ask her outright, so I just answered vaguely, "Not sure. Actually, I just realized I should probably—"

"I was thinking that, too," Molly said before I could finish. Her gray eyes were wide and troubled.

"I'll, uh, see you guys later," I said to Bri and Deb, who were looking really curious by now. Explanations—meaning, whatever I managed to make up—would have to wait.

Molly and I took our trays, dumped our uneaten lunches and

headed for the exit.

"What *is* going on?" I demanded quietly the second we were in the hall. "Do you know?"

"Not exactly, but I think it's my fault," she said miserably, walking so fast I had to trot to keep up. "After he got back from walking you home last night, Sean asked what we'd been talking about because he'd overheard the last little bit. I told him and he, well, I don't know when I've seen him so upset. He seemed calmer this morning, but I'm afraid—"

Though her worry was contagious, her explanation didn't seem to make sense. "Wait, you mean you told him what I said about Rigel and me being bonded? Why should he be angry about that? What does it have to do with him?"

She didn't answer, but gave me a look that was almost scared. Did that mean Rigel was right, that Sean already had a crush on me or something? But that was crazy. He barely knew me!

Before I could demand more information we reached the courtyard, which was empty except for Sean and Rigel. They weren't fighting—yet—but they definitely didn't look happy with each other. I pushed open the door and stifled a hiss when the cold wind hit me in the face. It was freezing out here! But half a second later, the cold was the last thing on my mind.

"—some nerve, barging in here and throwing around accusations," Rigel was saying. "None of this is any of your business, anyway."

Sean loomed over Rigel until they were almost nose to nose. He was several inches taller, though Rigel was broader through the chest and shoulders.

"The Sovereign's welfare is the business of *all* of our people. You'd know that if you were any kind of patriot. You can't put your own selfish feelings ahead of her safety."

"I'd never put *anything* ahead of M's safety!" Rigel nearly shouted. "You don't have a clue about anything you're assuming. Maybe you should—"

"I should what?" Sean said, leaning even closer.

They both shifted their stances, squaring off against each other, their hands clenching into fists. This was *not* my idea of civilized!

"Um, guys?" I said, loudly enough to distract them from each other.

They both whipped their heads in my direction, then relaxed slightly, taking a half step away from each other—but their fists didn't unclench.

"Get inside, M," Rigel said to me. "You shouldn't be here right now."

I heard Molly gasp from just behind me, and at the same time Sean snapped, "Don't tell her what to do. Who the *efrin* do you think you are?" Then Sean turned to me and said, in a gentler voice. "It's cold out here, Princess. I'm sure you'd be more comfortable inside."

By now I was about equally irritated at both of them. "How about neither one of you tell me what to do? I'm not going anywhere while you two are acting like a couple of barnyard roosters. If this ridiculous display of testosterone poisoning is because of me, I absolutely ought to be here. Right, Molly?"

I glanced back at her. She gave me a deer-in-the-headlights look, but after a second she nodded. "Right. You guys need to calm down. You don't want to get in trouble, do you?"

Sean glared at her, jaw rigid and blue eyes blazing, but then he took a visible deep breath. "Molly, why don't you take Emileia back to the cafeteria?"

"Molly's not taking me anywhere," I informed him, feeling a hot rush of anger despite the cold. "Do you both *want* to get kicked out of school for fighting?"

The two of them looked at me, then at each other.

"Gee, who will protect me if both of you are suspended?" I deliberately laced my voice with sarcasm, but I could tell they both took the question seriously.

After a long, tense moment, Sean moved away from Rigel and took a step toward me. "I just wanted to explain to him that just because he happened to be the first *Echtran* you ever met, and the first one to tell you about . . . about everything, it doesn't automatically give him some *claim* on you."

"I never said it did." Rigel also moved my way, like he was trying to get between Sean and me. "But just because you happen to be Allister's precious nephew, you seem to think you've been appointed her protector or something. Like you have some claim on her yourself. You don't."

Sean rounded on him, fists coming up. "Talk about not having a clue—"

"*Both* of you stop talking about me like I'm some piece of real estate in a land dispute," I interrupted, trying to maintain my anger to keep away my fear. "Sean, Rigel and I are together. Bonded. Deal with it. And Rigel, that bond doesn't mean you have to go all macho on Sean. He hasn't threatened me in any way, I told you that."

But they both still looked like they wanted to start pummeling each other, glowering ferociously. "He's the one who—" Rigel started to say, at the same time Sean said, "You don't really think—"

"Hey!" I did shout this time. "Aren't I supposed to outrank you guys? Just stop it! I want you both to . . . to shake hands and then back away from each other."

I knew I was pushing it, but I didn't back down. I just waited.

And waited.

Finally, a little to my amazement, Rigel gave a quick nod and extended his hand, and Sean did likewise. It had to be one of the most perfunctory, unwilling handshakes in history. Then they moved away from each other, which was what really mattered.

"Good," I said. "And if I hear about you fighting later, I'll . . . I'll tell Shim and Allister to come up with some kind of suitable punishment, on top of anything the school does."

I wouldn't really do that, but I definitely wanted them to *think* I might. I turned to Molly.

"You'll let me know if they do, won't you?"

She nodded vigorously, her eyes still wide. Then the warning bell rang and she seemed to snap out of her trance, or whatever it was.

"Come on, Sean, let's go," she said to her brother.

He sent one last, warning glare at Rigel, then nodded, first to her and then to me—though the one to me was more like a little bow—and followed her out of the courtyard.

I let out my breath, only then realizing how on edge I'd been. Then I turned to Rigel. "So what was that about? Really?"

He didn't meet my eyes right away, so I reached out and took his hand. The second I touched him, I gasped at the roiling emotions I sensed—anger, fear, jealousy, and again that tinge of sadness I didn't understand.

"Rigel?" I prompted, alarmed.

He looked at me then, apology written on his face. He'd clearly registered my worry. "I'm sorry, M. I really need to learn to control my feelings better."

I gently tugged him toward the courtyard door, since we needed to get to class. "I don't *ever* want you to hide your feelings from me, Rigel. But you can't let Sean—or anyone else—goad you into doing stuff you shouldn't. What did he say to get you that upset?"

We went inside, into the lovely warmth of the hallway. Rigel put an arm around me and rubbed my arm to warm me faster. "It's my fault you're cold, too."

"Never mind that. I'm fine. Answer me."

Rigel sighed, then nodded. "Okay. As far as I can tell, Sean totally freaked out when he heard we were bonded. He doesn't believe it— thinks I just made it up, like some kind of come-on line, to take advantage of you."

I snorted. "Molly didn't believe it either," I told him, "but I thought she'd at least decided to give me the benefit of the doubt. Guess Sean wasn't willing to do that."

I was kind of ticked Molly had told him at all, since it had led to so much trouble, but that wasn't fair. It's not like I'd asked her not to. In fact, I'd half hoped she *would* tell him, so he'd be less likely to flirt with me. I definitely hadn't expected it to backfire like this.

"Still, I shouldn't have let him get to me like that," Rigel said. "It put you in the middle and that's not fair."

"No, *he's* the one who put me in the middle," I pointed out. "Except I'm not really in the middle at all. I'm on your side, Rigel. Always. No matter what."

To my relief, I felt the negative emotions start to drain out of him.

"Thanks, M," he said as we reached the door to our History class. "I'll do my best not to make you put that to the test."

"I appreciate that," I answered with a grin. "And I'll do my best not to make that promise harder for you to keep."

I wished I could believe Sean would help with that, too, but I knew I couldn't count on it. My pleasant fantasy of all four of us becoming good friends was apparently just that—a fantasy. Unless I could somehow fix things.

Of course, Bri and Deb both wanted to know what was going on as soon as we joined them in History, and I'd totally forgotten to come up with something to tell them. Luckily, Bri made a guess of her own before I could say anything too stupid.

"It's something to do with Rigel's party Saturday, isn't it?" she asked as I stammered.

I immediately seized on that. "Yeah, actually, it was. He, um, had an idea for something kind of crazy, and I needed to talk to him about it, make sure he didn't commit to anything without asking his parents. I didn't want him to get in trouble on his birthday. Right, Rigel?"

"Yeah, and she was right, just like she usually is," he said, managing a chagrined smile. "I think we'll keep things simple after all."

"But if you can't go crazy on your sixteenth birthday, when can you?" Bri protested. "Don't wimp out."

I sensed Rigel tensing beside me and knew he was thinking of Sean instead of his party. Quickly, I changed the subject.

"Trust me, it's better this way. Hey, did you do the reading last night? I'm betting Rosa Parks will be on the final. Don't you just love everyday heroines like that?"

Deb jumped in with an enthusiastic agreement and a tidbit about Rosa Parks she'd found on Wikipedia, which kept us on safe topics until class started.

Molly, I noticed, didn't say a word during any of this and seemed preoccupied all during class. I wondered if she was still worried about the possibility of Sean and Rigel fighting—and whether she had a reason to worry that I didn't know about.

Sean was on the other side of the room, which meant at least I didn't have to worry about him saying anything that might blow my cover story or get Rigel upset again. Not for the next forty-five minutes, anyway.

13

fine (feen): *genetically related subsets of Martian population, each with certain attributes*

I wanted to talk to Molly privately to find out what Sean's problem was, but I didn't get a chance that day or the next. She had cheerleading, and I was trying to spend every moment I could with Rigel. Besides the usual reasons, I wanted to keep tabs on his emotions . . . and keep him away from Sean.

Then, on the the bus ride home Friday afternoon, Molly sat with Trina (no cheerleading practice on Fridays) while I sat with Bri and Deb. I started to wonder if Molly was avoiding a one-on-one chat, but the moment we both got off the bus, she turned to me.

"M, I think we need to talk. Would it be okay if I came over to your house for a little while? Your aunt won't be home, right?"

I was surprised she suggested my house instead of hers, then realized it made sense. If we were going to talk about Sean, we wouldn't want her parents overhearing us, or Sean himself coming home from practice right in the middle of things.

"She won't be home for at least an hour. And . . . I think you're right." A minute later, I unlocked the front door. "Let's talk in the kitchen," I suggested. "I'll get us some milk and cookies."

My aunt might be a pain in a lot of ways, but she did like to bake and kept the cookie jar filled most of the time. Today it was chocolate chip-walnut cookies that she'd made just last night.

"So," I said, settling myself across the table from Molly, "what's going on with Sean? Why is he so . . . *hostile* to Rigel? I really though they were going to get into a fight the other day."

To my surprise, she blushed. "I was afraid they would, too," she admitted. "I'm so glad you managed to talk sense into them before they did anything really stupid. You were amazing, by the way, how you handled them both."

Now it was my turn to blush at the frank admiration in her eyes. "I mostly just distracted them long enough for their brains to start functioning again," I said. "They're both smart guys. Way too smart to let their emotions get them in trouble. I know why Rigel was upset. He's basically jealous, no matter how much he denies it. But Sean seems to be deliberately saying stuff to *make* him jealous. That's what I don't get."

Molly's gaze slid away from mine. "It's . . . complicated. And hard to explain to someone who didn't grow up on Mars. Like, what a huge deal it was to find out you were alive after all, when everybody had thought there was no legitimate heir to the last Sovereign. So Sean feels—all of us feel—kind of . . . protective of you. Especially after the story came out about how close we came to losing you again last month."

"But Rigel has done a super job of protecting me! Seriously. He literally saved my life twice last month. You'd think Sean would be *grateful* to him. Instead, he acts like Rigel's the enemy or something."

Molly bit her lip. "Not the enemy, no. But it does seem disrespectful, the way Rigel acts around you. To someone from Mars, I mean, especially someone Royal. Sean's a really, really great guy, I swear, so please don't think he's—"

"Is it because he doesn't believe in the *graell*?" I interrupted her. "He thinks it's what you told me Tuesday night, just a . . . a line Martian boys use on girls?"

"Pretty much."

I waited for her to continue, but she didn't. "And you don't believe me either. You acted like you did, but . . ."

She shrugged, not quite meeting my eye. "I didn't want to get into an argument, especially where Sean might overhear us. But that's the main reason I wanted to come over. I need to explain to you why this thing you think you and Rigel have can't be the *graell*."

"Why it—" I stared at her, confused. "But it is! It's not just that we felt drawn to each other—I know that can happen between Martians apart from the *graell*. But honestly, Molly, you should have seen what I was like before I met Rigel. I was such a loser. A total klutz, with acne and glasses and a permanent bad hair day. I'm practically a different person now—because of my bond with Rigel."

Molly smiled, though she didn't look any less skeptical. "Yeah,

Trina mentioned that. She thinks your aunt and uncle paid for contacts and a dermatologist. She also, um, thinks you and Rigel are sleeping together."

I sucked in my breath. "That little—! Well, we're not. Shoot, we hardly ever even get to be alone together, my aunt is so strict. Not that we would if we could, of course," I quickly added. Though I couldn't pretend I'd never fantasized about what it might be like to—

"Oh, I didn't believe her, and I told her so," Molly assured me. "I just thought you should know what she's telling people. But, M, if you were never around any other *Echtrans* before Rigel, it wouldn't take the *graell* to make you change. We all tend to resonate with each other to some extent. It's why most *Echtrans* live in villages and neighborhoods together, and why we can feel it when others are nearby."

"The *brath*. I know. But it's *different* with Rigel. It's hard to describe since you haven't felt it, but I . . . I just know what we have is special." My words sounded lame even to me.

"No, I can't know exactly what you feel, but there's still a lot you don't know about our people—how we've evolved, how our society works, all kinds of stuff. Once I explain some of it, maybe you'll get why Sean is so upset."

Mystified, I just motioned for her to go ahead.

"Okay. You know that we've been evolving independently of Earth humans for more than two thousand years, right? Ever since the original colonists were abducted from Ireland or thereabouts by an alien race we know almost nothing about."

I got up and refilled our milk glasses and the cookie plate, since I had a feeling this might take a while. "Rigel and his folks told me that part, yes, and your parents told me more. They said those aliens did genetic experiments?"

"That's what we think, yeah. But after they left for good, fifteen hundred years or so ago, we continued with what I guess you could call eugenics—selective breeding—to enhance our natural abilities. It's why we're mostly stronger, smarter, more empathic, et cetera, than the *Duchas*. Over time, our society developed a structure based on our genetic differences."

"Wait—selective breeding?" I repeated, recoiling at the idea of arranged marriages, or worse. Nobody had mentioned that! "You mean you're forced to . . . to breed with whoever some scientist or computer program says you have to, for the good of the, uh, race? That sounds awful!"

"No, it's not like that! Not really," she assured me, her gray eyes wide and earnest. "It's more like . . . I guess you could call it tribes, or clans. A long time ago, like a thousand years, our people divided into different *fines*—" she prounounced it *feens*— "or bloodlines, according to innate genetic abilities.

"The smartest, most talented people formed the very first one, and became our natural leaders. A few generations later, that first group split into the Royal *fine* and the Scientific *fine*, which still form the basis for our two-party government system. Then those *fines* split into sub-*fines*. Nowadays, besides the Sovereigns, the Royal *fine* includes all our administrators, legal scholars, historians, and local government officials. The Scientific sub-*fines* are physicists, healers, engineers, geneticists, things like that.

"Meanwhile, everyone else separated into *fines* and sub-*fines*, too. Agriculture, manufacturing, mining, maintenance, arts, communications, systems management, groups like that. This must sound pretty complicated, huh?"

But I was fascinated, if still somewhat appalled. "So people are expected to marry within their own clan or, uh, *fine*?" I asked, trying to get back to her original point.

She nodded. "Abilities are stronger when both parents are from at least the same *fine* if not sub-*fine*. Everyone wants their children to be successful, so that's a real incentive to stick to tradition."

"Okay, I get it. Rigel's parents aren't Royal, so we aren't supposed to be together. But we're on Earth, not Mars, so what difference does it make? And what does it have to do with the *graell*? Other than the fact that you think it's fictitious, I mean."

She set down the cookie she'd just picked up. "Not fictitious, exactly. My mom says there have been a *few* documented cases over the centuries, though it's really, really rare. I mean the, um, fairy tale kind that happens fast, like love at first sight. The other kind, which a lot of people also call *graell*, is more common, though still pretty rare. That's where people, usually married couples, gradually form a physical and psychic bond over years together. A few have supposedly even developed the *shilcloas*, um, a telepathic link, though apparently only in the Royal family."

I opened my mouth to tell her that Rigel's parents had that, and that Rigel and I were getting close, but she went on without pausing.

"But the instant kind of *graell*? Even though there are fairy tales about it happening between way different *fines,* the few *documented* times it's ever happened have all been between people of the same *fine,* even the same sub-*fine*. And of really pure blood, besides. You and Rigel—"

"I know. He's Scientific and I'm Royal. Whole different *fines*."

"Not only that, according to Uncle Allister, his parents are from different Science *fines*—his dad from Informatics and his mom from Healing, which means he's not even from a pure-blooded sub-*fine*."

Now I was confused again. "But his grandfather, Shim—his dad's father—is a geneticist. Isn't that a kind of doctor, too?"

"That's what he does here, but Mum says he was Informatics back home, analyzing genetic and astrophysics data. But even a pure genetics researcher on Mars would be a separate *fine* from Healing. Healers—what you'd call medical doctors—have innate healing abilities that go beyond using treatments and medicines."

I blinked. "Wow, like . . . laying on hands? I didn't know that." Could Dr. Stuart really do that? I realized I'd never had an opportunity to find out—and since she was an OB/Gyn, I probably wouldn't. Though I supposed I could ask.

She nodded. "Most people have some kind of special, *fine*-related ability that no *Duchas* would have."

Not exactly like choosing a college major, then. Mars was apparently a society of savants, with very deep but very narrow skill sets born into them. I found that both cool and disturbing. "Like what?"

"Well, Engineers have super precise spatial skills, Mechanicals have an affinity with machines, Informatics instinctively understand computer languages and data sets, Agriculturalists make plants grow —though, um, I never have. Things like that."

"Wait, you're not a Royal? I thought—"

"No, my real parents were Ags, farmers in Glenamuir. They died when I was a baby. The O'Garas adopted me and assumed their identities—in the database, anyway—so Faxon's people couldn't track them down as Royals. Though I've more or less been raised as one."

Molly didn't seem upset about it, though I wondered if she really was. "So what about Royals?" I had to ask. "Do they have any special abilities?"

"Well, duh!" She grinned. "Most Royals are good at influencing people—like what you did Wednesday in the courtyard. And the closer you are to the Sovereign line, the stronger that ability tends to be, which makes sense, since the Sovereigns always have the purest gene pool."

"Influence people how?" I asked. "Like, clever with words?" I'd never considered that one of my talents—certainly not in the sense of ever having a snappy comeback when I needed one.

"Partly. Also charisma and intelligence and the ability to quickly analyze a situation and make snap decisions. Oh, and a sort of psychic 'push' that makes people more likely to agree with you. It's why hardly anyone ever argued with the Sovereigns—until Faxon."

My head was starting to spin but I tried to get back to the original point of this conversation. "Okay, I get now why you—and Sean, and Allister—find it so hard to believe Rigel and I can possibly be *graell* bonded. But I haven't told you all the reasons I think we are."

Molly picked up another cookie, took a bite of it, then a sip of milk. "So tell me." I could see she didn't expect to be convinced—at all. So much for any special Royal power of persuasion.

I took a deep breath. "Rigel and I can sense each other's emotions, especially if we're touching." I decided not to mention the telepathy thing, since we hadn't told *anybody* about that yet. "And on three different occasions, we've generated electricity, like . . . bolts of lightning. Two of those times, it saved our lives."

Now Molly was staring at me, mouth slightly open, cookie forgotten. "Seriously?" It came out in a whisper. "Why didn't you tell me *that* before?"

"I didn't have time, remember? I take it those supposedly common teenage resonances don't include that?"

Slowly, she shook her head. "The lightning thing, especially . . . that's straight from the fairy tales. The kind of *graell* that should be *completely* impossible for you two."

"Hey, it's not like I ever read any of those fairy tales, so there's no way I got the idea there. Besides, there were lots of witnesses the last time we did it—it's how we disabled that Ossian Sphere." I paused, then said, "Does this mean you finally believe me?" It was surprising how much I needed her to.

She held my gaze for a long, probing moment, then nodded, still wide-eyed. "I . . . guess I have to. I'm *so* sorry I—"

The back door slammed. "Marsha, are you home?" Aunt Theresa's voice preceded her into the kitchen. "Oh, hello, Molly. It's nice to see you again. I hope Marsha has been helpful with your school work."

"Um, yes, she has, Mrs. Truitt, thank you." Molly looked slightly alarmed, like she was worried we might have been overheard. "I, um, guess I should get home."

"Marsha why don't you see her to the door, then get back here and rinse off these dishes." My aunt dropped a stack of papers on the end of the table.

"Oh, I'll do that," Molly exclaimed, jumping up.

"Don't be silly," Aunt Theresa said. "You're a guest."

Molly sat back down with obvious reluctance while I put our plates and glasses in the sink and turned on the water.

"I'll walk Molly home, if that's okay, Aunt Theresa," I said over my shoulder.

She pursed her lips but nodded. "Mind you come straight back. I want the beds stripped so there'll be time to wash, dry and replace the sheets before bedtime. Oh, and since the lawn won't need mowing again this year, you can take over the weekly bathroom cleaning—though that can wait till morning."

Molly was staring at her with something like outrage, so I quickly nudged her toward the front door. "Let's go. I'll be back in a few minutes," I called back to my aunt.

As soon as we reached the sidewalk, Molly turned to me, still looking upset. "Does she always order you around like that?"

I shrugged. "Pretty much. It's not like she knows, uh, who I am. To her, I'm just some orphan she got stuck with a dozen years ago."

Molly's distress turned to wonder. "Wow. You really are like some fairy tale heroine. Like . . . Cinderella or something."

I laughed, though her words startled me. I'd often pretended to be Cinderella when I was younger, while mopping the floors or weeding the garden. It kept me from getting bored or feeling sorry for myself.

"Right. But with Trina and her friends instead of wicked

stepsisters," I joked, shaking off the coincidence. "They tell Earth fairy tales on Mars, too?"

"Some of them," Molly said, relaxing enough to chuckle along with me. "Along with our own. I guess Cinderella is pretty universal."

We'd reached the corner by then. "I should get back," I said. "Thanks for coming over, Molly. I, uh, learned a lot today."

She opened and closed her mouth, with such a strange expression on her face that I wished I could sense her emotions the way I could Rigel's.

"I learned a lot, too," she finally said. "We'll talk again soon. Maybe tonight?"

"Maybe." It was Friday, but I didn't have any plans since Rigel was still busy at home in the evenings. And there was obviously tons more I needed to know about Nuathan society, the Royals—and exactly what people expected me to do eventually.

Walking slowly back, I thought over everything she'd told me. Now that she finally believed me about the *graell*, she could help me convince Sean, too. Then the friction between him and Rigel should go away and we could all be friends after all.

Unless there was something else Molly wasn't telling me.

14

twilly: *obnoxious person; jerk*

When I suggested going over to the O'Garas' again after dinner that night, I expected an argument since Aunt Theresa was usually suspicious if I wanted to do anything on a Friday night. But to my surprise, she agreed immediately.

"I'm glad to see you making the effort to be a good neighbor to the O'Gara children, Marsha," she added. "Lili told me they all appreciate it, as they came here knowing no one."

"Yeah, they're, um, really nice. So you've been talking with Mrs. O'Gara some more?"

Her smile seemed strangely sincere. "Yes, she came by the flower shop last night and we had a nice chat. I encouraged her to join the choir at church and she seems open to the idea."

"Really? That's great. What time do I need to be home tonight?"

"As it's a Friday and it's just around the corner, I suppose you can stay till ten. Tell Lili I said hello."

"I will," I promised, fighting a sense of unreality. It was positively weird for Aunt Theresa to be acting so . . . so *nice*. If it was Mrs. O'Gara's influence, I couldn't help but appreciate it.

Walking to their house—it was cold tonight, but with no hint of the rain we'd had off and on for over a week—I wondered if Sean would even be there. Surely a guy that popular would have better things to do on a Friday night than hang around home? But when I rang the bell, he was the one who opened the door.

"M! I'm *so* glad you came," he greeted me, with a smile that looked both relieved and contrite. "I was such a *twilly*, I mean, such a jerk on Wednesday, I was afraid you wouldn't, even though Molly said— Anyway, I really, really wanted to apologize."

"Really, really?" I echoed with a reluctant smile.

He laughed, looking even more relieved. "Okay, I'm pathetic, I admit it. But I am sorry. Really, really sorry," he added with a grin that showed his perfect teeth. "Molly!" he called up the stairs. "M's here!"

She came clattering down with a smile as big as her brother's. "You came! Yay!" She surprised me with a hug, then surprised me again by jumping back like I'd burned her. "Sorry, sorry! I shouldn't have done that without asking. It's just—"

"No, it's okay," I said. "Don't go all weird and respectful on me. Please? Just let me be M with you guys, like you have so far."

They exchanged uncertain glances, then Sean said, "I guess it's okay when it's just us. But when we're around other *Echtrans*, don't get upset if we observe the forms, yeah? It'll look bad if we don't."

"Oh. Sure. I don't want to get you guys in trouble. So, um, any chance I can see more pictures of Mars?" I asked to change the subject, and was relieved when they both relaxed.

"I already picked some out." Sean led the way into the living room, pausing to close the curtains.

"Mum and Dad will join us later. They figured you might have questions they can answer better than we can. Here, have a seat." He indicated the sofa, now clear of boxes.

Molly and I sat down together, but then Sean squeezed between us, saying, "It'll work better if the omni is in the middle."

I immediately felt that tingle from him, but since I really did want to see the pictures, I just scooched an inch or two away and tried to ignore it.

Sean kept talking, apparently unaware of the tingle or my slight withdrawal. "Since you've never been to Mars, I thought this might give you a better feel for it than regular pictures. Plus, it's pretty cool."

He punched up the control screen and this time, instead of a little video projection, we were suddenly in the middle of a pinkish stone courtyard dotted with what looked like shiny black picnic tables and at least twenty teenagers milling around. There was sound, too—I could hear people laughing and talking in a language I didn't understand.

I glanced left, right and behind me—sure enough, the scene was three-sixty. The courtyard was surrounded on three sides by a one-story building of the same pinkish stone, opening out on our left to a view of the same green countryside I'd seen in the picture Tuesday night.

"Whoa," I breathed. "Is this, like, a holodeck?"

"A what?"

Feeling like a huge geek, I explained about Star Trek holodecks—
I'd been hooked on STNG reruns for the past couple of years. "But
I guess you guys wouldn't know about our old TV shows, would
you?"

To my surprise, they both nodded. "We do watch some Earth
television on Mars. It's even required for Earth Studies class," Molly
told me.

"But no, this isn't a holodeck like you described," Sean said then.
"It's just images, nothing solid that you can touch. This is—was—
our school back on Mars. Our cafeteria, I guess you'd say." I could
hear a note of wistfulness—homesickness?—in his voice.

As I watched, two girls and a boy walked toward us. They were all
very attractive—of course—and all dressed in similar but not quite
identical shimmery, pale blue outfits that fitted them well.

"Uniforms?" I guessed.

"Yeah," Molly replied. "The upperclassmen's are way cooler than
what I had to wear. That's Liam, Gwynne and Doranna—good
friends of Sean's."

Sure enough, just as she said that, they stopped a few feet away
and grinned right at us. One of the girls said something in a pleasant,
teasing tone of voice, but the only word I recognized was "Sean."

"Can . . . can you talk to them?" I asked.

"Unfortunately, no," Sean said. "Wish we could—you'd really like
them. The hologram's not interactive, just a video loop like the
picture you saw before, but on a larger scale. Gwynne was asking
why I had to make a recording when she was having a bad hair day."

Gwynne's short blond hair looked fine to me. And they did all
look like nice people. "Are they still on Mars?"

"Yeah. Though Doranna's folks were talking about leaving if
Faxon put many more rules on them. They're metallurgists and he
was demanding more and more resources for his military buildup—
the one he keeps officially denying." Sean snorted. "But they'd been
pulled off their research enough times to do stuff for his engineers
that they knew what was really going on."

"And Liam's older brother was drafted into Faxon's security force

—which was getting to be more and more like an army," Molly added. "They hardly ever got to see him after that. He had to go live in Thiaraway, the capital city."

The scene looped around then, blinking Sean's friends back to where they'd started. Sean had apparently stopped recording just after Gwynne's complaint. I couldn't help wondering if she'd been his girlfriend. There was something about her expression . . .

"So nobody speaks English on Mars?" I asked then, wondering if I'd be expected to learn Nuathan.

"Oh, yeah, pretty much everyone does," Molly assured me. "It's all the media ever uses, in fact. We're just required to use Nuathan in school—though Faxon was threatening to change that, claiming English is more useful."

I grimaced. "Probably because he was planning to invade Earth and bring pretty much everyone here. Luckily, Rigel and I—"

"Here, I'll show you part of Thiaraway," Sean said before I finish. "It's where you would have lived. I mean, if Faxon had never . . . you know."

I nodded, a sudden lump in my throat diverting my thoughts from last month's battle. If Faxon hadn't killed my whole family, Sean meant. For the hundredth time, I wondered what my life would have been like if Faxon had never existed, or if he'd been stopped before he got all that power.

The scene around us abruptly changed to a city scene, though it looked like no city I'd ever seen. The street was narrower than city streets on Earth and there were no cars, just wide walkways on either side and a metallic grid running down the middle.

A building that looked like it might be made out of rose quartz towered at least a dozen stories high on our left. Similar glassy skyscrapers were visible in the near distance, along with smaller buildings of brick, stone and metal. People hurried along the sidewalks on both sides, and a silver bullet-shaped train whizzed down the center track, making a whooshing sound as it passed.

"This is just an old promo vid," Sean explained. "It's not quite like this now, unfortunately. The trains hardly run anymore, except when Faxon needs someone or something moved quickly. And his troops are everywhere, keeping people from congregating on the streets. My dad says Thiaraway isn't as clean as it used to be, either. Guess that's not one of Faxon's priorities." His voice was scornful.

I was still gazing around, rapt. "So this is what it looked like when my . . . I mean, before Faxon? It's wonderful."

"Yeah, it really was," Molly agreed. "Look behind you."

I turned and caught my breath. It was a stunningly beautiful palace —a pink diamond palace, astonishingly like the one I used to imagine when I was little. Or had always assumed I'd imagined. "I remember this," I whispered disbelievingly. "How can I remember this? I was just a baby when I left."

"Most of us can remember things well into infancy," Sean told me. "And it's possible your parents showed you pictures after you came to Earth. Before—"

"Before they were killed," I finished, swallowing hard. Seeing the palace, so real and close it seemed I could walk right into it, suddenly made my shadowy past real in a way it had never been before. I had *lived* in that palace! For my first year of life, anyway.

"Once Faxon's finally overthrown, which he will be," Sean said confidently, "Thiaraway can be restored to what it used to be. *Echtrans* who want to can go home, and research on extending Nuath's habitability can resume. So much important work has stopped under Faxon. And so many people have had their lives ruined—or worse."

"Once he *is* overthrown, he'll be . . . punished, right?" I'd almost said "executed," but recalled what Shim had once told me about Mars' alternative to a death penalty. "They'll do that . . . that memory wipe thing?"

Sean nodded. "Yeah, the *Scriosath*, um, *tabula rasa*. Blank slate. That's the complete wipe, as opposed to the short term ones they use for lesser crimes. It hasn't been used in like a century, but if anyone deserves it, Faxon does." He gave a little huff. "Sorry. I get a little wound up about this stuff."

"No, it's okay," I said. "I get why. And I agree."

He smiled, but it was a serious sort of smile. "I'm glad. Because you really are our best hope for putting things right. I know it seems scary right now, but there are tons of people who'll help you. Once the government is reestablished, you can even live in that palace again. If you want to."

Such a weird thought! But . . . if not for Faxon, I'd have grown up in that beautiful pink diamond structure. In fact, I probably never would have come to Earth at all.

Or met Rigel.

"I really appreciate you showing me this stuff, but can we talk about something else for a minute?"

"Sure." Sean switched off the hologram and the living room reappeared.

I was startled by a pang of loss when the palace disappeared, but I didn't let it sidetrack me. "Earlier today, Molly and I had a talk. Did she tell you?"

"I tried to." Molly frowned at her brother. "He wasn't big on the listening."

Sean stood and ran a hand through his hair, making it stand on end with a comical look he clearly didn't intend. "Look, I said I was sorry about Wednesday. I know you think you and Stuart have a *graell* thing going on. And . . . I guess he actually believes it, too."

"Because it's *true*," I insisted. "Molly believes me now, don't you, Molly?"

Molly looked uncomfortable, but she nodded. "If everything M told me today is true, I think they really do have the bond, Sean. I'm sorry."

Sorry? "Why—?" I started to ask, but Sean shook his head almost fiercely.

"I don't mean to be disrespectful, M, but I just can't buy it, no matter what symptoms or whatever you think you've had. I . . . I know how easy it can be for people to convince themselves of stuff they want to believe. Did you tell her about Penny?" he asked Molly.

"Um, no. But you never told me the whole story, remember?"

"Oh, yeah. I forgot you were only thirteen. Well, Penny was the twin sister of a good friend of mine, back on Mars. A *twilly* named Godrick convinced her they were *graell* bonded, even though they were barely sixteen, and nobody could talk her out of it. She pretended to feel all kinds of vibes off him, claimed he'd even changed her eye color, though nobody else could see it. When she found out he was laughing about it to other guys, bragging how he'd . . . Well, she came unglued, actually tried to kill herself. Last I heard, she was still under a Mind Healer's care and pretty messed up."

Even though it was obvious what he was implying, I couldn't help saying, "That's terrible! What did they do to that Godrick jerk?"

"Nothing . . . officially." Sean's fists clenched, reminding me of his confrontation with Rigel two days ago. "He denied everything and his buddies backed him up, even though a lot of people knew the real story. By then Penny was acting so crazy, her word wasn't worth much as evidence. But her brother and I made sure he regretted what he'd done." He smiled grimly.

I sucked in a breath. "Sean, I'm really sorry that happened to your friend, but I promise you that's *not* what's going on with Rigel and me."

He shrugged. "Maybe not. But . . . you're the Sovereign, M. Even if it was somehow possible, it still wouldn't . . . I mean, they'd never allow . . . Look, can we not talk about it any more right now? If we do, I'm . . . afraid I'll say something that'll get you mad at me all over again."

I'd been about to remind him of the lightning thing, which was what had convinced Molly, but he looked so uncomfortable I stopped myself. "Okay, I guess I sort of understand. But *none* of this is Rigel's fault, even if it makes you feel better to think it is."

Sean sighed heavily. "I'll try to remember that. And I really am sorry I came down so hard on him before. It just seems so . . . presumptuous, the way he is with you, touching you without asking and stuff. I know he didn't grow up on Mars so he doesn't have our same ingrained reaction to who you are, but—" He broke off and took a steadying breath. "So . . . more pictures?"

Though I really wanted to finish convincing Sean about the *graell*, I decided not to push it right now. I could try again later. And soon I was completely distracted by more holograms of Nuath: the area around Glenamuir, classrooms, hydroponic gardens, orchards, and all the people Sean and Molly had known there.

Around nine, their parents came in, Mrs. O'Gara bearing a tray of herbal tea and adorable little lemon biscuits. While I nibbled, they told me how life had gradually changed after Faxon came into power, how he had dissolved the government by degrees until he was the sole authority.

"So, before that, there were two legislative houses, right?" I asked, glancing at Sean.

"Right," he said. "The Royal House, sort of like the Senate here, or maybe more like the House of Lords over in England, and the *Eodain*. Similar to the House of Commons, whose members are popularly elected."

"The People's House," Mrs. O'Gara clarified. "That's the closest English translation, I suppose, though it's primarily elected from among the Royal and Science *fines*. Each house had a mix of conservative and progressive members, though historically the Royal House has been the most conservative and the *Eodain* primarily progressive."

Mr. O'Gara took up the explanation. "Of course, the old government is in shambles after Faxon's depredations—assassinations and arrests, with most others in hiding or here on Earth. Even after he's overthrown, it won't be an easy task to rebuild it. I *wish*—"

"I know, dear." His wife patted his arm soothingly. "We'll go back as soon as we possibly can."

They spent the next half hour telling me more about how the Nuathan government was structured, with ministries for bizarre things like Terran Obfuscation (a whole branch devoted to keeping Earth from finding out about the colony), Gravity/Antigravity, Water Reclamation, Hydroponics and Animal Husbandry.

"Agriculture is still pretty big there," Sean explained when I looked surprised at the last two. "Though the Sciences have overtaken Ags and Husbandry as the biggest *fines*. Um, has anyone explained to you about *fines* yet?"

I nodded, shifting uncomfortably. "Molly did. Sort of like genetically predetermined career paths and clans and a social hierarchy all in one." And self-enforced gene pools, though I didn't say that.

Mrs. O'Gara chuckled. "That's rather a clever way to put it, dear, and not far off the mark."

I was grateful that they never once, during the whole conversation, put any pressure on me, never made me feel like they expected me to *do* anything, the way Allister Adair did. Still, I couldn't help suspecting the reason they were telling me all this was so I'd sympathize more with their cause. So I'd *want* to do something eventually.

Worse, I was worried that it might be working.

15

Cinnwund Rioga (KIN-wund ree-OH-gah): *Royal Destiny*

I tried to hurry through my chores Saturday, hoping I might be able to get to Rigel's party a little early. Already our walk—and makeout session—the day before yesterday seemed forever ago.

But Aunt Theresa kept thinking of more and more things for me to do. At least my taekwondo class in the middle of the day gave me a chance to swing by Glitterby's on the way home, to pick up the present I'd had made for Rigel's birthday. I thought it was gorgeous, but worried he might think it was too girly.

Talking so much about the *graell* yesterday made me even more aware of how "off" I felt when Rigel and I were apart. By late afternoon, I was positively antsy to see him again.

Finally I finished mulching the roses, my last chore. I showered, put on the outfit I'd carefully selected—a top in shades of green that Rigel had once said he liked and dark khaki slacks—and primped until I felt ready. Anticipating Rigel's smile when he saw me, I practically skipped down the stairs.

"Can you take me over to Rigel's now?" I asked Uncle Louie, who'd gotten home from the car lot a little while ago.

"Oh, your friend Brianna called while you were in the shower," Aunt Theresa informed me, coming out of the kitchen. "Her father offered to pick you up, so they'll be here in about half an hour."

I tried not to let my irritation show. "Oh. Okay. Thanks." So much for getting a few minutes of private time with Rigel. Knowing Bri, it would be more like an hour before they got here, so the party would be well underway. I went back upstairs a lot more slowly than I'd come down, to pass the time with homework.

"Allister probably wouldn't have let us be alone for more than two seconds anyway," I mumbled to myself. Not that it was much comfort.

Sure enough, a solid fifty minutes passed before I finally heard the doorbell. I grabbed Rigel's present and raced downstairs, reaching the door just as Aunt Theresa opened it.

"Ready?" Bri asked.

"Duh. Let's go," I said, hurrying to the car ahead of her.

She laughed as she followed me. "You've still got it bad, don't you? You just saw him yesterday, you know."

I just slid into the back seat next to Deb. "Hey, Deb. Thanks, Mr. Morrison." *Thanks for making me so late*, I added silently.

When we arrived, the long driveway leading to the yellow farmhouse was already lined with cars, a couple dozen, at least. Definitely no alone time with Rigel tonight.

"Huh. Somehow I thought their house would be fancier," Bri said as we headed up the front walk.

"Why? He told you it was just a big old farmhouse. They've fixed it up, though." Including a few "special" renovations, but of course those were well camouflaged.

"Do you realize this is the first party Rigel's ever had?" Bri commented. "Almost every other guy on the team has had at least one since the start of the year."

Since Rigel and I had been together, Bri and Deb had gone out with a few football players and Bri, especially, had been going to a lot of parties. The one or two times I'd mentioned it, she'd shut me down immediately, which worried me a little.

"What are you giving Rigel for his birthday?" Deb asked, distracting me. "I hope he'll like the Jewel Jaguars football mug I got him."

"How could he not?" I rang the doorbell rather than answer her question, worrying again my present was stupid.

But then Rigel opened the door and my jitters disappeared. "Hey, M." His smile was the one he reserved just for me. For a long moment we were lost in each other's eyes, but then he remembered his manners. "Hey, Bri, Deb. Glad you could come." He opened the door wide for all of us to enter.

As the others went past him into the house, he touched my arm and murmured, "I should warn you, some friends of my parents came and I don't think they're really here because it's my birthday."

96

I cringed. "You mean . . . because of me?"

He nodded, but then gave me a quick kiss that drove every other thought from my head—for a moment. I followed him into the house, trying to be upset that he knew so well how to distract me. Because even though I now understood better how most *Echtrans* felt, it was *not* okay if virtual strangers had come to gawk at me. Today was Rigel's big day, not mine.

But we hadn't taken three steps before Rigel's dad came up with three strangers in tow, two women and a man. "Ah, here you are, M," he greeted me. "Some friends of ours would like to meet you."

"Hello." I tried to hide my discomfort, glad Rigel was still beside me.

The three exchanged glances with each other and one of the women actually giggled. Finally, the man spoke. "So very, very pleased to make your acquaintance, your—" He broke off when Mr. Stuart frowned and shook his head. "That is, um, I'm Girard Neeson. Allow me to present my wife, Brenna, and her sister, Doreen Gilley. We've known Rigel and his family since . . . well, for years."

Sixty years? Seventy? Just as well he hadn't said, since several of our classmates were within earshot.

"Marsha Truitt," I said, extending my hand to each of them in turn. I felt the usual faint tingle from each of them, nothing like what I got from Rigel, or even Sean.

They were all very attractive, of course, and looked to be in their early thirties, though they could be a hundred, for all I knew. Somehow, given that giggle, I doubted it.

"Marsha?" Doreen—the giggler—echoed. "Is that—?"

"My friends call me M for short." Hadn't the fact that I'd been raised under another name circulated along with the news of my existence?

"How very . . . informal." Girard looked faintly scandalized. "We won't keep you. I'm sure there are others, ah, that is, it's been an honor, er—"

"It was nice meeting you," I said firmly before he could add anything that would be difficult to explain if overheard. With another carefully polite smile, I turned away to find Rigel hovering, ready to whisk me into the living room, where most of the guests were.

"Thanks," I murmured. He squeezed my arm in response and the awkwardness of the moment faded at the simple pleasure of his touch.

A moment later we were surrounded by friends from school, including the whole football team except, not surprisingly, Bryce Farmer. He had already resented Rigel for taking over Bryce's quarterback spot, but after Rigel and I accidentally zapped him senseless—something he totally deserved, by the way—he and Rigel barely tolerated each other.

Kind of like me and Trina who, unfortunately, *was* here, along with most of the cheerleading squad, though I didn't see Molly. Or Sean. Did they maybe think it would be awkward to come, after Wednesday's incident? If Sean could just bring himself to apologize to Rigel . . . but I wasn't sure he was up for that.

Allister didn't seem to here either, though I assumed Rigel would have told me if he'd left town.

"Oh, hi, Marsha," Trina greeted me with a syrupy, insincere smile. "You made it. Not quite a perfect party after all, but one can't have everything." Then, to Rigel, with a more genuine—though still syrupy—smile, "I just love your house, Rigel! It's like it was made to entertain. You *so* need to have more parties."

"I'll mention it to my parents," he said, then immediately turned to talk to a couple of football buddies, leaving Trina pouting. The past week or two she'd mostly flirted with Sean, but in his absence she'd been willing to revert to Rigel.

Between Allister's absence and the Stuarts keeping the Neesons away from me, I was able to relax and enjoy myself for most of the evening—until Rigel started opening presents. He saved mine for last, and I held my breath as he unwrapped it. Would he laugh?

"Wow, M, this is really special," he said, gazing at the crystal sun catcher etched with the constellation Orion. "Thank you so much." He leaned over and gave me a quick kiss.

His mother—who always looked way too gorgeous to be somebody's mom—came forward. I half expected her to frown about the kiss, but she was smiling as she examined the ornament. "Look, Rigel is blue, so it stands out." She pointed at Orion's left foot—the star Rigel. "What a thoughtful gift."

I let out the breath I hadn't realized I was still holding. Maybe it hadn't been a dumb idea after all.

People started to drift back to the buffet table and Rigel threw an arm around my shoulders. "Why were you worried?" he whispered. "You should have known I'd love it. I'm going to hang it right over my bed, where the morning sun will catch it. Then I'll wake up every morning thinking of you—though I do that anyway."

A wonderful rush of warmth went through me, partly from his words and partly from the love I could feel radiating from him. I knew he could feel the same from me. Everything was going to be fine. I was sure of it.

By nine-thirty, people started to leave. I knew some of them—especially the cheerleaders and most of the football players—were going to a later party at Nicole Adams's house. From ten feet away, I could clearly hear Bri and Deb whispering, discussing whether they could convince Bri's dad they were getting a ride home from another parent and really go to Nicole's party. The only problem with that plan, apparently, was me.

"You know she won't go," I overheard Bri say. "Even if her aunt would let her stay out that late, she never goes *anywhere* without Rigel."

Sometimes my enhanced senses weren't exactly a benefit. I turned away so Bri wouldn't notice my hurt—just in time to see Allister Adair enter the room, followed by all of the O'Garas.

"Sorry to be so late," Allister said smoothly to Shim, who had stayed mostly in the background during the party, tag-teaming with Mr. Stuart to keep the Neesons away from me. "I hope you saved us some birthday cake?"

"Of course," Shim said, just as smoothly. "It's good to see you again, Quinn, Lili." He gave a little half-bow to the O'Garas, then nodded to Sean and Molly as well.

I quickly scanned the room and saw Rigel talking to Matt Mullins near the buffet table. He clearly hadn't seen the O'Garas yet so I hurried over to join him. Even though Sean had apologized—to me, anyway—I wanted to be ready to intervene if necessary.

Rigel clearly felt my approach because he turned to me with a smile just before I reached him—then glanced over my shoulder and froze.

"What is *he* doing here?" he practically growled.

I gave Matt a quick apologetic smile and pulled Rigel off to the side, away from anyone else in the thinning crowd.

"Allister brought them—he's related, remember? Now, be nice. Yesterday I managed to convince Molly about us and by now she's probably convinced Sean, too. He already told me he was sorry for Wednesday, so maybe he's here to apologize to you, too." That would be an excellent birthday present, in my opinion, but Rigel just looked skeptical.

Sure enough, when Sean and Rigel greeted each other a few minutes later, no apology occurred, but at least they were polite. The girls crowding around to greet Sean probably helped. I tried not to be bothered that Bri was among them, flirting with Sean almost as outrageously as Trina usually did.

Bri saw me watching and came over. "Hey, M, the O'Garas say they can drive you home since you live so close. Would that be okay? Deb and I were kind of thinking we might look in at Nicole's on the way home since Justin offered us a ride."

My unease increased. Justin Blake was a senior and a known player. Even I'd overheard him bragging about the girls he'd scored —and about how much he drank at parties. "Are Nicole's parents home?" I blurted out before thinking.

Predictably, Bri scowled at me. "Jeez, M, you sound like my mother. I don't know. Probably not, knowing Nicole. Does it matter?"

Coward that I was, I backed down. "No, you're right. Sorry. Sure, you guys go on. I'll be fine with the O'Garas."

Her expression cleared immediately. "Thanks, M. See you Monday!"

A few minutes later, she and Deb left with Justin and several others. Soon the only people left were the Stuarts, the O'Garas, Allister and me.

Allister hadn't spoken to me since arriving, but almost as soon as the last non-*Echtran* left (the Neesons had gone half an hour ago), he came toward me with a smile that put me on edge—not that Allister ever did much that *didn't* put me on edge.

"Princess, it is good to see you again," he said, making the elaborate bow, right fist over heart, that was reserved for the

Sovereign. I'd seen it several times by now, but it still weirded me out. "I regret I have not had opportunity to pay my respects during my current visit to Jewel."

I pasted a smile on my face that probably didn't fool anyone. "Um, that's okay. It's . . . good to see you, too, Allister."

The slippage of his smile told me I sounded as non-Royal as ever. I knew I should try harder around him, but he was so pompous he made me *want* to antagonize him. I really needed to fight that urge, at least until I knew exactly how much power he had over me—and over Rigel. I forced my face into a polite, expectant expression.

Allister immediately pulled his smile back into place, then motioned Sean over. Sean moved to his side, but with a reluctance that bordered on suspicion, which struck me as odd. Oblivious, still smiling at me, Allister clapped a possessive hand on Sean's shoulder.

"Excellency, though you have already made the acquaintance of my nephew, he has not been *formally* introduced to you. I now take that office upon myself, belated though it may seem."

Taking a step back, he bowed elaborately to both of us and declared, "Princess Emileia, sole heir to Sovereign Leontine through his son Mikal, I hereby present to you Sean O'Gara, scion of the Second Royal House . . . your destined Consort."

16

Cheile Rioga (KEE-luh ree-OH-gah): *Royal Consort*

I noticed Sean's expression—startled, angry and embarrassed—about a quarter of a second before Allister's words penetrated.

"Wait. What?" Surely I couldn't have heard him right. Maybe it was just a Martian word that sounded like—

"Your *Cheile Rioga*. Your destined Royal Consort," Allister repeated. "I presume you have not yet been educated, Princess, about our customs for pairings?"

I swallowed, glancing wildly at Molly, who looked as embarrassed and upset as her brother. "Um, Molly told me people usually, uh, pair up within their own clan. Er, *fine*," I stammered. She'd said "married" but I wasn't using that word. Nuh-uh. No way. I was *fifteen* for Pete's sake!

"Did she tell you that the more important the *fine*, the more important that tradition is?"

I shrugged, not willing to admit to anything more. I could feel Rigel's hand in mine, feel the anger and frustration flowing from him. I imagined he could feel something similar from me, along with big doses of fear and confusion. What could Allister possibly be suggesting?

Sean, still beet red, leaned over to Allister. "Uncle, I *asked* you not to—" he began, but Allister waved him to silence.

"I know, Sean, but I felt it necessary to make the situation perfectly clear before things, ah, progress any further." He turned to Rigel and me with a disapproving glare, his gaze lingering on our clasped hands. "I presume from your confusion, Princess, that Molly did *not* enlighten you as to the pairing requirements for the Sovereign and his or her heirs?"

Numbly, I shook my head, gripping Rigel's hand more tightly, as if he might be forcibly torn away from me at any moment.

"Our traditions are quite specific when it comes to the upper echelons of the Royal *fine*, particularly for our Sovereigns. While the Sovereign is always a direct descendant of the previous Sovereign, the Royal Consort is traditionally the ranking person of the opposite sex, of the same generation, from the Second Royal House—in this case, descended from the Sovereign of four generations prior."

It sounded as complicated as the family trees in the appendix of *The Lord of the Rings* trilogy.

"So, wait," I interrupted again. "Does that mean Sean is my . . . cousin or something?"

"Fourth cousin, yes. You both trace your lineage back to Sovereign Nuallen, father to Sovereign Aerleas, who was mother to Leontine. Which means you share a great-great-grandfather."

Not *totally* icky, then, but there was still no way on Earth—or Mars —that I was okay with this. "So Sovereigns don't get to choose their own . . . Consorts?" I glanced at Molly again, but she was no help. She just looked upset and helpless and wouldn't meet my eye.

I'd thought the Stuarts would come to my defense, but though they looked shocked and disapproving, they didn't say anything at all. And Mr. and Mrs. O'Gara just stood off to the side, like they weren't involved at all. Cowards. Weren't they supposed to be famous heroes or something?

"With great power comes great responsibility," Allister intoned, like he was reading off a script. "The Sovereign has a duty not only to shepherd our people, but to safeguard their future. Maintaining the Royal bloodline is one of those safeguards. In the past, the designated heir to the Sovereign has known almost from birth who his or her destined Consort would be. The two are introduced as young children and encouraged to form bonds of friendship and, later, of love, enhancing their ability to jointly lead our people when the new Sovereign takes power.

"You, Princess, have unfortunately been denied that opportunity due to the unconscionable behavior of the usurper Faxon. Therefore, the sooner you and your Consort become well acquainted, the better—for you, for our people, and for the future of our race."

He finally stopped talking and smiled, like he expected I would thank him or something. Uh, no.

Drawing strength from Rigel's hand around mine, I said, "That's all very interesting, Allister, but I don't see how it applies to me. I mean, we're on Earth, not Mars. I don't have a 'people' to shepherd and probably won't, since the Martians are all moving here over the next few decades anyway. So how can any of this really matter?"

Allister finally lost his smile completely, clearly taken aback by my response. Sean didn't look happy either, though I wasn't sure if his frown was more for his uncle or for me.

"Sorry, Sean," I told him—and almost meant it. "You're a nice guy and all, but . . . I'm with Rigel. You know that. No Martian tradition is going to change how I feel."

Rigel gave my hand a squeeze—subtly enough that no one else would notice, but it boosted my courage enormously. No matter what happened, *he* was on my side.

But Allister wasn't giving up that easily. "Princess, you don't understand what is at stake, nor the enormity of what you propose. Never, in nearly a thousand years, has a Sovereign paired with someone outside the Royal *fine*. It simply isn't done—for a multitude of reasons."

"Right." I wasn't buying it. Not even a little. "Traditions. Customs. Stuff that doesn't matter diddly-squat to me. Sorry."

Allister sucked in a shocked breath. "There is much more involved than simple tradition, Princess! For dozens of generations, the Royal *fine* has been carefully maintained to maximize leadership qualities. This next century will be a critical one for us all, perhaps the most pivotal period since the colony began, as we make the transition from Mars to Earth. At this, of all times, we *cannot* risk our people losing any shred of confidence in their Sovereign or in the Royal line."

I opened my mouth to restate my position, but Rigel beat me to it. "Sir, I'd say M has made her wishes clear. No matter how stubbornly you refuse to believe it, she and I are bonded and you can't just . . . undo that for political reasons."

At the word "bonded," both Allister and Sean scowled at Rigel.

"You'd better not mean you've—" Sean began, but again his uncle waved him to silence.

Advancing menacingly on Rigel, Allister snarled, "Young man, if you have done anything to compromise the Princess, I assure you there are penalties in place—"

Now it was my turn to interrupt. "Oh, stop it. Rigel hasn't done anything to 'compromise' me. You guys sound like something out of a Victorian novel. Sheesh! We were bonded from the first time we touched. Hands!" I clarified quickly. "And there's plenty of evidence that we really are bonded—most of which you've already heard."

I looked to Shim for confirmation and he nodded.

"They're right, Allister, for all your unwillingness to see it," he said. "There were a dozen or more witnesses to what these two did to Faxon's Ossian Sphere several weeks ago when Morven attacked. Nothing short of a true *graell* bond could have accomplished that, I assure you."

But Allister snorted dismissively. "No Royals among your witnesses, of course, only people with a vested interest in raising the profile of the Progressive *fines*. I maintain that the Sphere was fundamentally unstable and that Morven's mishandling caused it to explode. Not that I'm ungrateful for the role all of you played in defending our Princess against him, of course."

Rigel was trembling with anger now, then I clearly heard: *Let's demonstrate.*

Startled, I glanced at him. Did he really mean we should zap Allister, right here in his parents' living room?

He gave me a tiny nod, his expression grimmer than I'd ever seen it. The idea of deliberately attacking another person, even one as obnoxious as Allister, made me recoil, but I was as desperate as Rigel to finally *prove* our bond—to Allister and to Sean. Steeling my resolve, I took a deep breath and tightened my grip on Rigel's hand. Maybe, if we were careful—

"Rigel." It was Dr. Stuart, her voice soft but firm. "Don't."

"Your mother is right," Shim said. "Violence is never the proper answer. Any kind of violence. Let go of M's hand and come over here, please."

How had they known? I felt Rigel's frustration, but also a bit of relief that echoed my own. He was still angry, though, and afraid, just like I was. After a long, rebellious moment, during which everyone in the room stared at us with varying degrees of disapproval, Rigel finally, reluctantly, released my hand and took a few steps away from me.

We exchanged a long look, silently reaffirming our love, then I turned to face Allister again.

"It won't make any difference if you try to keep us apart," I told him. "I'm not going to let you force me into some perverted arranged marriage. We're in the United States, in the twenty-first century, and I'm only fifteen. Things like that are illegal here."

Allister tried to arrange his face into some semblance of a fatherly smile—failing utterly, as far as I was concerned.

"Of course no one is going to *force* you into any such thing, Princess," he said, his tone as reasonable as he could make it. "I simply want you and my nephew to become better acquainted. It may be that when the time comes—years from now—you will find the idea anything but repugnant. Teenage relationships are notoriously short-lived, after all. I'm confident this one will run its course naturally, removing what you now, in your inexperienced youth, see as an insurmountable obstacle."

Sean now looked more embarrassed than pissed, but when Allister nudged him, he stepped forward and cleared his throat. "Like he said, M, the *last* thing I want is to pressure you to do anything you don't want to do. I just . . . want us to be friends. To stay friends. That will be okay, won't it?"

He looked sincere, even cute. My glance involuntarily strayed to Rigel, who looked like his grandfather's hand on his shoulder was the only thing keeping him from launching himself at Sean. He was obviously *not* on board with even friends, but I didn't see how I could refuse such an innocuous-sounding request.

"Friends is fine," I finally said. "But *just* friends. I'm telling you right up front that it's never going to be anything more."

A little to my surprise, Sean didn't seem upset by that. "It's all I'm asking," he said.

I suspected there was an unspoken "for now" in there, but if he was determined to cling to false hope, I couldn't stop him. All I could do was remind him where my true love and loyalty lay, every chance I got.

Suddenly, Mrs. O'Gara came to life. "I'm so glad we finally have this settled! Allister, I should have known you'd make a right hash of things, with your high-handed attitude and your ultimatums. None of this will become truly important for years and years, you know, so there was no need whatsoever to upset the children tonight."

She gave me a motherly smile that was meant to be comforting, but I couldn't help looking past her to the Stuarts. They didn't look nearly as complacent as the O'Garas did, though they seemed less upset than before. Dr. Stuart caught my eye and smiled reassuringly, but I thought it looked a little forced.

"And now, I suppose we'd better get Emileia home, hadn't we?" Mrs. O'Gara continued. "Goodness, it's after eleven o'clock! I hope your aunt won't be too upset with us, dear."

After tonight's revelations, that should have been the least of my worries, but I winced out of habit, knowing how mad she'd be—and not at the O'Garas.

"Yeah, I guess I really should get home," I mumbled, feeling like a wimp for agreeing.

"Thank you for coming tonight, M," Mr. Stuart said then, the first words he'd spoken since Allister dropped his bombshell. "I'm sorry things became so . . . awkward." He sounded like he was barely controlling some strong emotion.

"Thanks for inviting me." I encompassed Rigel and his parents with as pleasant a smile as I could summon under the circumstances, not wanting them to worry about me. "It was a great party. I'll . . . see you all soon."

Rigel took a step toward me at the same time I took a step toward him, but his grandfather didn't let go of his shoulder—and Mrs. O'Gara put a hand on mine.

"We'd better hurry, dear." I was pretty sure I wasn't imagining the anxiety in her voice. I was also pretty sure it didn't have anything to do with Aunt Theresa getting pissed.

Rigel and I weren't even going to be allowed a good-night kiss? My gaze locked with his. *See you tomorrow?* I thought at him as clearly as I could.

He gave me an almost imperceptible nod, but I also heard the word, *Somehow*. Like he didn't think it would be that easy. I hoped he was wrong.

No one spoke as we walked out to the O'Garas' van. Molly still seemed afraid to look at me, and I was careful to keep my distance from Sean. But when we got in, I somehow ended up sandwiched between the two of them in the back seat. I resolutely ignored the tingle from Sean, about three times stronger than the one from Molly.

As Mr. O'Gara started the engine, Sean cleared his throat. "M, I'm really sorry. I begged Uncle Allister not to say anything about this. I knew it would freak you out."

Before I could decide how to reply, Mrs. O'Gara twisted around in her seat to face me. "Yes, dear, I need to apologize for my brother. Allister handled this extremely poorly and we're all sorry about that. No one wanted you upset, I promise you."

I glanced at Molly, still silent and still not looking at me, then at Sean, then back to Mrs. O'Gara. "But you knew? All of you knew, this whole time?" I knew I sounded accusatory, but I couldn't help it. I *felt* accusatory!

Mrs. O'Gara nodded. "We've known since you were born, dear. Of course, like everyone else, we thought you'd been killed along with your parents when you were small."

"Molly?" I asked. She gave me one quick, distressed glance before looking away again, but it answered my question—and it hurt, because I'd really, truly thought we were becoming friends. I'd told her most of *my* secrets, after all.

I turned to Sean. "And you?"

He at least had the courage to meet my eye, though he was clearly uncomfortable. "Yeah. I grew up knowing that if you'd lived, we'd eventually, um . . . But you have to believe I never meant to spring it on you like this!"

I couldn't think of anything else to say. The very idea that they'd all been . . . *conspiring*, while acting oh-so innocent every time I'd been to their house over the past two weeks, made me feel both betrayed and foolish. Not that I could possibly have known.

Had Rigel suspected? He'd always seemed more jealous of Sean than I'd thought reasonable at the time. And Sean's animosity toward Rigel was now completely explained. He must have come to Jewel practically thinking of me as his property! That thought made me even angrier, but I seethed in silence.

"Here we are," Mr. O'Gara announced a few minutes later, pulling into my driveway. "Lili, would you like to go to the door with M to explain why she's so late?"

Sean climbed out of the back seat so I could follow, then hesitated.

"No, dear, you stay in the car," his mother told him. He obeyed without question. Not the first time he'd surprised me tonight.

I opened the front door a moment later, hoping against hope that Aunt Theresa had already gone to bed, but I wasn't that lucky. She stormed out of the kitchen almost the second I stepped over the threshold.

"Young lady, do you have any idea—" she began, then spotted Mrs. O'Gara and immediately became less strident, though she still looked angry. "Oh, hello, Lili. I didn't realize—"

"Theresa, I came in to apologize for bringing Marsha home so terribly late. You know how young people can be when they're having fun, totally losing track of the time. We suggested she come home with us, as we were all leaving and we live so close by."

"Thank you, Lili. I should have known not to depend on Dave Morrison. He lets his daughter wrap him around her finger. Missy, you are lucky we have conscientious neighbors who don't allow *their* children to stay out till all hours."

"Yes, ma'am," I mumbled, since there was no way I could explain exactly how much this *wasn't* my fault.

And instead of making up some excuse that would let me off the hook, Mrs. O'Gara just patted me on the shoulder and said, "Speaking of which, I'd better get my two home before they fall asleep. Will we see you at church tomorrow?"

"Of course." Aunt Theresa was all smiles now. "And thank you again, Lili. Good night."

With a nod and a last, motherly smile at me, Mrs. O'Gara left.

The second the door was closed, Aunt Theresa rounded on me, her smile disappearing as though it had never existed as she prepared to lower the boom.

17

Rigel (RY-jel): *Orion's left foot*

Wow. Happy birthday to me.

The second the door shuts behind M and the O'Garas, I shake Grandfather's hand off my shoulder.

"Is this how it's going to be now? I can't even say goodnight to M? Will you homeschool me, too, so I can't see her at all?"

"Of course not, Rigel," my father says. "Nothing needs to change that drastically. Does it?" He directs the question at Allister, which pisses me off even more.

"We can't have the boy interfering with affairs of state. This pairing will go a long way toward reassuring those who question the suitability of a Sovereign raised on Earth."

"*Pairing?*" I explode. "So much for *just friends.*"

"Precisely what do you have in mind, Allister?" my mother asks before I can continue. She doesn't look happy either. "M—and Sean —are far too young for pairing, as you yourself admitted. Even if they were so inclined."

Allister puts on his usual, superior look. "Not to worry, Ariel. I simply meant what I stated earlier—that the Princess and my nephew will spend time together, as they would have on Mars had Faxon never existed. As our Sovereigns' heirs and their Consorts have always done. Why does this come as such a surprise to everyone?"

I swing around to face my parents and grandfather. "Did you know? That M would be expected to—"

Mom cuts me off again. "We didn't know until tonight, Rigel. Not about Sean. Sovereigns have always been expected to make certain alliances of course, and we did worry that could pose a problem eventually. But Allister never mentioned that his *own nephew* was the one intended for her. Rather a glaring oversight, I can't help thinking." She narrows her eyes at Allister. I'm glad I'm not the only one pissed at him.

"I didn't want to alarm the Princess or prejudice her against her destined Consort by an injudicious word, and I felt certain that anything I shared with any of you would quickly reach her ears. I wanted to explain the importance of the pairing to her before that could happen."

"You seem to have failed in that goal rather spectacularly, Allister," my grandfather says, the lines in his face deepening with disapproval. "Perhaps had you ever raised children of your own, you might have handled this better."

Allister just waves a hand in the air. "No doubt the O'Garas will soothe any ruffled feelings. I saw more to lose than to gain by waiting. Already, this boy has wormed his way into her affections to an alarming degree."

"Wormed—!" I turn to glare at my grandfather. "I shouldn't have let you stop me."

"Of course we had to stop you, Rigel," my mother says. "Once you calm down, you'll realize why. You may even thank us eventually."

"Thank you for what? For making me stand by while you let these people screw up M's life almost as much as Faxon would have?" Now I'm glaring at all of them.

My grandfather shakes his head at me. "No, Rigel. For preventing you from doing something both you and Emileia would doubtless have regretted for the rest of your lives. Think of the burden you would have placed on her shoulders, along with your own."

He looks into my eyes and makes me really listen to what he's saying. I hate when he does that and I especially hate it now. Because much as I don't want to admit it, I know he's right. I could tell M didn't really want to zap Allister. She felt reluctant, even shocked, when I "suggested" it. After a couple seconds I manage to yank my gaze away from Grandfather's, shrugging rather than admit anything.

"Will one of you please explain what you're talking about?" Allister sounds peevish. "If the boy threatened to harm me in some way, he should surely be evaluated for mental stability before he is allowed near the Princess again."

Grandfather gives Allister one of his patient looks. "Did you hear a threat, Allister?" he asks mildly, like he himself didn't just accuse me of exactly that.

Allister frowns, looking back and forth between my grandfather and my parents. "No, but you all spoke as though—"

"For a moment, I believe Rigel may have been tempted to, ah, demonstrate the strength of the bond he shares with Emileia," my grandfather calmly explains. "The setting seemed inappropriate, however, so we discouraged him from doing so."

"Bonds again! Are *all* of you so credulous as to buy into what is clearly a teenage fantasy? Or are you merely cognizant of the effect on your family's status, should your grandson form an alliance with the Sovereign? I would hate to think such worldly considerations could sway your judgement on a matter so important to our people."

"Our people!" I blurt out, tired of his posturing. "What about M, and what's good for her? Does that even matter to you?"

"The good of the Sovereign and the good of our people are one and the same," he says, more pompous than ever.

I can't help rolling my eyes. "You can't even think of her as a person, can you? To you, she's just a . . . a chess piece you want to manipulate. But if she's really the Sovereign, she should have final say in pretty much everything, shouldn't she?"

Allister looks down his nose at me like I'm a bug or something—though he has to tilt his head back to do it, since I'm taller than he is. "Eventually, she will. But it is imperative that before she takes up her authority she be thoroughly educated in the intricacies of Nuathan politics and her own duties."

Duties that apparently include her hooking up with Sean.

"So what she wants doesn't matter at all?"

Instead of answering me, he turns to my parents and grandfather. "I've told you repeatedly, the boy has been allowed too much freedom and far too much access to the Princess. If he has convinced her that they share a *graell* bond, it is likely he means to persuade her to an intimacy she is by no means ready for—if he has not done so already. Such an egregious act could seriously undermine a delicate political situation, as well as centuries of—"

"Allister!" my mother snaps, startling me—and everyone else as well. "It is clear you cannot be expected to share a roof with someone you are determined to mistrust so thoroughly, nor will I stand by any longer while you insult my son. I think it best if you spend the remainder of your time in Jewel elsewhere."

"I beg your pardon?" he blusters, looking to my dad and grandfather to intercede.

They don't.

He makes a few outraged noises, then says, "If that is the way you feel, Ariel, I won't trespass on your *hospitality* another moment. I'll pack my things at once."

My mom is a little pinker than normal but her jaw is as rigid as I've ever seen it and she doesn't back down. "I'm sure if you call the O'Garas they will be willing to put you up for the night."

Allister gives them all another disbelieving glance, then storms upstairs. No one says a word for the two minutes it takes him to get his suitcase and come back down. He doesn't say anything either, just grabs his coat, gives everybody one last glare and slams out the front door. We hear the engine of his rental car start, then fade into the distance.

Finally, my mother lets out a sigh. "I suppose I shouldn't have done that."

"Don't apologize, Ariel," my grandfather says. "Allister's behavior tonight has been execrable. I'm surprised you allowed him to stay as long as you did, if he has been this unpleasant since his arrival."

"He has," I say, not adding that it's mainly been aimed at me.

My dad just shakes his head. "I don't blame you either, Ariel, but I hope he won't make us all regret this. He may not have the power here he had on Mars, but he does wield quite a bit of influence with the Council. And the O'Garas—"

"Will surely understand," Grandfather finishes. "None of them seemed pleased with the way Allister handled things this evening. And no wonder. He had no business saying the things he said."

"So . . . it's not true?" I can't quite keep the hope out of my voice, even though I know I'm grasping at straws. "What he said about Sean and M?"

The looks they all give me are pitying in varying degrees and my brief hope sputters out even before my grandfather answers.

"I'm sorry, Rigel. While Allister was both precipitate and clumsy with tonight's revelation, I can't imagine he would have made such a claim were it not true. Certainly all past Sovereigns have paired in the manner he described."

Betrayal slams me in the gut like one of my own uncontrolled football passes. "So you *knew* about this arranged marriage crap and never said a word to me? Or to M? What the hell?"

My mother puts a hand on my shoulder but it doesn't help much. "We knew about the custom, yes, but not about Sean. It seemed unlikely after Faxon's purges that anyone of the appropriate age and lineage had survived, so we assumed that M would be able to pair as she chose, without regard to the old customs." Her voice is soothing —which just irritates me, because I can tell she's *trying* to soothe me, with that special power she has.

"Faxon was very thorough," my father explains. "The O'Garas had to conceal their lineage in order to remain there, heading up the resistance. People became so tight-lipped about things like Royal bloodlines that I doubt anyone but Allister knew they were members of the Second House. In fact, it's likely that the reason they finally left Mars was to keep Sean safe. It was incredibly brave of them to stay as long as they did, under the circumstances."

The *last* thing I want to hear right now is another paen to the wonderful, heroic O'Gara clan. "Does that mean M really *doesn't* have any choice, like Allister said?" I probably sound as appalled as I feel.

"I wouldn't put it quite that way," my grandfather says. "At least, I know of no case in our history where a Sovereign was forced to pair against his or her will."

"You must realize that this is a unique circumstance," Dad reminds me. "As Allister said, all previous Sovereigns knew from childhood who their Consort would be, and also grew up with full awareness of Nuathan pairing customs."

Grandfather gives a little snort. "Customs that fly in the face of accepted genetic principles. I've argued for over a century that we should—" He breaks off. "But that's neither here nor there. The point is, Sean does exist, and most of our people will expect the Sovereign to honor tradition."

"Eventually," my mother adds, frowning at him. "Surely there's no need to require any sort of commitment while they are still minors?"

He sighs heavily. "Of course no one will expect a teen marriage, but once word gets out—and I have no doubt Allister will see that it does—there will be pressure to follow tradition as closely as possible. Which means encouraging Sean and Princess Emileia to spend time together, to facilitate emotional bonding."

"And discouraging her from spending time with anyone who might interfere with that? Like, say, me?" I can't keep the bitterness out of my voice. My gut feels like it's on fire.

"I'm sorry, Rigel." My grandfather sounds like he really means it. "I honestly believed this situation was unlikely to arise. When it became clear that you and Emileia had formed a *graell* bond—which is not quite so rare as Allister would like to believe—" he glances at my folks— "it seemed that you and she were genetically destined for each other. It is unlikely, however, that many of our people will see it that way."

My dad weighs in again. "The question is, what course will best serve our people in the long run? The first priority, of course, must be completely removing Faxon from power. But after that—"

Suddenly, I can't take it anymore.

"I'm going to bed. You can all plan the fate of 'our people' without me." What I need to plan is how to see M privately, so we can figure a way out of this mess. Maybe even tonight, if I can sneak out without—

"Rigel." Grandfather's voice stops me halfway to the stairs. "Promise me you won't do anything foolish."

Not for the first time, I wonder if he can read my mind. Or maybe, after almost three hundred years of experience, he can just read *people*. Either way, it's awfully inconvenient sometimes.

"No, sir." Not lying. I won't do anything *I* consider foolish.

He watches me for another second or two, then nods, apparently satisfied.

A minute later I shut myself into my room and stare at all my stupid model spaceships hanging from the ceiling without really seeing them. Foolish? Foolish would be risking what M and I have together. Especially since risking our bond means risking our lives, whether anyone else believes that or not.

Which means I can't afford to play by their rules. Neither of us can.

18

shilcloas (shil-CLO-ahs): *hearing another's thoughts; telepathy*

"Didn't you hear me calling up the stairs?" Aunt Theresa greeted me when I dragged myself down to the breakfast Sunday morning after an almost sleepless night. "I was starting to think you intended to pout rather than come to church today. Here—you have time for a quick bowl of cereal, and then we need to go."

Fifteen minutes later we were turning right on Emerald, then the block past the Town Hall to the old-fashioned white wooden church I'd attended as long as I could remember. We were walking quickly, because of the cold, and my mood improved with every step. Even if the Stuarts didn't sit with us because of Allister, I'd at least be able to *see* Rigel and soak up some of his vibes from across the sanctuary. Maybe we'd even be able to snatch a few seconds to talk.

Almost the only people at church this early were choir members, ushers and their families. And the O'Garas.

Aunt Theresa hurried forward and, to my amazement, actually *hugged* Mrs. O'Gara. I could count on one hand the number of times she'd ever hugged me. "Lili! Does this mean you've decided to join the choir? I'm so glad."

"It seemed a good way to get to know people," Mrs. O'Gara replied. "Will it be all right if my family sits with yours again?"

"Of course! I can't imagine why you even needed to ask."

She led them back to our pew, where Uncle Louie seemed more effusive than necessary, too. Then Aunt Theresa and Mrs. O'Gara went to join the choir downstairs while the rest of us sat down. Somehow Sean ended up next to me.

"Hey," he whispered as Uncle Louie and his dad talked across us. "I hope you're not still weirded out about last night."

I stared at him. "Seriously? I'm way beyond weirded out. Nothing about this is *remotely* okay." Uncle Louie was oblivious by nature, but I still used my less-than-a-whisper voice—which I'd never used with anyone but Rigel. That I was able to use it now made me resent Sean even more.

"I didn't make the rules," he said in the same barely audible tone. "Blame history, or even Uncle Allister. Not me."

"But you *knew*. You've known all along, all of you." That betrayal still rankled—a lot. "Where is dear Uncle Al, anyway? Coming with the Stuarts to make sure Rigel and I don't get anywhere near each other?"

Before he could answer, Molly peered around from Sean's other side. "Did you say something?" she whispered.

I just shrugged and shook my head, her question a reminder that now there were way too many people around who could hear stuff I didn't want heard. Sean didn't say anything else and I was glad, since just having him next to me was unnerving enough.

Five minutes before the service started, when I'd nearly given up hope they were coming, the Stuarts finally arrived. No Allister, but all three glanced quickly our way—Rigel the longest—then went to sit on the other side of the little sanctuary without saying a word.

Still, just having Rigel in the same room gave me a boost, both physically and mentally, like I'd received some nutrient I'd been lacking. That sensation reassured me that no matter how much everyone was against our relationship, they could never break our special bond.

"Hey, Marsha, you and your guy Rigel didn't have a fight, did you?" Uncle Louie asked in a perfectly audible tone. "How come they're sitting over there?"

He *would* pick this one time to be observant.

"No! I, um, told him Aunt Theresa would be mad about me coming home late last night, so he's probably just trying to keep me from getting into more trouble."

He just nodded and grunted. "Think she overreacted, myself," he confided, "but I can't claim to know much about raising kids." Clearly uncomfortable, he let the subject drop with a shrug.

A small sigh escaped me. My life would have been a lot easier over the years if Uncle Louie had ever been willing to take my side against Aunt Theresa instead of just muttering behind her back. Not that she was easy to stand up to. In fact, very few people in town had the nerve to oppose her, since she was well known for her quick-temper and sharp-tongue.

Except with the O'Garas. For some unfathomable reason, she'd taken to them immediately.

The sermon seemed extra long today, impatient as I was to snatch a private second or two with Rigel, or at least get close enough for a bigger dose of the strength he always gave me. The moment everyone stood after the benediction and dismissal, I started moving in his direction. Or tried to.

"What's your hurry?" Sean asked as I attempted to nudge my way past him into the aisle.

I gave him an impatient glance. "I just need to—"

"M, dear, do you think you could introduce Sean and Molly around to some of the younger people?" Mrs. O'Gara asked before I could make something up. Not that I should have to explain myself to Sean anyway.

"What? Oh, um, sure. C'mon."

Determined to use this to my advantage, I led them in Rigel's direction, even though the only other teenagers were at the back of the sanctuary, near the exit. He saw me coming and smiled, then frowned—probably because Sean was right behind me. Still, he moved toward me, edging past his parents. We were just a few yards apart when Mr. Stuart put a hand on Rigel's shoulder, stopping him.

At the same time Sean said, "Uh, M? Probably not the best place for another showdown."

I rounded on him. "Showdown? I just want to say hi. Or isn't that *allowed* anymore?"

Unfortunately, I hadn't noticed that Aunt Theresa was right behind Sean and Molly.

"Perhaps it shouldn't be, Marsha, after last night," she snapped.

I stared at her. "What, I can't even be *polite* to him? In *church?*"

She primmed up her lips. "We'll discuss this at home, Marsha. Now, weren't you going to introduce Molly and Sean to your youth group friends?"

With tears pricking behind my eyes, I swung back around to look at Rigel, who was still facing my way, looking as frustrated as I felt. Apparently his parents didn't want to risk a scene in church either.

Forcing down my anger and humiliation, I focused on him as hard as I could.

Arboretum? I caught the word clearly in my mind.

I nodded quickly and thought back, *Midnight.*

He gave me a quick nod back to show he understood, then turned away just as his mother started to frown at him.

"If that's how it's going to be, let's go." I could tell he was pretending to be more upset than he really was, so they'd be less suspicious. I hoped it worked.

Following his cue, I tried to hide my relief that we had a plan. With one longing look over my shoulder, I mumbled, "Yeah, okay, there are a few kids near the door. Come on."

Most of the teens had already seen Sean and Molly at school, but I introduced them around for the benefit of the watchful adults. Two guys started flirting with Molly, while nearly all the girls glommed onto Sean. I tried to ease away, still hoping to snag a quick word with Rigel, but Aunt Theresa intervened before I'd taken two steps.

"Lili suggested it might be nice to go out for lunch." She wore a delighted-looking smile, which looked weird on her face. "We should hurry if we want to get a table at the Lighthouse Cafe."

I blinked at her in surprise—and irritation. Two different Sundays the Stuarts had suggested going out after church, and both times my aunt had made up some excuse. I'd figured it was because of the money, but apparently not.

The seven of us walked out into the overcast, chilly day, heading for the Lighthouse Cafe, which was opposite the Town Hall on Diamond. Just before we went in, the Stuarts drove past and Rigel and I locked gazes for an instant. Even that tiny contact helped center me so I was able to smile when Molly complimented my new-ish skirt.

We managed to snag a table by the back wall as another group left and Sean maneuvered to sit by me again, even though I'd completely ignored him during the walk here.

"I'm kind of looking forward to my first snowfall," he said as I opened my menu.

Startled, I glanced at him. "What? You mean it never snows in . . . in Ireland?"

He shook his head, his expression serious, though his eyes

twinkled mischievously. "Not on the coast, where we were. They get a bit inland, especially to the north."

Uncle Louie, down the table, let out a guffaw. "By March, you'll have seen more than you ever wanted, boy, especially if you're the one who shovels the drive. We get a fair bit of lake-effect snow here."

The adults started comparing Ireland's and Indiana's weather and while my aunt and uncle were distracted, Sean leaned over and whispered, "Actually, it still gives me the willies a bit, how stuff just falls from the sky here."

I was still upset, especially with Sean, but that got me wondering what kind of weather, if any, they *did* have in Nuath, what with it being underground and all. I hadn't thought to ask during my visits to their house.

We ordered lunch, and the conversation changed—Uncle Louie and Mr. O'Gara talking about the local economy and Aunt Theresa and Mrs. O'Gara commiserating about the headaches of raising teenagers.

"Honestly, you can't take your eyes off them for a moment," Mrs. O'Gara said with a laugh. "Would you believe, I once caught Sean climbing out his bedroom window—a second story bedroom, mind you!—after midnight? Wanted to meet up with his friends and a bonny lass he'd just met, he did."

I felt my stomach clench as Aunt Theresa replied, "If Marsha ever tried such a thing, she'd be grounded until she leaves for college."

Could Mrs. O'Gara have guessed what Rigel and I were planning tonight? That story was as badly timed as if she'd done it on purpose.

"The lass wasn't all *that* bonny," Sean said in a joking undertone.

I glanced at him in confusion. "What?"

He leaned toward me, a coppery wave of hair falling across his forehead. "You looked a bit upset at what my mum just said. Didn't want you thinking I'd been casting about for girls the whole while I was in Ireland."

"The thought hadn't even crossed my mind," I assured him with complete honesty.

He just grinned and shrugged. "If you say so."

All I could do was shake my head. "Are you really that

delusional?" I whispered.

"Not delusional. But you'll find I *can* be persistent." He gave me a wink and took a big sip of his soda.

I looked past him to Molly and it was clear she'd heard the exchange—and equally clear she was uncomfortable. I wondered what her real thoughts were on the matter, but couldn't very well ask at the moment.

Like that first night the O'Garas had come to our house, I felt a weird disconnect between what I knew was true and how things appeared on the surface, with conversations on everyday topics like weather and the upcoming basketball season. No one, especially my aunt and uncle, would ever believe most of our group was composed of extraterrestrials.

Sometimes I wasn't sure I completely believed it myself.

Walking home an hour later, I caught Molly's eye and the two of us dropped a little behind so we could talk. Unfortunately, Sean slowed down, too.

"Do you mind?" I asked pointedly. "We need a little *girl* talk."

His eyes twinkled down at me as he arched a skeptical eyebrow. "Let me guess. About me?"

"Sean, not *everything* is about you," Molly informed him.

He just laughed. "Probably about Stuart, then. Either way, I'd as soon hear it. Need to know what I'm up against."

My mood was already in the pits and at that, I snapped. "Fine. It's on you if you hear something you don't want to. Molly, how long do you think it will take Sean to accept the fact that Rigel and I really are *graell* bonded?" I intentionally spoke as though Sean wasn't there, but he replied anyway.

"I'm guessing a few hundred years. Because it's not possible."

I still refused to look at him. "You know," I said to Molly, "Shim Stuart is probably the top geneticist on Earth, maybe even Mars, and *he* seems to think it's possible. And he doesn't strike me as the delusional sort."

Without warning, Sean reached over and grabbed my hand. I snatched it away, but not before I felt that jolt again.

"Sean!" Molly gasped, clearly shocked that he'd touched me without permission.

But Sean didn't apologize. "Try to deny *that*. I felt our connection the first time you shook my hand—and I know you felt it, too, even if you were afraid to say anything because of Stuart. Are you going to pretend you feel anything like that when *he* touches you?"

I could feel my cheeks burning, but I lifted my chin and looked him right in the eye. "No. What I get from him is at least ten times stronger." Maybe I was exaggerating a little, but not much.

Sean clearly didn't believe me. "How long did it take him to convince you of that?"

"I didn't need any convincing. Like I told Molly, we both felt it the very first time we touched and it totally freaked Rigel out. He didn't tell me what it meant for a couple of weeks—not until *after* we accidentally shot a lightning bolt at Bryce Farmer."

Sean frowned but didn't argue any more and the three of us walked in silence for a few minutes. Then, as we reached my street, Sean murmured, "Molly did tell us how you get treated at home, M. I hope—we all hope—you can ignore the awkward political stuff enough to still escape to our place sometimes."

Molly nodded eagerly. "We can pretend we still need lots of tutoring. Your aunt already seems to like our mum, so—"

Sean had dodged the *graell* subject again, but I couldn't help being a *little* touched by their concern. "Thanks, Molly. Really. But it may be a while before I'm comfortable coming over after . . . everything. Sorry."

Her face fell, making me feel guilty for a second—but only a second. Because she'd been in on the deception, too.

"I guess I understand," she admitted. "But I hope you'll eventually forgive us . . . all of us—" she glanced at Sean— "and we can be friends again. Real friends."

Even if I shared that hope, at least as far as Molly was concerned, at the moment I was way more looking forward to meeting with Rigel tonight—alone.

19

udaris thusmithoir (oo-DARE-is thoos-MITH-er): *parental authority*

My aunt and uncle went to bed early that night but there was no point leaving for the arboretum before a quarter to twelve. If anything, that might increase my chance of getting caught, and I didn't even want to *think* what my aunt would do if that happened.

Just in case Rigel and I decided our only option was to run away, I stuffed a change of clothes and a few toiletries into my backpack. Then I picked out what I was going to wear to meet him, did my last little bit of homework and glanced at the clock.

Only ten-thirty? Really? Sighing with impatience, I flopped down on my bed and picked up *Jane Eyre*, which I was rereading for the umpteenth time.

And fell asleep.

I woke with a start and glanced wildly at my clock. Two minutes past midnight! Silently calling myself every kind of idiot, I jammed my legs and arms into my jeans and dark sweater, my feet into my running shoes, and yanked open my bedroom door.

No sound from my aunt and uncle's room, so I raced down the stairs as quietly as I could, through the kitchen, out the back door, and started running toward the arboretum, five or six blocks away. I was halfway there before I realized I'd forgotten my backpack, but there was no going back for it now.

Instead, I ran faster, my shoes slapping the pavement. Now that I was away from the house, I was a lot more worried about getting to the arboretum before Rigel gave up and left than I was about making noise. Which is probably why I didn't hear a car pulling up behind me just as I reached the arched entrance covered with dormant rose canes.

"Rigel!" I called out in a loud whisper. "Are you still here?"

"M!" came his answering whisper, along with the sound of his feet quickly approaching. "I was starting to think you couldn't—"

Before he could finish, I heard a car door slam behind me and wheeled around—to see my Aunt Theresa heading toward me. I shrank back, hoping maybe I could hide in the arboretum, but it was already too late.

"Marsha Truitt! *What* do you think you're doing out on the streets in the middle of the night? Jewel may be small, but it's certainly not safe for you to go running at this hour—and on a school night! Of all the foolish, irresponsible— Why, *anything* could have happened to you, a young girl out on the streets at midnight! Alone! Completely alone!"

Heart pounding in my throat, I clung to a shred of hope that I could at least minimize the damage. "I'm sorry, Aunt Theresa, I know it was stupid, but I was so keyed up I just needed to run and I . . . I didn't want to wake you."

"You could have been mugged!" she continued to rant. "Or raped, or even murdered!"

"It's okay, Mrs. Truitt." Rigel emerged from the arboretum, dashing my fragile hope. "She wasn't alone. I would never let anything happen to her."

I closed my eyes. Rigel was trying to help, but he'd just made things ten thousand times worse. Sure enough, my aunt went totally ballistic.

"You!" she practically screeched. "Marsha, you know full well I don't approve of this boy, yet you deliberately sneaked out of the house—at midnight!—to meet him? I've raised you better than to act like a . . . a common little tramp! I can't even *begin* to tell you how disappointed I am—in both of you. Young man, you will call your parents at once, and I will speak to them."

Rigel stared at her and I could feel the panic and fury rolling off him even though he was several feet away. "What? No!"

"This instant, young man! If you don't have a cell phone with you, we will return to our house and you can call from there. I intend to nip this . . . this immoral behavior in the bud!" Even though she was much shorter than Rigel and not a fraction as strong, her anger made her intimidating.

Slowly, reluctantly, with a long, apologetic glance my way, Rigel pulled out his phone and called. I could hear it ringing several times on the other end before a sleepy voice answered.

"Hey, Dad, it's me. Yeah. I'm, uh—"

Aunt Theresa reached out and took the phone away from him. "Mr. Stuart? This is Theresa Truitt, Marsha's aunt. I have just caught my niece and your son meeting secretly at the arboretum in town— yes, at midnight. We need to discuss what should be done about it."

I could hear Mr. Stuart's voice, no longer sleepy, saying something that sounded decisive.

"Very well," Aunt Theresa responded. "I'll take them both back to our house and you can join us there." She handed the phone back to Rigel and turned to me. "Marsha, front seat. Young man, back seat. Now."

Rigel hesitated. "Um, my bike . . ." He glanced over his shoulder.

"Your parents can retrieve it later. In the car. Both of you."

Until that moment, "quivering with rage" was something I thought only happened in books. I'd never seen my aunt so angry— and I'd seen her angry a lot. Her lips were a thin slash across her face and her small, gray eyes sparkled with something that almost looked like unshed tears, but was probably fury. I got into the front seat without a word and Rigel got in back.

I desperately groped for *any* explanation for why I needed to meet Rigel in the middle of the night, but even with the boost in clarity his nearness gave me, I was too panicked to think straight. We were so totally, monumentally screwed.

I'd expected a lecture, but Aunt Theresa didn't say anything at all during the brief drive. She braked in the driveway with a spray of gravel and turned off the ignition. "We'll wait inside until the Stuarts get here."

She made a point of walking between us so we couldn't so much as brush fingers as we went up the front walk. I was dying for even the slightest contact with Rigel and knew he was feeling the same. But what could we do?

The next ten minutes were the most awkward I'd ever spent in my life. Aunt Theresa directed us to chairs on opposite sides of the living room, then sat between us on the couch. Once or twice she made little hmphing noises and I thought she would finally start lecturing, but then she didn't.

"Mrs. Truitt," Rigel said at one point, "please let me explain—"

But she cut him off with a glare and a sharp, "When your parents get here."

Neither of us tried to say anything else after that, just sat and fidgeted. I wondered at one point whether Uncle Louie was still asleep or if he was just hiding upstairs to avoid the conflict. Either would be totally in character.

Finally, after what felt like years, we heard the sound of a car pulling into the drive. With one quelling look at both of us, Aunt Theresa went to open the front door.

"Please come in," she said in a voice that could have frozen hot coffee.

Both of Rigel's parents had come. As they followed her in, I realized it was the first time they'd ever been inside our house. Our living room seemed even smaller and shabbier than usual as I mentally compared it to theirs.

"I'm sure you'll agree that these children need to understand just how deplorably they have behaved tonight," my aunt continued icily before they even sat down.

"We certainly do," Mr. Stuart said, frowning thunderously at Rigel.

Even Dr. Stuart, who was usually so nice, looked seriously angry. "I must apologize for our son's part in this," she said. "You can be sure such a thing will never happen again."

"It most certainly will not!" Aunt Theresa exclaimed. "For my part, I intend to keep an extremely close eye on Marsha for the foreseeable future, in addition to the restrictions I'll be putting on her activities. I'd like your assurance that you'll do the same with your son."

Dr. Stuart turned pink but I couldn't tell whether she was ticked that Aunt Theresa was telling her what to do, or just mad at Rigel. And me.

"I'd like to add my apology to my wife's," Mr. Stuart said before she could reply. "In the past, we've found Rigel to be very trustworthy, but I assure you he will now have to re-earn our trust." He pinned Rigel with his eyes, then glanced at me, still frowning. "Both of you showed incredibly poor judgment tonight. I hope you realize that. I can't imagine what you were thinking."

I nodded and Rigel mumbled a "Yes, Sir," but I knew he was

seething inside as much as I was. The Stuarts knew perfectly well why we needed to talk, after that bombshell last night, then everybody keeping us apart at church.

Yeah, maybe it *would* have been smarter for us to wait until school tomorrow, but we needed to talk about stuff we couldn't risk people hearing. Stuff *they* wouldn't want anybody at school to overhear. They *had* to understand that. But neither of them looked very understanding at the moment.

Aunt Theresa turned her glare back on me. "Marsha, you are not to spend time in this boy's company again. I'm telling you in front of his parents so that they will know where I stand on this."

She glanced at the Stuarts and they both nodded. I looked in vain for some trace of sympathy in their expressions but didn't see any.

"Did you hear me, Marsha?" my aunt said. "I want your word on this—no contact."

I stared at her incredulously. "What? You mean, at *all*? But we—" I stopped myself just in time from blurting out that we'd both get sick. The Stuarts knew, though. Didn't they? "We have some classes together at school," I finished, squashing down my panic so I could sound reasonable. "We . . . we can't stay *completely* apart."

"Which is why I want your word, Marsha. Other than absolutely necessary communication for strictly academic reasons, you will keep your distance even at school. Am I clear? Or must I contact your teachers about this?"

I felt tears welling up at the injustice, at the thought of how awful this would be. I didn't try to stop myself from crying, hoping if I was pathetic enough, the Stuarts might relent even if Aunt Theresa never would.

Instead, Mr. Stuart said, "Rigel, I'd like the same promise from you. I agree it will be best if you two avoid each other for a while."

Now Rigel's head snapped up. "But—"

"No buts. Not now. Promise me."

Even from across the room I could see Rigel swallow, feel the anger, fear and desperation flowing from him. But his father held his rebellious gaze until he reluctantly nodded—then immediately sent a glance my way that held both apology and defiance.

"Marsha?" Aunt Theresa demanded.

"Fine," I muttered. I refused to give her more than that, since this was a promise I had no intention of keeping. I was just glad the Stuarts hadn't asked for my promise, too, since I'd feel a lot worse breaking my word to them. Not that it would stop me.

For a long moment, all three adults just looked at us. I stared at my lap, so I couldn't see their expressions—or Rigel's. I just hoped he was as determined as I was to find a way around this horrible new restriction.

With a surge of mingled hope and fear, I suddenly remembered my backpack upstairs. Running away was still an option. Maybe our our only option.

"Very well," my aunt said at last. "That will do for now. I'll leave it to you," she said to the Stuarts, "to determine any further punishment for your son. I appreciate you coming."

Since that was clearly a dismissal, they rose, still looking relentlessly grim. Rigel and I managed one more long, desperate glance as they moved to the door, but if he was trying to send any thoughts at me, I was too upset to receive them.

Then they were gone.

20

cannarc (KAN-ark): *rebellion; mutiny; resistance*

My eyes were crusty when I woke up the next morning, and it took me a few seconds to remember why.

Oh, that's right. I'd cried myself to sleep. And now, as the disastrous events of last night came crashing back, it was all I could do not to start crying all over again.

Aunt Theresa had lectured herself hoarse about just how thoroughly I'd disappointed her by sneaking out, enumerating all the reasons my friends, and especially my boyfriend, were "bad influences." I'd tuned her out early on, but there was no tuning out the consequences.

I was grounded. More than grounded. I wasn't allowed to go *anywhere* but school and church, not even taekwondo, for the rest of the semester. Instead, I'd have a whole bunch of new chores around the house. Worst of all, I was forbidden to see Rigel or even any of my friends outside of school, until further notice.

My life was going to suck beyond all reason for the foreseeable future.

"Wow, M, you look awful," Bri greeted me when she and Deb got on the bus. "You're not sick again, are you?"

I knew she was referring to the few weeks in September when Rigel and I had pretended to break up and had stayed away from each other. Both of us had been a mess then, mentally and physically.

"No." I would be soon, though, if I adhered to the letter of my restriction. Which was one reason I had no plans to do so. "I'm grounded, though. My aunt got super pissed when I came home late from Rigel's party."

I saw no point telling them about last night. I'd been careful to sit well away from Molly, and Sean hardly ever took the bus anymore, getting rides from teammates with cars.

129

"Guess it's just as well you didn't come with us to the after-party at Nicole's, then," Deb said.

Bri nodded. "Yeah, we didn't leave there till midnight. But what a party! Deb had to do some quick talking to convince her mom we'd been with you, then spent too long at my house picking up my stuff for our sleepover. But how is your aunt grounding you? I mean, it's not like you're ever allowed to do much of anything anyway."

Like I needed reminding. "Now I'm *really* not allowed to do anything. She'd even be mad if she knew I was talking to you guys right now. I'm supposed to be in seclusion or something—not talk to *anybody* except when I absolutely have to for school. She practically made me take a vow of silence."

"And celibacy?" Bri giggled. Then, at my look, she added, "Oh, come on, M, I'm kidding. But you've already told us your aunt doesn't approve of Rigel."

"Yeah, well, she approves even less now," I said glumly. "He's number one on the list of people I'm not allowed to talk to."

Bri waved a hand. "Pfft! It's not like she can watch you at school. She already wouldn't let him come to your house, or you to his unless his parents were home. How is this so different?"

Her breezy attitude was irritating, but it also cheered me up a little. Maybe it *wouldn't* be all that different? "Unless Rigel takes her rules too seriously."

"You told him?" Deb asked.

"Aunt Theresa told his *parents*." I had the dubious satisfaction of seeing them both look shocked. "Yeah. That's how pissed she was."

Maybe I wasn't being *totally* fair, since sneaking out at midnight on a school night was arguably worse than coming home late from a chaperoned party. But I wasn't in a mood to cut my aunt any slack.

"Wow, that's low." Bri shook her head in sympathy. "How awkward was *that*?"

"You have no idea." I cringed again at the memory of last night in our living room.

Surely, *surely*, the Stuarts had just been playing along when they'd agreed to Aunt Theresa's terms? *They* knew she had no clue about the truth—who I really was, or about Rigel and me. They couldn't *really* intend to enforce Rigel's promise to stay away from me. Could they?

I shouldered my way through the crowd as soon as I was off the bus, so I could ask Rigel before class started. To my relief, he was waiting on the sidewalk outside, which would give us a few precious extra minutes.

But as I hurried over to him, he suddenly looked wary, making me worry all over again. "Hey," he said, sounding as cautious as he looked.

"Hey!" I tried to make up for it with my own enthusiasm. "There. Now we've already broken the rules, so let's talk."

Rigel let out a breath in obvious relief, then took my hand. I could feel the tension leaving him even as I felt my own nerves unknotting at his touch. "I was afraid you'd—I dunno—"

"Feel like I had to follow my aunt's stupid rule? No way. Just one more thing she doesn't have to know about. But what about you? Your parents? Do they really expect—?"

He shrugged as we started walking toward the building. "I'm not sure what they expect," he said in the whisper only I could hear, "but I got a lecture to end all lectures on the way home. About how I'd risked your safety, about betraying their trust, a bunch of crap about Martian politics. I stopped listening about halfway in."

"You, too?" I was in complete sympathy. "I thought my aunt would never shut up and go to bed. But . . . I don't think I've ever seen her so mad."

He was quiet for a moment. Then, as we reached my locker, he turned to me, pain in his eyes. "M, I am so, *so* sorry. This whole thing is my fault. If I'd stayed hidden, you probably could have talked your way out of the worst of it. At least, your aunt probably wouldn't have forbidden you to see me. And my parents wouldn't know about it at all."

"You were defending me," I reminded him. "It was actually kind of sweet. Though, yeah, it probably would have been better if you hadn't."

Rigel gave a half smile, but then shook his head fiercely. "No. I should never have suggested that meeting in the first place. We could have held out till today, and then we wouldn't—"

"If you hadn't suggested it, I would have. This is *not* your fault, Rigel! You didn't make up all those stupid Martian rules, or move the O'Garas to Jewel, or . . . or even intend to get yourself bonded to

131

me." I stopped at the look on his face.

"You think I regret that part?" He sounded almost angry. "No matter what happens, I'll *never* regret that. You're the best thing that's ever happened to me, M, don't you know that by now? But I'm worried I've totally screwed things up for you. Screwed up your future."

I shook my head as fiercely as he had. "I don't *want* any future that doesn't include you, Rigel. Period. We'll run away first. Screw whatever political—"

I was cut off by the warning bell. Maybe just as well, since we were getting so intense people were shooting curious looks our way, even though (or maybe because) our whole conversation had been in inaudible—to them—whispers.

"We'll figure something out. Somehow," Rigel promised.

He hadn't responded about running away, but I couldn't help thinking about it during Geometry. And the more I thought about that particular solution, the less scary and the more obvious it seemed.

We had three classes together before lunch, but no more opportunity to talk even semi-privately. We swung past the courtyard on the way to the cafeteria, but an icy drizzle had started falling. So after we got our lunches, I made a quick excuse to Bri, Deb and Molly about needing some alone time and we grabbed a table in the corner.

"Finally!" Rigel said as we sat side by side, facing the lunchroom so we could see any potential interruptions coming. "Okay. First off, I want to know what the O'Garas said Saturday night, after you left my house. What are they going to make you do?"

I frowned at him in confusion. "Make me do? They can't *make* me do anything. And they didn't say much, except to apologize for Allister. I still pretty much lambasted Sean—well, all of them—for knowing about this stupid Consort thing all along and not telling me."

"Yeah, I came down pretty hard on my parents, too," Rigel said. "They swear they had no idea about Sean, but they did know about the whole Consort thing. I can't believe they never said a word to either of us, just let us go on thinking we could . . . that it was . . ."

"You said we'd figure something out and we will," I reminded him, taking his hand. "It *will* be okay, Rigel. You'll see."

The pain was back in his eyes when he looked at me. "Will it, M? I just can't see how. We can't *really* run away—though I won't say I haven't thought about it."

"So have I—a lot. And why can't we?" I demanded. "Seriously, if running away is the only way we can be together, I'm totally in."

He grabbed both of my hands. "Really, M? You'd do that?"

"Absolutely."

He smiled a little—the first real smile I'd seen from him today—as he realized I meant it, but then he turned serious again. "I can't tell you how much that means to me, but . . . we need to find another way. Think of the uproar it would cause—not only the O'Garas and the Council and all, but your folks and the town and the school and everything. It might even break everything—everything!—out into the open."

Even if he was right, at the moment I hardly cared. "Being together matters more to me, Rigel. More than absolutely *anything* else."

He stroked the back of my hand with his thumb. "Same here." But the sadness was back.

Something niggled at me, and after a moment I realized it was the familiarity of the expression in his eyes. It was the same sadness I'd noticed last week, only more pronounced now. "You suspected, didn't you?" It came out almost as an accusation. "After the O'Garas got here, I mean. You knew all along something was up with Sean."

He shrugged, still sad. "I didn't know about *this*—this Royal Consort business. But them coming here, the way Sean was acting toward me, it forced me to really think about who you are. Your position, I mean. And to wonder just where I could fit in, longterm."

I tightened my grip on his hands. "With me! That's where you fit in. Always with me. How can you doubt that? You think, what, all this Sovereign stuff will go to my head and I'll think I'm too good for you or something?" I let out something between a laugh and a sob at the absurdity of the idea. "Every girl in this lunchroom wishes she was sitting here with you, Rigel. I am totally aware, every minute of every day, just how lucky I am!"

He managed a grudging smile. "Thanks, M. Sorry I'm being such a downer. It's just . . . the thought of losing you makes me a little crazy."

"Ditto." I was emphatic. "But that's *not* going to happen. No matter what. So let's eat. And strategize how we're going to get around this grounding thing for the next few days."

He nodded, but then frowned across the cafeteria. I followed his gaze and saw Sean sitting at our regular table, next to Molly, talking to Bri and Deb. As we watched, the whole group turned and looked at us.

Feeling both pissed and amused, I waved cheerily at them, then turned back to Rigel. "Gee, wonder what they're all talking about?" I couldn't quite keep the sourness out of my voice.

Oddly, he was suddenly more upbeat than just a moment ago. "Who cares? Because you're right. We're together *now*, no matter what happens later. I'll talk my parents around—half of that grounding thing was a show for your aunt anyway—and you can work on convincing her we can be trusted."

"Oh, sure! Piece of cake. Running away would be a whole lot easier."

"Hey, I didn't say it would be easy. Baby steps. We're still way ahead of where we were a few weeks ago, when we thought were about to die. Right?"

I couldn't disagree. "Right."

"There you go, then. Eat."

And I did, soaking up all the Rigel-ness I could while I had the chance.

21

breag fíonn (brag fin): *discover a lie; detect a falsehood*

Rigel and I didn't get another chance for private conversation that day, except for a few seconds just before boarding our separate buses to go home, when we managed a quick goodbye kiss.

"Guess I won't see you till tomorrow," I said wistfully.

"Guess not. But I'll be thinking about you constantly till then," Rigel promised. "Love you, M."

He boarded his bus and I turned reluctantly to mine. It was going to be a long afternoon, evening and night.

Molly came running up as I joined Bri and Deb in the line for our bus. I half hoped she'd seen that kiss, but if so she didn't mention it.

"I have to be at cheerleading in a minute," she panted, "but you're coming over tonight, right?"

"I can't." My regret was only partly feigned. "I'm, like, totally grounded right now."

Her eyes got big. "What? Why? Just because you got home a little late Saturday night? Your aunt seemed mostly okay about it yesterday."

I just shrugged. I hadn't told Bri and Deb the truth, and I definitely didn't want to tell Molly. After all, what was the point? All they needed to know was the result.

"Do you want my mum to talk to your aunt?" Molly persisted, like a dog with a bone.

Aunt Theresa would undoubtedly spill the beans if she did, so I shook my head. "I think we'd better let her cool down first."

Not that anything they could say would change her mind—or like any of the O'Garas would even *want* to change Aunt Theresa's mind if they knew the point of my grounding was to keep me away from Rigel. Still, if they *could* get her to lighten up a little, he and I might manage an occasional clandestine meeting.

"Maybe in a day or two?" I suggested.

"Absolutely," Molly agreed. "I'm sure Mum can make her see reason. She thinks your aunt is so strict because she worries about you. Plus she, um, doesn't seem to relate very well to teenagers."

Bri and Deb burst out laughing at this massive understatement. "I think M's Aunt time-traveled here from the 1930's," Bri declared between giggles. "They don't come any more old-fashioned."

"Yeah, she's pretty old school," I agreed. "Thinks kids should be seen and not heard, never out past ten until they're either twenty-one or married, that sort of thing."

"We'll still try," Molly promised as she turned to go, then whispered to me, "We'll use the tutoring excuse if nothing else works."

When I got home to a long list of chores and explicit instructions not to use the phone, the idea of running away appealed more than ever.

At bedtime I tried to comfort myself by rereading the endings of a couple of books where the main characters had gone through hell before finally getting their happily-ever-afters. It only helped a little.

By the next morning I was ready to tell Molly I was willing to accept any help she or her parents could give me. Unfortunately, Sean was waiting at the bus stop, too, and they both wore such troubled expressions, I was immediately distracted.

"Hey, guys, what's wrong?" I greeted them.

"Why didn't you tell me the real reason you were grounded?" Molly asked, hurt evident in her gray eyes. "It wasn't about the party at all."

I had a serious *oh, crap* moment but tried to hide it. "What do you . . . I mean, who . . . what did you hear? And from who?" Okay, so I didn't hide it all that well.

"Your aunt told our mum about you and Stuart sneaking out at midnight Sunday night." Sean looked totally judgmental. "What were you thinking? What was *he* thinking?"

Irritation wiped out embarrassed confusion. "We needed to talk—privately."

"Like you can't do that at school? Like, say, during lunch

yesterday? Without taking any stupid risks with your safety?"

Even though he was right, even though Rigel had pretty much said the same thing, I flared at him. "Why is it any business of yours? Or your mother's?"

Sean glanced down the street. The two other kids—both freshmen —who boarded at our stop were heading our way, so he lowered his voice. "You know exactly why it's our business, *Emileia*. Anything that puts you at risk is the business of every *Echtran* who cares about our people's future. But maybe you don't count as one of those?"

"Sean!" Molly hissed at him, clearly aghast. "Of course she cares!"

I just glared at both of them, since the two freshmen were close enough to hear us now. Plus I wasn't sure what to say in my defense, since I *didn't* care as much about the future of the Martian people as they clearly did. Not as much as I ought to, if I was ever going to be their Sovereign.

But hey, it wasn't like I'd grown up steeped in all this stuff, or like I even *wanted* to be their stupid leader. And if they expected me to do it without Rigel, I never would be. They could find themselves another Sovereign and let unprepared, disloyal me go my own merry way. The O'Garas would probably consider my thoughts blasphemous, but I didn't care.

I boarded the bus with a combination of rebellion, fear and guilt churning in my stomach.

Sean sat in the back with a couple of other jocks but Molly, to my surprise, sat next to me. The guilt got worse, since none of this was her fault. I *had* lied about the reason I was grounded, and then I'd snapped at her along with Sean when he went all protective and patriotic on me. I was groping for a not-too-embarrassing way to apologize when she beat me to it.

"M, I'm sorry if I sounded judgmental, and I'm sorry Sean got so sarcastic and all. He really does mean well, I swear! But I should warn you our mum made us both promise we'd, ah, keep an eye on you at school. She said your aunt asked if we could, and she gave her word. Only it would've been nice if she'd asked us first!"

Outrage immediately swamped all traces of guilt. "Wait. So you and Sean will blab to your mother if I talk to Rigel at school? And then she'll tell Aunt Theresa, so she can make my grounding even *worse?*"

Molly nodded, looking completely miserable. "We told Mum it wasn't our place to spy on you. But she kept after us till we both promised."

"That's just great," I said, facing forward again to avoid looking at her, my insides burning and churning again. "Did I tell you how sick Rigel and I get when we can't be together?"

Her gasp made me glance at her. She looked horrified. "Sick? No! I though the *tinneas* part of the *graell* stories was totally made up."

"Shh!" I cautioned. She looked even more upset at her slip, which made me feel mean, though I hadn't meant to be.

"Sorry, sorry," she whispered. "I'm not used to this, having so many people around who aren't . . . who shouldn't . . . who, um, don't know."

I faked a smile, to reassure her. "I know. Just . . . try to be careful, okay?"

She nodded vigorously but didn't have the nerve to say anything else before Bri and Deb got on the bus and joined us. While the three of them chatted about school stuff, I wondered what it would be like to live around people who all *knew*, like Molly and Sean had all their lives. A lot like being at the Stuarts' house, I decided. In other words, wonderful. But would I ever be *allowed* to go to the Stuarts' house again?

I tried to remind myself that I wouldn't be fifteen forever. In March I'd turn sixteen. (Interestingly, my adoption papers had listed my birthdate as a week earlier than it really was, probably to throw off anyone trying to track me down.) And in two more years I'd be eighteen and out from under Aunt Theresa's thumb. But two years was an awfully long time.

Rigel was waiting for me again when I got off the bus, and with a defiant glance at Sean and Molly, I walked over to talk to him.

"Hey," I said as we clasped hands, and knew he was feeling the same relief I was at the touch. I savored it for a long moment, then spoke quickly and quietly. "I just found out my aunt and Mrs. O are making Sean and Molly *spy* on us and report back if we don't keep our promise. Maybe we should run away after all."

He frowned at them over my shoulder. "*Making* them? Like they have no choice but to spy? I bet *he* was only too happy to go along with that."

I shrugged. "Molly just told me on the bus. *She* doesn't seem happy about it, and . . . it was nice of her to let me know."

"Nice. Right." I could feel his frustration building. "So if they blab to your aunt, you get in more trouble. And now *my* folks are saying it's important we keep our distance until things get sorted out—whatever that means. Meanwhile, Sean gets to spend time with you and I don't. Just like Allister wanted."

"What, like that'll suddenly make me fall for him? Not a chance." I sent love and reassurance his way as hard as I could, and he relaxed a little.

"You're right. I'm sorry. I guess let's pretend to cool it for a few days, see how it goes. Maybe if you can convince your aunt you're playing by the rules, she'll lighten up, and— Crap! There's the bell."

I squeezed his hand, then let go. "See you in class. We'll get through this, Rigel. We've faced worse, remember?"

He gave me a quick nod, then sprinted off without a backward glance and I had a sinking feeling that pretending to "cool it" might be as hard as our fake breakup had been. At least for me.

Molly wasn't in Geometry, English or Science, so we could at least sit near each other there and talk a little. Not that we did, much. We were both still trying to process everything, decide what we could reasonably get away with, and what risks we were willing to take. As soon as we headed to lunch, Rigel murmured something about working on a project in the library.

"What? Really?" I was so startled I forgot to whisper. "You're not even coming to the cafeteria?"

He gave a quick shake of his head and glanced behind me. Again I felt that combination of frustration and sadness from him. "I think that would be . . . harder. See you in History." The lingering look he gave me before hurrying off comforted me more than his words did.

I glanced back and wasn't particularly surprised to see Sean headed my way. Though he frowned after Rigel, his expression when he turned to me was perfectly friendly.

"I'm really sorry, M, for the way I went off on you this morning. I was totally out of line and it won't happen again." He remembered to whisper, showing more emotional control than I'd just managed with Rigel.

Not feeling particularly gracious, I just shrugged. Undeterred, he fell into step beside me as I headed to the lunchroom.

"Molly said she told you what our mum made us promise. Believe me, I don't like it any more than Molly does. I may not be a fan of you and Stuart as a couple, but I'm no snitch."

"Except you are," I pointed out. "Or won't you keep your promise to your mother?"

He didn't answer for several seconds, which made me unwillingly glance at him. He looked troubled.

"I'll do my best to fudge. Mol will, too. But you should know our mum, well . . . she always knows. Guess you could say it's one of her special abilities."

I blinked at him. "What, like a built-in lie detector?"

"Yeah, you could call it that. All she has to do is concentrate and . . . busted." He didn't look happy about it, which I could understand. Because how inconvenient would *that* be?

But right now it sucked worse for me and Rigel than for him and Molly. I huffed out a frustrated breath. "Fine. We'll try not to do anything you'll have to lie about, but we do have four classes together, so it's not like we can totally avoid each other."

"I know. I get that. As long as you at least *try* to stick to your aunt's rules, I think Mum'll be okay with it. And we really will do our best to cover if we can."

I was unexpectedly touched by his equally unexpected earnestness. "Thanks, Sean." This time I kept the sarcasm out of my voice.

"No problem." His smile seemed both sincere and relieved. "So. Lunch?"

22

Rigel (RY-jel): *a variable star with pulsations powered by nuclear reactions*

I'm already heading for the only corner of the media center where people are allowed to eat when I realize I should have grabbed something from a vending machine, since I didn't bring anything from home. So much for my noble gesture. Guess it's true, no good deed goes unpunished.

Trying to ignore my stomach grumbling—it was fine until I *thought* about food—I sit down, thump open my history book and try to concentrate on the reading I'm supposed to do for next period. Instead, I keep thinking about M in the cafeteria without me. Probably sitting with Sean O'Gara, since no way he'll pass up this chance to get on her good side.

Was she maybe right yesterday, and we should just run away? I know all the reasons we shouldn't, but the longer I have to stay away from her, the less important those reasons seem. Maybe if we plan it really, really well?

The Korean War can't compete. Especially since it's all boring dates and names and politics, instead of actual battle stuff. I finally give up and pull out a sheet of paper so I can at least write a note to M and slip it in her locker. That shouldn't break any of her aunt's stupid rules. Or my parents.'

Their betrayal still infuriates me. First keeping secrets from M and me, then going along with her aunt and all the O'Garas to keep M and me apart. Clenching my teeth, I pick up my pen.

My special M, is all I've written when a wrapped tuna sandwich lands on my open history book. I look up and Molly O'Gara is standing there, holding out a carton of chocolate milk. Confused, I take it without thinking.

"I figured you were probably hungry, since you didn't stop by the

141

cafeteria for anything before coming here," she explains.

Though she looks all friendly and sincere, I don't smile. "M told me you and your brother are reporting back to her aunt about us," I say, so she'll stop trying to make nice and go away.

Instead, she sits down across from me. "I figured she had, but that's not *quite* true. Our mum just made us promise to keep an eye on you guys. Please don't think we like the idea. Either of us. Or that we'll tell her any more than she forces out of us."

"Forces?" I don't even try to hide my skepticism. Like little Mrs. O could "force" seven-foot Sean to do anything?

Molly kind of shrugs, making her hair bounce. "Mum always knows if we're telling the truth or not. But if she doesn't ask direct, specific questions, we can probably get away with general stuff that won't be incriminating."

I think how my grandfather sometimes seems to almost read my mind. If Mrs. O can do that, I can see how it would be hard to get around. Not that it makes spying on us okay. At all.

"So why are you here?" I ask. No point beating around the bush.

She turns a little pink and looks away. "I think you're getting a really bum deal out of this whole situation, Rigel, and it's not fair. You had no way to know about . . . well, the politics involved, or . . . or anything."

"No, I definitely didn't know your family came here to ruin my life. And M's."

I think for sure that will tick her off enough that she'll leave me alone. But no. She does look upset, but also more determined. I try not to sigh out loud.

"Nobody wants to ruin your life, Rigel, you have to believe that." She's so earnest it's almost funny. But not quite. "I know Sean has been . . . kind of a jerk to you, but he really does want what's best for —" She breaks off and glances around, then lowers her voice to the kind of whisper M and I use when we need to talk privately. "For our people," she finishes.

"Screw our people," I say just as quietly, though it feels weird to use that special whisper with anyone but M. "They can take care of themselves. M can't. She needs me."

Molly twists her mouth for a second, then says, "I keep forgetting you grew up here." She obviously means Earth, not Jewel. "So I guess it makes sense you wouldn't care as much about our people back home as we do. They probably don't even seem real to you. But they're very real to us, and we *do* care. All of us."

"Yeah, okay, fine. I get that. My dad's way invested in all that stuff, too, so I hear about it a lot. But M's happiness matters more to me than some nebulous 'future.' And none of this is making her happy."

"Is it really her happiness you care about, Rigel? Or yours?"

I start to say they're the same thing, but she's watching me intently and I realize they're not—at least, not necessarily and maybe not always. But if I have to choose, it's no contest.

"Hers. If I really thought she'd be happier with me out of the picture, I'd leave her alone no matter what it did to me. But that's not the way it is. Nobody who's never felt the *graell* can really get it, so there's no point trying to explain. But M and I just aren't . . . complete without each other. Which means we *can't* be happy apart. Neither of us."

Now Molly gets that syrupy romantic look girls sometimes get. "That's so incredibly sweet, Rigel. M is a lucky girl." She sighs dreamily, then says, "And I really am sorry about . . . about everything. I just wanted you to know that."

Right. Like I believe Sean's sister is feeling sorry for *me*. But before I can throw her stupid apology in her face, she suddenly stands up. "I'd better let you study—and eat. See you in class."

She walks off and I stare after her, wondering what the hell that was really all about. Then I realize I only have ten minutes to eat the sandwich Molly brought and finish my note to M. I start writing between bites.

23

giola uresal (gee-OH-la OO-ree-sal): *a menial servant*

"So, are you ready for the big season opener on Thursday?" Bri leaned in close to Sean, blatantly flirting even though she was supposedly going out with Matt Mullins. I made a point of noticing, to distract myself from worrying about Rigel.

"I guess so," Sean replied after he swallowed a last bite of pizza— his third enormous slice. "Coach seems happy with my shooting, anyway. You all coming to the game?" His glance encompassed all of us.

"Grounded," I reminded him sourly, but Bri nodded vigorously.

"Are you kidding? We wouldn't miss it for anything! You're going to be amazing."

"Paul Jackson says you're practically a one-man team." Deb agreed, referring to a guy on the basketball team she'd hung out with a few times. "He says sometimes you're so quick it seems like you're in two places at once."

Sean looked a little uncomfortable, probably because that meant he'd been using abilities no "normal" athlete would have. "Hey, I hope nobody thinks I'm, like, a glory hound or anything. No matter what Paul says, we need the whole team out there to make things happen. They're good guys."

"Oh, he didn't mean that," Deb immediately assured him. "They all like you a lot, I can tell."

Before Sean could respond, Molly slid into the seat next to me, on the side away from the others. "I talked to Rigel a little when I gave him that sandwich you got for him," she murmured, then took a quick bite out of her pizza.

"How's he doing?" I whispered, my attention immediately snapping back to more important matters than basketball. I was glad the others kept discussing the upcoming scrimmage, so we could talk semi-privately.

Molly swallowed and took a big sip of skim milk before answering. "Fine, I think. Studying, making good use of the extra time."

"'Fine?'" I echoed. What a useless word. "What did he say?"

She shrugged, scarfing down more of her lunch. I tried not to let my impatience show since she *did* only have a few minutes before the bell and she *had* done me a favor delivering food to Rigel.

"He, um, says if it's for the best that he be out of the picture, he's okay with that," she finally replied.

"What?" I accidentally said it too loudly.

"What's going on?" Bri asked.

Without hesitating, Molly said, "I just told M about a rumor we're having a pop quiz in History. I don't think it's true, though. Sally Jorgensen is just worried because she didn't do the reading."

I nodded, impressed and a little startled by how quickly Molly had covered. I could never think stuff up that fast.

"Shoot, I'd better glance over it just in case," Deb said, pulling out her book.

Bri did the same, while Sean devoted himself to the rest of his huge lunch. The bell rang before I could ask Molly again what she'd meant about Rigel so I hurried to class, determined to ask *him* exactly what he'd said to Molly and why. Quick as I was, she and Sean were right behind me, so the best I could manage was to "accidentally" brush against Rigel as I took my seat.

He must have picked up on my worry, because he looked at me questioningly but my thoughts were way too complicated to send to him silently. We'd have three classes without O'Garas tomorrow, but I needed to know *now* if he was concocting some stupid noble gesture that would destroy our happiness forever.

Mrs. George broke into my anguished thoughts by announcing a pop quiz. Incredulous, I glanced at Molly. How had she known? But she looked as surprised as I was.

Coincidence or not, the quiz took my mind off of my worries for the next twenty minutes. When class ended, I took what fortification I could from Rigel's quick handclasp before we had to go our separate ways for the rest of the day. It wasn't nearly enough, but it reassured me that he wasn't feeling desperate. Just frustrated, like me.

At the end of the day I found a note from Rigel in my locker, which helped a little more. It was short but very sweet, promising that no matter how he kept his distance, he was thinking of me every moment. I tucked it into my bra and went to board the bus with a secret smile.

My glow faded when I got home and found a very *not* sweet note from Aunt Theresa with another list of chores and, again, explicit instructions to stay off the phone.

"She'd probably have it tapped, if she knew how," I grumbled.

Which made me realize—duh—that she *didn't* know how. Which meant she would never know— I was dialing before I finished the thought. Though I half expected to find his cell number blocked, the call went right through.

I sucked in an ecstatic breath, ready to pour out my heart and ask my questions . . . but his dad answered instead.

"Oh, um, hi. Is Rigel there?" I kept my voice totally casual. It didn't work.

"I think it's better if we all abide by your aunt's rules for now, M, and I'm sure those don't include you phoning Rigel," Mr. Stuart said.

I was glad he couldn't see me flushing with mortification. Since the only alternative was a lie he wouldn't believe anyway, I mumbled an apology and hung up.

With furious tears running down my cheeks, I ran up to my room and pulled out my old backpack from middle school and began a much more systematic packing than my hurried one Sunday night. By the time I finished, renewed determination had dried my tears. The backpack securely hidden under my bed, I went back downstairs to organize the pantry.

Making concrete preparations for a last-resort escape with Rigel improved my mood so much that I actually started making a game of just how over-the-top obedient I could be. I had just finished alphabetizing the spices when Aunt Theresa got home.

"Hm. That'll do." She sounded both grudging and surprised as she peered into the pantry. "Is the linen closet done?"

"I'll do it right after my homework." Would it kill her to actually compliment me?

Apparently. "See that you do," was all she said, hanging up her coat and washing her hands to start dinner. "Whatever you can't finish tonight, you can start on tomorrow."

I raced to Geometry the next morning to ask Rigel exactly what he'd meant about being "out of the picture." But when he touched me it felt so good, so calming, I suddenly couldn't bring myself to do it. Besides, whatever he'd said was probably just to throw Molly off. No point ruining these precious few minutes.

So, after all that rushing and worrying, I just asked how he'd spent his evening.

"Driver's Ed and homework. And fooling around with the telescope. It . . . it makes me feel closer to you."

I melted, any lingering uncertainty evaporating. "That's so . . . Thanks, Rigel. I wish I had something at home to remind me of you, too." Not that I needed it, since I thought of him constantly anyway.

He gave me that crooked smile I didn't see often enough lately. "I'll work on that."

"Oh! I didn't mean— You don't have to—"

"I know you weren't fishing for presents, M. But I want you to have something to remember me by, too." His smile faded.

"Don't put it like that!" I whispered fiercely. "You make it sound like you're going to . . . to disappear or something." Molly's words from yesterday took on ominous meaning again and sudden panic gripped my chest. "You're not, are you?"

To my relief, he shook his head emphatically. "Not by choice. I promise you that!"

"Do you mean—?" I began, then realized class had started and no one else was talking. I'd ask later.

But Sean was waiting just outside the door when class ended, then casually walked me to Computer class, forcing me to wait till English to talk privately again with Rigel

"What you said first period, did you mean someone might *make* you leave?" I asked urgently, the moment I could.

He shrugged. "No one's actually said that, so I'm probably just being paranoid. But it's no secret some people think it would be better for . . . you know . . . if I were out of the picture."

That was *way* too close to what Molly had said. "Not better for me!" I hissed, infusing my words with every ounce of certainty I

147

could summon so he'd believe me. "Never, *ever* for me!"

"I know, M. Not for me, either. Don't worry, okay?" But his smile was sad again.

"Okay." I *was* worried, though. What did he know, or suspect, that he wasn't letting on? I knew I could get it out of him if I had time, but with these stupid restrictions, we never seemed to *have* any time.

Molly intercepted us in the hallway on the way to Science, then she and Sean both showed up almost the moment *that* class was over, to walk with me to lunch. Rigel went to the media center again, this time with a sandwich he'd brought from home. It was almost like they knew I needed to talk to him and were tag-teaming to prevent it.

No, not "almost." They knew.

"What's wrong, M?" Bri asked almost as soon as she sat down at the lunch table. "You look worried."

Since I couldn't explain, I shook my head. "Just thinking. A lot on my mind these days." I glanced at Molly and Sean, but they both did an enviable job of looking clueless.

"You and Rigel aren't fighting again, are you?" Deb asked in a half whisper. "Is that why he's not eating with us again? You guys looked kind of . . . intense earlier."

"It's only been two days, and no. We're not fighting. Since my aunt made us promise to stay away from each other, he's working on a paper for extra credit. He's hoping to finish it today."

I was a lousy liar and Deb still looked doubtful, but it was Sean who startled me by saying, "Don't let him jerk you around, M. You deserve better than that."

I stared at him incredulously. How hypocritical was that, when it was because of *him* all this stuff had happened in the first place?

"Rigel has never jerked me around," I informed him, making every word distinct. "Ever."

His blue eyes held mine for a long moment but I refused to blink or look away, and after a few seconds he finally shrugged. "My mistake."

"Did you ask your aunt about going to the game?" Bri asked then, apparently oblivious to the moment of tension.

I shook my head. "I was going to, but she was in such a bad mood I chickened out." In fact, I hadn't even thought about it. "I'll ask tonight."

"You *have* to come, M!" Bri insisted. "It's Sean's big debut!"

"Guess that makes Sean a debutante, huh?" I was still ticked by his remark about Rigel.

But he just laughed along with the others. "I guess it does." His grin didn't hold any hint that he minded my teasing—if anything, the reverse. I quickly looked away.

History class was as frustrating as yesterday, with both Sean and Molly watching us, then Molly walking with me to French afterward.

"I asked Mum to use the tutoring excuse to invite you over this evening." Maybe she was trying to be nice, but all I could think was how awkward going to their house would be now.

"It won't work, what with Aunt Theresa's Infinite Chore List. You wouldn't believe the stuff she has me doing."

Molly's eyes widened indignantly. "That is *so* wrong! You should have people serving *you*, not the other way around." At least she remembered to whisper.

"Yeah, well, tell that to Aunt Theresa. Or don't," I added quickly, worried she just might. "She can't know the truth. Much as I sometimes wish she did."

"I know, but it really bothers Sean and me. You should hear what he says about it. Our parents, too. I told them the kind of stuff your aunt makes you do, like a *giola uresal*—that's, like, the lowest level of servant."

I shrugged. "I'm used to it, so it's really no big deal."

Still, I couldn't help hoping—just a little—that Mrs. O'Gara really could talk her around. What I *really* wanted was to spend time with Rigel, but anything that got Aunt Theresa to lighten up would be welcome at this point.

Mrs. O'Gara must have worked some magic, because the first thing Aunt Theresa said when she got home that afternoon was, "Molly O'Gara needs your help with some more schoolwork, so you'll be going over there after dinner."

"What about my grounding?" I was careful to sound sulky.

"The terms are for me to decide," she snapped. "The O'Garas are neighbors and you'll do this favor."

"Sure, fine, whatever." My spirits rose at the thought of getting out of the house for an evening. Awkward or not, this visit had to be better than scrubbing bathtub grout. Maybe Sean wouldn't even be there.

After doing the dinner dishes I headed over, hoping for some real girl talk with Molly—like more detail on what *exactly* Rigel had said to her at lunch yesterday. Unfortunately, Sean answered the door the same as always.

"M! I was worried your aunt might find some reason to keep you home at the last minute."

He looked so pleased I *almost* smiled. "I acted all upset, like it was part of my punishment," I admitted. "Where's Molly?" I didn't care if he was offended.

"Oh. Molly. She, um, got invited to some kind of cheerleading party at Trina Squires' house."

I took a step back. "You mean she's not home? At all? Then why —?"

"You wanted to get out of the house, didn't you? Out from under dear auntie's thumb? Molly offered to stay home since you were coming, but I could see she really wanted to go to the party so I said I'd entertain you instead. That's . . . okay, isn't it?" he asked, vivid blue eyes worried and pleading, like he'd be crushed if I said no.

Though I was sure it was an act, I shrugged and came inside. "I guess it's better than going back home," I said ungraciously. "But Molly should have told me."

"I wouldn't let her." He still wore that pathetic puppy-dog look. "I was afraid you wouldn't come, and hated to think of you cooped up doing chores another whole evening."

"How thoughtful." I didn't even try to keep the sarcasm out of my voice. "Maybe it's just as well. It gives you and me a chance to put all our cards on the table."

24

aisling (AYS-ling): *fantasy; daydream; imagination*

"Cards on the table? What cards?" Sean looked genuinely puzzled.

"It's just a saying. It means we tell each other what our real agendas are, instead of tiptoeing around and pretending."

His expression cleared. "Oh. Hadn't heard that one before, but aye, yeah. It is time we had a real talk, now that you know . . . how things are. C'mon." He started to reach for my hand, then changed his mind and just held his hand out to me, instead. I didn't take it. After a moment's hesitation, he gave a little shrug and headed into the living room.

I followed, gathering my courage for the coming confrontation, wishing I'd had time to rehearse for it. Sean sat on the couch and looked up at me expectantly but I pulled a chair over and sat across instead of beside him. I'd think better that way.

"Look," he began, "I know I apologized Saturday night for the way my uncle sprang this Consort thing on you, but I want to say sorry again. I've thought about it a lot since then and realize how we all must seem to you. Me, especially. It must look like we came into town under false pretenses and pretended to be your friends, when all the while we knew this huge thing you didn't, that was going to turn your life upside down. I don't blame you for being mad about that. For being mad at me."

"Well . . . yeah," I admitted, surprised he'd described it so perfectly.

"You must have felt the same way about the Stuarts back in September," he continued. "When you found out the truth about your identity, I mean."

I immediately bristled. "No! I never—" But then I broke off, because he was right. I *had* felt the same sense of betrayal when I'd first learned they'd come to Jewel specifically to find me. It might even have been stronger, because of the way I felt about Rigel—but

151

only until he convinced me he felt the same way.

"That was different," I finally said. "They didn't know for sure I was in Jewel when they came here—or if I was even alive. And Rigel definitely didn't plan what happened between us."

For a second, Sean's blue eyes blazed. "What happened—!" Then he caught himself. "Oh. Right. You mean that bond you two think you have."

"That we *do* have," I corrected. "That's part of what I need to get across to you tonight."

Instead of responding to that, he said, "You have to believe the last thing *any* of us wanted was to upset you or mess up your life. Especially me."

Especially him? "Yeah? Convince me."

He hesitated, long enough for me to become unwillingly aware of his *brath*, even from here. I ignored it, staring past his shoulder at the shelf of Martian books instead of at him.

"Well?" I prompted as the silence lengthened.

"Um, remember I told you I grew up knowing about you, about what would have been expected if . . . But of course, everybody thought you'd been killed by the time I was old enough to understand it."

I nodded.

"So up until a few weeks ago, you were never exactly real to me. Except, well, you kind of were." When he didn't continue, I glanced at him, to see he'd turned red and wasn't quite meeting my eye.

"What do you mean?" I finally asked, when the pause started to get really awkward.

He darted a look at me, then gave a sheepish sort of grin. "This part is embarrassing, okay? If I tell you . . . well, I don't want to make you uncomfortable or anything, I promise. But maybe it'll help if you know where I'm coming from in all this."

Now I was really curious. "Tell me what? C'mon, Sean. What is it?"

After hesitating again, he finally gave a quick nod and continued, still not quite looking at me. "Okay, then. For most of my life, I sort of, well . . . fantasized about you. Even talked to you. When I was a kid, I mean. Like having an imaginary friend. Later I imagined you as the ideal girl. Er, girlfriend."

Now I felt my own face flushing, which was ridiculous. "But that wasn't really *me*," I protested. "Just somebody you made up who happened to have my name."

Sean shrugged. "Maybe. Technically. But it *was* you, too."

"Huh?"

"See, I knew—or found out—pretty much everything about you. Pictures of you as a baby, what your parents were like growing up, exactly when and why they left Mars with you, your last known location on Earth. I even, um—" He raked a hand through his copper hair. "I even ran an age-progression program on you."

"A what?"

He turned even redder. "Using the last picture of you that existed, plus pictures of your parents at different ages. It extrapolated approximately what you would look like, as you grew up. And . . . it wasn't far off." His expression was frankly admiring.

I dropped my gaze in sudden embarrassment, trying to decide if I was flattered or totally creeped out.

"Sorry," he said quickly. "I shouldn't have told you that part. But I couldn't help pretending . . . hoping . . . you were somehow still alive and I wanted to know what you looked like, so if I . . . I ever found you, I'd know you."

I swallowed, but didn't say anything. Had the Stuarts had something like that, when they were searching for me? Of course, before Rigel, I wouldn't have looked much like they'd expected, what with the glasses and acne and all.

"In fact," Sean continued, "you were so real to me that when the news broke that you actually *were* alive, I wasn't even surprised. It was like I'd known it all along. So when Uncle Allister insisted we should come here, I was totally on board with the idea. I couldn't wait to meet you. For real." He finally met my eyes.

"I . . . I don't . . ." I groped for words to express all my feelings, positive and negative, but came up empty.

Sean misinterpreted my hesitation. "No, I get it. I sound completely crazy, don't I? Making up all that stuff when I was a kid, imaginary conversations and all."

"No! That's not it at all," I was forced to reassure him. "I, um, did a lot of that kind of thing myself when I was younger. So I get that part. It's just . . . knowing all this only makes it harder, Sean. I'm

153

sorry."

He lifted a shoulder resignedly and looked away again. "Yeah. It was stupid of me to think you'd have some kind of instant affinity for me, just because I had it for you. It's not like you'd ever even *heard* of me, while I'd been thinking of you my whole life. Of course, I had no idea about . . . about you and Stuart. Uncle Allister didn't tell me," he added, clearly annoyed at that omission. "He just said it was important I get to Jewel as quickly as possible. I only realized later that was why."

"I'm sorry, Sean," I repeated, and was surprised to discover I meant it. "Who knows? Maybe if I'd met you before I met Rigel . . . But I didn't. And I can't undo my bond with him, even if I wanted to. Which I don't."

He just nodded, still not looking at me, which somehow made me feel even worse. It seemed cruel now to give him my side, but it was still important. Necessary. "It's my turn now. I need to convince you that Rigel and I really do have a *graell* bond. Because until you believe that—"

"Look," he interrupted. "Can we . . . not do that right now? Please? I don't think I . . . I mean . . ." He closed his eyes for several long seconds, then opened them and said, with a sort of desperate, forced cheerfulness, "Hey, I said I was going to entertain you tonight, remember?"

"Right." I couldn't bring myself to press the issue when it so clearly pained him. "What did you have in mind?"

With an obvious effort, he summoned a grin. "Come and see. I think you'll like it." He stood up and walked over to the desk on the other side of the room.

Curious, I followed him and saw several weird-looking items assembled there.

"You were so fascinated by my omni, I thought you might like to see a few other fun gizmos." He picked up something that looked vaguely like an electric hot plate, but without a cord. "Mum does at least half her cooking with these—she has close to a dozen, all different sizes." Turning, he held it out to me.

Careful not to touch him, I took it. Forcing myself to focus on the item instead of his unsettling revelations, I turned it this way and that. It was flat, maybe half an inch thick and less than a foot square, with a big red circle on one shiny white side and a button on one edge. "How does it work?"

"Sort of like a microwave oven, only better and faster. You put a pot or a serving dish on it, then set it, so." He pushed the button and a little holographic screen much like the one from his omni popped up. "It instantly heats, cools or cooks whatever is in the pot or on the plate. You can even put different stuff on one plate, like with leftovers, and it'll make everything the right temp—potatoes hot, applesauce cold, like that."

"Convenient," I admitted, trying not to act *too* impressed since I was still uncomfortable around Sean for a whole variety of reasons. "What's this thing?" I pointed at something that looked like a leather scroll, maybe eight inches long.

Sean picked it up. "This would have been a lot more gee-whiz a few years back, but someone leaked the technology a decade or two ago. Now electronic readers are everywhere here on Earth, but we've had them on Mars for over a century. This is what I think of when you say the word 'book.'"

He touched the end of the "scroll" and it snapped flat and rigid, then touched it again and lettering appeared all over one side. He handed it to me.

"Wow." It was harder now to hide my awe. "This is Martian, right?" I asked, looking at the same strange characters I'd seen on some of the books on the shelves.

"Yeah, but it'll also display in English. Or any other language. It has a translator."

I watched as he demonstrated, the text switching to English—it looked like one of Shakespeare's plays—then to something I guessed was German or Dutch, and then to Chinese or something similar. Okay, I was impressed. Bri's Kindle sure couldn't do *this*.

"And it'll hold more than two million volumes," he told me, rolling it back up with another touch of a button. "Videos, too, but since the omni came out, nobody really uses books for that anymore."

This time his finger did brush mine, though I couldn't tell if it was intentional. I tried not to jerk away from the thoroughly disturbing jolt I felt, since I didn't want him to make a big deal about it.

"Yeah, the book thingy is pretty cool. But what's with these?" I asked, picking up what looked like an ordinary pair of eyeglasses with thin metal frames. "I thought all Martians had perfect vision naturally." I hadn't, of course, but I did now—now that bonding with Rigel had "fixed" me.

Sean just chuckled. "Try them on."

I did. Everything looked the same. But then Sean reached over—I managed not to flinch—and touched the frame. Suddenly everything got huge.

"Here, look," he said, holding his finger about six inches in front of me. I could see every pore in his finger and the ridges of his fingerprint looked like a mountain range.

"So they're like a microscope?"

"That's not all. Check this out." He crossed the room and flipped the light switch, plunging us into darkness.

Which was super creepy, after what he'd told me earlier. "Hey!" I protested.

"Touch the upper outside corner of the left lens," he said.

I did, and suddenly I could see everything in the room just as clearly as when the lights were on. "Whoa. How—?"

"Infrared, like night goggles or security cameras. It'll also see into the ultraviolet spectrum on another setting, and do telescopic vision, though not as well as a real telescope, of course. More like good binoculars."

He flipped the lights back on and I removed the glasses, feeling a little foolish about my moment of panic.

"And nobody would ever suspect." I looked more closely at the glasses. The buttons, or sensors, or whatever changed the settings, weren't even visible. "But I guess that's the point? Nobody's *supposed* to know about this stuff, right? Regular Earthlings, that is."

"Well, no, but it's not like I'm showing this stuff to anyone at school, and you're not going to mention it to Bri or Deb, right?"

An hour ago I'd have wanted to make him sweat, but now I shook my head without hesitation. "Of course not. It's not like I've told them about myself."

"No, I know. Though it must be tempting at times. Even more tempting to tell your aunt and uncle, considering the way they treat you. Hell, I've been tempted myself!"

I shrugged, trying not to feel touched by his concern. "They'd never believe you. And they'd believe it even less if I told them."

"I guess. So, um, can you also not tell Stuart about this stuff? He might make trouble with some of the higher-ups if he knows we have all this."

Immediately, my original irritation at Sean surged back. "Higher-ups? Isn't your precious Uncle Allister one of the highest-up guys on the planet? Anyway, I don't keep secrets from Rigel."

Sean's mouth twisted, but whether with anger or chagrin, I couldn't tell. "But you want me to keep secrets from my mum, right?" Before I could retort, he backed off. "No, sorry, that was out of line. I'm really not trying to put you on the spot or anything. Come on into the kitchen—I've got a couple other things to show you."

25

teachneoc (TEEK-nee-ok): *technology; gadgetry*

Sean's sudden shift from accusatory back to friendly and apologetic defused my flare of anger, almost against my will. And I *did* want to see more, so I followed him. Mrs. O'Gara was in the kitchen, frosting a yummy-looking chocolate cake.

"Ah, you're a wee bit early, Sean. I was going to bring this out as soon as the tea was ready. But now you're here, will you get out the cups?"

"I'll do it, if you tell me where they are," I offered, but Mrs. O'Gara looked horrified.

"You'll do no such thing, Excellency! It won't hurt this overgrown son of mine a bit to help out in the kitchen for a change."

Sean just grinned. "It's okay, M. Besides, it gives me a chance to show you something else." He opened a cabinet and took out a teacup, but instead of setting it on a saucer, he dipped a finger into the frosting bowl, laughing when his mother swatted him away. Then he daubed chocolate on the cup and put it back in the cupboard.

"Watch this," he said. He closed the cabinet and pushed an unobtrusive button underneath, waited a second, then opened the cabinet again. As I expected, the cup was now clean.

"Cool dishwasher, huh?"

I nodded, trying not to feel smug. "Yeah, Rigel . . . um, told me about these. Very cool."

Maybe Sean would worry less if I told him the Stuarts had Martian gadgets of their own, but it didn't feel right to share something that wasn't my secret to tell.

"I'll just have to find something else to show you, then," Sean said, making me realize I should have acted more impressed.

Mrs. O'Gara pulled out a chair at the kitchen table. "Have a seat, M, do. As you're in the kitchen already, you may as well have your tea here."

158

Sean set out teacups for all three of us while his mother cut thick slices of chocolate cake. It all smelled heavenly, though I hadn't been hungry until now.

"There, now. Do let me know if you need more sugar, or anything at all," she said comfortably, sitting down at the table with us and pouring the tea.

I smiled at her, though being fussed over still felt weird. Nice, but weird. "Thanks, Mrs. O'Gara. And, um, thanks for getting me out of the house tonight."

"T'was the least I could do, dear, after our family disrupted your life so. I hope things weren't awkward with Molly away, and that you and Sean have had a nice chat?"

I wondered if she'd been able to hear everything we said, but it seemed rude to ask. "Um, yeah, I guess so," I replied, though "nice" wasn't the word I'd have used to describe it.

"Well, that's just grand." She seemed more pleased than my lukewarm response called for. "By the bye, I believe I've convinced your aunt to let you come here as often as you like, provided you finish whatever tasks she sets you first."

"Really? Thanks! That's great." The evening *had* started out awkwardly, but now I was genuinely grateful I could have this regular escape.

I heard the front door open and close, then footsteps, but they sounded more like Mr. O'Gara's than Molly's.

Mrs. O glanced that way, then turned back to me with a concerned smile. "I'd prefer Theresa stop giving you menial jobs altogether, as it's simply not fitting, but with her not knowing who you are, I can scarcely explain why."

"That's super nice of you, Mrs. O'Gara, but it's okay, really. I'm, uh, pretty much used to it. And it won't last forever. I hope."

The look she gave me seemed both fond and a little sad. "The way you've held up all these years is a marvel, Princess. A credit to your breeding, it is, fitting or not. And now you do know who you are, I hope you won't take it amiss if we try to help you understand some of what you've missed out on, being raised the way you have."

"No, of course I don't mind! I love learning more about Mars. It's all fascinating to me."

A voice behind me—a voice that made my stomach instinctively clench—said, "I'm glad to hear that, Excellency, because your instruction definitely needs to proceed more quickly. Time may be getting short."

I whipped my head around and sure enough, the very last person I wanted to see was standing there: Allister Adair, looking as pompous and sure of himself as ever.

"What are you doing here?" I blurted out before remembering Allister was Mrs. O'Gara's brother. Then I did remember, and gave her a quick, apologetic glance before turning back to Allister. "I mean, um, how long have you been listening?"

To my surprise (and secret satisfaction), he looked a little chagrined. "My apologies, Excellency. I didn't mean to eavesdrop. I should have revealed my presence at once. But I was so pleased to hear that you are eager to learn more about your people and duties that my feelings got the better of me."

I refrained—barely—from making a snarky comment about him *having* feelings. "What did you mean, time is getting short? Short for what?"

"Nothing alarming, I assure you," he said, trying for that fatherly smile he sucked at. "Simply that a regular, even accelerated, schedule of study is long overdue, as you have missed so many years of education already. Thrice-weekly visits, perhaps?" He looked questioningly at Mrs. O'Gara.

She gave him a quick frown but nodded, then turned to me with a smile. "If you're willing, M? You did say you wanted to hear more, and it would get you away from your aunt more frequently."

"I guess so, if you really think you can convince Aunt Theresa to let me come that often. But . . . will *he* be teaching me?" I shot a suspicious glance at Allister.

"Only occasionally," he assured me. "I'm a busy man, after all, with duties in both Washington and Montana. When I am in Jewel, however, I would be pleased to teach you about certain topics for which I am particularly well-suited. If that meets with your approval, of course."

It was the most deferential he'd ever been toward me, but I still didn't trust him. "That depends. What topics are you talking about?"

His jaw twitched, but he kept his tone surprisingly polite. "Primarily Nuathan governmental structure, traditions and procedures. Things vitally important for you to learn about, especially given—"

Out of the corner of my eye I saw Mrs. O give a quick shake of her head and he broke off.

"Given what?" I prodded, sure now that there was something he wasn't telling me. "What's changed? Why the sudden urgency?"

"Allister means that we have no way of knowing how soon you may need this knowledge, given the, ah, increasingly uncertain state of things in Nuath," Mrs. O'Gara replied, with another frown for her brother.

"Yes, better safe than sorry." Allister's suddenly jovial tone only made me more suspicious. "Are you willing, Princess?"

My first instinct was to refuse, but the more I knew about all their convoluted rules, the better chance I'd have of finding ways around them—legitimately or not. Maybe I'd even discover a loophole that would allow Rigel and me to stay together.

"I suppose," I said. "Though I'd probably learn more from someone else. Anyone else."

After just the slightest pause, during which he again seemed to be biting back an instinctive rebuke, he nodded. "I understand. It is unfortunate that you and I began on such poor terms, Excellency. I intend to do my best to remedy that."

I wanted to tell him that the *only* remedy would be for him to stop being such a jerk about Rigel, but that would just lead to another big argument, and it was getting late.

"Right," I said. "But I'd better head home, if I want my aunt to let me come here again."

"Yes, of course." Mrs. O'Gara looked relieved. "We mustn't antagonize her unnecessarily at this stage."

I felt like a wimp, not challenging Allister the way I wanted to, but maybe I'd have better luck changing his mind about Rigel by degrees, if I could manage to keep my temper around him. I owed it to Rigel —and to myself—to try.

I was so distracted, I forgot to protest when Sean put on his coat to walk me home. In fact, I was barely aware of him walking next to me, I was so busy mulling over the evening's revelations and wondering what Mrs. O had kept Allister from saying.

"Hey, you want to see a new omni trick?" Sean asked abruptly when we were halfway to my house, snapping me back to the present.

"What? Oh, um, sure."

He pulled it out and I was surprised all over again at how small it was, not even as big as his thumb. He brought up the first screen, hit a button to bring up another screen, hit two buttons there, then stuck it back in his pocket.

"So . . . what did you do?"

He grinned down at me, his hand hovering above my shoulder. "May I?"

Though my first instinct was to refuse, I knew by now that some of the omni's functions required contact. I nodded, steeling myself against the tingle I always felt. Then, suddenly, I heard music. But not through my ears, exactly. More like it was playing in my *brain*.

"Waltz of the Flowers," I murmured. One of my favorite classical pieces. Did Sean somehow know that? Probably. "How does it do that? Can anyone else hear it?"

"Nope." He took his hand off of my shoulder and the music disappeared. Then he touched me again and it came back. "Way better than earbuds, huh?"

"Way," I had to agree.

We reached my house before the Tchaikovsky piece ended, making me wish the walk were longer. Only not really, because the *last* thing I wanted was to spend more time with Sean. Between his disturbing confession and all that Martian technology, the jerk had somehow managed make me forget I was mad at him. Was I really that easy to manipulate?

"Thanks," I said, stepping away from him and cutting off the music. "Tell Molly I said hi, okay?"

I headed up the front steps without a backward glance, half expecting him to stop me. He didn't, though, and when I finally peeked as I closed the front door, he was already halfway down the street. Telling myself firmly that I was relieved rather than disappointed, I went upstairs to get ready for bed.

26

ateamh rioga (ah-TEV ree-OH-gah): *persuasive
ability possessed by some of Royal blood*

I tried to ditch Sean and Molly as soon as we got off the bus the
next morning. I wanted to tell Rigel about my visit to the O'Garas'
before Sean could, plus all this staying apart was starting to give me a
headache and the first hints of queasiness. But the two of them
tagged along, talking to me, until I had to hurry to get to class before
the bell. I was sure it was on purpose.

Rigel was already in the classroom, looking as impatient as I felt.
Before either of us said a word, we clasped hands like we were
rescuing each other from drowning—which was almost what it felt
like. Being apart from Rigel was a lot like not having enough air, and
we'd been apart way too much lately.

After a few seconds of that wonderful relief, he gave me a
crooked grin. "I hear you went to the O'Garas' house again last
night."

"What?" I glanced wildly around but of course didn't see Sean or
Molly. "How did—? I was just about to tell you!"

"Quinn O'Gara came by our house last night. I figured you knew."

I shook my head. "Mrs. O told my aunt Molly needed more
homework help." I was debating whether to volunteer the
information that Molly hadn't been home when the bell rang.

After class, Deb immediately started asking me questions about
the assignment, then Molly met us in the hall before I had a chance
to say anything else to Rigel. Then Bri got to English before Rigel
did and was all about tonight's basketball scrimmage, so I still
couldn't ask him what Mr. O had been doing at his house.

I hoped I'd have a chance in Science, since Rigel sat right behind
me, but Trina had an ironclad excuse to monopolize him, since she
and Rigel were lab partners and we had to turn in topics for our final

geology projects next week. I tried to ignore the smug smirk she gave me every time I glanced back.

I'd given up and started talking with my own partner, Will, about our project, when Trina's words stopped me cold.

"You seem to be holding up really well, Rigel, considering how fickle a certain someone seems to be. I guess some girls are all about novelty."

I swiveled around to glare at her. "Sounds like you're describing yourself, Trina," I snapped. Because it really did.

She gave me one of her nasty, syrupy smiles. "I don't know what you mean, Marsha. *I'm* not the one who ran after the new boy, then dropped him like a rock when someone even newer came along. Everybody knows you're with Sean O'Gara these days. It's all over the school. But it won't be long before he sees through you, just like Rigel did." She turned her smile to him, losing the nasty tinge.

"I am not—!" I started to retort, but Trina cut me off.

"Oh, come on. Walking you to class, sitting all cozy together at lunch? You've practically got him on a leash. He told Nate Best you've even been spending most evenings at his house lately."

She hadn't said anything Rigel didn't already know—except that untrue "cozy" crack—but I could feel anger, jealousy and frustration start to build in him. I focused, thinking as hard as I could, *Not true! I love you!* He gave a terse little nod, but didn't send anything back, maybe because he was too upset at the moment to communicate that way. I *needed* to talk, really talk, to him alone. Soon!

I followed him from the room after class, hoping to get my chance the moment Trina was out of earshot, but there was Sean, waiting to walk me to lunch again. Any sympathy I'd begun to feel for him last night was swallowed up by annoyance, especially when he shot a smug look Rigel's way.

Before I could say anything, Rigel brushed past Sean, bumping him—hard—with his shoulder.

"Hey!" Sean said, shoving him back. "What's the idea?"

"Like you don't know." Rigel squared his shoulders and Sean did the same, reminding me vividly of their almost-fight in the courtyard last week. Already a small, interested crowd was starting to form.

I jumped between them before things could escalate. "Rigel. Sean. Stop it. Now." I didn't shout, but I spoke *really* firmly.

They continued to glare at each other for a long moment, but then Sean relaxed and shrugged. "He started it."

"That's debatable. Rigel?"

He shrugged, too, though he didn't really relax. "Whatever. See you later, M."

Before I could say another word, he strode off down the hall. I started to go after him, but Sean cleared his throat.

"Better let him cool down. Besides—"

"I know. My aunt's stupid rules—and your spying duties."

Sean looked unhappy, which was fine with me. "I told you it wasn't my idea. Anyway, Stuart needs to control that temper or he could risk . . . well, everything."

I glared at him. "Maybe it would be worth it. Get me off the hook."

"What do you—?"

"Never mind," I snapped, walking quickly toward the lunchroom.

He didn't get a chance to ask me again what I meant, what with everyone at lunch talking about tonight's scrimmage, which was fine with me. Less fine was the way he and Molly hovered all the way to History, then watched Rigel and me like a pair of hawks, so we couldn't even get two seconds alone.

My only consolation was another note in my locker at the end of the day, but all it said was: *This is driving me nuts! Gotta figure a way to talk SOON. Miss you. —R*

I agreed completely, but didn't have a solution—except to think longingly about the backpack under my bed.

On the bus home, Molly, Bri and Deb were all determined to get me to that night's scrimmage somehow, though if I couldn't be with Rigel, I didn't much care. Already my Rigel-deprivation headache was creeping back.

Because I'd promised, as soon as Aunt Theresa got home, I asked if I could go. And of course she said no.

"Have you forgotten you're grounded, Marsha?" she asked, pointing me toward the laundry room. "Helping Molly O'Gara with homework is one thing, but going out with your friends to a sporting event is completely different. You'll stay in and iron those curtains you washed yesterday."

I didn't bother to argue.

I was just finishing the first curtain when the doorbell rang, and a moment later I heard Mrs. O'Gara's voice. As always, aunt Theresa sounded delighted to see her. They went into the living room and I couldn't hear them anymore. I kept ironing. Twenty minutes later, when I was nearly done, I heard the front door close and then Aunt Theresa's footsteps.

"Because it means so much to Sean and Molly O'Gara, I've decided you can go to the game tonight, on the condition you sit with the O'Garas," she announced.

"Really?" I stared. This was twice in two days Mrs. O'Gara had convinced her to lighten up! I stopped myself in time from commenting on her complete one-eighty. "Um, thanks, Aunt Theresa."

She sniffed. "Just see you keep your distance from that Stuart boy. The O'Garas will pick you up in an hour. Finish what you're doing and make yourself a sandwich for dinner."

She walked away and I ironed faster, thinking hard. Aunt Theresa had only known Mrs. O'Gara for three weeks, but in that time she'd started acting completely out of character—always right after talking to Mrs. O. This could *not* be coincidence.

When Molly had talked about the Royal *fine* having powers of persuasion I'd discounted, since she'd been talking about me, but the O'Garas were Royals, too. If that's what Mrs. O was doing, I definitely needed to figure out how to use it myself!

Of course, Molly seemed to think I *had* used it, when I'd stopped Rigel and Sean from fighting last week. And again today? I certainly hadn't *tried* to channel any special "power," but both times they'd backed off more readily than I'd expected. Hm.

Whatever Mrs. O had done, it was getting me to the game—which I suddenly realized might give me a chance to see Rigel after all, if his parents let him go, too. On that thought, I turned off the iron and rushed upstairs to change—and to figure out a strategy to talk to Rigel alone, if he was there.

"Thanks for convincing Aunt Theresa to let me go to the game, Mrs. O'Gara," I said as I got into the back seat with Molly half an hour later. "When I asked earlier, she said absolutely not."

I didn't dare ask if she'd used any special power on my aunt, but

Mr. O turned to wink at me from the driver's seat and said, "Lili can be very persuasive when she wants to be." Which definitely lent weight to my theory.

"Your aunt feels strongly about discipline," Mrs. O'Gara said, "which would be well and good were you a normal teenager, but for our Princess, some occasional leniency is in order. Anyway, Sean and Molly wanted you to come very much, and your aunt allowed that it wasn't fair to punish them for your lapse in judgment."

I wasn't sure how to respond, since she apparently agreed I'd had a "lapse in judgment," but then I realized this might be a chance to find out about that powwow at the Stuarts' house last night. Except if I let on I knew Mr. O had been there, they'd know Rigel had told me, since none of them had.

Maybe I'd better not tip them off, since I was hoping to slip away to talk to him during the game. If Rigel *wasn't* there tonight, I'd definitely ask about that meeting on the way home. As Sovereign, surely I deserved to know if anything big was going down.

We made our way to the gym, Molly peeling off to join the cheerleading squad as soon as we got there. Sean was already on the court with the team, warming up. It was the first time I'd seen him in his jersey and I was startled at how muscular he looked. Not skinny at all—that was an illusion because of his height.

I obediently followed Mr. and Mrs. O'Gara to the bleachers, turning my attention from the guys on the court to the spectators. I was still searching for Rigel when Bri and Deb spotted me and hurried over.

"You made it!" Bri exclaimed, practically wriggling with excitement. "C'mon, we have great seats, right down front."

I glanced at the O'Garas. "Um, I can't. Unless you have room for all three of us?"

"We'll make room," Deb promised. "You're Sean's parents, right? You should sit close to the court anyway."

I belatedly introduced everyone as we went back down and squeezed into the prime section of bench Bri and Deb had saved with coats, despite a few grumbles from other students.

"He looks good, doesn't he?" Mrs. O'Gara said to her husband, but I barely heard her, because at that moment I spotted Rigel, heading obliquely our way. His dad was with him.

Knowing Rigel wouldn't be looking for me, I sat as tall as I could, trying to catch his eye without being so obvious that the O'Garas—or Mr. Stuart—would notice. When that didn't work, I took a deep breath and tried to project my thoughts—and my *brath*—toward Rigel, doubtful it could work from this distance.

To my surprise, he immediately looked up and around, then spotted me. Coincidence? I smiled and gave a little nod. He grinned back and started toward me, then obviously noticed the O'Garas, because he stopped and frowned, his expression questioning. I gave a tiny shake of my head, looking meaningfully at his dad, then the O'Garas.

With a quick glance at his dad, he nodded almost imperceptibly to me, then veered off to his right, motioning his dad to follow. A moment later some of his football buddies saw him and waved him over. I watched out of the corner of my eye to see where he sat.

"Oh, look, M, there's—" Bri suddenly exclaimed, but I quickly stepped on her foot. "Ow! What—?" Then she caught my wide-eyed glare, and the quick shift of my eyes toward the O'Garas and seemed to get it.

"Is something wrong, dear?" Mrs. O'Gara asked from my other side.

"Um, no. Just, um, sat on a coat button." Bri gave me a conspiratorial smile when Mrs. O looked away and I smiled back and mouthed *thanks*.

The game started a couple of minutes later, but I was way more focused on Rigel, several rows up and to the left. I didn't dare crane my neck, but did sneak glances back when everyone else was watching the court. On my third peek I managed to catch his eye for an instant and shoot him a quick smile, which he returned with a tight one of his own.

Immediately, I put my plan into action. "I'm sorry," I said to Mrs. O'Gara with a grimace I hoped was convincing. "I really need to go to the bathroom. You and Bri tell me anything I miss, okay?"

She looked at me with concern. "Are you feeling all right, dear?"

I shrugged. "Just really need to go—it hit kind of suddenly. I'll be fine . . . after."

The slightest hint of suspicion crossed her face, but then a big cheer went up as Sean sank a three-pointer, which drew her attention away from me. I cheered along with everyone else, then got up and hurried for the exit, praying that Rigel would follow me . . . and that Mrs. O'Gara wouldn't.

27

streach suas (stretch SOO-ahs): *resist oppression;*
underground resistance

I didn't look over my shoulder until I was out of the gym, since
doing so might make Mrs. O even more suspicious. At least she
wasn't right behind me. Yet.

"M!" Rigel called from down the hall and I whirled around, relief
flooding through me. "I went out the other way so it wouldn't look
like—" He broke off as I ran to meet him halfway and flung myself
into his arms.

But only for a second.

"C'mon. Let's find someplace more private in case anyone comes
after us."

"Good idea," he agreed. "Not a hundred per cent sure my dad
didn't see you leave."

Hands firmly clasped, we headed down the hall halfway between
the two gym exits, then around a corner into another empty hallway,
where we ducked into the first open classroom we came to.

And then, finally, we were kissing. It was absolute heaven.

"I can't tell you how much I've missed this," Rigel breathed when
we came up for air a minute or two later. "Can you get away at *all*
over the weekend? I'm dying for some serious alone time."

"Oh, so am I, Rigel. So much! But the *only* place I'm allowed to go
these days is the O'Garas.' Which reminds me—" I pulled just far
enough away to talk, keeping my fingers entwined with his. He felt *so*
good. "You never got a chance to tell me why Mr. O'Gara was at
your house last night."

"It was some last-minute thing. Shim got a message from Mars
and called him over so they could all discuss it."

"I wonder if that's what Allister was talking about? He was at the
O'Garas,'" I explained with a grimace. "Wonder why he wasn't at

your place, if something big is going on?"

Rigel smiled, though it was a grim smile. "Yeah, well, my mom kind of, um, threw him out of our house after my party."

"Wow, did she? Good for her! He totally had it coming, he was so awful to you. Is that why she did it?"

"Mostly," he admitted. "He got even worse after you and the O'Garas left."

I huffed out a breath. "Allister is *such* a jerk! But what was that message from Mars about?"

He shrugged, but I could sense the darkening of his mood. "Not sure. They were pretty tight-lipped, but I think the rebellion is heating up. I heard your name mentioned a few times before my mom caught me listening and sent me upstairs."

"Yeah, Allister let something slip last night about time being short before Mrs. O shut him up. I'm getting the impression they might expect more of me sooner than they said."

Rigel's grip on my hands tightened, pulling me closer. "What do you mean, expect more?"

I leaned against his chest, listening to the rapid beating of his heart. "I don't know yet. Maybe you and I should just take off before any—"

"There you are!" Mrs. O'Gara exclaimed from the doorway of the classroom. "I was afraid of this. I'm disappointed in you, young man," she said to Rigel. "You know full well that M's aunt has forbidden the two of you to spend time together. I understood that your parents had done the same."

"It's not his fault," I flared at her. "We just . . . just happened to run into each other."

She just looked at me, and after a moment I guiltily let go of Rigel's hands. I was sure the only reason she didn't accuse me of lying was because of who I was.

"I think we'd better head back to the gym." she finally said, more gently than I expected. "I imagine you'd rather I not mention this, ah, lapse to your aunt."

Rigel sent me a last glance that warmed almost as much as a touch. Then he gave Mrs. O a respectful nod and left us without a word. Maybe he was afraid of what he might say.

"It's not fair," I mumbled, mostly to myself.

"I know, dear. And I *am* sorry. I realize this is hard for you—for both of you. We never wanted that, despite what Allister implied. But it's for the good of our people, difficult as that may be for you to understand right now. Let's get back to the game, shall we?"

I felt another stab of guilt for making her miss several minutes of Sean's debut. None of this was really her fault. But it wasn't mine, either!

We made our way back to our seats and almost immediately Mrs. O started whispering to her husband in that super-quiet Martian whisper. Straining my ears, the few words I managed to pick up worried me: "together" and "could have been seen" from Mrs. O and "delicate situation" from her husband. *What* situation, I wondered? What had changed?

Finally, reluctantly, I started to watch the game. Even though I didn't understand much about basketball, it was obvious as soon as I paid attention that Sean was way better than any other player out there, on either team. He wasn't the tallest—one of our guys and three of theirs were taller—but he almost never missed when he threw at the basket, which he did a lot.

Next to me, Bri repeatedly squealed about how amazing he was, reminding me uncomfortably of Rigel's first football game. I forcefully pushed away my sense of *deja vú* because Sean was *not* any kind of replacement for Rigel. No matter what anyone "expected." So what if his touch affected me a *tiny* bit like Rigel's? It wasn't the same at all.

I started watching Molly instead, doing cheers on the sidelines with the rest of the squad. As I expected, she was also really good—maybe the best out there, even though it was her first time cheering. Watching her didn't give me any weird, guilty feelings, either.

Part way into the second half, Mr. O pulled out his cell phone and made a call, but I couldn't hear any of it over the yells of the crowd. Probably tattling to Allister, I thought sourly. Glancing back, I also noticed Rigel was no longer sitting with his dad—or anywhere else I could see. I kept checking, but he didn't come back for the rest of the game.

At the final buzzer, the gym practically exploded with cheers and everyone rushed the floor. Or, rather, rushed Sean, to congratulate him on his spectacular performance. Bri chattered nonstop as she dragged Deb and me in his direction.

"That's the biggest basketball win Jewel has *ever* had! Sean was *incredible!* He's even better at basketball than Rigel is at football. I mean, we didn't win Rigel's first game, right? But wow, we could win State if Sean keeps playing like tonight! How awesome would that be?"

She kept talking, but I stopped listening as soon as she dissed Rigel. Yeah, Sean had practically been a one-man team out there, but he only had four teammates to hold him back. Rigel had ten, plus he couldn't do anything at all when the offense wasn't playing.

Bri had me by the hand, but I was frantically scanning the mob around the court for a glimpse of Rigel, hoping he was still here. Even if I couldn't talk to him again, with the O'Garas right behind me, I wanted to *see* him.

I didn't, though, and then we reached Sean, who was smiling and nodding and answering questions, clearly enjoying his new celebrity enormously. Way more than Rigel had enjoyed his, I was sure. Just as I thought that, Sean spotted me.

"M!" he exclaimed, heading toward me with a huge grin, his arms coming up. "I was so juiced when I saw you in the bleachers! I didn't think you could come."

For a panicked second I thought he was going to hug me, but when I took a step back he immediately dropped his arms.

"Your Mom, uh, talked my aunt into letting me," I explained, edging nonchalantly behind Bri and Mrs. O'Gara. "It was really nice of her."

Bri wasn't the least bit reluctant to step into that aborted hug. "Sean, you were *amazing!*" she cried, throwing her arms around him. "You looked like an NBA player out there tonight."

He returned her hug but quickly released her, his ears reddening. "Not quite that, but thanks," he laughed, then turned to his parents who had to practically shoulder Bri aside to reach him.

"We're really proud of you, son," his dad said as his mother and Molly hugged him—hugs he returned more enthusiastically than he had Bri's. I was glad. For Bri's sake. "You played a great game."

Other people pressed in on him, slapping him on the back and congratulating him, but after a few minutes he turned back to his parents—and me. "Coach wants to see us in the locker room for some post-game stuff, but I should be ready to go in a few minutes. Meet you in the parking lot?"

"We'll wait just inside the East entrance," Mrs. O'Gara said, "in case you take longer than you expect. It's cold outside."

I didn't think it was all that cold, nearly fifty degrees. But then, I'd grown up in Indiana, not a climate-controlled underground habitat.

"Guess we'll see you at school," Bri said, reluctantly, I thought. I wondered if she'd been hoping for an invitation to something after the game, then immediately felt guilty for thinking that.

To make up for it, I gave her, then Deb, a quick hug. "Yeah, see you guys tomorrow. Maybe by next weekend I'll be ungrounded and we can go shopping or something."

"Absolutely!" Deb said, returning my hug. "Let us know if there's *anything* we can do to help, okay?"

"Promise," I said, touched.

We left the gym and Mrs. O put a hand on my shoulder, startling me, since the O'Garas were all about not touching me. Then I saw Rigel and his dad, about twenty yards away, and realized she must have seen them first. That's what I got for being distracted. I sent him all the love and longing I could and was almost sure I felt the same coming back from him.

"We should probably start making our way to the exit, don't you think?" Mr. O said with an *almost* imperceptible glance Rigel's way. "We don't want to get M home any later than necessary."

Molly caught up with us then, smiling hugely. "Wasn't that a great game? Didn't Sean look wonderful? Mom, Dad, the cheerleaders are having a celebration party with some of the players and Amber offered me a ride. Can I go?"

Her mother immediately shook her head. "I've heard about those parties, Molly. I don't think it's a good idea. Speaking of which, were any parents at home for last night's gathering?"

"What? Of course!" Molly said so quickly even I didn't believe her. Mrs. O just looked at her for a second or two and Molly blushed. "Okay, sorry. No. But I didn't do anything I shouldn't have, I promise!"

After concentrating another moment—using her "lie detector"—Mrs. O relaxed and smiled. "I'm glad to hear that. But no, I don't want you going to another party tonight, Molly. I'm sorry. Besides, we have M with us."

Molly glanced guiltily at me and I quickly said, "It's okay. I don't blame you for wanting to go."

To her credit, Molly shrugged. "It's no big deal. Some of those girls are kind of, I don't know, fake. Not like you."

"Or like you," I assured her. "But that doesn't mean they don't have fun parties."

Her smile was more grateful and relieved than necessary, but I barely noticed because I was watching Rigel out of sight as they headed to the other exit.

It was nearly ten minutes before Sean joined us, his hair damp and wearing a fresh t-shirt under his open jacket. I steadfastly ignored the clean-boy smell he gave off.

"Hey, everyone! Ready to go?" His question was to all of us, but his smile seemed mostly for me. I didn't meet his eye.

As we headed outside, I wasn't really surprised that Sean walked next to me, though I was glad he didn't try to touch me. When we were halfway to the car, though, he leaned close and whispered, "If you're cold, I have my omni in my coat pocket."

He had it here? At school? Really? "I'm fine. I grew up here, remember? It gets a lot colder than this, trust me." I said it loud enough that the rest of the family heard.

"That will be a new sort of challenge for us all, won't it?" Mrs. O'Gara said cheerily. "I must say, I prefer that to the sort that put our lives at risk."

Mr. O'Gara chuckled. "Those days should be behind us, Lili. Though different challenges await."

In the car, I somehow ended up sandwiched between Sean and Molly, Sean's thigh touching mine—through his jeans and mine, which *should* have made it okay. But then he threw an arm oh-so-casually across the seat behind me. "So, did my folks tell you about what's going on back on Mars?"

"Sean!" his mother exclaimed before I could respond. "Under the circumstances it seemed . . . premature."

"What?" I immediately asked. "*What* do you not want to tell me?"

Nobody said anything as I glanced back and forth between Sean and Molly. Like always when she got stressed, Molly wouldn't meet my eye, so I focused on Sean. "What?" I repeated.

Though he looked a little embarrassed, at least he didn't refuse to meet my gaze. "They say Faxon's grip is slipping and the resistance is growing faster than ever. And that once he's out, you—um, we—will have, er, more responsibilities."

"Responsibilities? What responsibilities?" I stared at him, then at the O'Garas in the front seat.

His father finally answered. "He means, Excellency, that the moment there is a power vacuum, it will be absolutely essential for our people to know their Sovereign is prepared to assume her proper role. To prevent chaos, you will need to declare for Acclamation immediately. In company with your destined Consort. On Mars."

28

Rigel (RY-jel): *a bright star, most visible in winter evenings in the northern hemisphere*

Even though I didn't get near enough time with M, it was enough that I'm feeling *physically* better than I have since my party. Only physically, though. Between Allister's hints to M, the bits I overheard last night at home, and my dad spending most of the second half on his cell phone, I'm seriously worried our time together is running out way sooner than either of us expected.

Waiting for Dad after the game, I decide I was a coward to duck out of the last ten minutes. A real man should be able to sit there and watch the girl that means more than life to him watch another guy do the super-jock thing. But I kept seeing Sean O'Gara through M's eyes—because of our link or my own paranoia?—and it just got to be too much.

As Dad and I cross the parking lot, I see M getting into the O'Garas' car. I try not to grind my teeth as Sean gets in right next to her. It would make more sense for him to get in first and let Molly sit in the middle, since M will have to get out first. Not that he cares. Probably plans to walk her to the door or something.

I know from experience how great a guy feels after winning a game the way Sean did tonight—like you can conquer the world. I also know how attracted some girls are to that kind of confidence. Not that *M* would ever react that way to anybody but me. No way.

I'm tempted to ask Dad to swing by M's house on the way home, but I don't. No matter how much this Sean thing bothers me, I'm not going to go all stalker. I may not trust him, but I trust her. Completely.

"You missed a great finish, by the way," Dad says once we're in the car, like we were in the middle of a conversation or something. "It looks like Sean O'Gara really is the *wunderkind* everyone is saying. I'm glad I decided to come."

I just grunt.

"I'm sorry, Rigel," he says, surprising me. "I shouldn't have said that. I know this is terribly hard for you."

Duh. I just shrug. Even if it might help to talk this stuff out with my dad, I can't bring myself to do it.

"Sometimes I forget what it was like to be sixteen," he continues when I don't answer. "Of course, I never had the kind of bond you have with M—at least, not until I was much older. I'd like to think your mother and I have something similar now. I'll try to keep that in mind."

"Thanks," I force myself to say. From his tone I figure he's in the mood to do the father-son talk thing and I can't decide if that's good or bad.

He clears his throat, like he does when he's uncomfortable. "I should tell you that we'll be going to your grandfather's for Thanksgiving."

"What?" I practically shout it, caught totally off guard. "To DC? Why isn't he coming here? We have more space." Plus our house isn't six hundred miles away from M! But I don't say that.

"In light of, ah, recent events, some feel it would be best if we leave Jewel for a few days."

"Recent events?" I get a nasty sinking feeling, which he immediately validates.

"Political events. And the fact that you and M don't seem able to abide by the rules we've set out, even for a few days."

Crap. So it's *my* fault. "Who tattled? Mrs. O?"

"Does it matter, Rigel? Given your lack of control, it was agreed a more enforced separation is in order."

Now I'm suspicious as well as furious—and scared. "Agreed by who? Allister and the O'Garas?"

"Not only them. I talked with Shim during the game as well, and the entire Council agrees that our presence here right now could . . . complicate things."

"Complicate things?" Suspicion, rage and fear all ramp into overdrive. "You mean between M and Sean O'Gara, don't you?"

"That's only a part of it. The situation will be explained more fully once we get to Washington. Until then, please don't jump to any conclusions, Rigel. Your mother and I are trying very hard not to."

I stare hard at him, wishing I could sense stuff from my dad the way I can from M. But I can't. "So they're not telling *you* everything, either?"

"No. Just that more *Echtrans* are moving to Jewel, along with an uptick in, um, tourism. And they're not just here to gawk at M."

I suck in my breath. "So why *are* they here?"

"Various reasons." Again he hesitates and clears his throat a couple times, which scares me even worse. "It has to do with the unrest in Nuath and the general expectation that Faxon's days are numbered. People smell a change in the air. Those who can't be on Mars want to speed it along by doing what they can here on Earth."

I'm not quite following. "Speed it along how? You mean they'll want M to do Sovereign stuff right away? She's not even sixteen yet!"

"She will be soon," he reminds me. "And there have been Sovereigns in our past who have had to assume at least a measure of power at that age, though not recently. Perhaps a greater concern is that not everyone is in favor of immediately installing a new Sovereign—especially one so young."

"You mean they'll want to get M out of the way? Like Faxon tried to do?" I try to fight down a wave of pure panic, but it's hard. Someone might be going after M *right now* and I'm not even allowed to protect her! Why did I talk her out of running away? Maybe there's still time . . .

But Dad shakes his head. "No, no, I don't think anyone will try to harm her. But many may try to influence her, in one direction or another, while others want to, well, observe her. To get a feel for just who she is and how they feel about her as Sovereign."

"So they'll what? Be following M around and sending reports or something? Will they tell M what they're doing?" I definitely will, as soon as I see her at school tomorrow.

"Possibly. As I said, it's early days yet, but people want to be sure we have a leader who can take over once Faxon is gone."

"I thought that tribunal thing back in September, with all those tests, did that?"

Again he shakes his head. "I'm not talking about the legalities here, Rigel. I'm talking about the will of the people. No Sovereign can lead effectively without the support of the majority. After our experience with Faxon, our people are understandably worried by the thought of another incompetent ruler. I imagine most are simply hoping for reassurance. That Princess Emileia will turn out to be exactly what they—what we—need."

I still don't like the way this is sounding, since I don't see how I fit into any of it. "And what if they *aren't* reassured? What will they do?"

"It's really too soon to say. If enough people are convinced M isn't ready to lead, or that she may never be ready to lead, they may look for alternatives. Someone else of Royal blood—though Faxon's depredations will make that difficult—or an alternative to the monarchy altogether."

"Like an elected leader? A president or a prime minister or something?" I can't keep the hope out of my voice, since that would solve everything, as far as I'm concerned. "Would that necessarily be a bad thing?"

"Perhaps not." But he looks troubled. "Anyway, I thought you deserved to know what's going on, given your attachment to M. And hers to you," he adds when I tense up. "Keeping you in the dark hasn't had particularly good consequences in the past, so your mother and I—and your grandfather—have agreed to bring you into the loop as much as possible."

"Thanks." But what I'm thinking is, *About time.*

To my surprise, he chuckles. "No promise not to make us regret it, eh? Guess I can't blame you, when there's so much we don't know yet. And Rigel, I do understand. More than you probably realize."

I just shake my head. Because, how can he?

"Yes, I do," he repeats. "Things weren't always smooth for your mom and me, either. In fact, opposition to our match was the reason we left Mars shortly after we married."

"What?" They never told me that! "Why would there be opposition?"

"You know about *fines.*"

"Yeah, they're the reason M is supposed to hook up with Sean O'Gara. They're both Royals and I'm not."

"Yes, but even outside of the Royal line, *fines* are an extremely important part of Nuathan culture. Even more so before Faxon. Your mother and I—"

"Are from different *fines?*" I think for a second. "Yeah, I think you did tell me that one time, but I didn't know it was any big deal."

He gives another chuckle, but this one sounds more sarcastic than amused. "We didn't understand how big a deal, either—until after we'd fallen in love. She was training as a Healer in the same facility where I was designing a new integrated medical information system. We started talking over lunch one day, and, well, before we knew it, we were pretty far gone on each other. Our parents weren't exactly pleased, especially at first."

"Even Grandfather? But he's so . . . so . . ."

"Progressive? Yes, and he was our strongest advocate, once he got over his instinctive shock. He was already lobbying for more intermixing of *fine* bloodlines, even back then. But it's one thing to advocate for a theory and another to have it disrupt your own family."

Imagining Shim, of all people, on the horns of a moral dilemma like that, I almost laugh. But I don't. Because *my* problem can't be solved that easily.

"Thanks for telling me, Dad. I guess you do kind of get it." But it doesn't mean he'll be able to fix things. That's up to me . . . and M. "I'm still not cool with this trip to Washington, though. You want to what? Leave after school next Wednesday?" That should give M and me enough time to plan, especially if we pretend to go along with—

"No, I'm sorry, didn't I say? We leave tomorrow."

29

spiare (spee-AH-ray): *spy; snoop*

"You're all out of your minds. I'm not going to Mars!" I told the O'Garas as we pulled out of the school parking. "I have a life *here.*" Which included Rigel. But adding that wouldn't help my case, except maybe with Molly.

"Calm down, M." Sean put his hand over mine, which was anything but calming.

I wrenched it away, glaring at him. "You're kidding, right? In what universe would I be calm about this?"

He didn't try to touch me again, but his expression was so intense it was almost as bad. "Nobody's going to bundle you into a ship in the middle of the night against your will or anything. It's not even a launch window right now. We just . . . need you to start thinking about the future, and your part in it."

"You mean Mars's future. Not mine."

"You *are* Mars's future," Mr. O'Gara said firmly—so firmly I half believed him. Okay, maybe quarter believed him. "You are the hope we've all needed. The one thing that can unite our people at this critical time."

"Gee, no pressure." I accidentally said it out loud.

To my surprise, Molly laughed. "She's right, you know," she said, surprising me even more. "This is an awful lot to put on a high school sophomore who *just* found out who she is a couple of months ago. I don't think you're being fair, expecting her to automatically be okay with all of this."

"Thanks," I murmured. She reached over and gave my hand a quick squeeze of reassurance. I didn't jerk away.

Nobody said another word until we pulled into my driveway. Then, her voice gentle and motherly, Mrs. O'Gara said, "I hope we haven't upset you too badly, M, as that's the very last thing we want to do. We're very excited to see our work of the last fifteen years finally coming to fruition, of course. At the same time, we mustn't lose sight of your feelings. They do matter to us."

What could I say? "I understand." Even though I didn't think I'd *ever* understand. Not really.

Sean got out of the car and I followed. He turned toward my house, like he was planning to walk to the door with me, but I shook my head.

"I'd rather you didn't." I said it quietly, but he could tell I meant it and didn't argue. As he got back into the van I said, to the whole family, "Thanks for getting me out of the house tonight. I really do appreciate that."

But that was the *only* thing I appreciated, and only because it had given me those wonderful few moments with Rigel.

I rushed to Geometry for the third morning in a row, this time to tell Rigel about this latest development, which would surely make him agree we should run away. Like always, the first thing we did was clasp hands, soaking up each other's essence. But I'd barely felt that first wonderful rush of relief when I sensed such a strong negative emotion that I leaned away to get a better look at his face.

"What?" Though I suspected I knew. "Did they tell you about—?"

"I have to go to Washington for Thanksgiving, to my grandfather's place. Today. At lunch. They weren't even going to let me come to school, but I swore I wouldn't go at all unless they let me at least say goodbye to you first."

My heart practically stopped, this was so much worse than I expected. "But . . . Thanksgiving's not till next week! You *can't* be gone that whole time?"

He looked as miserable, as devastated, as I felt. "Ten days. Ten whole days. Assuming—"

"What?" My alarm spiked even higher. "You think they won't let you come back? Is this because of last night? Mrs. O told her husband and then he called somebody . . . This is *my* fault, isn't it?" It was all I could do to keep my voice at the necessary sub-whisper.

"No! *Not* your fault, M, not at all! It's just stupid politics."

My hands tightened convulsively on his. "That's it, then. We have to run. Now. *Before* they can—"

The bell cut me off. We reluctantly separated and took our seats.

Deb, I noticed gratefully, hadn't tried to talk to me during my few precious minutes with Rigel. She didn't even act upset that we'd ignored her, like Bri would have. Instead, she was staring at the teacher so intently I turned to look, too.

My gut clenched. Standing next to Mr. Benning was a woman I didn't recognize—but who was unmistakably Martian. I knew the only reason I hadn't felt her *brath* when she'd come into the room was that I'd been too busy absorbing Rigel's.

"Class, please welcome Ms. Harrigan. She's a student teacher and will be observing this and a few other classes until the holidays. She'll also be able to offer help to anyone who needs it when I'm otherwise occupied."

Everyone murmured a greeting, the boys more enthusiastically than the girls. Because Ms. Harrigan (or whatever her real name was) was gorgeous, with shoulder-length blond hair and wide, gray-green eyes with impossible lashes. Even without her vibe, I'd have guessed she was Martian.

I felt Rigel's worry and knew he was remembering "Mr. Smith" just like I was. Even if Ms. Harrigan wasn't here to try to kill me, her presence couldn't possibly bode well for either of us.

Halfway through class, she confirmed that assumption when she stopped by my desk as she wandered around the room. Leaning over, pretending to help me with my assignment, she spoke in a voice only I could hear.

"I can see you're nervous about my presence, Excellency. Please don't be. I'm only here to observe, and to advise you if necessary. Your actions and alliances matter to a great many people."

With an effort, I kept my eyes focused on my paper. "So you're here to spy on me? And to report back?" I murmured just as quietly.

"Spy is an ugly word, Excellency. But someone in your position can't expect to be a private person. Surely you know that."

Before I could respond she moved on, pausing briefly by Rigel's desk, too. I couldn't hear anything but could tell from his expression —and the wave of uneasiness I felt from him—that she'd said *something*.

I was dying to find out what, but as soon as the bell rang, Ms. Harrigan oh-so-casually moved between the two of us and managed to stay there as we made our way to the door. And Molly was waiting in the hallway.

Of course, she immediately recognized Ms. Harrigan as another *Echtran*, though she couldn't say anything—not out loud. But she smiled and nodded, and the "student teacher" smiled back before we started walking.

"So, you know her?" I demanded. Rigel had started to turn away, but paused to hear the answer.

Molly shrugged. "Not really. I saw her in Ireland. I heard she was nearly killed in an early uprising against Faxon, back, um, home. Her face was all over the news—the underground news—a couple of years ago. She left for Earth a month before we did."

So they'd brought in another gung-ho revolutionary to pressure me to step up and act like a leader—and to keep me away from Rigel.

"What are you guys whispering about?" Deb asked from behind us, and Molly and I both started.

"Just that new student teacher," Molly said truthfully and completely naturally.

Rigel and I locked glances for a moment, silently vowing that we'd talk as soon as humanly possible and that we weren't giving up no matter what. Then, after sending me a burst of love and longing so powerful it left my whole body humming, he headed off down the hall.

"Did you see how all the boys were practically drooling over her?" Molly continued.

Deb snorted, successfully distracted. "Boys are so shallow. All it takes is pouty lips and a hot body and they turn into idiots."

We all took turns boy-bashing until we parted ways for second period.

I spent Computer class desperately working up a plan for Rigel and me to escape before he left in two hours. Though I hadn't worked out the details, I hurried to catch Rigel in the hall before English.

"Let's cut. I've been thinking, if we can just—" I broke off my urgent whisper when Ms. Harrigan suddenly appeared in the doorway.

"Let's not linger in the hallway," she said sweetly, though there was something distinctly *not* sweet in her expression. She watched us pointedly until we reluctantly went into the room, then followed us in. Apparently she was "observing" this class, too.

Not only that, she suggested a new project to Ms. Thurston—the latest in a string of subs we'd had since Mr. "Smith" left—which had us all pairing up to do contrasting critiques of *The Bell Jar*. Needless to say, I was *not* paired with Rigel. Just like in Geometry, Ms. Harrigan managed to oh-so-casually keep us well away from each other.

Rigel sent me several frustrated glances from across the room, where he was paired with Trina, of all people. Unfortunately, Trina saw me looking back and gave me a nasty, smug smile. Worse, she made a point of walking from English to Science with Rigel, preventing us from managing so much as a word between our last two classes together.

Ms. Harrigan wasn't in Science, but Mr. Ferguson was all excited to announce that right after Thanksgiving, some big expert on exogeology was coming and would be with us till the end of the semester. Not hard to guess that would be another Martian. Did they plan to monitor every class Rigel and I had together for the rest of the year?

Trina didn't leave Rigel alone for a moment as we worked on our final geology projects. My own partner, Will, who I usually liked pretty well, seemed unusually irritating today. He kept insisting that because our project was a simulation of terrestrial impact craters, my astronomy hobby made me more of an expert—meaning he wanted me to do most of the work.

When the bell rang, I distinctly heard the word *wait* in my mind. I glanced at Rigel and he gave me a little nod, so I hung back while the room emptied. Trina lingered for a few seconds, but when Rigel took both of my hands in his, she gave a disgusted snort and left.

"I'm supposed to go to the office now, so my folks can sign me out." The mix of desperate emotions flowing from his touch was so intense it made me gasp.

"No! I thought you'd have lunch, at least."

He shook his head sadly.

"Then we *have* to run away. Now!"

"On foot? How far would we get? My parents are probably already here. If we try and get caught, they might not bring me back at all."

I knew he was right, but the idea of ten days apart was terrifying. All I could do was stare at him, tears prickling my eyes.

A spasm of pain twisted his face, then he manufactured a smile clearly intended to reassure me. "We'll get through this, M. I'll see you a week from Monday. Stay . . . stay safe, okay?"

"Safe?" I stared at him incredulously. "We'll be lucky if this doesn't kill us both! Don't they understand that? I thought your folks believed!"

His jaw clenched. "I don't know if they believe that part. I tried to hide it last month and only told them about it last night, so now they think it's just an excuse. Anyway, I don't think they have much choice. This whole plan came from higher up."

"Allister?" I hissed. "That *bastard!* He's—"

"Not just him, Dad says. Look, if there's any way I can convince them to come back sooner, I will." He didn't sound very hopeful, though.

"Maybe if you get sick enough . . . But I hope you don't!" I was sure, though, that we both would. I wished I was as sure that it would make a difference to the people messing with our futures. Our lives. "Stay as healthy as you can. And safe! Okay?"

I was terrified now that some Martian radical might do something awful to Rigel if they thought he was screwing up their plans. What if this whole trip was a trap? What if—?

Rigel leaned forward and kissed me, halting my spiraling panic. "I'll be safe, and I'll be back. I promise. If you can survive this, I can."

Not wanting terror to be the last emotion he sensed from me, I forced it down, trying to project confidence instead. And love. "You're right. We . . . we can do this. But oh, Rigel, I'll miss you so much!"

I could see Sean hovering in the hallway, but I threw my arms around Rigel anyway. The O'Garas, or at least his Uncle Allister, were to blame for this separation. Besides, what difference would it make if word got back to my aunt? I wouldn't see Rigel for more than a week, no matter what she did.

"Ditto," Rigel murmured, hugging me back. "I love you, M. Never forget that."

"I won't. Never. Don't ever forget that I love you, too." Sean could probably hear us, but I didn't care.

There was nothing else to say, so after embracing for a dozen more heartbeats, we separated. I felt a physical wrench, and knew Rigel felt it, too. Then, with a neutral glance at Sean and a quick, brave smile at me, Rigel headed for the front office.

"So, you two have decided to ignore the rules completely now?" Sean asked when I joined him in the hall.

I glared at him. "Why does it matter? Playing by the rules didn't keep you guys from sending him away."

To my surprise, he looked genuinely startled. "Sending him away? Away where?"

"He has to go to Washington, DC, for Thanksgiving—almost a whole week early. Are you going to pretend your uncle didn't have anything to do with that?"

Sean didn't answer right away, walking beside me in silence until we had nearly reached the cafeteria. "I guess I can't promise he wasn't involved, but I can absolutely promise I didn't know anything about it," he said at last. "Sorry, M. But . . . it's probably for the best, you know? With all these the new folks coming to town and all."

I whirled on him. "Best? Don't tell me what's best for *me!* Because you have no idea. I guarantee you, being separated from Rigel will never be *best* in any way, shape or form." I turned away and stalked to the lunch line, so angry I was on the verge of tears—and I was *not* going to give Sean the satisfaction of seeing me cry.

A tiny voice whispered that he wouldn't really be satisfied to see me cry, that he liked me too much for that, but I resolutely ignored it. The only voice I wanted to hear in my head was Rigel's, not my stupid, disloyal conscience.

30

dhualgis cumann (doo-AHL-gus koo-MAHN):
benevolent duty; royal obligation

I spent the rest of the school day careening between misery and panic and trying not to let any of it show—not until I could figure out what to *do*. Because there had to be *something*! I'd never survive ten whole days completely apart from Rigel, and neither would he, no matter how much we'd tried to convince each other we'd be okay.

By the time I got home, I was mentally and emotionally wrung out. My head was starting to pound and my heart felt bruised and battered. I went straight to my room to curl up in a ball and be miserable, now that no one was watching me for signs of weakness. When Aunt Theresa got home I dragged myself downstairs, only to be told I was going to the O'Garas' again tonight.

"Do I have to?" I didn't have to fake my reluctance this time. That was the last place I wanted to go, especially if Allister was going to be there.

"I can't imagine why you wouldn't want to, after they did you such a favor last night by taking you to that basketball game," my aunt replied. "Refusing to help Molly with her schoolwork would be the height of ingratitude after that."

I'd temporarily forgotten that I was supposedly doing a good deed by going over there. I considered telling her I wasn't feeling well, which was true, though I suspected it was because I'd been crying for an hour. And because I was already imagining how awful I *would* feel after a few days without Rigel. No, better save that excuse for later. I'd need it.

"Sorry. You're right. Sure, I'll go," I said dully.

As usual, I headed over as soon as I finished the dinner dishes. My feet were dragging despite the cold, I was so not looking forward to their reactions to Rigel's leaving. Would they be smug?

Condescendingly sympathetic? I just hoped I could keep from either crying or losing my temper if they brought it up.

Sean answered the door, but the whole family was waiting in the living room. And sure enough, they all seemed oppressively cheerful when they greeted me. At least Allister wasn't there—yet. I sat next to Molly on the couch and was relieved when Sean sat in a nearby chair instead of beside me.

"We still have some pie left from dessert, M, if you'd like a piece," Mrs. O said with a wide smile. "And I've just brewed a fresh pot of chamomile tea."

"Um, just tea, thanks." I hadn't been able to swallow much dinner but didn't feel the least bit hungry, even though Mrs. O was an even better baker than my Aunt Theresa.

As she poured, her husband said, "I'm sorry if we seem a bit overly excited tonight, Excellency. It's just . . . we've received some rather good news today."

Molly turned to me in surprise. "Oh! I totally forgot that you wouldn't know, M. And, um, I guess you're probably not in the best mood right now, huh? What with Rigel leaving and all."

"You mean that's not your good news?" I didn't even try to keep the bitterness out of my voice. All this grinning was pissing me off.

Molly's surprise turned to shock. "Of course not! That would be so mean. Can I tell her?" she asked her parents.

Mrs. O'Gara nodded, still smiling.

Practically bouncing in her excitement, Molly said, "There's been a real uprising against Faxon back on Mars. Some of his guards have even deserted him and joined the resistance. Mum and Dad told us as soon as we got home from school today. They're pretty pumped about it—we all are."

"We are, indeed," her father agreed. Sean and Mrs. O also nodded enthusiastically. "We didn't want to say anything until the preliminary reports were verified and it's still too soon to know all of the ramifications," he continued, "but Faxon is quickly losing support. When he finally falls, it will change everything. It's what we've hoped for, been working for, for years. Almost since the usurper seized power."

That explained why they were so secretive last night—that meeting at the Stuarts' must have been because of those "preliminary reports." My panic started creeping back, but not because of Rigel this time. Or not only because of Rigel.

"So . . . what does this mean, exactly?"

"It means we can go home!" Sean burst out, looking positively ecstatic at the prospect.

"Not yet, dear," Mrs. O'Gara cautioned him, "but soon, we hope. Once we know for certain what the political climate is like. Unfortunately, things are likely to become even more dangerous in Nuath before they get better. Faxon is unlikely to step down without a fight."

"With the news reports so vague and confused, how will we be able to tell?" Mr. O sounded frustrated.

His wife patted his arm. "It's still very early days. We'll know more soon. Besides—" She broke off and glanced at me.

"Besides what?" I prompted. "I *need* to know this stuff, don't I?"

"Yes," Mr. O'Gara said decisively. "That's why you're here, after all. To learn as much as possible about 'this stuff,' as you put it." He chuckled, his frustration apparently no match for his good mood.

It sort of made me want to smack him. Smack all of them, with their stupid grins.

"It's why we're so anxious to get back," he continued. "There is an enormous amount of work to be done, work we can help with."

I was perfectly fine with *them* leaving to rebuild the government or whatever, but clearly that wasn't all they had in mind. "What kind of work?" I asked suspiciously.

"Bolstering the resistance, now that it's finally taking hold. Organizing protests, so that Faxon can be deposed with as little bloodshed as possible. Bringing together the various factions that oppose him, so they can work effectively together."

I waited, knowing there was more, and that I wasn't going to like it. I was right.

"Needless to say, once Faxon is removed—which could happen at any time—we'll need to act quickly before the resulting power vacuum degenerates into anarchy or even civil war, which could tear our people apart. In other words, the moment it's safe, we need to bring back the exiled Royals."

Which obviously included *me*. But not the Stuarts, since they weren't Royals and not exactly exiled, having been on Earth for

191

seventy-five years. And if the "authorities" wanted Rigel away from Jewel right now, how much more would they want to keep him on Earth if I went to Mars?

The panic I'd been fighting now grabbed me by the throat. I tried to force my brain to function so I could argue my side convincingly.

"Look, I know this is really important to you and all, but you can't possibly expect me to just . . . just walk away from everything I've ever known, everyone I care about, to become some . . . figurehead for your cause."

"Not a figurehead!" Mrs. O'Gara seemed shocked. "Not at all. It may seem that way at the moment, because you don't yet know enough and aren't yet old enough to truly lead. But our Sovereigns have been anything but figureheads. Surely you've learned that much by now?"

"Sovereigns in the past, maybe. But this new government will be starting from scratch, right? Even Allister has said no one expects me to actually *lead* until I'm older. So what would that make me, exactly, if not a figurehead?"

She and her husband exchanged glances and I got a sense they didn't really want to answer. But I kept waiting and finally Mr. O'Gara said, "I won't deny that at this moment you are primarily a . . . symbol to our people. A symbol of hope, and a rallying point. But even as a minor, a Sovereign has certain powers."

Mrs. O'Gara cleared her throat and he broke off with a guilty glance at her.

Immediately, I pounced on what he'd started to say. "Powers? What powers *do* I have? Right now?" Maybe enough that I could at least make them bring Rigel back?

"Well . . ." Mrs. O'Gara pursed her lips and sent her husband a quick frown. "Once you're properly Acclaimed Sovereign, you'll likely appoint a Regent to serve until you reach your majority. Depending on your age, you can invest certain powers in that Regent while reserving others to yourself, but it's been many generations since a Regent was required, so I'm not certain exactly where the dividing lines are."

I stared at her, fervently wishing I had her ability to tell if someone was being truthful. Even without it, I had a gut feeling there was a lot she wasn't telling me. Especially when she sprang to her feet the moment I opened my mouth to ask more questions.

"I'll just get a fresh pot of tea, shall I?"

I doubted I'd get more answers out of her tonight but I wasn't *about* to let the subject drop for good.

At breakfast the next morning, Aunt Theresa informed me that I could go to taekwondo that day after all. No doubt she'd learned Rigel was out of town, and didn't want the money she'd paid for those classes to go to waste.

Not that I wanted to argue. Whatever her reason, I was eager to go someplace other than the O'Garas,' someplace I could burn off a bit of my frustration. I headed out as soon as I finished my morning chores.

After warmups and kicking drills, Master Parker split us into pairs for sparring practice. I found myself opposite Darlene, a black-belt in her early twenties, one of the most aggressive sparrers in the school, even counting most of the guys. I hadn't sparred with her since I was a yellow belt, but the memory made my stomach clench. She'd knocked me down twice, hard, and I'd come away with a couple of really nasty bruises, even with all the pads we had to wear.

"Master Parker says you've gotten better lately," she whispered as we bowed to each other. "Let's see whatcha got."

Though nervous, I smiled grimly as we shifted to fighting stance. I *was* better now, and I was in a mood to prove it. Master Parker gave the Korean command to begin, and Darlene immediately led off with a lightning-fast roundhouse kick, followed by a back-spinning kick to my head, which I barely ducked before missing her completely with a roundhouse kick of my own.

She came at me again and I forced myself to focus, imagining her as one of the people trying to keep Rigel away from me. My momentary fear vanished, replaced by anger and an unexpected surge of confidence.

Darlene's next kick seemed to happen in slow-motion, giving me all the time in the world to fade back and counter with a solid back kick to her midsection that sent her flying, landing on her backside.

She was up again before I could worry that I'd hurt her, coming at me with renewed determination—and a hint of respect in her eyes. She feinted a bit, watching for an opportunity, then lunged in with a vicious axe-kick that would have knocked me to my knees if it had landed. Again, I had no trouble sidestepping and delivering a roundhouse to her chest pad, followed by a back-spinning kick that connected solidly with her padded helmet.

This time, she didn't get up. Time abruptly returned to normal as concern spiked through me. "Darlene?" I said uncertainly, and to my relief she started to stir. She was struggling to sit up when Master Parker blew his whistle and hurried over.

"Just sit still for a moment," he told her, then looked at me. "Marsha, are you *sure* you don't want to spar in the upcoming tournament?"

Darlene was clearly still dazed. "What *was* that? It felt like a baseball bat."

"Sorry," I said in a small voice, appalled by what I'd done, legal move or not. Now I understood how Rigel and Sean must feel when playing sports against regular Earthlings. But if I couldn't control myself any better than that, I definitely had no business trying to be a leader.

Just like I'd tried to tell everyone from the start.

Between freezing drizzle and no Rigel at church, Sunday was dreary. Especially since I was feeling the first twinges of headache and nausea from going too long without seeing him.

The only diversion occurred when several of Jewel's more prominent citizens gathered for the latest gossip after the service. I tuned it out at first, wrapped up in feeling sorry for myself, but then a few words caught my attention.

"What I don't understand is, why now?" Mrs. Billingsley was saying. "Mid-November isn't exactly tourist season in Indiana, and the Jewelry Festival isn't until May."

Her husband put a hand on her shoulder. "Let's not look a gift horse in the mouth, Belinda. I've sold three houses in two days, which has never happened in my life. You said sales at the bookstore are up, too."

"So are my sales," chimed in old Agatha Payton. "And have any of you noticed? I probably shouldn't say this in church, but most of these out-of-towners are awfully good-looking." Aunt Theresa and one or two others looked slightly shocked and Agatha tittered. "Hey, just 'cause I'm old don't mean I'm dead!'"

The Billingsleys had owned Belinda's Books on Diamond since way before I was born, and Mrs. Payton owned and ran Glitterby's a few doors down. All were at least third generation Jewelites, so their opinions carried weight in town. Mrs. Batten and her mother, who owned and ran Quilt World, nodded their agreement. I glanced at the O'Garas, who all looked impressively clueless.

Was Jewel going to become the next Martian enclave? I used to think it would be cool to have lots of other *Echtrans* around, like Sean and Molly had always had, but not if they were mainly here to pass judgment on everything I did—and who I spent time with.

"Marsha!" Aunt Theresa broke into my thoughts in a tone that made it clear she'd already said my name more than once. "It's time to go. Those baseboards won't scrub themselves, you know."

The O'Garas' obvious struggles to hide their horror at my aunt's words might have been amusing if I hadn't had a headache. Aunt Theresa was clearly scrounging now to find extra jobs for me around the house. Would she unground me if she ran out of ideas?

Not that it would matter, if Rigel never came back.

I went to the O'Garas' again that night and this time Allister *was* there. He spent the first hour shoving facts down my throat and the second hour making me regurgitate them.

"Show me the proper response of the Sovereign to the traditional salute by the people." He demonstrated that salute as he spoke, bowing with right fist over heart.

I inclined my head to the precise degree he'd drilled me on, my chin tilting down until I could just barely feel tension at the front of my throat. "It is my benevolent duty to guide my people into our best future."

"Better. Now, in Nuathan."

I did my best, but my Nuathan was a long way from coming naturally yet. *"Is a mo dulgas cumann chun treoir a thabert istich inner nadaoine is fearr sa todhchaí?"*

"Dhualgis," he corrected me. *"And thabhairt isteach inár.* Again."

With a tiny sigh, I said the words again, trying to get the pronunciation right.

He nodded, though he didn't look completely happy. "For a first lesson, I suppose that will do. Say it with authority, mind you, not as a question. You must instill confidence. Now, what are the two primary cities on Mars?"

"Thiaraway and Monaru."

"How many villages?"

"Eighteen. There were twenty-three, but five have been evacuated to conserve power. Which is why orderly emigration to Earth over the next century is essential," I added, though he hadn't asked. It was getting late and I was tired and achy and just wanted to get this over with.

He regarded me suspiciously with his little gray eyes, then gave a small shrug. "Very well. That will do for tonight, Excellency, but we have scarcely scratched the surface of all you must know. Please do not grow complacent."

I nearly snorted. "I'm not," I assured him. "Not even a little."

The weather was still undecided between freezing rain and sleet. Mr. O'Gara drove me the short distance home, since Allister wouldn't let Sean use his omni to keep us warm and dry for the walk.

"Please thank your aunt and uncle again for inviting us to Thanksgiving dinner," Mr. O said when I got out of the car. "We're all very much looking forward to it."

"I will. Um, me too." I knew I wasn't convincing but didn't much care.

I dragged myself up the porch stairs and into the house, every step an effort. Allister had given me a Martian "book"—one of those scroll thingies loaded up with a gazillion texts on Martian history, government, laws, sociology, you name it. I needed to get started on it, but all I wanted to do was sleep.

In fact, I wished I could sleep away the next seven days and not wake up until Rigel was back. Since that wasn't an option between school, Thanksgiving, and Aunt Theresa's increasingly imaginative chore list, it was going to be a long, long week.

31

tinneas (TIN-es): *physical illness, rare among Martians except in the very elderly*

I could swear my alarm went off only seconds after I turned out my light, but according to my clock, I'd slept more than nine hours and it was time to get ready for school. Despite all that sleep, I felt even worse than when I went to bed.

"What's wrong?" Molly asked when I reached the bus stop.

"Not feeling great. I told you this happens when Rigel and I can't be together."

She bit her lip, looking distressed. "Already? But you just saw him Friday."

I just shrugged, not feeling up to explaining that it seemed to take less and less time apart before symptoms started, the stronger our bond became.

Sean wasn't on the bus. Probably getting a ride with a friend. I was vaguely disappointed, only because seeing me like this might finally make him believe in the *graell*. No biggie. He'd have plenty of other chances to be convinced this week.

Normally I hurried to Geometry but today there was no point. Still, my steps quickened as I got close and experienced an irrational hope that Rigel might be there after all.

He wasn't.

Ms. Harrigan was, smiling at me as soon as I came in. Since she was one of the ones who wanted Rigel out of the picture, I didn't smile back.

I felt steadily worse as the day wore on, finding it hard to focus on anything but my desire to see Rigel again. I went through the day on automatic, nodding and answering questions when necessary. No one but Molly asked if I was okay, so I must not have looked as bad as I felt.

I hadn't heard from Rigel at all since he left, not that I'd expected to. I'd checked my e-mail every chance I got but after my initial disappointment, I realized he was probably being watched even more closely than I was.

Still, I decided on the bus ride home, what did I have to lose by trying his cell phone? They couldn't punish us much worse and I just might die if I couldn't at least hear his voice soon. I punched in his number the moment I got home, renewed hope making my heart beat faster than it had all day.

My hope started to drain away when it rang twice, three times, four. Then Rigel answered!

"M?" he whispered. "I've had my phone on vibrate, in case you were able to call. Had to get away from everyone before I could answer. How are you doing?"

I almost blurted out the truth, but realized that would upset him. "Better, now that I can hear your voice." Which *was* true.

"Me, too." I suspected he was editing as much as I was. "I can probably only talk a minute or two."

I was just about to pour out my feelings to him when he asked, "What's going on in Jewel?"

"I guess you've heard what's happening on Mars?"

"Yeah, it's all anyone's talking about here. Are they . . . putting more pressure on you?"

"Guess you could say that. Allister's trying to cram as much info into me as fast as he can and the O'Garas are all excited they'll get to go back soon. But no matter what they say, I'm not going with them, so don't worry."

"I'll try. M, I'm so sorry I talked you out of running away. I really wish we had."

My heart caught at the longing in his voice. "Oh, me, too, Rigel! So much. When you get home, I promise we'll figure some way—"

I broke off at the sound of another voice at his end, his dad's, asking what Rigel was doing. Then Mr. Stuart said into the phone, "I'm sorry, M. I know this is difficult for both of you, but please don't try calling Rigel again. I'll be keeping his phone with me for the rest of our stay here."

"Wait!" I cried. "At least let me tell him—" But the line was dead.

I let out a scream that the neighbors could probably hear as it echoed through the empty house. *Why* hadn't I told him I loved him, very first thing? Or talked about some other way to communicate? Now I'd gotten him in trouble and it would be even more impossible.

Furious at myself as well as at everyone trying to pull my strings, I stomped upstairs, pulled out that Martian e-book thing and snapped it open, determined to find *something* I could use to my—and Rigel's—advantage. I clicked to the index, searching for anything about the authority of underage Sovereigns.

All too soon, though, my anger-fueled energy started to ebb and the words began running together. With a sigh that was equal parts frustration and exhaustion, I shut off the book and dragged myself back downstairs to tackle my afternoon chores.

Tuesday mostly went by in a blur, other than the pinch of disappointment I still felt in every class that should have had Rigel in it.

"Honestly, M, snap out of it," Bri said at one point. "I've asked you like six times whether you're coming to the game tomorrow night, and you give a different answer every time."

I blinked rapidly to bring her face into focus. "What?"

She gave an exasperated sigh. "Are you coming to the game tomorrow or not? Matt's driving me, and he needs to know whether to pick you up."

"Oh. Probably not. If so, I'll probably ride with the O'Garas again."

"*Thank* you," she said with a little huff. "All I needed to know. I'll tell Matt."

It wasn't until much later that I realized the main point of her asking was so I'd ask about her and Matt, since this would be their first real date. Oh, well.

At lunch I was vaguely aware of Sean and Molly watching me with concern as I sat there with nothing but a juice box, staring into space. Maybe it should have surprised me that neither of them said anything to me. But to the extent I could think at all, it was about what Rigel might be doing in Washington at that moment and what a relief it would be when he got back.

Aunt Theresa had me doing even more extra cleaning stuff at

home to get ready for Thanksgiving, since the O'Garas were coming over. She even dug out her mother's—probably her grandmother's—silver that I'd seen maybe twice in my life and made me polish it.

At least it was mindless, so I could stay busy without having to think or deal with awkward questions from my aunt about my absent-mindedness. As we sat down to dinner, I was already looking forward to bedtime, when I could at least dream about Rigel. Then Aunt Theresa said the O'Garas were expecting me again tonight.

What with Sean's game tomorrow and Thanksgiving the day after, I hadn't expected that. "I'd really rather not. I'm not feeling all that well. Can't I just go to bed early?" I looked hard at her, trying to use whatever persuasion powers I might have, though they were probably as weak as everything else about me right now.

To my surprise, my aunt regarded me uncertainly for a long moment. "Well, I suppose if you— Oops! Louie, be careful!" she exclaimed as my uncle spilled some gravy on the table.

She turned back to me, her concentration broken. "I already told Lili you'd go, Marsha. Molly is getting a bit anxious about the exams coming up. If you're tired, you don't need to stay long."

Arguing was too much effort so I just nodded, then played with my food until Aunt Theresa and Uncle Louie were done and I could wash the dishes. I was halfway to the O'Garas' when I realized I should have suggested that maybe I had something contagious, in which case my aunt wouldn't want me to go over and give it to them. I'd use that excuse later, if I needed to.

If I could still think at all by then.

Mrs. O'Gara opened the door instead of Sean this time, then carefully ushered me inside like I was made of glass. "Molly told us you weren't feeling well, dear," she said, leading me to the cushiest chair in their living room. "No lessons tonight, I think—I've suggested Allister stay away. I'll bring you some tea and biscuits and you can just relax a bit, eh?"

Molly sat in the chair next to me as her mother bustled off to the kitchen. "What's wrong, exactly?" She seemed genuinely curious. "Are you sick to your stomach, or what?"

"Yeah," I admitted, "and it's getting worse. The headache started Sunday. And now I'm getting really . . . fuzzy. More than I remember from the last time."

She frowned at me for a long moment. "You mean the time you told us about, when you and Rigel pretended to break up for a few weeks?" I nodded. "But how can it be *worse* already? I mean, it's just been three or four days."

I shrugged. "I don't know exactly how it works. The other time we were in classes together, even if we weren't talking or touching. Maybe that's the difference. Or— Oh, hi, Sean," I broke off as he came in with a plate of cookies.

"Hullo, M. Moll said you weren't feeing quite the thing, and I could see at school you were a bit out of it." He set the cookies on the coffee table and sat on the couch across from us. The cookies were pretty, with pink and white frosting and sugar sprinkles, but didn't tempt me at all.

"Did she tell you *why* I'm not feeling well?" I made myself ask.

He gave a sort of half shrug. "I figure it's probably that bug that was going around last week. Half of my calculus class had it."

"Sean." Molly's tone was chiding. "You know we—*Echtrans,* I mean—don't get sick. M wouldn't catch some Earth virus."

"Yeah, well, she's lived separate from other *Echtrans* most of her life. That probably screwed up her immune system. You've been sick before, haven't you, M?" His expression was almost pleading.

I answered truthfully. "I had a sore throat once, when I was six. And a tummy ache once or twice from too much Halloween candy. Other than that, um, no. Not even a cold. Except back in September, and I already told Molly about that."

Clearly, that wasn't what he wanted to hear. "Yeah, I know what you've *convinced* yourself is going on, but I don't buy it. I told you about Penny—"

"The girl who got tricked into thinking she had the *graell* with some guy, yeah. But I'm *not* imagining my bond with Rigel." I winced. "Or this headache." All this talking was making my temples throb.

"Look, I didn't mean—" he began, looking genuinely concerned, but his mother came in with the tea tray before he could finish.

"Here we are, then." She set down the tray and poured out three cups of tea. "This will make you feel more the thing, dear," she said, handing me my cup. "Everyone has an off day now and then, after all."

So she was in denial, too.

"Thanks, but the only thing that'll make me feel better is Rigel coming back. Sorry."

She drew back a bit, frowning. "Now, dear, there's no need to let your imagination run away with you. I'm sure you miss the Stuart lad, it's only natural, but it hardly seems fair to blame him for how you're feeling tonight."

"Blame *him?*" I repeated. "I don't blame Rigel at all! I blame whoever made him leave Jewel. Were you in on that?"

For a long moment, she stared at me, chewing on her lower lip as though deciding whether to answer—which was an answer all by itself. Finally she sank down onto the couch next to Sean with a heavy sigh.

"Excellency, I'm still not sure you fully understand what's at stake right now. Perhaps if I explain to you what Quinn and I have been up against for the past dozen years . . ." She trailed off uncertainly.

"Okay, go ahead. Explain it to me. Because you're right—I don't understand why it's so terrible for Rigel and me to be together, especially when it makes us both feel so terrible to be apart."

Mrs. O'Gara gave a quick, decisive nod. "Very well. Perhaps you're not aware that most negative tendencies—some might call them vices—that plague humankind have been systematically bred out of our people over the centuries."

"Shim mentioned it when he talked down Boyne Morven and his followers last month—that Martians aren't supposed to be greedy or violent or whatever. But Faxon—"

"Is an anomaly," she assured me. "Unfortunately, while sublimating our baser qualities brought millennia of peace to Nuath, it also left us poorly equipped for dealing with . . . anomalies. Most of us tend to be, for want of a better word, pliable. Except for the Royal *fine*, as resolve is necessary to lead. It's why Faxon worked so hard to systematically eliminate as many Royals as possible. Those who didn't flee to Earth faced arrest, convenient 'accidents,' or simply disappeared. Some, however, changed their names—even their appearances, in some cases—and went into hiding."

I frowned, trying to remember what Molly had told me about that. "But . . . you lived in a village, didn't you? And Sean and Molly went to a regular school and all?"

"Yes, once we had established new, fictitious identities as members of an Agricultural *fine*. Friends in Informatics helped us and certain other Royals to create new family histories that went back generations, inserting our real names on flight manifests so that it appeared we had gone to Earth along with most of the other exiles."

"So your last name isn't really O'Gara?"

Sean answered. "No, it is. We left Mars last year because resistance records had been seized, so once we got to Ireland there was no point in keeping our fake name. Which was Mulgrew, in case you're curious."

"During our years as the Mulgrews, Molly's birth parents," Mrs. O continued, "Quinn and I worked tirelessly, often thanklessly, to rouse our people to rebel against Faxon. The vast majority were sympathetic to our cause, particularly when conditions worsened and Faxon's oppression became more ruthless. But because of their inbred passivity, motivating them enough to rise up, even in their own interest, was beyond us.

"Oh, we managed small pockets of resistance, along with a few leaks and propaganda campaigns that embarrassed Faxon and publicized our cause. But though we had countless allies, distressingly few were willing to actually *do* anything. We were already on the verge of giving up when we were forced to flee. It seemed no matter what we did, we came no closer to creating the spark our people needed. Until you."

"News that I was still alive, you mean?"

She nodded, giving me a fond, almost misty smile. "It was overwhelming, you know, learning you survived. Bailerealta held a festival that went on for ten days. The enclave in Montana had a great celebration, as well. I can only imagine the response on Mars once word filtered back—though of course Faxon tried to suppress it. Only in recent weeks has your existence become common knowledge there, and it did what we spent so many years trying to do: it has electrified our people to throw off the yoke of tyranny at last!"

Her words resonated with such fervor, such feeling, I actually felt a flicker of what could only be Nuathan patriotism—unwilling and unfocused as I was. That unfamiliar feeling was immediately followed by a more reasonable one: guilt. Because I couldn't possibly be what they needed.

Again, Molly seemed to understand my feelings best. "Mum, this is a lot to dump on M at once. I'd hate to feel like the future of a whole race depended on me. I'd probably hide under my bed!"

Mrs. O'Gara didn't look amused. "You don't have Emileia's bloodline, Molly. She was bred from many generations of leaders and I have no doubt she is completely up to the task—or will be, once she grows accustomed to the idea and receives the proper training. I'm not frightening you, am I, dear?" she asked me.

"Um." I glanced at Molly, then Sean, then back to Mrs. O before answering truthfully, "Not exactly. Maybe because I feel so crappy right now. But I do know there's no way I can live up to any of this. How could anyone? Especially somebody like me, who wasn't raised to it? I can't even speak Martian, er, Nuathan yet. Not to mention knowing how to do all the stuff you say I'd have to do. You claimed I wouldn't just be a figurehead, but I don't see how I can possibly be anything else, at least for a long time."

Mrs. O'Gara only hesitated for a second. "Well, of course you'll need more instruction before you can take on your proper duties. That's why Allister is pushing you so hard. But even now—"

"But what *are* my 'proper duties'?" I pressed. "What authority *do* I have? Right now?"

She'd weaseled out of that question Friday night and now she looked so uncomfortable that Sean said, "Mum, you don't have to —"

"No, she has a right to know," she said, half to herself. "I'm just not sure . . ."

"That you want me to know?" Now I was getting angry again.

Her eyes flashed with an emotion that might have been anger of her own, or fear—but it was gone before I could decipher it. "No, dear, of course not. I simply don't want to give you wrong information. While there must be laws and customs pertaining to an underage Sovereign, I'm not terribly familiar with them."

More than ever, I wished I could tell for sure when someone was lying. Surely, once they'd found me, Allister and the rest of the Council would have dug out those old laws? They *had* to know.

Another wave of exhaustion made me go fuzzy again. Once I felt better—after Monday—I'd read more of the stuff Allister had given me and see what I could figure out on my own. For now, I just nodded.

"Okay. Maybe Allister knows. But . . . I don't feel up to talking to him tonight."

Her smile became motherly again as she relaxed. "Of course, dear. He's not here anyway. He and Mr. O'Gara are, ah, visiting with some of the newer *Echtrans* tonight, getting to know them better. Would you like Sean to walk you home now?"

"I am pretty tired." I wondered if she'd almost said *meeting* instead of *visiting*, and if so, what that might be about. "Thanks for the tea and cookies."

And for confirming that I had *some* kind of power, even if she didn't want to tell me what. If it was more than the O'Garas or Allister wanted to let on, maybe I *could* do something about this enforced separation from Rigel. But I kept that thought to myself. For now.

32

athshondis (ath-SHON-dis): *resonance*

Sean and I walked in silence. Which was fine, since I didn't feel like
talking to him. But halfway to my house, he suddenly said, "Hey, I'm
sorry if I sounded like I didn't believe you were sick. I can tell you
are. I just—"

"Don't believe it's because I'm away from Rigel," I said flatly. "I
know." I knew I should use this chance to argue my point, but I just
didn't have the energy.

"After everything Mum said, don't you get why nobody wants to
believe you two have a bond? It's not just me being jealous or
possessive or anything."

I didn't really care if that last part was true or not. "Yeah, I get
that she thinks it'll screw with their plans if word gets out about our
bond," I snapped, anger giving me another little energy boost. "So
the strategy is to deny it, cover it up, and keep Rigel as far away from
me as possible. Gee, maybe it would even work . . . if only it *wasn't* a
real bond and I wasn't getting sicker and sicker. How inconvenient
for you all."

"Being sick sure hasn't messed with your sarcasm." He sounded
more amused than upset, which just pissed me off more.

"Yeah, I'm contrary like that. I'm sure it would be easier for
everybody if I was just an obedient little Sovereign. Sorry about
that."

He snorted. "*Obedient* isn't a word I've ever heard used to describe
a Sovereign, so it's good you're not. We need a leader, not some
puppet who does whatever she's told. But a *real* leader has to put her
people first, ahead of whatever she'd rather do—or any attachments
she might have. Think about that."

Sean turned on his heel and left me standing in my driveway,
staring after him with my mouth open.

Even though I was ridiculously tired, I tossed and turned for a long time after going to bed. I was dying to sink into oblivion or, better yet, wonderful dreams about Rigel. Instead, Mrs. O'Gara's words, and Sean's, kept replaying in my mind.

It was overwhelming, you know, learning you survived. Bailerealta held a festival that went on for ten days. . . it has electrified the people to throw off the yoke of tyranny at last!

A real leader has to put her people first, ahead of whatever she'd rather do . . .

But I didn't *want* to lead! I never had. From the start, I'd told them they needed to find someone else, that I wasn't qualified to be their Sovereign, no matter what some stupid blood test said. I *couldn't* let them suck me into their cause. I wouldn't. Trying to be what they wanted could only lead to heartbreak for Rigel and me and disappointment for everyone else.

An hour later I finally fell into an exhausted sleep. But my dreams, when they came, weren't only of Rigel. Somehow, images of him were intermingled with those of Mrs. O'Gara's impassioned face, and Sean's . . . and a pink crystal palace.

"Marsha, you look terrible," Aunt Theresa greeted me when I dragged myself downstairs for breakfast the next morning. "Are you sick?"

All at once, the idea of forcing myself through another day of school without Rigel was unbearable. "Yeah. I must have caught that virus that's been going around. Maybe I should stay home."

She scrutinized me for a long moment and I held my breath. I'd never in my life stayed home sick from school, which probably helped—along with the fact that Rigel was still out of town. She finally nodded.

"Would you like me to make a doctor's appointment for you?"

I shook my head. What would a doctor find? "If it's that virus, it seems to last a few days, then go away on its own. If I'm not better by next week, I'll go to the doctor, okay?"

"All right." She was clearly relieved. Doctors were expensive. "I recommend you sleep as much as possible today. Then perhaps you can join us for Thanksgiving dinner tomorrow, though you'll need to keep your distance from everyone. I hope you haven't already infected the O'Garas."

"Me, too. And yeah, I'll sleep," I promised, beyond eager to do just that. My headache had reached epic proportions and my stomach was roiling. I forced down some tea and a few bites of toast, then headed back up to my room.

"Lots of fluids," Aunt Theresa called up the stairs. "Call the school office if you decide you need a doctor after all."

I was already back in bed when she left for work a few minutes later.

When I woke again, it was past one o'clock. Six extra hours of sleep had helped some. My headache was a little less pounding, my tummy not *quite* so gross and mind clearer. I pulled on my robe and made my way down to the kitchen to brew some more tea.

I nibbled a cookie while I sipped it, worried if I didn't eat anything at all I'd be too weak by Monday to properly appreciate Rigel when he got back. I just hoped I could keep it down. With my brain halfway working again, I glanced at the phone on the wall. Would Rigel's dad have given him back his cell by now?

No, I'd gotten him in trouble once. It would be safer to email, though I doubted he'd be allowed to read it. Still, it would make me feel better to try. I carried my tea and cookie to Uncle Louie's office and booted up the computer.

When I logged into my account and saw *two* emails from Rigel waiting, I felt totally stupid. *Why* hadn't I checked again after Monday's cell phone debacle? Okay, yeah, my brain had been wrapped in fog, but still. I clicked open the first email, dated Monday night, and started reading.

Hey, M, hope you get this! I know you don't check email much. Really wish I'd had time to tell you I might manage an email or two before my dad grabbed my phone.

Anyway, like I started to tell you earlier, all kinds of important folks have been dropping by. Sounds like some big meeting is happening later this week. Never realized before just how important Grandfather is. I'm trying to listen to everything I can, since a lot of the talk is about you, no big surprise. Hoping to hear something useful, since I bet they're not telling you everything, either. I'll clear my outgoing mailbox as soon as I send this, just to be safe. Ditto for future emails. If you write back, do the same thing, okay?

I'm kind of achy without you, but some of it's probably just in my head. We

*went longer than 10 days without touching back in September, so this should be
a piece of cake, right?*

*Hope you're keeping busy and your aunt's not dumping on you too much. Tell
the O'Garas I said hi. (Not really.) And take care of yourself, okay?*

Every last bit of my love,
Rigel

I read it over two or three times, smiling, then opened the second
email, dated yesterday.

*Hey, M, haven't heard back so don't know if you got my first email or not.
Really kicking myself for not talking faster yesterday! Since I deleted it right
after sending I'm not positive what I wrote. My memory seems fuzzy without you,
isn't that weird? Aching worse, but hey, we're down to less than a week now!
Can't wait to see you Monday!*

*Now it sounds like that big meeting won't be until after we leave. I think part
of the reason is they've noticed me paying attention when they talk. Should have
been sneakier, I guess. But it sounds like all kinds of stuff's going down on
Mars these days, faster than they expected. Maybe you're hearing about it from
the Os, too? Bet they're all kinds of excited. :-/*

*Since I don't feel much like going sightseeing without you, I've been looking
through Grandfather's books, digging into old laws and stuff, hoping I might find
something we can use. At least, when I can stay awake. It's nuts how tired I am!
My mom's acting a little worried but I think she's afraid to ask what's wrong.
Probably afraid I'll go off on another rant. I kinda did that already when they
acted like us being apart was no big deal.*

Email me back if you get this, okay? And stay safe and healthy—for me.

Love you amazingly,
Rigel

I didn't realize I was crying until I felt tears dripping off my chin.
Reading his words, I could almost hear his voice—that perfect voice
that did such wonderful things to me. I missed him so, so much. It
especially hurt to think he might be feeling as awful as I was. Even
though I wouldn't trade our bond for anything, I hated that it could
make Rigel sick. Ever.

Brushing a hand across my eyes, I started typing my reply. I played
down my symptoms, and also how much time I'd spent at the

O'Garas.' I told him I was researching from my end, too, since I was *positive* there must be some kind of loophole we could use. I apologized over and over for not checking my email sooner and promised I would every night from now on.

I wanted to compose a little poem or something that would make him smile but realized if I did, it would just kill him to delete it. My brain wasn't up to it right now, anyway. So I just said how terribly I missed him and that I was counting the seconds till he got back. I sent it and was hovering my finger over the delete key, thinking maybe I should read his messages just once more before erasing them, when the phone rang.

"Crap," I said aloud. The computer clock showed it was past three-thirty, so it was probably one of my friends. And my aunt would be home any time, unless it was one of her days for the florist's shop. I'd lost track.

With a silent apology to Rigel, I deleted his emails along with the record of my sent one and shut down the computer.

"Hello?" I answered on the fourth ring.

"Oh, you *are* there!" It was Bri. "I didn't wake you up or anything, did I? Are you feeling any better yet? Sean and Molly said you probably stayed home because you were sick. I'll bet that means you can't come to the game tonight, huh? That's such a bummer!"

"Hi, Bri," I said as soon as she took a breath. "You didn't wake me up, but yeah, I'm sick. Just some virus, I think. You guys have fun at the game and tell me all about it after, okay?" As if there was any chance she wouldn't do that anyway.

"We will. Oh! You want me to wish Sean a good game for you?"

"Um, yeah, sure."

"He'll appreciate that, I know. I'll give him a hug, too—from you, I mean. I hope you feel well enough to eat some turkey tomorrow."

"Thanks, Bri." I was glad she couldn't see my knowing smile. "Guess I'll see you Monday. Say hi to Deb for me, and you guys have a nice Thanksgiving."

I hung up, amused by how transparent Bri could be sometimes. But then I frowned.

Bri had all the signs of a major crush on Sean. I didn't think he would lead her on at all, but I didn't want to see her hurt. And if I tried to warn her off, she'd either think I was jealous or putting her down. Oh, well. Bri was always getting crushes, but they only lasted until the next crush-worthy guy caught her eye. She'd be fine.

Suddenly, the weariness I'd pushed back with all that extra sleep came crashing back full force and I sagged against the wall. It was all I could do to throw my cookie napkin away, rinse out my teacup and drag myself back upstairs to bed. I never heard Aunt Theresa come home, or Uncle Louie, either.

At one point I was dimly aware of my aunt opening my bedroom door and asking softly whether I wanted any dinner. I think I mumbled "no" because she left just as quietly and I didn't remember anything else until I woke up late the next morning.

Thanksgiving turned out both better and worse than I expected. I was there physically—I even set the table and stirred and basted a little, after disinfecting my hands under Aunt Theresa's watchful eye. But my brain was hovering between a mindless, miserable haze and wondering how Rigel's Thanksgiving in Washington was going.

The O'Garas—and Allister—showed up around three o'clock and everyone sat down to turkey and all the traditional fixings an hour later. I moved like a zombie to the dining room when my aunt called us in. Mrs. O'Gara, I noted dully, had taken over my traditional duty of carrying dishes from kitchen to table.

During the pre-dinner chit-chat in the living room I'd sat in a corner staring into space, only dimly aware of the concerned looks our guests kept shooting my way. I felt like I should reassure them somehow, but I couldn't remember why—or even if that would be a good thing. In fact, my head was pounding so loudly, I could hardly hear what anyone said. When Sean sat next to me at the table, I barely noticed.

"Quinn, would you like to say the blessing?" my aunt asked once everyone was seated. I was relieved, since she usually asked me, but couldn't bring myself to care whether it was out of concern I'd screw it up or out of politeness to our guests.

As they always did for holiday meals, my aunt and uncle clasped hands and extended their free ones, indicating that everyone should do the same. Sean gave me a slightly nervous look and held out his hand. Since it would have looked weird not to, I took it, bracing myself for that irritating tingle.

And had to stifle a gasp.

Because in addition to the usual zing, the instant I touched Sean's hand, the pounding in my head lessened noticeably, and by the time the brief prayer ended, my stomach had started to settle, as well. When Mr. O'Gara said "Amen," I had to fight a crazy urge to cling to Sean's hand.

Out of the corner of my eye, I could see him looking at me curiously, but I didn't dare look back. What was going on? Nobody's touch but Rigel's should be able to make me feel better! Should it?

The turkey, stuffing, and green bean casserole were passed around, and I automatically took some of everything as I struggled with this confusing new development. Could this be something the O'Garas had planned, some Martian technology they'd used to make Sean's touch mimic Rigel's? But why would they do that, if they didn't even believe in the *grael*? It didn't make any sense.

When I glanced down at my plate a few minutes later, I discovered I'd eaten almost everything on it. How had that happened? I hadn't had any appetite since Friday night. My head still ached but it was just a dull throb, instead of feeling like someone was trying to split it with a sledgehammer. And while I was still weak and tired, my mind was clearer than it had been all week.

Only because thinking clearly would be to my advantage, I was tempted to touch Sean's hand again, to see if this bizarre healing effect might go any further. But I resisted.

Because I wasn't sure I really wanted to know.

33

Rigel (RY-jel): *a blue supergiant star, approximately 860 light years from Earth*

"Stop it, Mom. I said I'm not hungry."

But, embarrassing as it is in front of all my Grandfather's Thanksgiving guests, my mom keeps her hands on my back, doing everything she can to "heal" me. I guess I appreciate that she wants to help, but her Healer powers obviously don't have any effect on my withdrawal-from-M symptoms. Why can't she just accept it?

"I can sense the pain in your head and joints, and your nausea." She sounds more frustrated than ever. "If I can sense it, I should be able to alleviate it."

"Leave the boy alone, Ariel," Grandfather says from the head of the table. "We've already discovered that some of the supposedly legendary aspects of *graell* bonding were recorded in the old scientific texts, even if they were never explained. As I recall, this is one of them."

One of the guests, a woman I don't know, stares at my grandfather. "Shim! Did you say *graell* bond? Whatever do you mean by that?"

"I'm sorry, Glynnis." He's using his soothing voice—one I've heard a lot the past few days. "I forgot you wouldn't have heard yet. It appears my grandson and Princess Emileia have formed a *graell* bond, politically awkward as that might be."

"Awkward is putting it mildly." Glynnis is staring at me now, like I might suddenly morph into a monster or dance on the table. "Why —how—was such a thing allowed?"

I want to tell her it's none of her business. Or that nothing could ever have stopped our bond once M and I met. But I'm afraid if I open my mouth again I might hurl, so I let my folks handle it.

"If you recall, Glynnis, Rigel is the one who finally located our

213

missing Sovereign, after several years of searching," my dad says. "As another adolescent *Echtran,* it was hoped he would be able to sense her more strongly, but no one had any way of predicting they could form such a bond."

Teague Sullivan, across the table from me, nods. "Aye, most of us never even suspected the *graell* was possible, outside of fairy tales, so how might the Stuarts be after preventing something no one even believes in these days?"

He seems like a nice enough guy. Pretty sympathetic compared to most of the dignitaries who've been in and out of Grandfather's house. But his accent always reminds me of the O'Garas, which keeps me from completely trusting him.

"I'm not sure I believe in it even now," puts in Kyna Nuallan, one of the Council members who was at our house when they verified who M was, back in September. She wasn't all that nice then, either. "I know you mean well, Shim, but—"

"You've heard my evidence, Kyna," Shim reminds her. "You all have, except for Glynnis, here. I'm afraid there is very little room for doubt."

I stare at my plate, wishing it was empty since the sight and smell of turkey and oyster dressing makes my stomach roil. It's not like I *planned* to screw with their politics.

Little Nara Gilroy speaks and I look up. "If poor Rigel is so affected by being separated from our Princess, does that mean she is suffering similarly?" She looks really worried and I remember Nara was the very first member of the Council to believe M was who they all hoped she was.

I swallow a couple of times, then force myself to reassure her—a little. "She'll be fine once we see each other on Monday. But yeah, she's probably not feeling so hot right now."

"Which will complicate things quite a lot, there's no denying," Teague says. "Unless a solution can be found?" That's clearly directed at my grandfather.

"Our researchers are exploring options."

My mind's fuzzing out again—it's been doing that a lot the past couple of days—but that word startles me alert. "Options? What kind of options?"

"It's too soon to say, so I won't worry you unnecessarily, Rigel."

He looks around the table with a smile that looks totally forced. "But enough of politics, everyone. This is supposed to be a social occasion, so I propose we treat it as such. Happy Thanksgiving!" He raises his glass and everyone else does the same, though most of them look as unsettled as I feel.

What possible "options" can he be talking about? Does he mean some kind of medical procedure to undo our bond? No effing way! And even if some Martian scientist *does* figure out how, I wouldn't let them. Neither would M. They have to know that. It must be something else, maybe something to make her feel better when we're apart.

I think about that and feel even sicker. Because if they can, shouldn't I *want* that? My brain starts to fog again and I decide there's no point worrying about it until I know more—not that I have enough energy to do much worrying right now, anyway.

After an awkward silence, Teague asks the others about their travel plans over the upcoming holidays. I decide I don't need to listen anymore and gratefully zone out. I wish I could just sleep, but that would be way rude, so I just stare into space and miss M with every cell in my body. Literally.

I don't wake up until noon the next day. My first thought is that I'm glad nobody made me get up. My second is that I feel even worse than yesterday. Even though my stomach is empty, I lurch to the bathroom for yet another round of dry heaving.

Afterward, I manage to drink a glass of water and brush my teeth before heading to the kitchen to see what's going on. Nobody's there but I find a note from my mother.

Rigel, we've all gone to the Natural History museum, and then we're meeting a few people for drinks. We should be home by five, certainly in time for dinner. We didn't want to wake you, but there's plenty of leftover turkey in the fridge.
—Love, Mom

Leftover turkey sounds disgusting, but I make myself some tea, remembering M said it made her feel a little better. Plus it makes me feel closer to her. Which reminds me I haven't checked my email since Wednesday night, and this is the perfect chance.

Sure enough, there's another note from M, sent just this morning, replying to my reply from late Wednesday night.

My poor Rigel,

I hate that you're feeling awful, too! This has been the longest week of my whole life and I SO can't wait until Monday! I hope your Thanksgiving was better than mine. The whole O'Gara family came to our house, including Allister. He totally creeps me out, it's like he's watching my every move, just waiting for me to screw up so he can be snarky about it later. Did I tell you he's giving me TESTS now on all the Martian stuff he's teaching me? There was kind of a weird thing that happened at dinner, too, but I'll tell you about it when you get home.

Oh, it was really sweet of you to offer to have your dad or Shim send me stuff on Martian history and politics, but the O'Garas gave me an e-reader, one of those scroll things, you've probably seen them, right? It's crammed with more history, genealogies and legal/political stuff than I'll be able to read in a lifetime. I've been too sleepy to read more than a tiny bit of it so far but I know I should, since I might find something that will help us—you and me, I mean. When you get home I'll be able to stay awake long enough to do that, for sure!

I love you totally and I'm counting every single minute until I can see you again! Please, please take good care of yourself and sleep lots—I think it helps a little.

Until Monday,
Your M

I read it over like ten times, wondering what "weird thing" could have happened that she didn't want to put in an e-mail. My first thought is it's something about Sean, since she wouldn't want to upset me, but it's stupid to jump to conclusions. Maybe she just felt too tired to type any more right then. This *is* a lot longer than the other e-mail she sent me, and way better written. She must have spent a long time proofing it. Pushing away my stupid suspicions, I slowly start typing, trying to make my e-mail as good as hers.

Over the next couple of days I get even more tired and achy and foggy-brained, to the point I don't want to do anything but sleep. My mom is seriously worried, I can tell, but when she asks what she can do to help me, all I can tell her is to get me back to Jewel. Back to M.

Like I've been saying all along.

I think it's sometime Saturday afternoon, though at this point I'm not positive, when I hear a bunch of voices downstairs on my way back from the bathroom. For a few seconds I just stand at the top of the steps, blinking, trying to remember why I should care about this.

Oh. Right. I told M I'd try to find out what they're talking about, in case it can help us later. Squinting against my jackhammer headache, I creep halfway down the stairs, every step a ridiculous amount of effort. So much for me being some kind of super athlete.

"—claims she seemed noticeably better Thursday evening," are the first words I hear clearly. It sounds like Teague's voice. "He's saying it's due to his nephew being near her, though why he'd think that if he doesn't believe in the *graell* in the first place, I'm not clear."

Now Kyna says, "Whatever the cause, it appears the Sovereign may not be as strongly affected as Rigel, which is all to the good. For our people, I mean, Ariel. Of course we're concerned about your son, as well."

"As long as we can be certain Allister is not merely reporting what he wishes to be true rather than the Sovereign's actual condition." It's my grandfather talking now. "He has shown himself capable of, shall we say, self-deception on this matter already."

"Has he seen her again since Thursday night?" Nara's voice, sounding worried but hopeful. "Does she continue to improve?"

I sneak down another two stairs, anxious to hear the answer.

"No," Teague says. I wince. "He said his sister called to ask about her this morning and was told she was feeling worse again, and sleeping. I suggested Lili visit her tonight or tomorrow, if possible, to give a firsthand account of her condition."

"Not Allister himself?" A male voice I don't recognize.

"Ah, it seems Allister hasn't exactly endeared himself to our Princess." Teague sounds almost amused, which pisses me off since they're talking about M being so sick. "Those of you who know him can probably imagine why."

"No need for imagination," my mom snaps. That almost gets a smile out of me. "Allister has behaved abominably to Emileia as well as to Rigel. He seems to think he has authority over her, rather than the other way around."

There's some indistinct murmuring in response, then I hear

footsteps approaching from below. Crap.

I pull myself back up the stairs as quietly as I can, then tiptoe into my little room and ease the door shut. Back in bed, I stare at the ceiling and ponder what I just heard.

So Allister thinks Sean can make M feel better when I'm not around? I snort. He wishes! Both of them wish! They'll see what better is when I get back—they all will. That thought calms me down enough that I start to drift off again . . . until another thought snaps my eyes back open.

M said in her e-mail that something weird happened at Thanksgiving dinner. Could that be it, that Sean made her feel better? Because she sure as hell wouldn't tell me *that* in an e-mail, knowing how crappy I already feel.

I feel another bout of dry heaves coming on.

When we finally head home Sunday, I'm so weak my dad won't even let me carry my own backpack through the airport. I sleep the whole way on the plane, waking up just enough to stumble to the car when we get to Indianapolis, then fall asleep again as soon as my dad starts driving.

Next thing I know, my parents are carrying the suitcases into our house. Dad makes two trips rather than ask me to help and I don't even argue. All I want is my bed. My mom seems sad, but I figure it's because I'm so sick. And then I'm asleep again.

Either I automatically set my alarm or one of my parents did, because it goes off at the regular time for school the next morning. I groan, but then I remember it's finally Monday, the day I'll see M again, and I leap out of bed.

And collapse in a heap on the floor.

Okay, maybe leaping was a bad idea, but I'm still super excited at the prospect of seeing M. Touching M. Talking to M. I drag myself upright and stagger into the bathroom to brush my teeth.

"Rigel! What are you doing up so early?" My mom sounds shocked when I appear in the kitchen ten minutes later.

"School," I say. Isn't that perfectly obvious?

"But . . . you're sick! I've already called the two most experienced Healers in the Midwest, and they'll be here this afternoon to see what they can do for you. Why don't you go back to bed until then?"

I stare at her. "Seriously? No way. Don't you get it, Mom? What I need is M. She's the only one who can make me better. I thought you and Dad got that."

She calls my dad into the kitchen and I have to say it again, which sucks since I'm still feeling like crap and don't really have the energy for this right now. Then the two of them do that telepathy thing for a long time—two or three minutes—and finally nod at each other.

"I'll take you to school," my dad says, "but if you're not feeling better by lunchtime, I want you to go to the nurse's office and I'll come back and get you. Your mother has patients this morning, but she'll be home this afternoon, before Fiona and Brody get here."

The Healers, I assume. "I'll feel a *lot* better by lunch," I promise. "Unless M's aunt doesn't let *her* come to school. Because she's been sick, too. Probably," I add, realizing too late that they don't know we've been emailing each other and I wasn't supposed to have heard those conversations between the bigwigs. Stupid fuzzy brain.

But it will all be better as soon as I see M.

"I'm ready," I tell my dad. "Let's go."

34

Miochan (mee-OH-kan): *healing; curing; a major Martian* fine

Even though I hadn't been able to stay awake for more than a few minutes at a time all weekend, when my alarm went off Monday morning I had *no* desire to go back to sleep. Finally, *finally*, I was going to see Rigel again! School couldn't happen soon enough.

But first I'd have to convince Aunt Theresa I was well enough to go.

The "cure" from Sean's touch at Thanksgiving was only temporary, wearing off before the O'Garas left that evening. Maybe I could have gotten another boost if I'd touched him again, but I didn't. It felt too much like betraying Rigel . . . and using Sean.

Even when the O'Garas came by after church yesterday (I stayed home, with Aunt Theresa's reluctant blessing), I was careful not to let Sean touch me. They acted so worried, though, I said I was sure I'd feel better within twenty-four hours. I could tell they didn't believe me.

I painfully peeled myself out of bed and stumbled into the bathroom to brush my teeth and put on way more makeup than usual, hoping it would make me look healthier than I felt. Squinting critically into the mirror, I added more blush, then went back to my room to put on a bright pink sweater on the theory it would impart some perkiness.

"Good morning," I greeted my aunt with all the cheerfulness I could muster when I reached the kitchen.

She frowned at me for a long moment, then smiled slightly. "You must be feeling better."

"I am!" I assured her, and proceeded to pour myself a big glass of orange juice and a bowl of cereal. I sat at the table and pretended to eat while she puttered around, finishing her coffee. When she left the kitchen a moment later to get her tote bag for school, I quickly dumped the cereal in the trash and half the orange juice down the sink and sat back down before she came back.

"I'm glad to see you have your appetite back," she said, glancing approvingly at my empty cereal bowl. "Are you up to taking the bus, or would you like me to drive you this morning?"

Trying not to let my relief show—or my surprise, since the elementary school was in the opposite direction from the high school —I smiled. "I'll be fine on the bus, but thanks, Aunt Theresa." I wasn't sure I could keep up the healthy act all the way to school, and did *not* want her changing her mind about letting me go.

Luckily, she left ten minutes before I did, so she didn't see me shuffle and wobble my way to the bus stop. Both of the O'Garas did, though.

"You're not seriously going to school today, M!" Molly exclaimed before I even reached them. "You're so sick!"

Sean was also frowning in obvious concern. "Yesterday you were practically at death's door and you still look awful—though I see you tried to hide it with makeup."

I was surprised he noticed. Exhausted from the effort of walking half a block, I just said, "I won't get better until I see Rigel again, so I *have* to go to school."

Molly gave a sigh that sounded sympathetically romantic (though it might have just been exasperated) but Sean glowered even more fiercely.

"That's ridiculous. Mum said Dr. Stuart is bringing in some top-notch Healer friends of hers today, and they'll take care of you while they're here. They'll probably want to see you first, in fact, so you should go back home."

"Healers?"

"Yeah. Stuart's acting sick, too, I guess."

"It's not an act," I ground out, sudden panic making me feel even sicker. What if this meant Rigel wouldn't be at school today after all? I knew he'd come if he possibly could, though, and no way was I giving up my only chance to see him if he did. "If I'm not . . . not better by the end of the day"—I paused for breath—"your precious Healers can see me then."

Which was exactly what Rigel would have told his mother. I

hoped.

"You're kidding, right?" Sean argued. "You look like you're about to fall down." He reached for me, maybe just to steady me, but I stepped away. Especially now, I didn't want Sean's touch doing anything to detract from my reunion with Rigel. Immediately, he dropped his hand. "Sorry. It's just . . . we're all worried about you, M."

An odd, unfocused sense of guilt made me snappish. "About me? Or about losing . . . your precious Sovereign?"

"Both," he snapped back.

Before I could pull a good retort from my sluggish brain, the bus came around the corner, along with the other two kids from our stop, at a jog. Climbing onto the bus was harder than I expected but after the way I'd just acted, I didn't dare ask for help.

I did, however, take the very first empty seat instead of heading toward the back of the bus, like I usually did. The freshman girl I sat next to gave me a curious look but didn't say anything. Neither did I.

Bri and Deb glanced questioningly at me when they got on at their stop, too, but since there weren't any empty seats near me, all we exchanged was a quick "Hi." I had to fight to stay awake for the rest of the bus ride, but I managed it.

We finally pulled up in front of the school and there, waiting for me on one of the benches in front of the school, was Rigel! He was shockingly thin and pale, and he swayed when he stood up, but he was still the most glorious sight in the world. I couldn't get off the bus fast enough. (Literally, since even though I was hurrying, I was moving like I was about ninety years old.)

By the time I reached him, everyone else on the bus had passed me and gone into the building, Bri and Deb with a backward glance or two. Just as well, since non-Martian witnesses to this reunion might be a bad idea. Not surprisingly, Sean and Molly didn't go in, but lingered, off to one side. I followed Rigel's glance and saw Sean looking skeptical, Molly eager, both of them curious.

But then, I only had eyes for Rigel.

"You're here," I said as I tottered forward, which was *so* not what I'd planned as my first words to him.

"You, too," he said, taking a few steps toward me with obvious effort. "I was afraid you'd—"

But then I propelled myself the last few feet and no more words were necessary. We clasped hands and gasped in unison. My headache was gone, *poof*, as if it had never been. Then Rigel kissed me and it was like all the power of the sun was pouring into me. It was the most wonderful, healing feeling I'd ever experienced: fireworks to someone who'd been blind and a hot bath to someone who'd been freezing, all at the same time. I could feel myself getting stronger, healthier, with every fraction of a second that passed.

It was Sean's voice that finally penetrated. "C'mon, you two, or we'll have to tell our mum about this."

I turned to face him, grinning, as Rigel threw an arm around my shoulders. "Go ahead," I said. "I *want* you to tell her—tell them all! Tell them how I looked on the bus. *And* tell them how I look now." Because I was sure I must be glowing, I felt so full of happiness and health.

Sean's jaw was clenched, angry, but he also looked stunned—and a little sad. Molly, on the other hand, was smiling, romantic stars in her eyes.

"That was beautiful," she whispered now. "I'm sorry I didn't believe you sooner, M."

"Oh, give over," Sean snapped at her.

Rigel looked out at the parking lot and gave a thumbs up and I turned to see his father's car pull away. He must have been watching our reunion, too. Good.

Sean frowned. "This doesn't change anything, you know. M is still grounded and you're still supposed to stay away from each other. Her aunt—"

"Sean!" Molly exclaimed. "How can you say that, after—" The warning bell rang, interrupting her.

Sean just glowered at her, then at Rigel and me. "I didn't make the rules," he muttered. "C'mon, we'd all better get to class."

Rigel and I grinned at each other—then shrugged. School just seemed so . . . *mundane* after the miracle that had just occurred. Really, what was the point?

Rigel, clearly picking up my thoughts, gave a little nod. "Wanna ditch?" he murmured too softly for Sean to hear.

"Absolutely. We can—"

"What are all of you students still doing out here?" It was Mr.

Pedersen, the vice principal, or, as half the school called him behind his back, The Warden. "Didn't you hear the warning bell? Oh, it's you, Rigel, Sean." He softened—star athletes got extra slack—but he didn't leave. "I'm sure none of you want to be late to class. You have —" He glanced at his watch. "—three minutes to get to first period. I suggest you hurry."

Since there was no ditching under The Warden's watchful eye, we followed Sean and Molly into the school—at four times the speed I'd managed when I got off the bus. I was tempted to see if I could fly, I felt that good.

"So do I," Rigel whispered, giving my hand a squeeze as we hurried to Geometry together. "I love you so much, M," he whispered then, and I could feel the truth of the emotion right through his fingers, still entwined with mine.

"Oh, Rigel, me, too. I've missed you more than I ever thought I could miss anything. Let's please not ever be apart again, okay?"

"Fine by me." He was grinning ear to ear, but then glanced at Sean, up ahead, and his grin faded slightly. "Though our folks—and certain other people—might have something to say about that."

I couldn't believe how incredibly, magically better I felt than I had just ten minutes earlier—like night had turned to day, rain to sunshine. My mind was also clearer than it had been in over a week, forcing me to realize he was right. Not that I cared at this exact moment.

"Well, we're together now. And it's awesome. *You're* awesome," I told him.

He laughed, and it was the most beautiful sound I'd ever heard. "You're pretty amazingly awesome yourself. In fact, I think you just saved my life."

"Ditto." That's sure what it felt like—like I'd been at death's door and now was bursting with health. I couldn't stop grinning, either.

I'd forgotten about Ms. Harrigan until we entered the classroom and the "student teacher" frowned at our still-clasped hands. We reluctantly released each other, but exchanged a last, secret smile as we headed to our seats. Even a Martian spy who wanted to keep us apart wasn't enough to spoil my fabulous mood.

Class started immediately, but all I could think about was Rigel and how wonderful it was just having him in the room. His vibe felt stronger to me than I could ever remember. Still, I was startled to suddenly hear his voice in my head.

I'm picking up your thoughts so well today! Can you hear mine if you try?

Involuntarily, I glanced at him to see him watching me with a questioning look. I gave him a tiny nod, then thought back, *I can! This is awesome! If we can do this, it won't matter if they don't let us talk in school.* Then, mainly to test this new, wonderfully enhanced ability, I asked, *Did your folks try to keep you home today, like my aunt did? Did you hear about these Healers that are coming to town?*

Yeah, my mom was all about that this morning. Guess we don't need them now, huh? His triumph and amusement came through with the words and I had to suppress a grin that the teacher—and especially Ms. Harrigan—might notice.

I sure don't. I feel fantastic! I love you, Rigel.

We continued "talking" like that through the whole period—off and on, since occasionally we did have to pay a *little* bit of attention to the teacher. It was wonderful. It also seemed to get easier and easier, the more we communicated this way. By the time the bell rang, we'd nearly caught each other up on our ten day separation, though we'd done some of that in emails already.

The one thing I didn't tell him about was the weird effect Sean's touch had on me at Thanksgiving dinner. I would eventually, of course, but for now I didn't want to do anything to spoil Rigel's—or my—euphoria.

When Molly met us in the hall on the way to second period, I gave Rigel's hand a quick squeeze and thought, *Now it won't be so hard to play by the stupid rules. See you in English.*

Can't wait. Love you, M! With a half-wink, Rigel headed off to his Spanish class and I walked with Molly most of the way to Computer Apps.

"I still can't believe how much better you look," she said wonderingly.

I gave her a huge smile that made her blink. "*So* much better. Didn't I tell you I would? Do you really, truly believe me now?"

"I do. I have to. I just didn't expect . . . But it's great. I think."

I could understand why she'd feel conflicted, between her loyalty to Sean and all the political stuff her parents kept pushing, but I wasn't conflicted at all. "It *is* great. See you at lunch!"

Once or twice during second period, I could have sworn I heard a faint echo of Rigel's thoughts and wondered if he was trying to think at me from a distance. I thought back, *I hear you, I think,* the second time, but didn't get anything after that. I'd ask him next period if I'd imagined it.

I hadn't.

Yeah, I wanted to test the limits, he admitted once English class started —with us again paired with different partners on opposite sides of the room. *Wonder if we can increase our range with practice?*

Worth a try, I thought back. How awesome would it be if we got to a point where we could communicate from different rooms . . . or from across town, even?

Let's test it at lunch, he suggested. *Since you're probably still grounded?*

I think so. Aunt Theresa hadn't actually mentioned it since I got sick, but with Rigel back in town, she probably would. Now that I was better, though, I was definitely going to try that "persuasion" thing on her if she tried to lay down more rules.

We "chatted" in Science, too, which was easy, since Rigel sat right behind me. The challenge there was trying to avoid the eye of our new exogeology expert, who was totally another Martian.

Not only was Mr. Gilliland impossibly young and hot for a teacher, but he kept staring at me, acting almost as starstruck at seeing the Sovereign for the first time as the *Echtran* tourists who visited Jewel. It was a huge relief when the bell finally rang for lunch. I headed for the door quickly, glad that our new "expert" was apparently too in awe to try to talk to me—yet.

Sean intercepted me before I'd gone three steps down the hall— how did he do that, anyway?—and Rigel immediately dropped back.

"I take it you're still feeling better?" he asked, dropping into step beside me as I headed for the lunchroom. "Or are you just putting on a good show?"

Fully aware that Rigel could hear every word with both his ears and his mind, I couldn't suppress a big grin. "I feel fabulous! Better than I did *before* Rigel went away."

He frowned down at me, clearly skeptical. "So, on the bus—"

"You can't think I was faking. I told you what would make me better, you just didn't want to believe it. And now you know: when you keep Rigel and me apart, you're literally making me sick. Are you really okay with that?"

Sean glanced over his shoulder at Rigel, now walking a dozen paces behind us, then back at me, clearly conflicted. "You know I don't want you sick," he whispered—as if that would keep Rigel from hearing. "I'd *never* want that for . . . for lots of reasons."

I figured he was referring to what he'd confessed about his lifelong fixation on me . . . something else I'd never mentioned to Rigel. I quickly diverted my thoughts before Rigel could pick up on them.

"Then help me convince everyone else that Rigel and I need to be together. Because that's the *only* way I'll stay healthy, Sean."

He didn't say anything else before we reached the cafeteria, but I could see he was thinking hard—and not liking where those thoughts were leading.

Rigel sat in the far corner of the lunchroom—part of his experiment, I assumed, though several football players joined him as soon as he sat down.

Can you hear me now? he thought at me as soon as I joined our usual table with Bri, Deb and the O'Garas.

Loud and clear, I thought back. We grinned at each other across the thirty yards or more separating us. This was *way* easier than before our separation and reunion. Cool.

"You still feel okay, M?" Molly asked, pulling me back to the group at *this* table. Despite her earlier words, she still looked slightly surprised.

"Yep, I feel great—now."

She and her brother exchanged worried glances but didn't question me further.

Bri had gone out of town for Thanksgiving, and Deb's grandparents and aunts and uncles had been visiting, so neither of them knew how sick I'd been. Which meant they didn't find anything remarkable about me being well today. But Bri was frowning anyway.

"You and Rigel aren't fighting again, are you?"

"Again? We never—um, no. We're not fighting."

"Then why is he sitting way over there?"

"My aunt—" I began, but Bri waved that away with one hand.

"Like she'd know whether or not you guys sit together at lunch? It's not like anyone here would actually *tell* her."

I looked pointedly at Sean, then Molly. Sean just grinned, admitting nothing, but Molly had the grace to drop her eyes.

"Are you kidding? She knows almost all of the teachers," I pointed out after an almost-awkward pause. "If we sit together at lunch it would totally get back to her and she'd make my grounding even worse."

Bri didn't look convinced, but Deb backed me up. "They were talking to each other in Geometry this morning, and it sure didn't look like they were fighting."

Of course that made Sean scowl, which made me wonder what he'd tell his mom, and what she'd tell Aunt Theresa.

Can they do anything worse to us than the last ten days? came Rigel's thought.

I glanced over at him and noticed that Ms. Harrigan was patrolling the cafeteria today, eerily reminiscent of "Mr. Smith" back in October. She couldn't possibly suspect that we were communicating right now, but I still felt a little shiver of apprehension . . . or maybe premonition.

I sure hope not, I sent back.

35

naesc geaniteach (nesh gan-it-EEK) *genetic affinity*

I'd been in the house maybe five minutes that afternoon when the phone rang. Hoping it might be Rigel—maybe wanting to test the range of our new, improved telepathy—I answered eagerly. "Hello?" It was Mrs. O'Gara.

"M, dear, if you're well enough, can you come to our house? Sean and Molly tell me you're feeling much better today."

"Um, I should probably ask my aunt—" I began, feeling strangely reluctant.

"I'm sure she won't mind," she said firmly. "She's said you can come here any time. Just leave her a note saying where you are, so she won't worry if she gets home before you do."

Her voice held a hint of command I'd never heard directed at me before, but I couldn't think of a reason to refuse. "Oh. Uh, sure. I'll be over in a few minutes."

I hung up, frowning. Every instinct told me something strange was going on. Another new development on Mars? Guess I'd find out when I got there.

It only took me a minute to drop my backpack in my bedroom and use the bathroom. Then, curiosity overcoming reluctance, I headed over to the O'Garas' house. Mr. O opened to my knock.

"Thank you for coming, Excellency. Nearly everyone is here already."

"Everyone?" I echoed. His use of my title increased my foreboding, but he was already heading into the living room. After a second's hesitation, I followed.

Not to my surprise, Allister was there, along with Sean, Molly and Mrs. O'Gara. And two others, a man and a woman I didn't recognize.

"M, dear," Mrs. O said, "this is Brody and this is Fiona, two of our most accomplished Healers, down from Chicago. We told them how ill you've been this past week, and they agreed you should be

229

seen. In fact, we came by your house earlier today and were surprised to find no one home. I understand you actually went to school today?"

I nodded, regarding the pair dubiously. "I had to. I mean, I feel fine now. Are . . . are you the Healers who are friends of Dr. Stuart's? I thought you were coming to Jewel to see Rigel."

"Yes, although Ariel tells us he is feeling much better, as well," the woman, Fiona, said.

"Um, did the O'Garas or Dr. Stuart explain *why* Rigel and I are both better today?"

Brody frowned as he replied, "Ariel Stuart mentioned something about a bond, but she was rather vague." That surprised me. Why wouldn't she just tell them the truth? Politics? "With your permission, Excellency, we would like to perform a medical scan to document what appears to be a rather remarkable recovery."

"Er, sure. But what about Rigel? Aren't you going to examine him, too?"

"We are indeed. The Stuarts should be here soon."

Even as he spoke, I heard a car door slam outside and a moment later Mr. O'Gara ushered Rigel and his parents into the room.

To the best of my knowledge, it was the first time Rigel had ever been in this house. It gave me a weird feeling, sort of like when his parents had come to my house for the first time, the night we got grounded. Did they know the O'Garas were in a shabby little house like mine, so different from their big, modernized farmhouse out in the country?

Weirdly, I felt almost defensive on the O'Garas' behalf, even while I wanted nothing more than to run to Rigel and wrap my arms around him. It was like two separate pieces of my world were colliding and I was caught between them. What I felt wasn't quite guilt—more like being pulled in two directions by conflicting loyalties. Except my loyalties *weren't* conflicted, of course. They were completely with Rigel. Always.

You okay? he sent, even as I thought that.

I started to nod, then decided we maybe shouldn't tip everyone off to our new ability just yet. *Fine. Just not sure what's going on. Do you know?* He didn't.

"Thank you for coming." Allister's stiffness reminded me that Dr.

Stuart had thrown him out of their house after Rigel's party. Had they seen each other since?

Dr. Stuart was apparently remembering that, too, judging by the disapproving look she gave Allister before addressing the Healers directly.

"I appreciate you coming to Jewel on such short notice to examine my son—and Princess Emileia, of course—though it now appears they've recovered to a remarkable degree."

"Which in itself is worthy of study, both in my opinion and in that of the Council," Fiona said with a smile. "We by no means consider this a wasted trip."

Brody nodded his agreement and I felt my spirits, already buoyed by having Rigel in the same room, rise even higher. This was our chance to prove to everyone, once and for all, that our *graell* bond was absolutely real. Then they'd *have* to let us spend more time together.

Picking up on my elation, Rigel thought to me, *Yes! Perfect. Bet old Allister didn't count on that.* It took all my self control not to nod this time, but I looked at him and grinned.

Meanwhile, his mother was saying, "I definitely agree that this unprecedented sickness and near-instantaneous recovery our Sovereign and Rigel have experienced should be independently verified."

"Independently?" Allister echoed. "By members of your *fine*, who also happen to be your personal friends?"

"Who would you suggest evaluate the recent dramatic changes in both Rigel's and Emileia's health, Allister, if not Healers?" Dr. Stuart asked mildly. "The Royal *fine* is as well represented in this room as ours."

"She's right, Allister," Mr. O'Gara said, with a frown for his brother-in-law. "It's in the interests of all our people that we get to the heart of this matter as quickly as possible. I, for one, am willing to accept the professional opinions of the Healers present, once they have examined the evidence."

Allister gave a terse nod and retired to a chair on the far side of the room, though he kept shooting dark looks at Rigel—and, occasionally, at me. Clearly, he still thought we were either making the whole thing up, or that we'd chosen to bond just to piss him off.

I tried not to look at him, afraid I might smirk once our claim was proven. Which it would be.

"Now, Rigel," Fiona began, "your mother tells us you have been extremely ill this past week, and we were able to verify that with several other *Echtrans* who visited Shim during that time. Can you describe your symptoms?"

Though he looked a little nervous—and no wonder, since he was essentially in the lion's den—Rigel answered readily, describing the headaches, nausea, fatigue and mental fuzziness I was all too familiar with by now. As he spoke, the two Healers nodded, making notes on little electronic tablets.

"Would you mind if we took a hair follicle or two for analysis?" was Brody's next, unexpected request.

"Um, sure," Rigel said, immediately plucking a few dark hairs from his scalp and handing them to the Healer.

Fiona turned to Dr. Stuart. "Ariel, did you bring any intact hairs or other cells of your son's from while he was ill, as we suggested?"

Rigel's mother nodded, pulling a tiny plastic bag from her purse. "I took these from his comb before he got home from school."

"Thank you. Excellency? If I might ask you some questions as well?"

I went through the same interrogation and gave nearly identical answers: from Friday afternoon on, I'd felt progressively worse—as the O'Garas and Allister could all verify—but after reuniting with Rigel today at school, I'd become perfectly well within minutes. I was tempted to mention our new, improved telepathy thing, but again thought better of it. For now. Just in case.

I also didn't mention the weirdness of Thanksgiving when Sean's touch had temporarily restored my appetite. In fact, I shut that bit out of my thoughts entirely in case Rigel was "listening." I'd much rather tell him privately, since I was sure he wouldn't like it.

"Finally," Fiona said, "and I hesitate to ask, Excellency, but might we have a hair follicle of yours?"

Nodding—this was nowhere as scary as that blood test the Council had insisted on back in September—I pulled a couple of light brown hairs from the side of my head and handed them to her.

Anticipating her next question, I said, "I can get some from this morning or yesterday from my brush at home, too."

"Ah, no need, Princess." Mrs. O'Gara held up a small envelope. "When we visited yesterday, I took the liberty . . . that is, I thought that a cellular analysis might help in diagnosing whatever illness you had, so I pulled a few hairs from the brush on your dresser."

"Oh." I felt strangely violated, even if it was just old hair from my hairbrush. I mean, why not just ask me? Of course, I'd been pretty out of it at the time . . . "Um, that's fine. Great." I tried hard not to be weirded out, since I believed she did care—about me, personally, and especially about me as a potential benefit to Mars.

Speaking quietly with each other, and occasionally with Dr. Stuart, the Healers fed the hairs into a small electronic device that had a pop-up holographic screen sort of like the omni's, but with a much more complicated display than anything Sean had shown me.

"Interesting," Brody murmured at one point. "See how the peptides have changed? I'm guessing the boy's will show something similar. And look at the matches along these two DNA strands, between—" Eyebrows raised, he glanced at Rigel, then at me.

"Yes, there does appear to be a genetic affinity. Very interesting," Fiona agreed.

Suddenly, Sean spoke for the first time since I'd arrived. "Um, do you think you could take a look at one of my hairs, too?" He plucked one and held it out. "Because I seemed to have a healing effect on her, too."

Everyone stared at him, though I noticed neither Allister nor the O'Garas looked surprised. In fact, Allister was nodding. Everyone else was clearly startled, especially me. Sean hadn't given any hint—

"At Thanksgiving," he clarified. "After we held hands to say grace, she looked a lot better and . . . and ate more than I'd seen her eat all week up till then."

So he *had* noticed. I was starting to realize Sean didn't miss much, when it came to me.

Fiona turned to me. "Excellency, is this true?"

Trapped, I bit my lip, hesitating. "Not exactly." Then I saw Mrs. O'Gara watching me carefully and remembered her lie-detector talent. Crap. "Well, sort of, I guess. I did feel a *little* better for an hour or two. Not back to normal at all, but . . . better. It wore off really quickly, though. Touching Rigel this morning made me one hundred per cent healthy instantly. And I still am. Healthy, I mean."

"Fascinating," Brody said, finally taking the short strand of copper hair Sean was still proffering.

He fed that into the device, too, and more muttering ensued. Dr. and Mr. Stuart seemed tense, though I didn't see why. They'd left me so completely alone since finding out about Sean and the Consort thing, I'd assumed they'd bought into the political necessity of keeping Rigel and me apart.

But these Healers were proving we *had* to be together to stay healthy. Were they upset because that would force people to rethink their precious Martian traditions? I'd assumed they'd be relieved to have proof Rigel and I really were bonded, but it didn't look that way. I swallowed the little lump in my throat, remembering how nice Dr. Stuart had been to me before the O'Garas came along. Motherly, even. I missed that.

"Well?" Allister asked from across the room. He looked tense, too, but that didn't surprise me at all. He'd been hostile about Rigel and me from the beginning.

The two Healers exchanged a glance, then turned toward him.

"Particularly considering this evidence from the O'Gara lad, I believe what you have suggested may be possible," Fiona told him, "though we won't know for certain until we perform a few *in vitro* experiments."

Rigel and I exchanged a confused glance. "What may be possible?" he asked suspiciously.

Allister's mouth twisted unpleasantly. "We can't have our Sovereign incapacitated by whatever genetic anomaly you seem to have produced in her. I, or rather the Council, has asked our Healers to find a solution to that problem." Then, to the Stuarts, "As soon as they do, the original plan can proceed as scheduled."

Mr. Stuart looked angry but it was his wife who spoke first. "We don't know enough to risk that yet. The whole idea is strictly theoretical at this point. I won't risk my son's life—or Princess Emileia's—on a theory."

"Of course not." Allister tried to speak soothingly, but he really sucked at that. "The Council doesn't expect your family to relocate until Christmas, by which time our Healers will surely have developed a cure and tested it—on both of them."

"Relocate?" I gasped. "What are you talking about?" Then, silently to Rigel, *Did you know about this?*

He shook his head fiercely, then, before it could be obvious it was in answer to me, he said, "No. I can't leave M. I won't. She needs me now more than ever. All these factions, people trying to—"

"Rigel," his father said warningly.

Allister positively smirked. "Just because you helped to protect the Sovereign against Faxon's assassins once doesn't mean you have been appointed her personal bodyguard, boy. We have people specially trained to fill that role. Not that she's in any danger at the moment, to the best of our knowledge—except from you."

Dr. Stuart looked seriously pissed. "We have to take more than Emileia's *physical* safety and well-being into account, Allister. It is no exaggeration to say that she—and Rigel—will suffer enormously if they are permanently separated, no matter what *solution* might be achieved medically."

Her husband nodded. "She's right. When we tentatively agreed to leave Jewel, it was before we'd seen the result of Rigel and the Princess being separated, then reunited. Now that we have—"

Mr. O'Gara interrupted him, his voice quiet and reasonable-sounding. "Van, Ariel, will you really endanger the future of our people—all our people—for the sake of a teen romance? No one expects you to leave before some treatment can be found for the physical symptoms, but you both know how critical appearances are right now. Loyalties are balanced on a knife's edge. Emileia *must* be seen as our future Sovereign, with all that entails."

There was a long, tense silence. I could tell the Stuarts were communicating and realized belatedly that Rigel and I do the same. I'd been so happy, so sure—

They can't really do this, can they? I thought at him, panicked. *There's no such thing as an . . . an antidote to the* graell, *is there?*

Sounds like they plan to create one if they can. The emotion that came through with his thought was both grim and scared, though I could tell he was fighting the fear. I tried to do the same, so I could think more clearly.

Dr. Stuart gave her husband a quick nod, then came over and surprised me with a hug. It clearly surprised everyone else, too; I saw various degrees of outrage on the faces around me, especially Allister's. I immediately hugged her back to demonstrate that I didn't mind a bit. In fact, it was exactly what I needed right then.

"I'm so sorry, M," she whispered as she embraced me. Her voice caught and I wondered if she was holding back tears. "We really thought— Please believe that the last thing we ever wanted was to hurt you."

It was incredibly reassuring to know they still cared about me. "I know. And . . . you can't leave. Really. I . . . I won't allow it." I could feel tears threatening, too, until sudden anger pushed back my fear.

I turned to the others. "Did you hear me? I won't *let* you send them away."

"The decision will be theirs, of course," Mr. O'Gara said. "But I'll be surprised if they choose to defy the will of the Council in this matter."

"I'm sorry," Dr. Stuart repeated, releasing me with obvious reluctance. "If there's any way—"

"Ariel, I think we should go." Mr. Stuart's voice held a note of warning. "Rigel, you, too. You'll still see each other in school these next few weeks. Beyond that, well, it will depend on what the Healers come up with, and on the Council. I'm sorry, too, M." I could tell he meant it.

But it didn't matter, because they were leaving. Leaving the O'Garas' house and, in just a few short weeks, leaving Jewel completely.

Unless I could stop them.

36

dilsacht (DIL-sok): *loyalty; allegiance*

I'll fix this somehow, I thought desperately to Rigel as his parents
herded him toward the door. *They can't do this!*

He looked back at me, frustration as clear on his face as it was in
his thoughts. *Be careful, M. I can't lose you. Not now!* Then, a little more
calmly—but I could tell he was forcing the calm, for my sake—
Tomorrow. We'll figure something out tomorrow.

I resisted the urge to nod, glad we'd kept *this* part of our bond
secret. *Tomorrow,* I thought back. Then, aloud, for everyone else's
benefit, "I'll see you at school, Rigel. And I'll try to have good news."

He grimaced, a mockery of a smile, and then they were gone.
Immediately, I turned to face the others.

"You can't do this. You can't *make* them move away, just like that,
just because of me. Dr. Stuart has a job here, she has patients. Rigel
has school." I didn't try to hide my anguish—or my anger.

Mrs. O'Gara came forward, her expression sympathetic. "M, dear,
I'm sorry it has come to this, and even more sorry you're so upset
about it. But surely you can see that it is necessary?"

"No! I don't see that it's necessary at all! What's the point? To trick
all these new Martian observers into thinking Sean and I are dating?
So they'll tell everyone I'm forming those *alliances* you care so much
about?" I was practically shouting but I didn't care.

I glared around at everybody in the room. Molly was staring at the
floor, her chin trembling like she was holding back tears. Sean looked
upset, too, and also wouldn't meet my eye. The two Healers were
quietly packing up their equipment, like they couldn't escape quickly
enough. Mr. O'Gara looked serious but determined and Allister—
Allister was smirking again. I wanted to slap him so badly my palms
itched.

"That's only part of it, dear." Mrs. O'Gara kept her voice and
expression soothing and apologetic. "Rigel is a distraction at a time

when you need to be focused on learning as much as possible about your people and your future duties."

"So this is because I haven't been *studying* hard enough?" I glared at Allister. "I've been sick this whole last week, remember? Because Rigel *wasn't* here. Obviously him being gone is *way* worse for my studies than having him here could ever be."

Finally, Allister spoke. "That won't be true once a cure is found for this . . . anomaly. And those alliances you speak of so dismissively are far more important than you yet realize. You will understand once you've learned more. How can we impress upon you what a critical time this is for our people?"

I clenched my teeth for a moment so my answer wouldn't be a scream. "I get it, okay? Faxon will be out of power soon and you . . . you *Royals* need to be able to hold me up as some kind of replacement before anyone else tries to take over. But you also keep telling me I'm too young, that I'm not ready, so excuse me if I don't see how who I'm dating is going to make *any* difference."

"You may be young," Mr. O'Gara said, his voice still oozing reasonableness. "But you *will* have responsibilities as soon as Faxon is out of power."

"Right. Okay. You want me to be a leader?" He nodded, as did the others. "Fine. Then I hereby forbid you to make the Stuarts leave Jewel."

Mr. O'Gara smiled. "I'm afraid you don't have that authority, M, not yet. That will be the Council's decision and then it will be up to the Stuarts to obey it—or not."

"Okay, then what authority *do* I have?" I challenged him. "Give me some examples."

I wasn't surprised when he hesitated, shooting a glance at Allister before replying. "Ah, as you are underage, one of your first duties when Acclaimed Sovereign will be to appoint a Regent until you reach your majority."

"Someone *appropriate* from within the Royal *fine,*" Allister added. "Someone with experience, who is familiar with issues on Earth as well as on Mars." His smug expression implied he fully expected to be that Regent.

Over my dead body.

"What else?" I prompted.

"Even as a minor, you will have ceremonial duties," Mr. O'Gara said. "You will be, in essence, the face and voice of our government, though your Regent will handle most of the day-to-day governance. Those powers will be transferred to you over time, as you gain experience, knowledge, and political connections."

That last word made me glance at Sean, who still wasn't looking at me. "And Sean? What would *his* duties be? Since you make it sound so important that he has to be—" I broke off, not willing to say the word *Consort* or anything similar.

Allister answered. "Traditionally, the Sovereign and his or her Consort have ruled jointly, dividing their responsibilities according to their individual strengths and interests. That is why the Consort must be from the Royal *fine* and House, and why he or she is also trained in government, history and leadership principles from an early age."

Now I spoke directly to Sean, forcing him to look at me. "So you've been studying this stuff all your life?"

Clearly embarrassed, he shook his head. "Not exactly. Not the way I would have if . . . well, everyone thought you were dead, remember? Which meant I was . . . nobody special."

There was an echo of old pain in his voice that made me curious what his childhood had been like, with him pretending I was alive— the thing that would make him special. Did he get teased, like when I "pretended" to be a Martian princess? Our reasons hadn't been all that different . . .

With an effort, I pulled my thoughts back to what really mattered. "What can I do to convince you that Rigel and I *need* to be together? Because we do." I tried to be forceful but was afraid I sounded whiny instead.

"We're not the ones you need to convince, dear," Mrs. O'Gara told me gently. "It's in the hands of the Council now—and the Healers."

Molly spoke for the first time since I'd arrived, though barely above a whisper. "What . . . what if the Healers *can't* find a . . . a cure?"

Fiona, on her way to the door with Brody, answered, surprising me slightly since she was so far away—but of course, she had Martian hearing. "I can't imagine anyone will force a separation in that case. But—I am sorry, Excellency—I'm reasonably confident we'll have something ready to test within a few days, as the Council has requested we devote all of our resources to this." The two Healers gave me the fist-over-heart salute and left.

"Stupid Council," I muttered, glaring at Allister again, since he was the only member present. Which reminded me. "Is Shim on board with this? With making the Stuarts move away from Jewel?"

Allister cleared his throat, looking just the slightest bit uncomfortable. "He may have dissented when we put it to a vote Saturday night, but that was before we had the Healers' assurance that they would be able to produce an antidote. When his grandson's health is no longer an issue, I'm certain he will see reason."

So Shim *had* believed in our bond all along. Though how that could help, with the rest of the Council so determined, I wasn't sure.

I suddenly felt drained by the drama of the past hour, but couldn't let them see any weakness. Not now. Not when staying strong might be the only power I had to change anyone's mind.

"I'm going home," I told them.

I worried that a night away from Rigel might cause a relapse, but I woke up the next morning still feeling light years better than yesterday morning—if not quite as good as when I was actually with Rigel. That was good, since I had some big decisions to make. Both of us did.

Like yesterday, Rigel was waiting outside the school when my bus pulled up. To my surprise, neither Sean nor Molly commented—or even looked particularly judgmental. Sean just gave him a quick nod as he went past, into the school, and Molly sent me a sympathetic, sad sort of smile before following her brother inside.

"Looks like you won *them* over, at least." Rigel twined his fingers through mine—always a fabulous relief after time apart. "What did you say after I left?"

"Hardly anything to them. I did kind of throw tantrum at the O'Garas and Allister, for all the good it did. They claim I don't have any real power yet, for all the Sovereign crap they keep yammering at me. Whether that's true or not, we can't let them get away with this. You *can't* leave me again." I looked pleadingly into his face, gripping his hands more tightly.

"Dead last on the list of things I ever want to do," he said with that crooked smile I loved so much. "But my parents . . . I don't think they'll defy the Council, M. We talked about it for hours last night. They hate it as much as we do—well, almost as much. But they won't put their personal feelings ahead of what they see as the good of their people."

"Well, I will," I said stubbornly. "You're *way* more important to me than a bunch of people I've never even met."

Rigel pulled me against his chest and buried his face in my hair. "And you're more important to me than anything at all, including my own life. I want to be with you more than anything in the world, M, but—"

The warning bell rang and he loosened his grip on me.

"But what?" I prompted, taking his hand again.

"C'mon. We don't want the Warden catching us out here again." He led me toward the front doors but I pulled against him.

"But what?" I repeated. "Rigel?" I could feel sadness and conflict from him, and it worried me.

He tugged on my hand. "We can talk later—silently, if we have to. Let's get to class."

It wasn't an answer, but I could tell he didn't want to say more when we were likely to be interrupted. Based on that conflict I felt, I suspected he also wasn't quite sure what he wanted to say, and needed time to think about it. Frustrated and impatient, I accompanied him silently to Geometry, trying hard to keep my doubts to myself.

Ms. Harrigan was already there, which meant no out-loud talking. But once class was underway, I thought to Rigel, *What were you going to say earlier? Can you tell me now?*

Just trying to figure what's best for you, M. We can't let them screw up your life, but I don't want to accidentally do that, either. We'll talk later, for real.

When?

But he just shook his head, almost imperceptibly. I tried—hard— to tap into his thoughts, but either I wasn't as good at it as he was, or he was better than me at shielding. All I got was a jumble of emotion —worry, love for me, some unfocused fear, but no clue to what he was actually *thinking*. I pressed my lips together and tried to focus on the lesson, even though math had never seemed more irrelevant.

I was a little surprised neither Sean nor Molly showed up to walk me to second period, which meant Rigel could.

"Okay, give," I said as soon as I'd verified no one was close enough to hear—no one with Martian hearing, in other words. "What was that 'but'? What makes you think *you* could possibly screw up my life?"

Rigel gave a half-grin, but I could tell his heart wasn't in it. "I know what you're thinking, because I've been thinking it, too. But all the reasons we couldn't run away before Thanksgiving still hold now, M."

"Before Thanksgiving, nobody was trying to make you leave town permanently!" I protested. "You got as sick as I did last week, Rigel. Maybe sicker. I'm not going through that again, and neither are you."

"They said—"

"Yeah. Some so-called cure they don't even have yet. Like I care. The sick part wasn't the worst thing about last week. Not for me." I left that hanging, almost a question.

He sighed. "Not for me, either. Being apart from you, well, it just might kill me, even if their antidote works. But I won't sacrifice your whole future because of my feelings."

"Then do it for *my* feelings." My voice rose above a whisper and I tried to control myself. "How many times do I have to tell you, Rigel, *you* are my future!"

He didn't say anything else until we reached my classroom. Then he whispered, "Okay. If it really comes to a permanent separation, we'll run. Meanwhile, lets both look for alternatives, okay?"

"Okay."

Since no spies were around, he gave me a quick kiss—enough to make my heart race—then headed off to his own class.

I didn't see Sean or Molly at all until lunchtime. Rigel and I had agreed—silently, because of that new *Echtran* "expert" in Science—that we'd talk for real at lunch, if we got the chance. Since Sean wasn't waiting to escort me like he'd been doing lately, we walked to the cafeteria together.

We got our food, then Rigel went to the same table he'd sat at yesterday while I swung by my usual table to let everyone—especially Sean and Molly—know I planned to sit with him today. Instead of objecting like I expected, Sean nodded, then got up and walked part way to Rigel's table with me.

"M, I want to let you know I won't . . . we won't . . . try to keep you two apart anymore," he murmured. "No matter what our mum says. I saw how sick you got last week and how much better you are now and I, well, I can't be part of that. Making you suffer."

Startled, I looked up at him. The pain in his eyes made me wince, but he also looked determined.

"Thank you, Sean. Thank Molly for me, too."

He gave a quick shake of his head, frowning now. "Don't. This doesn't mean I'm okay with—" He glanced at Rigel. "But I won't . . . make you hurt." For a moment he looked almost pleadingly into my eyes, then turned away abruptly and went back to his table, where the others were watching us curiously.

I stared after him for a second, confused and a little disturbed. But I could worry about Sean later. Right now, I had a precious chance to talk with Rigel and I wasn't about to waste it.

"What was that about?" Rigel asked as soon as I joined him. "O'Gara telling you not to sit with me?"

"No, actually. He said they're not going to try to keep us apart anymore. He and Molly, I mean. I'm pretty sure everyone else will."

Rigel frowned over at the other table. "Wonder what he's plotting now?"

I put my hand over Rigel's, making him look at me. "I don't think he's plotting anything. He's not a bad guy, Rigel. Just . . . committed. He and Molly have been really nice to me, running interference with Allister and even their mom. I consider them friends."

"Friends." I could feel jealousy and uncertainty from him. "One of whom can make you feel better, apparently. Whose DNA is helping those Healers concoct their damned cure. So what you said earlier, about leaving—"

"I meant it. I still do. You're *way* more than a friend to me, Rigel. You know that."

Finally he smiled, his negative feelings slowly dissipating, though sadness lingered in his eyes. "Glad to hear it. Because you . . . you're my life, M."

37

stochail (sto-KAYL): *preparation, as for a battle or journey*

Barely a minute after I sat down with Rigel, Ms. Harrigan entered the cafeteria, 'patrolling,' like yesterday. Sure enough, as soon as she spotted us, she headed our way, though casually, like she didn't want it to be obvious.

"So." Rigel spoke quickly, watching her progress. "We agreed to look for alternatives, right? The O'Garas gave you that book full of stuff and I can probably get more files from my dad. You e-mailed you were looking for loopholes. Let's both work on that."

I nodded. "I found out last night I can read even faster now than before you left. But so far it's mostly government structure, history, protocol, stuff like that. Allister probably edited it before giving it to me. But some of the laws are so convoluted, maybe there's something he overlooked."

"And I'll look at more recent stuff—news stories from the past twenty years, especially resistance news. My dad has tons of books and articles." He laced his fingers absentmindedly through mine as he talked. It felt delicious.

I'd have been happy just to enjoy the moment, but Ms. Harrigan was getting closer. "What if we *don't* find anything? Or not soon enough? Those Healers said they might have something to test in a week. We need a backup plan, so we can get away if we have to. It won't be easy, and we need to be ready."

He squeezed my hand reassuringly, then switched to telepathy, since Ms. H was getting close enough to hear us now. *We'll both work on that, too, and compare ideas tomorrow, okay? Don't worry, M.* He could sense my emotions at least as well as I sensed his.

Okay. We'll figure something out, one way or another, I thought back, just as Ms. Harrigan reached us.

"Are you sure this is wise, Excellency?" Ms. Harrigan whispered, frowning at our still-clasped hands. "I may be here merely to observe, but I feel I should advise you—"

"How about you don't?" I interrupted. Me, interrupting a teacher! Except she wasn't *really* a teacher, and we all knew it. "I'm being advised to death these days, thanks. And don't call me that—not here."

To my surprise, an embarrassed flush stained her flawless cheeks. "Of course. My apologies." With another frown for Rigel, she hurried away.

"Wow." Rigel was looking at me with something like admiration.

"What? I'm sick of all these . . . these *meddlers!*"

He grinned. "Me too. But the way you stood up to her—that was great. You've changed more these past few months than you realize, M." His grin faded. "You really are becoming a leader."

I stared at him. "What, because I was rude to a teacher? Oh, yeah, they'll be bowing down to me for that. Don't be silly."

But his words made me wonder. I knew I'd changed physically, getting stronger and faster—and a little prettier. Plus this improved telepathy and my faster reading, all of it thanks to Rigel. But my personality hadn't changed, had it? I still felt like an insecure teenaged girl most of the time, which was about as far from a leader as anyone could get.

"Besides," I said aloud, "I don't *want* to be a leader. Haven't I said that all along?"

"Yeah, you have," he agreed, but he still looked thoughtful—and wasn't letting me read those thoughts, whatever they were.

Unsettled, I turned my attention to my lunch.

Sean had a game that night, so I didn't have to go to the O'Garas.' (I didn't even ask to go to the game, though I wondered what my aunt would have said if I had.)

Pleading homework, I went up to my room right after dinner and spent the evening poring over Martian legalities and traditions. Pretty boring stuff, but as I pushed myself to read faster and faster, I found myself sucked into parts here and there—especially the history.

Whenever I found anything that might be useful—an obscure clause in an old law or some historical reference to an exception to a tradition—I jotted it down in a notebook I'd started for that purpose. I also noted which years or even decades were skipped over, in case Allister had deliberately deleted stuff he didn't want me to see.

When I finally rolled up the scroll around midnight, I was amazed to discover I'd read the equivalent of six or seven whole books since getting home from school that afternoon.

Among other things, I'd learned that Sovereigns weren't expected to rule for more than a hundred years, though some had ruled much longer, while others had stepped down early in favor of a successor. Three different times, that successor wasn't the Sovereign's child, but a direct descendant of an earlier Sovereign.

There had been six underage Sovereigns in the history of Nuath, the youngest Acclaimed at the age of twelve, and their actual authority while minors (which on Mars meant under eighteen) had varied a lot. Based on what I'd learned, I probably *could* force my wishes on the Council, but that would obligate me to declare for Sovereign right now, which I was *not* ready to do.

Most importantly, I'd read about a few occasions where intended Consorts had been rejected by the Sovereign, once only days before the "joining," or wedding. In that case, the Sovereign in question, Vevilana, had gone on to rule solo for more than seventy years, Nuath's own Virgin Queen.

I fell asleep slightly more hopeful that Rigel and I would find our loophole in time after all.

The next day we compared notes at lunch. Though Ms. Harrigan didn't talk to me in the cafeteria again, she did keep wandering past, like she was hoping to overhear something. We both kept an eye on her, waiting until she was on the far side of the room to talk out loud about anything important.

What Rigel had found most encouraging from his research was the recent dissent among various factions of the underground resistance—which was becoming less underground as its numbers swelled.

"A sizable minority are opposed to installing another Sovereign at all," he told me, his eyes shining. "If they convince enough people to agree once Faxon's gone, you might never have to play ruler at all!"

I was startled to feel a spurt of resentment—almost anger—at those people. Which was just crazy. Sure, they were essentially dissing my grandfather, but I'd never even met him. And they sounded like my best hope for getting out of a job I totally didn't want.

"That would be awesome," I agreed, my smile only the tiniest bit forced. Before Rigel could tap into my conflicted feelings, I pulled out my own notebook and started sharing what I'd found last night.

"If you're reading as fast as I am, we'll get through all this stuff a lot quicker than I thought," I concluded. "I was right, though, that I hardly have any recent history, and I'm pretty sure there are parts that have been deleted. These are the gaps that made me suspicious."

He copied my list into his notes. "Doesn't surprise me. I wonder if it's just Allister who doesn't want you to know everything, or it's the whole Council? We may not have much of this older stuff at home, but I'll fill in any blanks I can."

Ms. Harrigan was meandering back our way, so as soon as he'd copied everything, he snapped his notepad shut and we turned our conversation to school-related topics neither of us cared beans about.

Back home that afternoon, I spent some time working out a plan for Rigel and me to run away, since neither of us had found anything yet that was a slam-dunk alternative—or even close. It was my night to make dinner and I nearly burned the macaroni, I was so absorbed in details to throw everyone off our track.

I listened more closely than usual to Uncle Louie's stories over dinner, gleaning a detail or two that might be useful later. I also hoped do some computer research after dinner on how to effectively disappear before diving back into my Nuathan texts.

Unfortunately, I'd barely started clearing the table when Mrs. O'Gara called, asking my aunt if I could come over. Of course, she said yes.

After what had happened here the last time, I couldn't suppress a sense of dread when I knocked on their door twenty minutes later. "So, what's tonight's bad news?" I asked Sean brightly when he answered the door.

"Bad news?" He looked genuinely confused, which was a relief. "What do you mean?"

"Never mind. Why am I here?"

Allister answered, which was bad news all by itself. "Now that you are recovered, Princess, I thought we should continue your education. There may not be much—"

"Time left. Yes, I've heard. Repeatedly. Where do you want to start?" I joined him in the living room, resigned to an unpleasant evening.

Mrs. O'Gara put a cup of tea in my hand before I could sit down, then set out a plate of amazingly yummy scones with jam. Probably trying to make up for my horrible last visit—as if anything could.

"Sean, why don't you join us?" Allister said as his nephew started to leave us alone. "Much of it will be review for you, but that will be no bad thing."

Meaning that Sean, as my supposed future Consort, would need to know this stuff, too. Sean's reddening ears showed he'd also caught his uncle's implication, but he sat down in the chair next to mine without a word.

Allister became all business then, launching into his lectures and questions without further preamble. Rather to my surprise, nothing he told me was new; I'd read it all in the scroll-book. When Allister started quizzing me, I made a point of answering quickly, and with painstaking accuracy.

"Nuathans first came to Earth shortly before the Renaissance— which they helped to spark," I responded at one point. "After that, ships came here at roughly twenty to thirty year intervals, always taking advantage of the closest synchronous orbits of the two planets."

He nodded, his brows rising higher with each correct answer I gave. Sean appeared frankly amazed—and admiring. I tried not to look at him.

"And our settlements in America?" Allister asked after only the slightest pause.

"We had representatives on both the *Santa Maria* and the *Mayflower*, but we first formed a real collective in New Hampshire in the eighteen hundreds, followed by a smaller one in Colorado just before nineteen hundred, then the big one in Montana in the nineteen-thirties."

Allister blinked, clearly surprised, since those were details he hadn't mentioned tonight. "I take it you are finally studying?"

"Yes, now that Rigel is back and I'm feeling *so* much better, I'm catching up. Which proves he's *not* a distraction to my studies. Rather the reverse." I glanced at Sean, who looked away, then at Mrs. O'Gara, who was sitting across the room talking quietly with her husband and Molly. She didn't look at me, but I was pretty sure she was listening.

"Hmph." Rather than acknowledge my logic, Allister resumed his questions. "How are the representatives for the People's House chosen?"

"The *Eodain,* you mean? They're elected—popular election—from among candidates put forth by each of the villages, usually community leaders from the Royal and upper Scientific *fines*, though the law allows for other *fines* as well."

"And the Royal House?"

"By blood, of course. Though specific positions in the *Riogain* are determined by Acclamation, based on demonstrated interests and skills. When there are multiple candidates for a position, a vote of the Royals is called, and if a two-thirds majority can't be reached, the Sovereign decides." One of those many duties they expected me to take on eventually. I couldn't even imagine it.

As Allister continued to quiz me on the intricacies of the legislature, I couldn't tell whether he was pleased I got all the answers right or irritated to have nothing to scold me for. He was clearly groping for more difficult questions when Mr. O'Gara interrupted him.

"Allister? There's a call for you." He held out one of those tiny cellphones most *Echtrans* seemed to use, though I assumed it wasn't *really* Martian technology since I'd seen them used in public.

"Thank you, Quinn. Excellency, I'd say you've earned a break. Well done." Allister actually granted me a thin smile before retreating into the entryway by the front door. Then, into the phone, "Yes?"

Sean went to get us more tea while I started spreading jam on a scone, straining my ears for all I was worth. My hearing was so much better since Rigel's return, I discovered I could even hear the voice on the other end fairly well.

"—need more time to isolate the exact sequence for the Stuart boy, but the serum for the Sovereign is almost ready to test." It sounded like Healer Fiona's voice.

Allister shot a quick glance my way, which I pretended not to notice, carefully wiping my knife on the edge of my plate.

"That's the important one," he said quietly. "Let's move forward with that."

"But . . . the boy? We promised Ariel—"

"It can't be helped," Allister snapped, then lowered his voice again. "Keep working on it, of course, but time is of the essence. We need to move ahead with what we have. How do we proceed?"

I heard a sigh from Fiona, like she wasn't happy with that decision —and no wonder. How could they even *consider* testing their so-called cure until they had one for Rigel, too?

After a pause, Fiona answered. "Have both children there Saturday. There's a slight chance the same serum will work for him as well. Once it's administered, we'll separate them for a week or two. If the Sovereign suffers no ill effects—"

"We'll be able to move ahead immediately instead of waiting. Excellent. Please extend my thanks to your team." Allister clicked off and came back into the living room with a completely phony smile. "You'll be pleased to hear, Princess, that there's to be a, ah, reception in your honor here on Saturday. As it's to be a happy occasion, your . . . friend, Rigel Stuart, is invited to attend as well."

The O'Garas all looked at him with varying degrees of surprise and barely-concealed skepticism. I tried to hide mine better.

"This is rather sudden, isn't it, Allister?" Mrs. O'Gara asked. Her "lie-detector" had to be buzzing like crazy, but she kept her tone mildly curious.

Allister nodded, his eyes darting to me, then back to her. "Yes, well, the Council feels it's long overdue." With sudden inspiration, he added, "Nara did especially request your lemon poundcake, if you'd be willing to make it."

Though Mrs. O *had* to know he was just making crap up, she nodded, looking convincingly pleased by the compliment. She was way better at this than her brother, making me wonder what position Allister had held in the Nuathan legislature. Because he had to be one of the worst politicians ever—maybe a casualty of that Royal inbreeding Shim worried about.

"How nice of her!" Mrs. O'Gara said, not letting on by even a flicker that this was all fake. "Of course I'll make it. What time Saturday?"

Again Allister was clearly caught off-guard, but he covered a little quicker this time. "I said I would check the Princess's schedule and get back to them. Princess?"

I tried to smile as convincingly as Mrs. O'Gara had done. "I have taekwondo at noon, if my aunt lets me go, then I'll have to shower, but I can be here by two o'clock. Gee, does this mean they're finally seeing things my way? About Rigel, I mean?" I infused as much hopeful excitement into my voice as I could.

"Perhaps so," he equivocated—badly. "In any event, I'm sure they'll be willing to listen to anything you have to say."

"That's great!" I grinned around at all of them, my mind working furiously. Glancing at the clock on the mantel, I blinked in obvious surprise. "Gee, look how late it is! I'd better get home. Thanks for the tea and scones, Mrs. O'Gara."

"You're welcome, dear." I watched her face, but she was still focusing on Allister, not me. "We'll see you Saturday, if not before."

"I can't wait!" I enthused.

She really did look at me then, with that same probing look I'd seen her use on Molly, then relaxed as she divined that I was being totally honest.

Because I really *couldn't* wait until Saturday. By two o'clock, I fully expected to well away from Jewel, along with Rigel.

Permanently.

38

ealu (AY-loo): *break free; escape; elope*

Tomorrow night, I insisted to Rigel the next day. We were supposed to be taking a pop quiz in Geometry, but I was filling in random answers so we could continue the conversation we'd barely had time to start before class.

We're not ready, he thought back, pretending to focus on his on quiz sheet. *The plan isn't ready.*

I shot him a quick glare, then looked back at my paper. *I don't care how many holes the plan has, we can't wait any longer! They plan to test their stupid antidote on Saturday, then separate us completely—take you out of school, probably out of Jewel. Even if it only works on me, I don't think they'll let you come back. Ever!*

I'd thought telling him they didn't even *have* an antidote for him yet would be enough to convince him, but he still seemed more worried about messing up my nebulous "future" than his own health or even his life.

To my relief, Rigel finally gave a tiny nod. *You're right. I don't see any alternative to running now.*

We spent the rest of that class and all of English and Science trying to solidify our escape plan, but it wasn't easy. For one thing, it kept getting more complicated, and for another, there were a lot of interruptions. I hoped eventually this kind of telepathy would become effortless but now, though single words were easy, it still required a *lot* of concentration to send and receive whole sentences.

At lunch, we headed straight to "our" corner of the cafeteria to work out the final details aloud, even though my aunt had pointedly reminded me I was still grounded as I was leaving for school that morning. Her rules and threatened punishments hardly mattered, if we were leaving Jewel forever the next day.

"So Allister lied right to your face?" Rigel whispered as we sat down.

252

"That surprises you? I don't know why. He's never cared the least bit about us—or even about me as a person. Just about politics and his precious position. For a race that's not supposed to be power-hungry, he sure seems to be. He even expects me to appoint him Regent as soon as Faxon's out."

"No, I guess I'm not surprised. It's just hard to believe any of this is true. So, will you appoint him Regent?" he teased, clearly trying to lighten my mood.

I couldn't help but laugh. "I won't be appointing anybody Regent, since I won't be around to play Sovereign for them. So. Back to the plan?"

To my relief, I felt his mood shift from worry to determination as everything sank in. "You're right," he said. "Let's plug up some more holes."

Unfortunately, just then a couple of football players plunked themselves down at our table, and then others drifted over, too, including Bri, Deb and Molly. Only Sean stayed away, sitting with some of the basketball team.

That forced us to wait till History, when we could at least go back to silent planning without acting noticeably odd. Still, I was confident we had everything major covered now. This *was* going to work. It had to!

My heart was starting to pound as I put the last dish in the drainer Friday night. Everything had gone according to plan so far, but the hardest part was still ahead.

"Okay, I'm done," I announced to my aunt and uncle, who were watching TV in the living room. "I'd better head over to the O'Garas'—they'll want to leave soon."

I ran up to my room and grabbed my old backpack, still packed from before, but with a few last-minute additions, then headed back downstairs. "See you guys tomorrow morning," I called out as I opened the front door.

"Be a good guest," Aunt Theresa cautioned me. "Offer to wash your sheets in the morning."

"I will." I left before she could notice how nervous I was.

It had been a gamble asking my aunt if I could go to Sean's game tonight, then spend the night with Molly afterward, but I'd focused all the persuasion I could onto her. To my amazement and huge relief, she'd agreed almost eagerly.

She did say something about calling Mrs. O to confirm, but when I told her she and Molly were out shopping but would meet me at their house in time to leave for the game, she accepted it without question, surprising me again. I could definitely get used to this new ability. Except I wouldn't be around to use it on her again.

I forced myself to a normal—okay, slightly quick—walking pace until I was out of sight of the front windows, then ducked across the street and jogged between two houses to make my way to Diamond. I absolutely didn't want the O'Garas seeing me when they left for the game, which would be any minute now. I'd told Molly my aunt made me choose between the game tonight and the "reception" at their house tomorrow, so I'd elected to stay home.

Keeping an eye out for anyone who might notice me and remember later, after I was reported missing, I skirted the garbage cans behind the Thurmonds' house and slipped through the gap in the fence into the service alley behind Dream Cream.

Rigel was already there with his own backpack. "Everything go okay?" he asked after a quick hug and kiss.

"Way easier than I expected," I admitted, clinging to his hand to absorb strength and confidence, which I was going to need tonight. "I didn't even have to go to Plan B." Which was to pretend to have a relapse from last week, go to bed early, then sneak out my window—which wouldn't have given us nearly as big a head start.

"Great! My folks think I'm at the game, too, with the football team, then going to a party after. Told my dad Matt Mullins would give me a ride home."

"So your dad dropped you in town?"

He nodded. "Some of the guys were meeting here at Dream Cream before the game and I joined them for the last few minutes. Pulled a switch as they were leaving, so Matt thinks Jeff is giving me a ride to the game and Jeff thinks I'm with Matt. They'll notice I'm not there, but I don't think they'll do anything about it."

"So that gives me until morning and you until what? Midnight? When are you supposed to be home?"

"Midnight, but I think I can push it till tomorrow, too. My parents were so relieved I want to socialize with the team again, they're going easy on me. They know I've been upset about all this. They are, too, you know."

I tightened my clasp on his hand and he returned it. "I know. But they can't—or won't—*do* anything about it. Which leaves it up to us."

"Yeah." For a second I got that worried, conflicted feeling from him again. "So, what's the least visible way to the car lot?"

Before answering, I threw my arms around his neck and kissed him again, hard. "For luck," I said in answer to his surprised—but pleased—response.

"Yeah, we're going to need it. For luck." He kissed me back, a real kiss that made me tingle all the way to my toes.

When he finally released me, he grinned at my undoubtedly dazed expression. That was some kiss! "Okay," I said breathlessly. "Car lot."

I led the way behind the businesses along Diamond, ducking when the back door of the Lighthouse Cafe opened and someone came out to empty the trash. They didn't see us.

Past the business district, the alleyway ran out and we had to use the street. It had been full dark for over an hour by now and it was also freezing, so nobody else was out walking. I hoped the predicted overnight snow showers would hold off, since that was the last thing we needed.

We didn't see anyone as we zigged up Emerald and then down Sapphire, heading toward the outskirts of downtown. A few cars passed, but we stayed far enough from the shoulder that the headlights didn't hit us. It took about forty minutes on foot, but we finally reached the closed car lot where Uncle Louie worked.

"You're sure they don't have a watchman, or dogs or anything?" Rigel whispered, the first words either of us had spoken aloud since we started walking, though we'd been sending loving—and calming —thoughts to each other.

I shook my head. "A couple of security cameras, but I know where they are. Come on."

The plan was to "borrow" a car from the lot—I knew the access code to the building, and where they kept all the car keys—and drive west. Or Rigel would. He'd taken some Driver's Ed and at least had his learner's permit. Of course, if we got stopped, we were toast.

We won't get stopped, Rigel thought to me, projecting more confidence than I felt at the moment.

"How do you do that?" I whispered. "I never hear your thoughts unless you're sending them to me, but you snag mine right out of my head!"

He shrugged, grinning a little. "Maybe I pay closer attention."

I hmphed—an unwelcome reminder of Aunt Theresa, who I'd probably never see again—then led him along the edge of the lot, where we weren't within range of the security camera out front. Once we passed the corner of the building, I angled back in, close along that side, and around to the back door. The back camera was focused on the cars, not the door, so if we stayed close to the building, we should be okay.

I listened carefully, in case anyone was working late in the service department, but everything was quiet. Nobody wanted to hang around on a Friday night. Satisfied, I punched in the easy four-digit code to unlock the back door. I was glad they'd installed this keypad a few years back. It meant Uncle Louie couldn't possibly be linked to what we were about to do. The last thing I wanted was for him to lose his job.

Everything was dark and quiet inside the dealership but I didn't dare risk attention by turning on any lights. I moved by memory and feel to the small office where the security equipment was, along with all the keys to the cars on the lot. First task was to turn off the recorder for the cameras.

"Just unplug it," Rigel suggested.

I reached to do just that, then paused. "This thing is a little glitchy anyway—Uncle Louie complains about it. How about we short it out, instead? That'll look more like an accident."

He nodded and I could tell he was impressed, which pleased me a ridiculous amount. We held hands, then Rigel touched the recorder. A spark flashed for an instant and it hummed to a stop.

"That should do it," he whispered.

"Yup! Let's pick out a car." I was as excited as if we were actually going to buy one instead of stealing a getaway vehicle. Or maybe that's *why* I was so excited.

Back outside, we headed toward the far back lot, where I told Rigel they kept the cars that needed work before sale, and all the foreign imports they couldn't sell.

"Check it out! A '75 Mustang," Rigel breathed in my ear.

I shook my head. "Too flashy. Plus it's a stick. Can you drive stick yet?"

"Um, no."

Chuckling—only half to myself—I kept walking. "Here. This old gray Corolla shouldn't attract much attention. And it already has a dealer plate."

"Let's swap the plate with another car anyway," Rigel suggested, sounding amazingly calm about all this. I tried to feel the same, for his sake as well as mine.

"Good idea. Then even if they do notice it missing, they'll give the police the wrong plate number."

He made the swap and we went back to the office, where I pulled out the tiny LED flashlight I'd stuck in my pocket and examined the keys. It only took me a couple of minutes to find the right one, though it felt like ages.

Making sure the door locked behind us, we went back to the Corolla, threw our backpacks into the back seat and got in.

"You *do* know how to drive this, right?" I fought to control a wash of panic as the enormity of what we were doing hit me. A few days ago, I'd surprised Rigel by being rude to a teacher. Now we were stealing a car!

"Hey, I've had two whole weeks of Driver's Ed and I'm a fast learner. It'll be fine, M," he assured me, but I could feel his tension. He wasn't nearly as calm as he was pretending to be, either.

I stayed quiet as he started the car, backed it out of its space and maneuvered it around the building and out to the road. He really did seem to know what he was doing, and it was my turn to be impressed.

"One last stop, then we're out of here," Rigel said. Maybe I imagined that hint of a quaver in his voice.

He drove us back into town and around the side of the now-closed post office, stopping by the Express Mail drop box. Glancing around to be sure no one was within sight, he pulled out his cell phone and dialed.

"Hey, Dad, it's halftime. We're winning—O'Gara's dominating again, of course. Huh? Oh yeah, I'm outside—it was too noisy in the gym to call. Anyway, Matt wants to know if I can stay over, some of the guys are gonna crash in his rec room tonight. That way he won't have to drive me till morning and you and Mom won't have to wait up. No, of course I won't be drinking, Dad, come on! Okay, thanks. See you tomorrow."

He hung up, then pulled a prepaid Express envelope out of his backpack. It was addressed to Shim, in Washington, DC. He sealed his phone inside and stuck it into the drop box.

"There." He sounded the tiniest bit breathless but not nearly as nervous as I felt. "It's a six a.m. pickup, so by the time they think to track my cell it should look like we're halfway to Grandfather's place."

We'd planned this part out earlier. Since Shim was the only member of the Council who'd voted against separating us, it made sense we might run to him. If that diversion worked, it should buy us a few extra hours or even a full day while they followed that lead.

As we'd agreed, Rigel headed east, then south once we hit the state highway, so we could pick up the interstate to Indy. From there, we'd go west.

"Do you think we should have gone to Shim after all, and tried to misdirect them in a different direction?" I asked worriedly, once we were past the town limits. It was one of the options we'd discussed.

He shook his head. "No matter how sympathetic he might be, he'd have to turn us over to the Council. If he didn't, I don't know what they'd do to him, but it would probably be bad. Then he wouldn't be able to help us at all. It's better if he doesn't know anything about this."

"Yeah. Yeah, you're right. Of course." The idea of having *no* adult support was unnerving, but I'd better get used to it. This was going to be my life—*our* lives—for a long time now. Maybe forever.

But as long as we were together, we'd be okay.

I hoped.

39

Rigel (RY-jel): *an important navigational star*

Every extra mile between us and Jewel, the safer we are—or so I keep telling myself as I drive West on I-70 out of Indianapolis. But I can't help thinking of all the things that can go wrong. Neither can M.

"What if one of the guys calls your house, asking why you're not at the game?" she says, forgetting she already asked me that.

"They'd call my cell, not the house," I reassure her, though I don't *know* that, since my cell will go straight to voice mail.

She nods, but she's still tense. We both are. Because it's *not* impossible they already know we're gone. M's aunt might have called or dropped by the O'Garas' house, or they could've called her. And if they do know . . .

For about the twentieth time, I stiffen as a car comes up to pass us, glancing out of the corner of my eye to make sure they're not staring, trying to identify us. I feel M looking at me, feel her worry, and force myself to relax again, projecting all the calm and confidence I can.

"Even if they figure it out tonight—which they *won't*—they can't know what we're driving, or even *that* we're driving. Or which way we've gone," I remind her. "We made it out of town. That was the hard part."

I wish I really believed that.

I wake up, my neck stiff from sleeping half sitting up, and glance at the old wristwatch I'm wearing. Crap! Two hours later than I thought. But when I glance down at M, still fast asleep, snuggled into the crook of my arm, I smile. How can one person be so adorable?

Before waking her, I give myself a minute to just love her. And then another couple of minutes to really *feel* all the emotions I've been trying to hide from her the past few hours: anger at everyone

259

trying to run our lives, worry about our future, *her* future, and just plain terror we'll get caught and separated. Because I don't see how that won't happen eventually. And it'll only be "eventually" instead of "immediately" if we're really, really lucky.

I watch her beautiful, peaceful face while I get my feelings back under control, taking deep breaths and focusing again on just how much I love M and how perfect we are together. Too perfect to even consider not staying together forever. One more breath.

"Hey," I whisper, jostling her slightly. "We need to get moving again, and I kinda need both arms to drive."

She stirs, then opens those amazing green eyes and gazes up at me through her long lashes, still bleary but with a smile on her lips. "Mmmm. Good morning. I love you."

My heart squeezes painfully, but I grin down at her. "I love you, too, M. But it wasn't supposed to be morning yet, remember? We slept for three hours."

Now she sits up and I can feel alarm from her—the same alarm I'm trying to suppress. "Three hours? I thought your watch was supposed to go off after one hour!"

"Yeah. Either it didn't or we both slept through it."

We'd driven all night, getting gas in St. Louis, along with a couple of awful hot dogs from the gas station, before continuing west until about five a.m. By then it was starting to snow, plus I was in danger of nodding off. So I exited near the western border of Missouri, found a church parking lot in the middle of nowhere, set my watch alarm and fell asleep. At least the snow has stopped. For now.

I realize I'm starving, plus I have to pee. I can tell M feels the same.

"Food and bathroom?" I suggest.

"Sounds great," she agrees. "Maybe not in that order."

I can't help laughing. It feels *so* great to be together, just the two of us, at least pretending it's for good. I try to keep my doubts buried deep, so she won't pick up on them.

"I think we passed a burger place when we first got off the highway," I say, to keep her mind on food. "Sound good?"

"Sounds perfect! Let's go." She scoots away from me and fastens her seat belt, making me miss the contact so much I reach over and squeeze her hand before starting the car.

There are only a few cars in the parking lot of the restaurant. The drive-thru would be safest but we both need the bathroom, so I park.

"Do you really think they're after us yet?" M must have picked up on my thought about the drive-thru. I need to be more careful.

"Probably not." I unbuckle my seat belt and open my door, trying to sound confident. "But they will be soon. When does your aunt expect you home?"

We both get out before M answers. "I didn't give her a time, but I wouldn't put it past her to call if I'm not back by eleven, since I'm supposed to have taekwondo at noon."

"So we're safe for another two or three hours . . . but then all hell will break loose. Hope they at least keep it quiet."

"Yeah." I focus and can tell she's thinking about everything that could go wrong—for us and for all the *Echtrans*—if the police get involved. The stuff we managed to ignore when we were so desperate to get away seems big and unavoidable now that we *are* away.

You're just gloomy because you're hungry, she thinks at me as we enter the restaurant. Then, out loud, "You want to order while I run to the bathroom? Or vice versa?"

"You go first. I'll order." Seems like the least I can do since I'm screwing up her whole future.

The stern look she gives me says she caught that—or at least the emotion that went with it. She's definitely getting better at picking up my random thoughts. Oops.

I go to the counter while M heads to the ladies' room. "Breakfast?" the girl behind the counter asks. She looks bored, which is good—means she's less likely to remember us.

"Yeah. Two egg sandwiches, biscuits, a Coke and a hot tea. To go."

She looks closer at me and smiles a little, but I avoid her eye and make like I'm watching for M to come out of the restroom. After a second, she punches in our order and gives me the total, looking bored again.

I hand her a twenty, doing the math in my head while she makes change, trying to figure how far the three hundred and sixty dollars I was able to scrape together will take us, if we're careful. Not far. I've already spent fifty on gas and food. Money's going to be an issue.

M's coming back, so I switch mental gears. "I've ordered and paid. You take over and I'll be right back, okay?"

"'Kay." She winks, forcing a grin out of me. I wish again this trip could go on forever.

She has our order in a bag when I get back and we head to the car. We wolf down our breakfasts—M actually surprised I remembered she likes tea—and plan the next leg of our trip.

"I've been watching you drive, and I think I can probably spell you some during the day," she says. "If it doesn't start snowing again, anyway. Then we can take turns sleeping and get farther, faster."

I frown at her, wondering how safe that would be since she's never driven a car in her life.

"Safer than you falling asleep at the wheel."

"Okay, now I know how you feel when I do that." I grin so she knows I'm not upset, though it means I need to work harder to stay upbeat inside my head. "And yeah, as long as you stay in the right lane, you'll probably do fine. But I'll drive for now. We can switch over at a rest stop or something if I get sleepy again."

Five minutes later, we're back on the highway. "Why don't you go ahead and get some more sleep so you'll be fresher if you have to take over?" I suggest.

"I'm not at all sleepy right now. How about I read some more of this scroll thing for a while instead? You know, just in case."

"Good idea." I try to keep my voice and thoughts light, but I know she's getting as much worry from me as I am from her. Nothing to do but keep driving. I continue to tense every time a car passes, though I know I'm being paranoid.

M just gives me an understanding smile, then snaps her book open and starts reading. Every now and then she reads something out loud to me, which is good since it keeps me from zoning out between panic attacks.

"Whoa! Did you know a Regent doesn't have to be a Royal?" she says at one point. "That's just a tradition, not law. Bet Allister didn't want me finding *that* out. Not that it matters," she adds quickly. "He can be the stupid Sovereign himself, for all I care." I can tell she doesn't really mean it, that she's more bothered than she lets on.

"Still, good to know," I say. "You know, just in case."

She grins at me, but the worry's still there underneath.

"Hey, can't hurt to have a few backup plans." I try to sound brisk and cheerful. "You want to brainstorm some?"

"Not yet." Her smile is gone now. "Let's stay positive, okay? We've made it a lot farther already than either one of us expected. We can do this, Rigel. We have to."

I nod, my eyes on the road. I don't need to say anything. We both know what the alternative is. I speed up just a little.

For the next hour or two, M keeps reading, faster and faster, but she stops to talk to me every now and then when she senses I need the distraction. I noticed I read faster, too, since Thanksgiving. Weird how that separation and reunion seems to have ramped up our bond and the abilities that go with it.

After another hour or so, M finally curls up, using her coat as a pillow, and tries to sleep again. I'm glad. Because by now folks back in Jewel have to know we've disappeared. Which means things will get way more dangerous from here on out. I'd rather M not think about that yet.

As her breathing slows, I let down my emotional guard just a little. I keep glancing in the rear view mirror, though what I expect to see, I don't know. Nobody can possibly have traced us this far yet. I don't think.

Truth is, I have no idea *what* kind of technology the Council might have for emergencies like this. No way they tagged this car, but what if they've tagged *us* somehow? Not impossible, from the kinds of stuff I've seen and heard about. It's good I didn't think of that while M was listening in.

A while later gas is getting low, plus I'm having more and more trouble staying focused on the road ahead instead of on the cars behind us. A few snowflakes hit the windshield. I'm watching exits for a gas station when M wakes up.

"How long did I—? Oh, crap! It's really snowing! When did this start?"

"Maybe fifteen minutes ago, but it's getting worse. I don't guess you'd better try driving after all."

She gives me a long look and I can tell she's gauging my mood. Between lack of sleep and being keyed up for hours, I'm too wiped to block her much.

"You're really tired." I feel her worry. "Do you think it would be safe to stop somewhere so you can get some sleep? I can at least keep watch."

I glance at the clock on the dash. Almost three. They'll have been looking for us for hours, now. "Not unless we find someplace really hidden." I shouldn't even consider it, but that three hours of sleep this morning seems like forever ago.

M feels even more worried now, but just says "Let's get gas and some lunch."

I pick a busy truck stop near the Kansas border, figuring we're less likely to be noticed than at some little mom and pop place. Because who knows what kind of word has gone out about us by now.

We buy hours-old turkey sandwiches and a couple of Cokes and I pay with cash. I wish I could use the credit card my parents gave me after my birthday, but it's way too risky.

"Want to eat here or in the car?" M asks, glancing at the dozen or so bright orange tables near the register.

"Car," I say aloud, then think, *Don't want to stay in one place too long, where someone might remember us.*

She just nods. I can tell she's worried by how tired I feel, but doesn't want to say so. She's not wrong, but we should put at least another hundred miles behind us before we think about stopping.

The snow's coming down harder than ever when we get back in the car.

"I've been thinking," I say as I unwrap my sandwich. "Colorado has some hippie-type communes in the mountains—I read up on it —so I'll bet we can find a place where they'll let us stay if we help grow food and stuff. We'd be impossible to find, then."

"That would be perfect!" M sounds—and feels—perky. I wonder if she's faking it. "I actually know stuff about gardening, too—Aunt Theresa always made me help in hers."

I throw an arm around her and try to sound super positive. "You can teach me, Indiana girl. I've never done any farming or gardening or anything."

M laughs and it's a beautiful sound. I want her happy more than I want anything in the world. My worst worry, the one I have to hide deepest, is that I'm wrecking her future happiness. But then I glance in the rear view mirror.

"I'm no farmer," M is saying, "but I can definitely— What?" She breaks off and I feel a surge of anxiety from her. "What's wrong?"

"That blue car. It came zooming up, but now it's creeping along like it's checking out all the parked cars. Get down."

She ducks down under the dash, then shoots me a terrified glance. "Did they see me? See us?"

I keep watching the mirror as the car crawls past us, then finally pulls into a space about four cars away. "I'm not sure, but we're outta here. Don't sit up until I say."

M nods. I hate the fear I can feel from her. I back out so fast I almost hit another car. The driver lays on his horn, but I just shift into drive and head out, still keeping an eye on that blue car. Nobody has gotten out of it yet, but I can see at least two people inside.

A few seconds later we're on the ramp to the highway. The blue car isn't behind us, so I tell M she can sit up now.

"Was it really them? Could you tell?" she asks as she buckles in, fear still coming off of her in waves.

I shake my head, starting to feel stupid, even though I'm still watching the rear view mirror. "No. Probably not. I just . . . panicked a little." I force myself to relax. "Sorry—didn't mean to scare you."

"I guess we're both kind of jumpy." Her emotions even out and I wonder if she's working as hard at it as I am. Funny how we're both doing that, for the other one's sake. Or maybe not funny.

"Why don't you take another nap?" I suggest. "If I get sleepy, I'll pull off somewhere, I promise."

She gives me a long look, then nods. "I can try. Wake me up if you need a distraction or if anything else happens, okay?"

"Promise."

Even though she clearly doesn't think she'll be able to sleep, she drops off in less than ten minutes. Her even breathing makes it harder than I expected to stay alert. I glance in the mirror again and my gut clenches. Is that the same blue car from the truck stop? I can't tell, but when I speed up a little, it stays the same distance behind me. I slow down until I'm going below the speed limit and it doesn't pass me.

Crap.

I speed back up, just a little, trying hard not to panic again since there's nothing I can do but keep driving. At least we have a full tank of gas.

Lots of other cars pass me, even though it's still snowing, but that blue car stays behind me, mile after mile, exit after exit. As it gets dark, the windshield starts to ice up, even though I have the defroster going full blast. I can barely see the road, and all I can see of the car behind me is headlights.

Scared as I am of possible pursuers, I start watching for another exit. Escaping won't do us much good if I crash and kill us both. I keep telling myself I don't know for *sure* that car is really after us. I don't believe me.

I take an exit for a farm road, then turn left, crossing over the highway, since all the lights are in the other direction. Sure enough, a car exits behind me—but it turns right, not left. A wave of exhaustion makes it way too easy to convince myself I was wrong all along.

Maybe three miles down the dark, deserted road I see a closed feed store with just a security light on. Nobody's following, so I pull into the parking lot, then around behind. Gratefully, I put the car in park and turn off the engine.

M sits up with a start. "Where are we? What's wrong?"

"Nothing." I project all the certainty I can summon. "I decided to take a nap, that's all. Tonight should get us through Kansas, but I can't do it without some sleep. Then, when we get to Colorado, we'll find a permanent hiding place in the mountains."

"Will we live in a tent?" M feels more excited than worried. I can't help but chuckle.

"Only if you want to. Might get cold, though."

"I won't be cold if you're with me."

Her smile and the wave of love and confidence I feel from her almost convinces me again that this whole thing can work. She snuggles against me and for the first time all day I really relax.

I'm just leaning over to kiss her when a blue car comes tearing around the corner, spraying gravel, at the same moment a truck rounds the other side of the building, headlights blazing. There are more cars behind both of them.

We're trapped.

40

cloigh (kloy): *overpower or overthrow; defeat; subdue*

Rigel and I only had time to exchange one glance and one thought: *Run!* before people started piling out of the cars suddenly surrounding us. Since I was already leaning against Rigel, we both bolted out of his door, me clinging tightly to his hand. We raced toward the trees and brush behind the parking lot as they converged on us from all sides.

One man made a grab at me, missed when I dodged, then another loomed up right in front of us and seized Rigel's arm, yanking him away from me. The first guy started to reach for me again, then hesitated. I didn't. I whipped around with a back-spinning kick to his head.

He went down with a satisfying thump and I lunged for Rigel's hand again. The second our fingers touched, we let loose an electric jolt that sent his captor flying six feet through the air.

"C'mon," Rigel said aloud to me, taking a better grip on my hand. This time we made it out of the parking lot, but I could hear feet pounding right behind us.

"Stop!" a man yelled. "Please! Don't make us shoot!"

Needless to say, we didn't stop. A second later I heard the sound of one of those energy weapons all the Martians used during that big battle in the cornfield in October. A charge zapped right between us. Warning shot, or a miss?

Faster! I thought to Rigel, since we were clearly outrunning them. Maybe they were lousy shots. Maybe we could—

Rigel grunted and his grip on my hand loosened as he stumbled and fell to his knees. He'd been hit.

Keeping a death hold on his hand with both of mine now, I turned to face our attackers, furiously sending all the healing and strength into Rigel I could. To my relief, he struggled back to his feet, but now they'd had time to surround us.

"Don't come any closer," Rigel warned them.

"Quiet, Stuart," one of the men barked. "You're in enough trouble as it is. Kidnapping a Sovereign is high treason." His words and his *brath* confirmed that these weren't random criminals looking to rob or kill us. Or hurt me, probably, since he called me Sovereign. But—

"Kidnapping?" Rigel and I said at the same time.

"Remember orders," another man snapped. "We're not supposed to let them say anything." He brought up his tiny silver weapon. "You two come along quietly and no one will get hurt."

"I don't think so," I snapped back at him. No way were they framing Rigel for kidnapping! I tightened my grip on Rigel's hand. *Let's zap them all!*

He gave a grim nod. We sent out another lightning bolt and the two closest to us went down.

Again? Rigel suggested, but now I hesitated.

If we accidentally killed somebody, they'd have a real crime to pin on Rigel. I sent him an anguished look, trying to choose between the lesser of two evils. Then someone in the back fired and we both went down. I felt like I'd been simultaneously kicked in the head and punched in the stomach. Before I could recover, two people grabbed me, one of them mumbling apologies, while two others grabbed Rigel, pulling us apart again.

A grim-looking woman moved toward Rigel, something shiny in her hand, saying, "Your youth might gain you some leniency, though I can't promise anything."

Rigel slumped into the arms of his captors as I watched in horror. "What did you do to him? Rigel? Rigel!"

But there was no response, either aloud or in my head. Terrified, I drove my elbow into the stomach of one of the men holding me. He grunted and loosened his grip. "Hold her!" he gasped as I wrenched partly away.

Without pausing, I elbowed the other one, then delivered a back fist to his face with the same arm. Amazingly, I seemed as strong as he was. He staggered back, almost letting go, but then the woman who'd just knocked out Rigel appeared at my side.

"My deepest apologies, Excellency," she said. I saw the flash of silver in her hand a half-second before I felt a pinprick in my upper arm. Then everything went black.

I came to abruptly, my first conscious thought the same as my last. "Rigel?" I cried out, snapping my eyes open and struggling to sit up on the soft surface beneath me.

To my surprise and overwhelming relief, that surface turned out to be the couch in the Stuarts' living room. Surely that meant Rigel was here too? I stared around at the sea of faces surrounding me—some concerned, some stern, most of them unfamiliar—but his wasn't among them. Nor were his parents'. My relief oozed away.

"Where's Rigel?" I demanded—though my voice sounded more pitiful than commanding.

Shim stepped forward and some of my relief crept back.

"He's not here, Princess. That you are is something for which we must all be extremely grateful. You can't know how very essential your safe recovery has been."

His grave tone and expression, even more than his words, popped my last little bubble of relief. I'd never seen Shim look at me so disapprovingly. But no amount of guilt could distract me from my primary concern.

"Where *is* Rigel? You, or someone, must be able to tell me that," I insisted.

Allister Adair, the *last* person I wanted to see, moved into my line of sight. "Rigel Stuart has been taken to a holding facility in Montana," he told me with no trace of sympathy. "He will stay there until a verdict can be reached."

"Verdict? What do you mean?" I didn't like the sound of that at all.

Allister's pale gray eyes grew even colder. "The boy has committed a serious offense. The *Echtran* Council has never before dealt with a charge of treason, so some deliberation will be required. It is possible that his youth will mitigate what would otherwise demand the ultimate penalty."

I stared at him, feeling the blood leave my face as my mouth opened and closed soundlessly.

"Allister," Shim snapped. "There have been no formal charges yet, merely an accusation. Let us not be precipitate. One thing at a time, please." He turned back to me and I could see the anguish behind his carefully stoic eyes. It was nothing to my own anguish, though!

"Ultimate penalty?" I gasped, finally finding my voice. That meant a complete memory wipe, unless . . . was there a death penalty that wasn't in the books? "What is he accused of?"

A woman I'd met once before—Kyna, that was her name— replied when both Shim and Allister hesitated. "Kidnapping, Excellency. Did he not take you from the O'Garas' protection against your will?"

"No! Of course not! Running away was totally *my* idea. He only agreed after I talked him into it. You *have* to let him go. Now!"

A surprised murmur ran through the people in the room, but all I could think about was Rigel. Was he being told the same thing? A new fear gripped me: if he thought it might help me somehow, would he *admit* to kidnapping me? What would they do to him if he did?

"I'm afraid it's not that simple, Princess," Allister told me. "Even if what you say is true, the boy is now a security risk. It must never be suspected that you ran away of your own volition; that you deliberately attempted to abdicate your responsibilities and position. That would completely undermine our campaign to present you as the logical choice for leadership now that Faxon's regime has collapsed."

"Collapsed?" The word caught me off guard, distracting me, but only for a second. "I don't care about your *campaign*," I informed him vehemently. "All I care about right now is Rigel. You can't make him stand trial—or *thrialach*—for a crime he didn't commit. I won't let you. I . . . I'll abdicate. I hereby totally refuse to be Sovereign, unless you let him go."

That seemed to startle, even alarm most of them, but almost immediately Kyna snapped, "That's not possible, Excellency. There is so much you don't understand, so much more at stake than—"

I turned my back on her to face Shim. "*You* won't let them do anything to Rigel, will you?" I pleaded, cutting Kyna off midsentence. "They *have* to let him come back! You know how sick both of us will get."

Instead of giving me the reassurance I craved, he turned to the others. "This is becoming needlessly, perhaps disastrously, upsetting for the Princess. I would like to speak with her—alone—to clarify the situation. The *entire* situation." His words seemed laden with a significance I couldn't grasp.

As the others hesitated, I finally had a chance to notice who was here. Besides the furiously frowning Allister and the disapproving Kyna, I recognized little Nara, watching me with sympathetic tears in her eyes.

Those three, plus Shim, had also been present when a blood test proved my identity in this very room back in September. The others were strangers to me. I wondered where Rigel's parents were, and the O'Garas.

"You may record our conversation if you wish," Shim said with a touch of impatience when the only response was Allister's quick head shake. "Or listen remotely from another room. My only concern is that the Princess understand everything she must, as quickly as possible. Nothing else can progress until then."

The others murmured their agreement though, at Allister's insistence, one of the men I didn't recognize set a small omni-like device on the mantel before they all filed out, leaving Shim and me alone in the living room.

He pulled a chair to face me and sat down with a weary sigh, looking somehow older than I remembered. I guiltily wondered if the stress caused by my running away might be the reason.

"First, my dear, let me say how genuinely happy I am that you are safe. And my grandson as well, of course." A smile flickered across his face. "We all imagined the worst until our trackers picked up your trail and were able to deduce what had happened."

"Um, how *did* you—?"

Shim held up a hand, silencing me. "Let's just say that we have techniques neither you nor Rigel were aware of. Right now, however, it is essential that I inform you as quickly as possible about all aspects of our current situation—and then get you home."

I glanced at the clock on the mantel. Three o'clock? Sunday afternoon, I assumed, since it was light outside. "How long was I out?"

"More than twenty hours, and if you're not home before five, the, ah, creative excuse Lili O'Gara has provided your aunt and uncle may not hold up. I'm sure you don't want their suspicions aroused any more than we do."

"Uh, no, I guess not. Excuse?"

"Again, that can wait. You'll be given the gist on your way home. The entire *Echtran* Council has convened here for a purpose that cannot be put off any longer. As you heard, Faxon has finally fallen from power. Though we knew things were tending in that direction, his ouster happened more quickly than expected when Royal sympathizers took advantage of an unexpected opportunity and most of his inner circle turned against him. Word reached Earth late Friday night, within hours of your leaving Jewel."

In other words, the power vacuum Allister and the O'Garas were worried about—and me nowhere to be found. Guilt stabbed me again, but I shoved it away.

"Okay, my timing really sucked, I get that. But the O'Garas—the Council—didn't leave us any choice! They were planning to separate Rigel and me permanently. Yesterday. Weren't they?" My question was an accusation, directed not just at Shim, but at the whole Council, listening in.

He nodded sadly. "Allister assured us you had no suspicion, but he has always tended to underestimate you—both of you. Yes, the plan was to test this new antidote yesterday, which would have entailed an immediate separation after its administration."

"Were the Stuarts okay with that? Were you? Where *are* the Stuarts, anyway?"

"On their way to Montana, to support their son in any way they can. And no. Ariel, in particular, was violently opposed to the plan," Shim admitted. "Nor was the Council unanimous, though only Nara and I actually voted against it after the debate concluded. I suspect our opinions were given less weight because of our personal feelings in the matter."

Though that helped a little, knowing wouldn't have kept me from running away. For all the good that did, since Rigel and I had been separated anyway. I refused to believe it would be forever.

"Okay, I'm here now, whether I want to be or not. What *exactly* am I expected to do? According to Allister, I won't be ready to actually lead for years, so I guess I don't see what the big deal is. I mean, why not just elect someone who's qualified *now* to take over, at least for the next ten or fifteen years, since you need a leader right this minute?"

I knew it wasn't quite that simple, based on all I'd learned about Nuathan government, but it still seemed like the logical solution in a unique emergency like this one.

"It's true that you are too young to step into a full leadership role immediately," Shim agreed, "but with several factions suddenly vying for power on Mars, it is *essential* that the majority of those factions unite, and quickly, before we are plunged into anarchy and civil war. You, my dear, are the obvious rallying point for that unity, young as you are."

"So it's like I said to the O'Garas before—I'm basically going to be a figurehead?"

He surprised me by nodding. "In that particular sense, yes, for the time being, though a symbolically important one. However, there is another matter of which even the O'Garas are unaware, one that makes you our only possible choice for Sovereign and representative of our people, completely apart from Nuathan politics."

"There is?" Something even the O'Garas didn't know? I'd figured they knew more about everything Mars-related than anyone, except maybe Shim himself.

"Until last night, this was known only to a small handful of our most trusted leaders and scientists," Shim said, his look impressing me with the seriousness of whatever he was about to tell me. "It was only revealed to the entire *Echtran* Council last night, when there was dissension about your, ah, fitness to lead because of your recent adventure. Prior to that, Kyna and I were the only Nuathans on Earth who had been fully briefed, due to the nature of our research contributions."

"So . . . really top secret stuff, huh?"

"Extremely." His look rebuked me for my light tone. "So much so, in fact, that it would be considered treason for you to mention this to *anyone* outside of the Council. That includes any of the O'Garas and my grandson as well, should you eventually be reunited."

Those last words created a bubble of hope that wiped out the rest until Shim's commanding gaze forced me to focus on everything he'd said. Slowly, reluctantly, I nodded. "I . . . I promise."

I had no idea how I could keep anything secret from Rigel, since he could read my mind, but I wasn't about to mention *that* with the rest of the Council listening in. They'd probably use it as a reason to never, ever let me see Rigel again.

Shim was watching me shrewdly, almost like he knew there were things I wasn't telling him, but then he nodded. "Very well. I must hold you strictly to that promise, Excellency. Once you hear the rest, you will understand why secrecy is so vital."

Again he paused, watching me carefully for any reaction. I was careful to keep all expression off my face and after a moment he continued.

"For more than four hundred years, we on Mars have scoured the galaxy for signs of other intelligent life. I realize Earth humans have been doing the same in recent years, but we had the advantages of more sophisticated technology and the certainty, due to our own history, that such life does exist."

"The Extra-solar Research Ministry. I know." I'd memorized all twenty-seven ministries since Nuathans were so into bureaucracy. "You mean they found something?"

"Indeed. Several somethings, most of which are known to the general population, as they are simply unconfirmed evidence of possible civilizations on far-flung planets. What most do *not* know, however, is that we ourselves were contacted approximately three hundred years ago and that a sporadic, ah, correspondence has continued since."

My breath caught and I stared at him. "Wait. Mars has been in contact with *other* aliens? For three hundred years? Are . . . are they the same ones that originally—"

"We believe so, based on how they originally contacted us, though even that is not absolutely certain. There is still much we do not know about the Grentl—an approximation of what they call themselves. They are not humanoid, though we have reason to believe they have something resembling DNA. They appear to exist as some combination of physical and energy-based life and have technology that surpasses ours by quite a bit more than ours surpasses that of Earth."

By now I was mostly past feeling like I was living in a science fiction novel but this threw me right back into that mindset. Boggled, I shook my head.

"How can we communicate with them at all?"

"That took nearly fifty years to work out," he admitted, "And it's still rudimentary. They don't use language in the same sense we do, but seem to understand us better than we do them. What they have primarily sent so far have been questions."

I thought about that for a moment, then asked what seemed like the most pressing question. "So are they . . . friendly now, or are they coming back to do more experiments?"

One corner of Shim's thin, dry lips quirked up, reminding me forcefully of Rigel's crooked grin. "That, unfortunately, is one of the things we have not been able to conclusively determine. I congratulate you, Excellency, on so quickly striking to the heart of the matter."

Had I? I shook my head, still confused. "But . . . what does it have to do with me? And why is it such a huge secret?"

"Interestingly, those two answers are bound together. It had always been our policy to only disseminate information about potential extra-solar civilizations after the ESR has drawn its preliminary conclusions, so as not to invite undue or premature speculation."

I had to suppress a snort. "I guess the Martian press isn't as persistent as ours."

"No, it certainly isn't. That has sometimes been a blessing, though in the case of Faxon . . . but again, that is a discussion for another time. When the Grentl contacted us—'us' meaning two ESR astronomers who happened to be on duty at the time—the protocol was to wait until we knew more before publicizing that fact.

"Over time, a two-way dialogue of sorts was established due to their sophisticated use of quantum entanglement. And the more we learned, the clearer it became that the general citizenry should *not* be told. For one thing, many of our people have beliefs rising to the level of superstition, even religion, when it comes to our original abductors."

That made sense, as primitive as the original colonists had been.

"For another, we discovered early on that the Grentl are—how to put it?—rather touchy. During preliminary communications with our scientists, there was a, ah, misunderstanding. Fortunately, young Sovereign Aerleas, your great-grandmother, was able to avert what could have been a diplomatic—or much worse—disaster, after which the Grentl made it clear they would deal only with her."

"But . . . what happened when she died?" I was caught up in the story, which felt more like fiction than anything real or personal.

Shim gave me another slight smile. "Ah, there we had a stroke of luck. The Grentl apparently reproduce by fission. Because of this, they perceive an offspring as essentially the same person as the parent. Therefore, your grandfather Leontine was able to pick up where his mother left off without the Grentl taking offense."

"And now he's gone," I whispered, suddenly seeing where this was going.

Shim nodded. "As is your father."

I swallowed. "So did Faxon—?"

"Apparently so, though we have no way of knowing yet what damage he has done to relations. Please believe me when I say that should the Grentl choose to take action as a result of perceived insult, it could well mean the end of life on Mars and, quite possibly, Earth as well."

All I could do was shake my head helplessly as he said the very last words I wanted to hear.

"Yes, Princess. The *only* person who can possibly prevent such a calamity . . . is you."

41

taigde (TAG-duh): *research; records*

It was a good thing I'd had those twenty hours of drugged sleep, since I was sure I wouldn't be able to close my eyes all night. I sat cross-legged on my bed staring blankly at the star charts on my wall —what I could see of them by the light of half a moon and my little nightlight—trying to wrap my brain all that had happened this weekend, and especially what I'd learned today.

After the Council took turns lecturing me on how the fate of two worlds was on my shoulders, Allister had driven me to the O'Garas,' with one last caution to say nothing about the Grentl stuff—which had clearly shaken him badly. Mrs. O didn't say much when she brought me home, except to give me the details of her story to Aunt Theresa about the impromptu mission trip Molly, Sean and I had supposedly gone on over the weekend.

Of course, that hadn't stopped my aunt from lambasting me the moment Mrs. O'Gara was gone, because I hadn't called and asked permission first. I'd finally pulled out all the stops, using every ounce of my fledgling persuasive ability to convince her I'd tried repeatedly but couldn't get through, and that the bus had been about to leave. That had stopped her tirade for the evening, though I doubted I'd heard the last of it. But that was the least of my worries right now.

My number one goal was to find an escape clause for Rigel—and for me. I was already feeling the first twinges of Rigel-deprivation, which meant he was feeling it by now, too. I'd been given the so-called antidote at the Stuarts' house, but they admitted it might be a day or two before it took effect . . . *if* it took effect.

I'd asked—demanded—whether Rigel was given the antidote as well, but nobody seemed to know for sure. His parents must be in Montana by now, and I wanted to believe they'd make sure he got it —but *was* there even any antidote in Montana? It killed me to think of him suffering again, maybe even worse this time, because of me.

277

Rigel worried about screwing up my life, but look what I'd done to his! If not for me, he'd still be the most popular guy in school, looking at two more fabulous years as quarterback, a full-ride college scholarship at a big-name school, probably an NFL career. It was entirely possible I'd taken that away from him. Permanently.

A sound from my aunt and uncle's bedroom made me stiffen for a second, thinking Aunt Theresa was getting up to say more awful stuff to me, before realizing it was just Uncle Louie starting to snore.

Since it was totally obvious I wasn't going to fall asleep anytime soon, I turned on my bedside light and pulled out my Martian e-book, grateful it had still been in my backpack, which had been brought back to Jewel with me. Snapping it from pencil-size to tablet, I found the spot where I'd left off in the car—then clenched my teeth against the sudden pain in my chest at that reminder of my brief, idyllic time with Rigel.

If I was going to save him, save both of us, I had to know *everything* I could possibly use to our advantage. Determinedly, I started reading again.

My alarm clock startled me awake, since I didn't remember falling asleep. I must have at some point, but I'd managed to read well over half the scroll first. I was glad my Rigel-deprivation hadn't slowed my reading speed yet. If anything, it was still increasing.

I'd taken more notes, though I realized now I could recall everything I'd read perfectly. Still, looking over the notes might help me craft a strategy, once I—

Crap. Another glance at the clock said I didn't have time, though going to school seemed stupidly irrelevant given the stakes I now faced on several fronts. But if I was going to keep my aunt and uncle —and all the other non-*Echtrans*—in the dark, I'd have to at least go through the motions.

"So, um, hey," Molly greeted me at the bus stop. "I see you, ah, got back okay."

Sean didn't say anything at all, just regarded me with a half-angry, half-worried frown.

"Yeah." I hoped they didn't expect me to act happy about being back. For a little more than twenty-four hours I'd allowed myself to believe my dream of being with Rigel for good had a chance of coming true. Now I'd never see him again unless I convinced the

Council to let him go. Which I would. Somehow. *Before* they wiped his memory.

Rather to my surprise, Molly sat next to me on the bus and Sean sat right behind us. The moment we started moving, Sean leaned forward between us and said, "So, nice weekend?"

The acid in his tone made me glance at him in surprise. He was looking more angry than worried now.

"A busy one, for sure," I answered carefully, since we were surrounded by other students.

"Yeah, us, too," he practically growled. "You're welcome." He sat back against his seat with a thump and didn't say a word for the rest of the trip to school.

I looked curiously at Molly, but she just shrugged, not looking much happier than Sean did. I wanted to ask exactly what had happened while I was gone, but this wasn't the place, especially since Bri and Deb would be getting on at the next stop. Besides, I didn't have the brain space to worry about it right now. I lapsed back into planning and worrying about Rigel.

His absence from school worried everyone not in the know. I overheard a couple of football players wondering if he was sick again, but didn't bother to reassure them. He probably was by now.

Ms. Harrigan didn't act worried. If anything she looked smug, though that might have been my imagination. Just as well she didn't say anything to me, since I'd have been rude and probably sent to the office. In Science, I couldn't tell whether Mr. Gilliland knew or not, since he always stared at me like that. I didn't really care.

I was a little surprised when Sean and Molly both showed up to walk me to lunch, after the way they'd acted on the bus. It's not like they had to keep me from spending time with Rigel now.

"How are you feeling?" Molly asked as we walked.

I shot her a sour look. "Lousy. How do you think?"

She bit her lip. "So it's . . . not working?"

"Takes a day or two, Moll. That's what they said Saturday," Sean reminded her.

Though I wouldn't admit it, I did feel a little better than last night, unlike the last time Rigel and I were apart. No nausea and just the slightest headache. Oddly, my lack of physical symptoms upset me more. It should hurt to be apart. That's how our bond was supposed to work.

Again, I wondered whether they'd given Rigel the antidote yet. If they had, if it really worked on both of us, would his parents try at all to get us back together? Why would they? I tried to fight down my panic at that thought.

To distract myself, I asked, "So, what *did* you guys do this weekend? What did you mean on the bus?"

"You don't know?" Molly sounded genuinely surprised.

"Should I?"

"Duh," Sean replied, still clearly pissed. "We spent all day Saturday and half of Sunday fixing up some old lady's trailer just outside of Kokomo, like Mum told your aunt."

I looked at Molly for verification. "You did? I thought that was totally made up."

"It sort of was, but we had to make it look good in case your aunt checked it out. So Mum called the church and got the name and address of somebody on the list for assistance and carted us up there. I even used your name so the woman would say I was you if anyone asked." She flexed her shoulders, like they were sore.

"What all did you do?"

Sean grimaced. "Fixed her steps and painted them, then fixed and painted the lattice around the bottom of the trailer, to keep animals out. Stuff like that. I had to leave Saturday practice early. Hope Coach won't make me do laps around the gym."

"Oh. Sorry. I didn't know."

He shrugged, but his expression softened. "We were all really worried about you, you know, even apart from the political stuff. I'm glad you're back. And safe."

Though I knew he meant well, I stiffened. "I was safe the whole time. I was with Rigel."

The softness instantly disappeared. "You both must realize now how stupid that was. How dangerous. What was he thinking? What were you? What if—"

"Sean," Molly cautioned him. He'd been getting a little loud and people were starting to glance our way. "Not here."

"Right." He shot a sideways look at me and ducked his head. "Sorry. Out of line. But you have no idea how scared I—we—were."

His earnestness touched me in spite of myself, but before I could think of any way to respond, Deb and Bri joined us in the lunch line, so we obviously had to change the subject.

"You don't think Rigel will be sick for long, do you?" Bri suddenly asked me as we reached our table.

I looked up, startled. "What? Why?" I hadn't denied it when she'd assumed in English he was sick, but I hadn't confirmed it, either. I hoped her words weren't a bad omen.

"The winter formal next week, silly! You guys are going, right?" Then, without waiting for me to answer, "How about you, Sean? Have you asked anybody to the dance yet?"

Clearly caught off guard, Sean shook his head. "Um, not yet. Who are you guys going with?"

Bri gave him such a flirtatious smile it was all I could do not to roll my eyes. "Depends on who asks me."

They bantered back and forth, then Deb and Molly joined in. The whole scene suddenly struck me as surreal. How could everybody act so . . . *normal* when Rigel was in prison facing who knew what, while super-advanced, non-human aliens might be preparing to wipe us all out of existence? Not that any of them knew that last part, but still.

Pretending to be interested in my friends' conversation, I focused on the first of those problems, determined to have Rigel back in Jewel by the end of the week. Finally, halfway through History, I hatched the beginnings of a plan. In Health class, I worked out more details while the teacher droned on about STDs. I was impatient now for school to end so I could get home to my scroll to double check a few things.

When I finally headed to the bus, I was startled to see Sean waiting by the curb. I knew he had basketball practice, so I hurried when he motioned me over.

"M, I should have told you this earlier, sorry," he murmured so no one else could hear. "But, well, I was still pissed at Stuart for going along with that dumb running-away thing."

"Told me what?" His worried expression put all my nerves on high alert.

He looked over my shoulder at my waiting friends, then back at me, pain and apology in his eyes. "Something my uncle said after you left our house last night. Not only does it sound like there's no way Stuart is getting that antidote thing, he hinted that some folks in

Montana might . . . take matters into their own hands. About his sentence, I mean."

I stared at him, stricken, feeling all the blood leave my face. "What do you mean? They might . . . lynch him or something?" I remembered what we'd studied in History about the Ku Klux Klan. "He might not even get a trial?"

Sean shrugged, looking more miserable than ever. "I'm not sure. I asked, but he didn't really answer, just looked . . . smug. I . . . thought you should know. I may not like Stuart much, but—"

"Thanks, Sean," I said with an effort, fighting the panic that threatened to choke me. "I . . . I appreciate you telling me. Really."

With a quick nod, he loped off to practice and I climbed onto the bus. When Deb asked me what was wrong, I just shook my head and pretended to listen to Bri's plans for a shopping trip.

Once home, I had a bunch of chores to catch up on after being gone all weekend, which was frustrating since now I *really* needed to finish working out my plan. Fast as I tried to work, Aunt Theresa got home before I was done and kept me downstairs to help with dinner and then do the dishes.

Finally, claiming I was still tired from all my "work" over the weekend, I escaped to my bedroom, where I immediately pulled out my scroll and my notes. First I reread a few things I remembered from before, then used the index to double check the wording on a couple of statutes.

My homework went completely undone, but that was the absolute least of my worries. By eleven o'clock, I thought my plan was solid. It was gutsy, but *should* work, since I had Nuathan law and precedent on my side. The only problem was, once I convened the Council there would be no going back.

I'd originally planned to go to the O'Garas' after school tomorrow and ask Allister to convene them, but after what Sean told me this afternoon, I was afraid to wait that long. Some of the Council might head back to wherever they lived, and any delay might give those people in Montana a chance do something awful to Rigel before I could act.

I put my ear to my bedroom door and listened until Uncle Louie was snoring good and loud, then I tiptoed downstairs to the kitchen, picked up the phone and dialed Rigel's land line. Late as it was, I wasn't surprised when it rang four times before Shim answered.

"Hello?" He sounded tired but also cautious, though I was sure caller ID told him who was calling.

"Shim, it's M. How quickly can you reconvene the Council? It's important."

"Ah, one moment, Excellency." There was a long pause, during which I could hear voices in the background. I hoped that was a good sign. Then, "Everyone is still in Jewel, though three members have early flights out of Indianapolis tomorrow. Perhaps next week we could—"

"No. It has to be before anyone leaves. Either right now, tonight, or they can cancel their flights and we'll do it tomorrow. No later."

There was another hushed conference at the other end of the line, then Shim said, "Very well, Princess. Shall I have Allister pick you up on his way here? He is at the O'Garas' tonight."

My heart pounded with anticipation and astonishment at my own audacity. "That'll be fine," I told him, hoping against hope I could pull this off. "I'll be waiting out front."

42

chabhil (KAB-vil): *negotiation; debate; (occ.)*
ultimatum

I ran upstairs to change into something more presentable than my
ratty sweats, brushed my hair and clipped it back, tucked the scroll-
book in my pocket, then hurried—quietly—back downstairs. I'd be
grounded till I was forty if Aunt Theresa caught me sneaking out
again, but with Rigel's freedom, memory, maybe even life at stake, I
was more than willing to take that risk.

The kitchen door was farther from my aunt and uncle's bedroom,
so I slipped out that way, then walked up the driveway to the street.
I'd only been waiting five minutes—wishing just a little for Sean's
omni and its personal climate control—when Allister pulled up.

"Thanks for the ride," I said as politely as I could manage as I
climbed in. I could tell Allister what I really thought of him after I
delivered my ultimatum.

He hmphed, not unlike Aunt Theresa, and pulled away from the
curb. "It's an honor to serve, Princess." His voice dripped sarcasm
but I didn't react. All my thoughts were focused on the meeting
ahead.

The drive to the Stuarts' house seemed longer than usual due to
the chilly silence in the car and my mounting nervousness. When we
finally got there, I didn't wait for Allister to open my door but got
out and walked ahead of him to the house.

Fake it till you make it, I told myself firmly. For the next hour I had
to act like I'd been brought up as royalty instead of a misfit
midwestern orphan. Rigel's life depended on how well I could carry
this off.

One of the Council members I'd just met yesterday, a tall,
absurdly handsome blond man named Connor, opened the front
door just as I reached it. "Excellency," he said, with that fist-over-

heart bow thing. I inclined my head exactly as I'd been taught, determined to look more regal than I felt. Allister followed me in and I didn't have to look at him to know he was scowling.

Everyone had convened around the dining room table, which conveniently seated eight. They all rose when I entered, then bowed to me in unison. Again I inclined my head, telling myself firmly that this was my due, not something that should weird me out.

Deliberately, ignoring the humility that had been drummed into me over the years by Aunt Theresa, I moved to the empty chair at the head of the table. Allister irked me by taking the seat at the opposite end, presumably because he was the "ranking Royal" as he liked to remind everyone.

Except now I was.

"Thank you all for meeting on such short notice," I said, proud that my voice held only the tiniest hint of a quiver. "We had to cut our discussion short yesterday and now I'd like to continue it. A lot of facts were laid out for me, but very few of my questions were answered. Tonight I want those answers, after which I have a proposition for you."

I paused for breath after my rehearsed spiel, half expecting some kind of protest from Allister or Kyna or someone. None came, so I continued.

"First, you must have found out by now whether Rigel has been given the same antidote I have?" I looked to Shim, who frowned unhappily.

"I did inquire, Excellency, and was told that no antidote was sent to Montana. Supposedly—" He shot a glance down the table to Allister— "that is being rectified?"

Allister, I noticed, didn't meet my eye. "I believe so, yes."

"You 'believe' so?" I echoed. "Not good enough. I want someone to verify for me—now—that Rigel has either been given the antidote, or that the antidote is on its way to him. Also, that it will *work* for him. Can you do that, Allister?"

He shifted in his seat uncomfortably. "I'll, ah, have to make a call, but it's awfully late—"

"It's two hours earlier in Montana. Make the call."

Reddening, he glanced around the table, clearly hoping someone would back him up or rein me in. When no one did, he took out his cell phone and got up to leave the room.

"No, here is fine," I told him. I knew I was pushing it, but I didn't trust him for a second to do what I asked if he was out of earshot.

With a quick glower at me, Allister made the call. "Yes, it's me. Have some of that antidote sent to Montana on the next available flight and tell them to administer it to the boy. . . . That's right. . . . No, never mind that. . . . Yes, yes, on my authority."

He punched off his phone. "There. It's done."

"Thank you, Allister."

Even though I'd clearly heard the man on the other end say, *You're reversing your previous order?* I decided to move on rather than confront Allister about it just yet. If things went the way I hoped, his agenda wouldn't matter. I took heart from the fact that some of the other Council members were now looking askance at Allister, too, since it was obvious even from his end of the conversation that he'd been less than honest before.

"Now that we've established that Rigel was *not* given any antidote," I continued, "I want him released and returned to Jewel. Immediately."

"But—" Allister motioned to his phone. Then several others spoke up.

"Excellency, that's not possible—or prudent," Kyna informed me.

At the same time, Connor exclaimed, "I thought you understood that he must remain there for now, if only for appearances' sake."

Even Shim, who had been frowning furiously at Allister a second ago, said, "I fear that could undermine our effort to have you quickly Acclaimed Sovereign by Nuath's citizens."

I let the storm of protests die down before responding. "Yes, I understand how important appearances are right now. You all made that clear to me, repeatedly. Believe me, I don't want to be the cause of a civil war on Mars, which is why I'm willing to propose a compromise. Even though I don't have to."

"What do you mean, Excellency?" asked Breann, a stunning brunette and another high-ranking Royal.

"I mean that I have the authority to have Rigel released and brought back without the Council's agreement—though I would rather have it."

Several heads started shaking.

Malcolm, another Royal I'd met for the first time last night, spoke first. "I'm afraid you are overestimating your current power, Princess. Not only are you underage, you haven't yet been Acclaimed or installed. There are very specific ceremonies—"

"That are traditional. I know. I've read all about them." I pulled out my scroll and snapped it open on the table. "But I've also read *all* of Nuathan law, the entire code, which isn't all that long. Not nearly as long as the hundreds and hundreds of pages of tradition and precedent—which I've also read. Isn't it true that law always supersedes tradition?" I looked around at them all, trying to hide the fact that I was holding my breath.

Slowly, Malcolm's head began to nod, then Breann's and Connor's, and finally, to my surprise, even Allister's. But he was the one who protested next.

"None of our traditions are contrary to codified law. They would never have become traditions if they were."

I couldn't bring myself to look Allister in the face for fear I'd say what I really wanted to, which wouldn't be regal at all. "Perhaps not contrary, at least under normal circumstances. But these aren't normal circumstances, are they? When was the last time you had an underage Sovereign, with no surviving ancestor, who inherited without warning?"

"Was that Arturo, son of Tiernan?" Malcolm hazarded.

I nodded. "Almost eight hundred years ago. But the law hasn't changed since then, nor has anything happened to overrule the precedent that was set. *Tradition* is different now, but not the law itself. Arturo took power at the age of fourteen, mediating disputes and confirming officials. He even started the space program that eventually led to the first exploratory mission to Earth. His Regent wasn't appointed for more than two months, according to your own historical records."

"But the Regent is always appointed—" Allister began, but I cut him off.

"According to tradition, yes. As soon as a new underage Sovereign is installed. But the two times since Arturo you've had an underage Sovereign, it was *not* unexpected. A Regent had already been chosen by Acclamation *and* confirmed by the previous Sovereign."

To my surprise, it was Nara, usually so supportive, who launched the next volley. "I won't deny for a moment that you have the right to issue whatever orders you see fit, Excellency," she said. "But please do try to look at the larger picture. We really do have your best interests in mind, as well as those of our people."

"What part of the larger picture?" I asked her.

"Specifically, your fitness to rule. Not that *I* doubt it for a second," she quickly added. "But it's terribly important that we convince the majority of our people, here and especially on Mars, as quickly as possible. If it were to become known that you ran away of your own volition—"

Now I saw where she was going. "You mean you want to use Rigel as a scapegoat so it will look like I was an unwilling victim."

"Only . . . only temporarily," she assured me with a placating smile.

I shook my head. "How am I more fit to lead if I was a victim instead of an instigator? The opposite should be true. Besides, how many people actually know I was gone? Did word get back to Mars about what happened?"

Everyone around the table exchanged glances, then Shim answered. "From all we've been able to determine, we believe not. Yet."

"But there's no guarantee it won't leak out," Kyna put in. "We had to call on the assistance of numerous people to track you down. If a single one of them should be indiscreet, much damage could be done."

"Then we deny everything," I told her, projecting all the confidence I could. My recent practice with Rigel helped. "Who will dare contradict the Council? And me?"

Though most of them looked uncomfortable, no one replied.

After a brief, awkward silence, Breann spoke. "There is another issue, Excellency, apart from what happened this weekend. Sean O'Gara, your destined Consort."

I nodded. I'd been expecting this. "Again, you're talking about tradition, not actual law. There's nothing in the Nuathan code that specifies who I have to eventually join with. Believe me, I looked *very* carefully for that! There *is* lots of tradition, added to over the centuries, but it was never codified into law."

I expected Allister to pipe up, so was startled when Shim spoke instead. "You're quite correct, my dear. And perhaps by the time you are of marriageable age some sort of accommodation can be made. But at the moment we must concern ourselves with your acceptance by the Nuathan people. That must occur before anything else can proceed."

"From all we've been told," Connor said, "if young Stuart returns to Jewel, it will quickly become apparent to any observers that you have no intention of honoring Nuathan tradition in this matter. Even limited observation has revealed your clear preference for Stuart over Sean O'Gara."

I glared at him. "So was it you who put spies into my very classrooms at school? How much respect does *that* show for the Sovereign?"

He sat back in his chair, blinking and stammering. "Ah, not me, personally, Excellency, I assure you! But interested parties felt it necessary—"

"It's not necessary, and I want them gone. Tomorrow, if possible."

Connor nodded, swallowing. "I'll, er, make your wishes known, of course."

"Excellency, I don't think this is wise," Malcolm said before I could thank Connor. "The reason there are observers at your school is to reassure those elements who are wary of an untried Sovereign after our unfortunate experience with Faxon. Those elements make up a not-insignificant percentage of our people who will need that reassurance if they are to wholeheartedly accept you."

Kyna nodded. "He's right. It's all very well—not to mention quite impressive—for you to quote chapter and verse on Nuathan law." I was surprised by the respect on her face, as she'd always been so critical. "However, as Shim just intimated, you cannot lead effectively, or at all, without the will of the people behind you. Particularly now, when they have so recently suffered a brutal and incompetent leader."

"Which is why it's so important for you to be seen forming a, ah, friendship with my nephew." Allister had been unusually quiet till now, after having his falsehood exposed. "The traditionalists are your staunchest supporters right now, which means the last thing you can afford to do is alienate them."

Everyone but Shim and Nara were nodding now. I felt my tenuous control of the situation slipping away.

"I understand that. I do," I told them all earnestly. "And I do want what's best for the Nuathan people." As I said those words, I was startled to realize I meant them. When had *that* happened?

"Then you'll agree to be guided by us, Princess?" Breann asked.

I looked her directly in the eye. "Guided, yes. Manipulated, no. And I absolutely won't allow Rigel to be railroaded for a crime he didn't commit, no matter what noble-sounding principles you spout to justify it. Besides, without him, I can't be what you want me to be. Because he and I are *graell* bonded and, antidote or no antidote, we can't live without each other."

"But—" Allister began, and a few others murmured as well. I held up a hand to silence them and to my surprise, it worked.

"I am, however, willing to offer a compromise." I paused, gauging their expressions. They ranged from irritated to skeptical to downright hostile, though a couple at least appeared willing to listen.

"Allow Rigel and his parents to immediately return to Jewel, with your blessing. Permanently, or until they *choose* to leave, without being pressured. In return, I will not only continue being friends with Sean and Molly O'Gara, but when in public—where other *Echtrans* might be watching—I will do my best to make it *appear* that Sean and I are becoming a couple. It will only be pretend, though, and I'll make sure both Sean and Rigel understand that. In private, and in reality, I'll still be with Rigel."

Heads started shaking all around the table. "Ridiculous," one of them snapped, followed by several murmurs of agreement. As I'd feared, they weren't going for it. And no matter what their laws might say, I couldn't *make* all these important people do anything. But I had to try. Steeling my resolve one more time, I played my very last card, the one that would seal my fate.

"If you accept this compromise, I will also promise to learn all I can, as quickly as I can, and to fulfill my duties as Sovereign. However, if Rigel isn't brought back—in fact, if *anything* happens to him—" I glanced meaningfully at Allister— "I'll abdicate. I won't cooperate, even as a figurehead. I'll have nothing to do with governing, or diplomacy with aliens or anything else, no matter *how* high the stakes are."

There was a long, disapproving silence. From their expressions, I could tell some didn't believe me and others thought I was acting like a spoiled brat.

Finally Breann, the highest ranking Royal after Allister, said, "For any compromise to be binding, we must put the Sovereign's proposal to a formal vote, with all—" She pinned me with her aquamarine gaze— "agreeing to be bound by the result."

As one, the others chorused, "Agreed."

"Agreed," I echoed, a huge knot forming in the pit of my stomach. I'd really done it now. I knew the law. If the vote went against me, they couldn't *make* me do the Sovereign thing, but I'd also be leaving Rigel to the mercy of a crazy mob in Montana, with Allister calling the shots. Even if he escaped alive, even if we someday saw each other again, he wouldn't remember me.

Feeling like I just might faint, I held my breath, praying I hadn't just jettisoned Rigel's future, along with my own.

43

Rigel (RY-jel): *an intense star expected to end in supernova at a relatively young age*

"Hey! Come back here!" I yell. "Where are my parents?" But the guard is gone.

I make a face at the sorry excuse for a dinner he left me—a hot dog and some carrot sticks—then glare around at my cell. It's absolutely a cell, a cinderblock room with a metal door and a tiny barred window the size of a missing cinderblock. I haven't left it since I got here. I only know "here" is Montana because my mom mentioned it during the ten minutes they let me see my folks this morning.

For the past twenty-four hours or more—I don't really know—my world has been this ten by ten room with a cot-like bed, dilapidated table, two chairs, and a chest with two drawers—not that I have anything to put in them. A bucket and a wash stand in the corner pass for a bathroom.

I glance again at the hot dog and push it away before it makes me heave. Separation from M is making me sicker faster this time, but I'm not about to give anyone here the satisfaction of mentioning it. They can keep their stupid antidote. If it even exists. Nobody's offered me any and I wouldn't take it now if they did. Though for M's sake I hope it does exist and that it works—for her.

Like I've done most of the day, I strain my ears to hear anything that will give me a clue whether she's here, too. It's more likely they took her back to Jewel, but my folks didn't know and the guard won't tell me anything, no matter how many questions I ask when he brings me food and empties my toilet-bucket.

There've been voices outside the door a few times, but too far away to make out words. I can reach the window by standing on the bed, but it looks out on a wall and I haven't heard anything from that direction at all.

I don't know what time it is, but it's dark. I fling myself down on the bed. Between nausea, headache and worry for M and my folks I'm pretty tired but doubt I can sleep. Then I hear footsteps.

Jumping back up, I go to the door, but before I can put my ear to it, it opens. A man I've never seen before, flanked by two other men, comes inside.

"So," he says, looking at me like I'm a bug—which immediately reminds me of Allister Adair, even though this guy is taller, younger, and better looking. "You're the Stuart kid."

"Yeah. So? Who are you?"

He flicks a glance at the larger of the men behind him, and he steps forward and smacks me across the mouth. It hurts, but I've had tackles hurt worse. I don't make any sound, just keep watching the first guy who came in, the one in charge.

"Clearly, you need to learn some respect," he says, tilting his head back so he can look down his nose at me, since he's no taller than I am. "But I knew that already, since no properly brought up *Echtran* would presume to imagine our Sovereign had some kind of preference for him."

I want to shout at him that what M has for me is way more than a "preference," but I clench my jaw instead. I'm not telling this asshole anything.

"Sit down, *Rigel*." He makes my name sound like something nasty.

I don't move, so the two guys with him grab me by the arms and force me into one of the chairs at the table. Then they step back and stand behind me, while the guy in charge seats himself across from me.

"I am Governor Lennox, magistrate of Dun Cloch."

The compound in Montana. Last I heard, there were five or six hundred *Echtrans* living here. This jerk's their governor?

"I am also," he continues, "the person who holds your fate in his hands. So I recommend you not only show me proper respect, but give prompt and truthful answers to anything I ask. This may be the only trial you get."

Trial? What the hell?

Lennox watches me for a minute or two, then folds his hands in front of him like he's settling down for a long talk. "So," he begins at last, "was it because she wouldn't go along with your little romantic fantasy that you decided to kidnap the Princess?"

I expel my breath through my nose in a snort. They have to know by now I didn't kidnap her. I heard my parents trying to convince someone about our bond this morning, before they were hauled away. Forcing myself to act calm, even though I don't feel it, I look him in the eye.

"What have you done with her? And with my parents? Whatever you think I did, they had nothing to do with it."

"There will be an inquest," he says, like that's supposed to reassure me. "For now, your parents are under house arrest for plotting to help you escape. We can't have that, obviously. You've done enough damage already."

My gut twists, thinking of my folks in a nasty little cell like mine when all they were doing was trying to help me. That *is* my fault.

"And M? Is she here, too?"

He shoots another glance at the big guy behind me and I get another smack across my mouth.

"How dare you?" Lennox sounds less calm now. "If you refer to her Excellency, you will call her Sovereign or Princess, and not by her given name. Or, worse, some disgusting diminutive of that name. I am Governor of the largest *Echtran* enclave on Earth and *I* would never presume to do such a thing. Who are *you?* Nobody. The Earth-born son of two longtime emigrants who were misfits even on Mars. Having a grandfather on the Council won't earn you any special favors in Dun Cloch, I promise you."

"She's not here, then, huh?" No way she wouldn't have set the story straight by now if she were. But she'd do that no matter where she is. Which means wherever she is, nobody's listening to her—or maybe even letting her talk to anyone. Are they keeping her drugged or a prisoner in Jewel? I *so* need to get out of here!

Though he's still glaring, Lennox finally answers my question. "No, the Princess is not here. She was safely returned to her home and to the Council, no thanks to you. Believe me, if she had been harmed—at all—while in your company, you would not be sitting here talking to me now. As it is, you are guilty of high treason, a capital crime."

Though I'm careful not to let it show, I feel like I've been punched in the stomach. Capital crime? What the hell? Grandfather told me Martians—or *Echtrans*—have never had a death penalty. Did they? Do they?

"It will be *my* decision," Lennox continues, "whether or not you deserve any sort of leniency. At the moment, I am inclined to think not. I am, however, prepared to listen. It's possible you may escape with only the *tabula rasa*. So, I ask you again. Why did you kidnap the Princess?"

Having my memory completely wiped, all the way back to infancy, doesn't sound much better than death. Maybe worse. I wouldn't even remember M. Which I guess would be incredibly convenient for everyone but us. The idea of seeing her again but not knowing her twists my heart.

"I didn't," I tell him. "Leaving Jewel was a mutual decision, hers as well as mine."

"Don't be ridiculous," he snaps. "Everyone knows the Princess has begun receiving the instruction necessary to lead her people. That's been widely publicized. Also that her personality and aptitude profiles are ideal, despite having been raised *Duchas*. What possible reason could such a promising Sovereign have to leave her instructors and her future Consort at the exact moment Faxon fell from power on Mars? The timing suggests that you are a sympathizer of his, seeking to undermine the resistance in its very moment of triumph."

My growing headache makes it hard to take in everything he just threw at me, but I do my best. "Wait. Faxon is out? Like, totally out? When did that happen?"

He looks like he's about to have one of his goons hit me again, but he doesn't. "Friday night," he finally tells me. "By Saturday morning, nearly every *Echtran* on Earth had heard the news. Do you expect me to believe you didn't?"

"How would I? How would either of us? M, er, the Princess didn't know, either. And the *last* thing I am is a Faxon sympathizer! Hell, his guy Morven tried to kill me, along with, uh, the Sovereign and my folks. Or didn't you hear about that?"

That does fetch me another clout to the head from one of the guys behind me.

"I know all about Morven, I assure you," Lennox tells me with a little smile. "Far more than you do, I imagine, as he's been in residence here for two months. The only reason he still possesses his memories is that the Council hoped he might recover enough to provide information on Faxon. Believe me, there are those here who feel strongly enough about what he attempted to take matters into their own hands. Most of them feel the same about you. And you still haven't told me why you abducted the Sovereign."

I roll my eyes to the ceiling. Is this guy deaf, or what? "I did tell you. I told you she and I left together. As for why, I know this will probably get me smacked around again, but it was because the Council was planning to separate us, probably permanently, and she didn't want that any more than I did. Don't you get it? We *need* to be together!"

I'm about to tell him about our *graell* bond, but he nods at the thugs behind me and this time they both hit me, one on the head and the other across the back.

"That was a warning," Lennox says. "I will *not* allow you to impugn the honor of our Princess by implying not only that she has romantic inclinations toward you, a nobody, when she has already been introduced to her Consort, but that she would put such inclinations above her duty to her people. That is tantamount to accusing the Princess herself of treason."

I want to yell at him to *ask* her, to call the Council or anybody who's talked to her since we were caught, but he keeps talking.

"If such a vicious rumor became public, it would seriously undermine the Sovereign's ability to lead, to gather the support she *must* gather, and quickly, now that Faxon is gone. In which case, instead of a vocal handful of a hundred or so, *every* Nuathan who cares about the future of our race, here and on Mars, would want you dead."

For the first time, I detect the fear behind Lennox's anger, which means he's even more dangerous than I thought. I'm not sure what to say, since the very last thing I want is make things worse for M. Who knows what she's going through back in Jewel? Getting endlessly ragged on by Allister, at the very least, but maybe worse than that. They can't accuse *her* of treason, can they? Wouldn't they just decide she's unfit to lead, instead? I guess that would be bad for Mars, but—wouldn't it be good for us?

Maybe it would be like my dad said and they'd have to elect somebody or appoint somebody or something. It's not like M ever wanted to be Sovereign—she's said so dozens of times. But I know deep down it can't be that easy. They aren't going to revamp their whole system of government because of a teen romance. And if shutting me up—permanently—is what it will take to prevent that, that's what they'll do.

But what about M? She won't sit by while they make me disappear. In fact, she's probably screaming bloody murder right now. In which case, won't the easiest way to shut *her* up be to tell her I'm dead? If she believes that—whether it's true or not, and it probably will be—she won't have any reason to stay on Earth at all. Then they'll get *exactly* what they want.

I look up at Lennox's implacable face and feel icy fingers of dread crawling up my back as I realize these people will never allow me to see M again. They see my very existence as a huge threat to their cause. And there's not a damned thing I can say that will convince them otherwise.

"Ah," he says, meeting my gaze. "I see you finally understand. Pity you didn't think things through several days earlier. If you had, we wouldn't have this mess to sort through and keep quiet."

Something in his eyes makes me realize another truth. "You knew. You knew all along I didn't kidnap her, that we ran away together. I'll bet you even knew about our bond."

He shrugs. "What I know—or believe—makes no difference, as nothing we say here will ever leave this room." He stands up. "Since it seems unlikely either you or the Princess will be able to keep your dangerous opinions to yourselves, my decision becomes obvious. If, as you claim, she also believes in this *bond*, a simple memory wipe won't suffice, despite our law."

Because our bond would still be there. The best way to control M is to kill me, so she'll have nothing left to fight for. Pain shoots through my heart at the thought of what she'll feel when they tell her. I wish I could spare her that, at least.

Lennox displays no emotion as he continues. "I'll allow you to say goodbye to your parents. In light of your youth, you'll be sedated before the execution. It will be as painless as a memory wipe."

"What about the law?" The words tumble out before I can stop them. "Won't the Council or somebody—"

"Not to worry." He actually smiles. "You will attempt to escape before the *tabula rasa* procedure and will suffer a fatal accident in the process. Such a pity."

Lennox and his goons leave the room and lock the door behind them. I stare at it for about ten seconds, then run to the bucket in the corner and throw up.

The next three hours are the longest of my life. I wish there was something in this cell to distract me—a book, a magazine, even interesting patterns on the walls. But there's nothing, so all I can do is think—and anticipate. Off and on I pray—yeah, I'm reduced to praying—that M will come out of this okay, that somehow she'll get over losing me, get over everything, and have a happy life, on Earth or on Mars. But mostly, I'm just scared to die and spend eternity without her.

After way too much time to think, I finally hear voices outside the door.

"You have five minutes," my taciturn guard says as the door opens and my parents rush into the room. The guard retreats and locks the door again.

"Rigel!" my mom cries, rushing forward to hug me. "It can't be true. They can't possibly do this. Performing the *tabula rasa* on a minor is counter to every principle of our people. Somehow, we'll —"

"Mom, it's okay," I manage to choke out, though her distress unleashes the tears I've held in check until now. "I'm not scared," I lie, trying to make this easier for her, grateful she doesn't know Lennox's real plan. "I need you guys to take a message to M for me."

My dad grips my shoulder, then hugs me, too, something he hardly ever does. "We'll do anything you need us to do, son, but this isn't over. I left a message for Shim before they took my phone away. I can't believe this ridiculous excuse for a trial and sentencing has the blessing of the Council."

I shrug, trying to calm him down, too. If they figure out Lennox's "accident" for me is faked, if they raise a stink, he'll probably have *their* memories wiped. Or worse. "Maybe not. But this Lennox guy —"

"Lach Lennox has never forgiven your grandfather for speaking out against him when he was nominated to the Council," Dad says, "though others must have voted him down as well. It's clear he's taking out his resentment on you, because of Shim."

"Does his reason really matter?" I ask. "If nobody's here to stop him, he'll still do what he's convinced is necessary."

Both of my parents look stricken, and my mom shakes her head convulsively, tears streaming down her face. Before they can protest again, I say what I need to say.

"Look, if you can stop him, that's great, and I hope you can. But if you can't, I need you to tell M that . . . that I love her, but that she has to move on. Maybe . . . maybe she can bond again." I swallow, hard. "Maybe with Sean. That's what everyone wants, and they're already friends. She needs to have someone close to her who cares about her as a person, not just the politics, and . . . I think maybe he does. I hope."

My mom hugs me again, chanting, "No, no, no," under her breath while my dad wraps an arm around her like he's keeping her from flying into pieces—and maybe he is. I don't even try to keep from crying, knowing I'm leaving everything, everyone I love, so soon. I wish with all my being I could see M one last time, to say goodbye.

"Time," the guard announces, and we all start. None of us heard the door open.

"Please," my mother pleads. "Just a few more minutes?"

When the guard shakes his head, my dad demands, "I want to speak with Lennox again. Now."

"I'm sorry," the guard says, his voice not completely unsympathetic, "but you have to leave now." Gently but firmly, he pries my mom's arms from around me and escorts them from the room.

I hear someone else talking to them outside, then all the voices recede just before the guard—I still don't know his name—closes the door again and turns back to me.

"Sorry, Stuart," he says, to my surprise. "I really hoped it wouldn't come to this. I . . ." He shakes his head almost angrily. "Not as proud of my people right now as I've been. Anyway, I have your sedative here, so at least you won't feel anything. Best I can do.

"Sorry," he repeats, coming toward me with a tiny silver syringe.

For the second time in forty-eight hours, everything goes black. My last thought before I lose consciousness is that my love for M will continue past death.

44

scriosath (SKREE-oh-sath): *memory erasure, up to and including the* tabula rasa *or "blank slate"*

As soon as everyone, including me, agreed to a vote on my proposal —or, rather, my ultimatum—Breann stood. "In keeping with tradition, a roll call vote will be taken, in order of seniority. Shim?"

"Aye," he said firmly. He didn't smile or look at me, but that wasn't what mattered right now.

"Allister?" Breann said next.

"Nay." He spoke just as firmly, but didn't meet *anyone's* eye.

I held my breath as Breann called on the others, knowing Nara's was the only other vote I could count on. The others' expressions didn't reveal anything at all.

To my surprise, Malcolm voted aye, as did Nara after him. I just needed one more.

"Kyna?"

She hesitated for a long, long moment, frowning down the table at me as she considered. My heart sank. Then she gave a quick, decisive nod. "Aye."

I tried not to let my breath out too obviously. Next Breann called on Connor, who voted aye without hesitation, then finally Breann herself voted—also in my favor. Allister's had been the only negative vote!

"Th . . . thank you," I stammered, my earlier bravado now gone. I felt like I'd just run a marathon. "Now what?"

"I'll make the call," Shim said, "if that's agreeable to the Council and our Sovereign?"

His expression, as he finally faced me, was not only kind, but respectful—more than I'd ever seen it. That respect was mirrored in the faces of the rest of the Council—except Allister's, of course.

"Yes. Please," I replied. The others—again excepting Allister—

301

nodded as well.

Shim took out his phone and called. "Yes, this is Shim Stuart, calling on behalf of the Council. I need to speak with Governor Lennox." The man at the other end said something that sounded like an apology. "No, now," Shim told him. "This is important."

There was a much longer pause this time, and then I could hear the same voice at the other end asking for Allister.

"Lennox is answerable to the entire Council, not to a single member," Shim said. "The Sovereign herself asked me to make this call. Now, get Lennox to the phone."

This pause was so brief, it was obvious Governor Lennox must have been right there. "Yes, what is it?" I could clearly hear him say. "I'm extremely at the moment." His insolent tone startled me, since I couldn't imagine anyone being insolent to Shim.

"Then you should be pleased to hear that the Council is relieving you of one of your many concerns," Shim said pleasantly. "It has been decided that Rigel Stuart is to be released immediately and he and his parents returned to Jewel. I believe you heard me." That in response to a shouted *What?* "Tonight, if at all possible."

There was more sputtering on the other end of the line, but Shim just listened without comment, finally saying, "You have your orders, Lennox. Implement them. Now." He was frowning as he hung up.

"Is there a problem?" Breann asked.

"I hope not." The concern on Shim's face scared me. "He tried to cite various procedural complications at his end, but it was clearly a delaying tactic. I'm not sure—"

Allister's phone rang. He pulled it out, glanced at the screen and, like before, got up to leave the room.

This time it was Breann who stopped him. "Allister, you can take your call here. We don't mind." Despite her phrasing, her tone implied it wasn't optional.

With a quick glare around the table, Allister answered it. "Yes?"

I was sure I wasn't the only one who recognized Lennox's voice on the other end, sounding agitated. Allister quickly cut him off.

"Sorry. I can't help you." He cut the connection before Lennox could say anything else.

"Wrong number?" Kyna asked, her voice dripping sarcasm.

Allister hesitated, clearly deliberating, then shrugged. "Lennox had, ah, already given the order. He, ah, *hopes* there is still time to countermand it."

"*What?*" I nearly shrieked it. "What order?"

Allister swallowed visibly, looking furtively around the table.

"Breann, perhaps you should handle this," Shim suggested. "Given my, ah, history with Lennox, I fear another call from me may do more harm than good."

She nodded and pulled out her own phone. "Lennox," she snapped as soon as he answered. "I want your personal assurance, this instant, that you will comply with the Council's orders. You should know that Allister is no longer in any position to shield you."

There was a lot of talking at the other end, most of which sounded like apologies. Finally, I couldn't take it any more.

"Tell him I want to talk to Rigel," I said. "Now."

Breann relayed my command, listened to more agitated apologies from Lennox, then said, "Very well, then. Tomorrow morning at the latest."

Disconnecting, she turned to me. "He claimed that Rigel is asleep, though from his choice of words I suspect he means sedated. He did, however, assure me that he is safe, and promised to have them all on a plane in short order."

"In the interim, Excellency, I should take you home," Shim said gently.

"No!" I cried. "Not until I know for sure that Rigel is safe. Why would they sedate him?"

"We will find out," Shim promised me. "But should your aunt and uncle discover you gone, implementing the terms of our agreement might become difficult. If all goes well, you will see Rigel sometime tomorrow."

I knew he was right. The last thing I wanted was for Aunt Theresa to put me under house arrest. And it was a pretty good bet nothing else would happen tonight. Slowly, I nodded.

"But you'll call me or . . . or come get me . . . if—"

"Of course," Breann said. Then, "No, Allister, I think you'd better remain here until Shim returns. We have a bit of unfinished business."

Silently, I accompanied Shim out to his car, trying not to let my anxiety cross the line into hysteria again.

"Do you really think Rigel will be back in Jewel tomorrow?" I asked Shim at one point during the ride. The look he gave me was sad and definitely sympathetic.

"I hope so," was all he said.

I wanted to ask more questions but something in his expression stopped me. I stayed silent for the rest of the drive. When we reached my still-dark house, I let myself in and quietly made my way up to my room with Aunt Theresa none the wiser.

Needless to say, I never slept a wink.

School the next day went by in a blur. I could tell my friends, including Sean and Molly, thought I was getting sick again, but it was really lack of sleep combined with frantic worry for Rigel. I almost wished I *were* sick, since it seemed disloyal, an affront to our bond, that I wasn't.

At the final bell, I bolted for the bus, glad that Sean had basketball practice and Molly cheerleading, so I wouldn't have to talk to them.

The moment I got home, I raced to the phone to call Shim—and saw the answering machine light flashing. All day I'd alternated between desperate eagerness for my reunion with Rigel and terror that something had gone horribly wrong in Montana and I'd never see him again. Would this message tell me which it would be?

My finger trembled as I pushed the button.

"M," came Mrs. O'Gara's voice, "please come to our house the moment you get this. Leave a note for your aunt, but erase this message."

And that was all.

I played it three more times, trying to figure out from her tone whether the news was good or bad, but I honestly couldn't tell—especially since what was bad news to me might possibly be good news to her. My heart clogging my throat, I scrawled a quick note to Aunt Theresa saying I was at the O'Garas' house, then ran out the door without even dropping my backpack.

Both Mr. and Mrs. O'Gara were waiting for me on their porch, which only ramped my anxiety higher. I slowed from a trot to a fast walk as I approached, my breathing much faster than my brief exertion could account for.

"What . . . What's going on?" I panted as I reached them. "Can you tell me?"

Mrs. O'Gara put a comforting arm around my shoulders, giving me a quick hug that scared me half to death. It *must* be bad news!

"We're supposed to take you to the Stuarts' house," Mr. O'Gara told me. "The Council is assembled there, and waiting for you."

I swallowed, hard, determined not to cry in front of them if I could possibly help it. "Is . . . is Rigel there? Is he . . . is he . . . back?" I'd almost said *dead* but couldn't get the word out.

"I believe so," Mrs. O said, giving me another squeeze. "These have been a terribly difficult few days for you, my darling Princess."

I stared at her, not daring to believe her halfhearted reassurance but wanting to, oh! so much. "Let's go," I said. Not until I saw Rigel—alive—with my own eyes would I really be sure.

The way they hurried to their van, I realized I'd made it a command.

Nothing was said during the ten minute drive, and I was out of the van almost before it had stopped, running up to the Stuarts' front door. The O'Garas followed more slowly.

I'd barely touched the doorbell when the door opened, and I nearly collapsed with relief when Dr. Stuart greeted me with a smile.

"You're back!" I cried, flinging myself into her arms, which closed around me in a wonderfully comforting way. "And . . . and you're smiling! That *must* mean Rigel is okay?"

"He seems to be," she assured me. "He should be waking up any moment now, and we all thought you'd like to be here when he does."

I looked toward the stairs longingly. "Yes! Please."

She led me to Rigel's room, which I'd only been inside once before, his parents were such strict chaperones. Shim and Kyna were standing just outside, and I could see Mr. Stuart through the open door, sitting next to Rigel's bed. Even better, I could see Rigel himself, looking pale and disheveled, but unhurt. I darted forward, but Shim touched my shoulder, halting me.

"Excellency," he murmured, "I must remind you of your promise. Not a word."

I was so focused on Rigel, it took me a second to realize he was talking about the aliens, the Grentl. "No, no, of course not," I promised quickly, never taking my eyes from Rigel's wonderful,

wonderful face.

"Very well, then."

He released me with a subtle nudge toward Rigel, which was more urging than I needed. I practically flew to his side.

"Rigel?" I whispered, tremblingly touching his cheek. "Can you hear me?"

My heart beat a dozen times before his eyelids fluttered open. Wonder filled his eyes as he saw me, then gazed around at his room, with spaceship models and the dreamcatcher I'd given him hanging above the bed, then at his parents, standing right behind me.

"Am I dead? Is this . . . heaven?" he asked, his voice gravelly.

I flung myself onto him even as I heard his mother give a little sob behind me. "No, no, you're *not* dead! I was so afraid—! But you're here, we're together, and you're alive. Oh, Rigel!" My voice broke on his name and the tears I'd been holding in check all day finally started to flow.

"M," he murmured. "My M. I thought I'd never see you again. I thought—" His arms came around me and then we were kissing, in full view of his parents and the Council members in the hallway, and I didn't care a bit.

45

comhriteach (KOM-ree-teek): *compromise*

I spent the next few hours sitting on Rigel's bed, most of the time with our hands clasped, since I could feel him regaining all his strength—and more—from the contact. His mom even brought up snacks and drinks so I wouldn't have to leave his side until I finally had to go home for dinner.

With so many people around, we didn't talk much. The whole Council was still in the house, plus the O'Garas for the first hour or so. I knew meetings were going on downstairs but couldn't feel guilty about missing them, I was so happy to be with Rigel again—this time without the threat of having him torn away from me forever.

Even our silent "talking" was minimal. We were both *feeling* too much to put into words, so we spent our time sharing those feelings, instead. Also, after the first rush of joy and relief at our reunion, I remembered my promise to Shim. I doubted I could keep that secret from Rigel indefinitely, but I owed it to Shim to at least try, after all he'd done for for us.

There was also the matter of how to tell Rigel about the compromise I'd made with the Council. I knew he wasn't going to like it, but it had to be done, and soon. If I waited too long, someone else might mention it to him or to Sean, even though I'd made it clear I wanted to tell them both myself. And if Sean found out first, then said something to Rigel . . . No, I couldn't risk that.

More than once, I tried to frame the words. But we never seemed to be completely alone and I didn't want to tell him in front of a way-too-interested audience. The most I managed was to warn him that we'd still have to pretend not to be together at school, because of the *Echtran* observers there. When he asked how long that would last, I shrugged but let him know silently that I'd tell him more later.

The next day at school, it was even harder to deflect his questions.

There was no way I could explain everything silently in the middle of class, or even out loud in the hallway. My aunt let me go to taekwondo that afternoon, though, and he was waiting for me when I came out.

"Walk you home?" he asked me with a grin. "Or is that still not allowed? I . . . couldn't face the whole afternoon and evening without seeing you."

I glanced around to make sure no one was watching, even from a window, then hugged him and returned his kiss eagerly. "I don't *think* we'll get in trouble, as long as my aunt doesn't find out." Or the Council.

"Let's swing by the arboretum for a few minutes," he suggested. He carried my gear bag and it was all I could do not to hold his hand as we walked there in silence.

The minute we reached "our" bench, Rigel set down my bag and gave me a penetrating look. "Okay, what is it? It's totally obvious something's still bothering you, so spill."

"You're right," I admitted, twining my fingers in his to bolster my courage—and to gauge his reactions better. "It's . . . It's about how I got you back to Jewel, how I, um, how I got them to let you go. Don't be mad, okay?"

Rigel pulled me to him for a hug and another quick kiss. "*Mad* at you? Impossible. So how *did* you get me out of Lennox's clutches? I really, really thought I was dead. He told me to my face it would look like I had some kind of fatal accident."

I gasped, fighting down my horror. I'd come even closer to losing him than I'd thought! "That's . . . I need to tell the Council that. I'm sure they don't know. Except maybe Allister." Was even *he* that fanatical? I shuddered again at our narrow escape.

"After you left, I asked my folks and my grandfather what you'd done, but none of them would tell me." He felt a little worried to me, now.

Bracing myself for worse, I plunged in. "That's because I wanted to tell you myself. I, uh, sort of made a deal with the Council to get you back."

Judging by his expression, he could feel my worry and uncertainty as clearly as I felt his. "What kind of deal?" he asked cautiously.

"Well . . . I offered to stop fighting the whole Sovereign thing if they brought you back and said I'd refuse to be Sovereign at all if anything happened to you. But they still went on and on about how incredibly important appearances are right now, to rally all the people behind me and the legitimate government before factions start splintering off and maybe starting a civil war on Mars. And part of that appearances thing involves . . . Sean."

I felt a jolt of anger and jealousy from him, and his fingers tightened convulsively on mine, though not quite painfully. "Sean. So you agreed to . . . what? Get engaged to him or something?"

"No! Of course not!" Now it was his turn to feel *my* anger, and it immediately undercut his. "But . . . I had to promise to *act* like I'm with him, in public. When other Martians are around, anyway. At least until the government is back on its feet."

When he started to pull his hand out of mine, I tightened my own grip so he couldn't. "Rigel, it's *only* for show! Part of my deal was that I'll *really* be with you, for now and for always, no matter how I make things look to everybody else."

He frowned, only partially mollified. "And how *will* you make things look? Are you going to . . . to go on dates with him and stuff? Hold hands in the hallways? And for how long? What if it takes years for them to put the government back together? Then what? You know Sean will take full advantage of this, try to make you—"

"Rigel." I put a finger on his lips to stop his tirade, which was getting a little loud, even for the deserted arboretum. "Nothing Sean can do will make me stop loving you. Nothing!"

He swallowed visibly, then nodded, his anguish receding somewhat. "I'm sorry, M. I know the only reason you made that deal was to save me—and it worked." His mouth twisted into a semblance of a grin, though not a happy one. "Guess you made them an offer they couldn't refuse."

"It was a little dicier than that, but yeah, I guess so. After a lot of arguing, they put it to a vote and agreed to my terms."

An echo of the desperation I'd felt during that all-important vote swept through me and in response, Rigel hugged me tightly and kissed me again, a real kiss this time. When he finally pulled back a little to look at me, I was surprised by the respect in his eyes.

"I guess they do have a real leader after all."

I felt myself blushing. But yesterday evening, as I'd been leaving his house, I'd overheard Kyna saying almost the same thing to Breann.

"Yes," her voice had come from behind a closed door, "I think we were all relieved to see the Sovereign demonstrate the backbone she'll need for the days and years ahead. I confess, I didn't think she had it in her and I'm delighted to be proved wrong."

Had I really "demonstrated backbone?" If so, it had been purely for Rigel's sake. But maybe . . . maybe it did mean I could eventually become what they needed me to be. As long as I had Rigel with me the whole way.

That evening after dinner, I went over to the O'Gara's house, ostensibly to work on a history paper. In reality, the Council wanted me to record a short video to reassure everyone on Mars that I was alive, healthy, and not crazy.

Breann gave me a suggested script, but said I could use my own words. Since it didn't sound much like me, I changed some wording but kept the gist, introducing myself and talking about how I knew it was a difficult time, but that I was sure they could pull together for the good of everyone, and that I was learning what I needed so I could help with that eventually.

After three takes, Breann seemed satisfied. Putting the tiny recording device in her pocket, went to the kitchen, where the O'Garas had been waiting, to say goodbye to them before leaving. A moment later Sean wandered in.

"Done with your first movie?" he teased. "Breann says you were great. They're doing some edits, I think, before sending it to the rest of the Council."

"I don't know about great, but I did it."

I suddenly realized this was a perfect opportunity to tell Sean about my bargain. In fact, it was possible Breann was keeping everyone in the kitchen to give me the privacy to do exactly that. Dreading his reaction, though not for the same reason I'd dreaded Rigel's, I launched into my explanation before I could lose my nerve.

As I explained the compromise, I repeated more than once that the whole thing would *only* be for show. By the time I finished, though, Sean was grinning like Christmas had come two weeks early.

"So let me get this straight. In the interests of peace and for the good of our entire race, we need to convince all the *Echtrans,* here and everywhere, that we're dating?" His grin widened further. "I'm in! You can come to my game tomorrow night and the party afterward. We can put on a good show for everybody."

I frowned. "I told you, Sean, it'll only be when *Echtrans* are watching, like at school. It doesn't mean I'll go with you to parties and stuff, when none of them are around."

Still smiling, he quirked an eyebrow. "Like word won't get back to them if everybody at school knows you're still going out with Stuart? For this to work, we have to convince *everyone,* not just the *Echtrans.* Think about it."

With a sinking sensation in the pit of my stomach, I realized Sean was right. To truly abide by my agreement, I *would* have to make everyone—even Bri and Deb—believe I was with Sean instead of Rigel. How had I missed that detail?

My insides squeezed at the idea of everyone at school thinking I'd dumped Rigel to be with Sean. It would be even worse than our other fake breakup, because now I'd be the bad guy. I could just imagine what Trina would say. At least Rigel would know the truth. And Molly. And there was one other super important bit.

"Part of my deal with the Council is that I'll *really* still be with Rigel, just not in public. So I'm only going to play along in front of everybody if I get alone time with him on a regular basis."

That finally erased Sean's grin. "You don't expect me to help with *that,* do you?"

"I at least don't expect you to sabotage it. And yeah, if you or Molly—or your parents—can help, I'll really appreciate it."

He grumbled but didn't outright refuse. I took that as a good sign and changed the subject.

"So, where's your dear Uncle Allister? Dare I hope he's left Jewel?" I'd heard yesterday at the Stuarts' that he'd been removed from the Council but I'd been too wrapped up in Rigel to ask for details.

"Didn't they tell you?" Sean seemed surprised. "He's been exiled to Montana for what he and Governor Lennox tried to do. Sounds like they're both going to face an inquest over this business."

I blinked. "Who told you that?"

"Mum. They invited her to take Uncle Allister's place on the *Echtran* Council, since her bloodline is the same as his, plus she did all that resistance stuff on Mars. She agreed."

"Really? That's great!" The idea of never having to see Allister again cheered me enormously. Mrs. O'Gara *was* an obvious choice to replace him—and she liked me, which couldn't hurt, though I knew she'd always put the Nuathan people first.

When Mrs. O'Gara brought in tea and cookies a few minutes later, I immediately congratulated her on being appointed to the Council.

"Thank you, dear. I'm just happy you're home safe and that everything has, ah, worked out." Clearly she knew about my compromise, but she managed not to look at all smug about it, unlike Sean.

Even better, she then promised to help convince my aunt to loosen up my restriction so I could spend more time with Rigel "as a friend." Startled and pleased, I thanked her profusely, then haltingly proposed we tell the *Echtran* community Rigel was my personal bodyguard, to explain him staying close to me. It was an idea Rigel had come up with while walking me home, though of course I didn't say that.

Mrs. O nodded after only a moment's hesitation, surprising me again. "That's actually quite a clever plan, dear. Particularly since everyone already knows about the role he and his family played in protecting you from Faxon's forces."

Molly sighed and murmured that it sounded terribly romantic. Though Sean scowled, it gave me hope that Molly, at least, would be a willing ally in helping me get some private time with Rigel.

Maybe this compromise thing wouldn't be so bad after all.

46

fedhmiu (FEY-mew): *implementation; application*

The next day Sean joined Rigel and me on the way to lunch, deftly inserting himself between us. "So, guess we all need to figure out how this new compromise is going to work in practice, huh? I heard they might be putting hidden cameras in the halls and cafeteria and stuff, so we should all start playing our parts." He reached for my hand.

Interestingly, the tingle wasn't nearly as strong with Rigel right next to me as it had been at Thanksgiving, when I was seriously Rigel-deprived. Rigel, not surprisingly, started scowling.

"If we want it to be at *all* believable," I said, easing my hand out of Sean's, "it should be gradual, don't you think? How about we all just act like friends for a while first?"

Now it was Sean's turn to frown. "That doesn't sound like what you told . . . *them*. Is it?"

I swallowed. Unfortunately, he was right—again. The Council was watching me now, whether with cameras or the spies they already had in place, and would know if I went back on my word. I'd promised them I'd make it look like I was with Sean, and now I had to follow through. Putting it off wouldn't make it any easier.

"Okay, fine," I snapped, making no effort to hide my irritation. Those stupid cameras weren't up yet. "But there's no way I'm staying completely away from Rigel, even at school. He's supposedly my bodyguard now, remember? So you guys will have to work really hard to make it look like you're friends."

Neither Sean nor Rigel seemed to like that idea much, but after a moment they both grudgingly nodded.

For the first time in ages, they both sat at the same lunch table, one on either side of me. They did a surprisingly good job of acting like friends, too, talking about sports across me, with Bri offering frequent opinions from her side of the table. Their former animosity

313

was so well concealed that I only felt the occasional stab of jealousy from Rigel.

Then, without warning, Sean turned to me and said, like it was the most natural thing in the world, "So, M, winter formal? What do you say? Will you be my date?"

Of course that stopped all conversation cold, every single head at our table whipping around to stare at us.

Biting back my instinctive refusal, I hesitated, trapped by Sean's bright blue gaze while Rigel's stunned fury mounted from my other side.

Crap! What should I do? I thought desperately at him.

Immediately, I could feel him struggling to control the anger and jealousy that had exploded at Sean's invitation. *Dammit! I don't know. Why did he have to—?* He hesitated for a long moment while he continued to rein in his feelings, then slowly responded, *I think you have to say yes, M. You did make a deal. Sorry. I'll . . . try to behave.*

"Um, sure, Sean, I guess so," I finally stammered after what had to be the longest, most awkward pause in history. "Thanks." I even managed a pathetic attempt at a smile.

The staring didn't stop. "Whoa," Bri breathed, looking from Sean, to Rigel, to me, over and over. I wondered what she saw on Rigel's face, but didn't dare glance at him. Up and down the table there was muttering, the gist of which was, "Didn't see *that* coming."

Molly, sitting next to Bri, looked only slightly less startled and a lot more concerned. "Rigel?" she said tentatively.

"Hey, it's fine," he said almost jovially, in stark contrast to the emotions rolling off him in gradually diminishing waves. "Actually . . . do you have a date yet, Molly?"

Her eyes got wide. "Oh! Um, not—I mean, I sort of half-promised, but—"

"Wanna go with me?"

Her eyes got wider.

"You know, as friends?" he added.

At those words, Molly's panicked confusion gave way to a smile. "Friends? Sure, Rigel, that would be great. Maybe we can all, um, ride together?" She looked at her brother and me.

"Yeah, let's do that," I said before Sean could refuse. Not that he necessarily would have, but I wasn't taking chances. "We'll all go together. As friends."

Sean quirked an eyebrow at me, clearly not as pleased by my amendment as Molly had been by Rigel's, but he didn't dispute it. "Sounds great."

Rigel and Sean both sat at my lunch table every day after that, and though they couldn't completely resist occasional minor sniping at each other, they mostly acted pretty civil. Molly and Deb were clearly delighted. Bri occasionally pouted a bit because Sean no longer flirted with her, but with so many football *and* basketball players regularly vying for her and Deb's—and Molly's—attention, she couldn't be *too* upset.

I found it easier and easier to pretend we were just one big circle of friends, even if I had to silently reassure Rigel about a dozen times a day that the new closeness between Sean and me was still strictly for show. Our table quickly became the most popular in the lunchroom, and I couldn't help gloating a bit when I caught occasional glimpses of Trina's jealous face.

Now that I was supposedly going out with Sean instead of Rigel, Aunt Theresa finally caved about my restriction, helped along by Mrs. O's "persuasion"—and my own. Rigel started coming over to the O'Garas' house some evenings, where he was allowed to sit next to me and even hold my hand while we studied and talked— something we could no longer do at school. It was always a wonderful relief, no matter how much Sean glowered.

One afternoon all four of us even went to Dream Cream together, just like I'd once fantasized back when Sean and Molly first arrived in Jewel—except that I had to sit next to Sean, with Rigel and Molly across the table from us. At least Rigel and I were able to carry on our own silent conversation during the lulls in the spoken one.

So while things weren't ideal, they weren't nearly as bad as I'd feared when I'd first made my compromise with the Council.

Even so, the winter formal was awkward.

Rigel's parents had volunteered to chaperone, so they drove the four of us to the dance. They knew all about the compromise and why I'd made it, which was good, since otherwise they'd probably hate me for what I was doing to Rigel.

"Emileia has to be home by eleven," Dr. Stuart reminded us before we parted at the gym doors, "so we'll meet back here at a quarter till. Have fun."

We all headed into the gym, which was festooned with paper snowflakes for the occasion. Fittingly, Jewel's first real snowfall of the winter was predicted to start later that evening.

You look amazing, Rigel thought to me for at least the third time since he'd seen me in my "new" (another of Bri's castoffs) electric blue sheath. It fitted me well, especially since I'd filled out a tiny bit in the right places over the past couple of months.

Ditto, I thought back with a grin. Rigel was heart-stoppingly gorgeous in his black three-piece suit. I was irresistibly reminded of Homecoming, my last (and first) dance with a date: Rigel. Everything had seemed absolutely perfect then, the bad guys vanquished and any Sovereign duties still comfortably far in the future. What a difference a couple of months had made.

"So, dance?" Sean asked, looking down at me with almost as much admiration in his eyes as I felt from Rigel.

It was a fast song, so I had no qualms about agreeing. Rigel and Molly hit the floor nearby, and a moment later Bri and Deb and their dates joined our circle, all of us exchanging compliments along with greetings.

By the end of the song I was feeling much less weird about the whole "first date with Sean" thing . . . but then a slow one started.

Even as I tensed, Sean put his arms around me with a grin I was sure would make Rigel want to punch him.

Yeah, but I won't. I don't think.

I resisted the urge to look around at Rigel's thought, instead murmuring to Sean, "Don't overdo it, okay?"

"C'mon," he said, still grinning as he moved me in time to the music. "It's me."

"Exactly." I tried to force myself to relax again.

Though now and then I felt one of his hands slide an inch or two up and down my back, Sean was a gentleman, never straying into questionable territory. As for me, I kept one hand totally motionless on his shoulder, the other on his upper arm.

"That wasn't so bad, was it?" Sean murmured when the song ended.

I rewarded him with a grudging smile. "I guess not. Thanks."

Several fast dances followed. Since it was common knowledge Molly and Rigel had come as friends, she was soon asked to dance by various upperclassmen and we barely saw her again. The rest of us swapped off occasionally, too, Rigel, partnering mostly cheerleaders —including Trina, once—as well as a dance each with Bri and Deb. More than an hour into the formal, he came up to me as I finished a dance with Jimmy Franklin.

"Just one, you think?" he asked softly.

I glanced at Sean, talking easily with Amber, the cheerleader he'd just danced with. "Sure. I don't think one dance counts as cheating, do you?"

His smile answered me just as another slow number started. Though it was bound to piss off Sean, I went ahead and put my hands on Rigel's shoulders as his went around my waist. *We just can't get carried away,* I thought to him, *as much as I wish we could.*

Got it. You feel incredible, though, M. I love you so much!

We spent the dance carefully *not* clinging to each other while we exchanged increasingly passionate thoughts, so that when the music stopped, I was flushed despite our (physical) restraint.

As expected, Sean was frowning when came up to us a second later. "Had to be a slow one, huh?"

"We didn't plan it that way," I told him. "Anyway, it's over now."

Another slow song began and his frown disappeared. "This one's mine, then. C'mon."

This time he held me tighter than for the last slow dance, and once I had to nudge his hand upward when it strayed a little too low on my back. Rigel, partnered with Molly again, sent something like a growl into my mind. I hoped he wasn't being *too* obvious, watching me while dancing with other girls.

"Thanks, M," Sean said when the song ended. "That was great. *You're* great." He still had his arms around me, his bright blue eyes sparkling down into mine.

I smiled back and something in his expression changed. Deepened. Slowly, he lowered his face toward mine. I realized just in time what he intended and pulled back, alarm shooting through me.

"Sean!" I hissed. "That's *not* in the bargain. Not now, not ever."

He straightened abruptly, frowning again. "I just . . . Sorry. Just wanted to make it look good?"

I shook my head, not buying that for an instant. "We don't have to make it look *that* good. Got it?"

"Yeah," he said heavily, an intense, hopeless longing painfully clear on his face. "Got it."

I couldn't help feeling a twinge of . . . of something. Because I did like Sean and hated hurting him, even unintentionally. But not nearly as much as I would hate hurting Rigel.

"Okay, then," I said. "Let's get some punch."

Nothing else happened to put me on edge for the rest of the evening, other than the occasional frustration I felt from Rigel—and definitely shared. I knew he was remembering Homecoming, too.

At ten forty-five on the dot, we met the Stuarts at the side door and headed out of the school to find snow falling thickly.

"Sean, look!" Molly squealed, and I suddenly remembered they'd never seen real snow before.

"Pretty, isn't it?" said Dr. Stuart. "We may have a white Christmas after all. I'm glad we brought the four-wheel-drive."

I glanced up at Sean, who had stopped dead at the sight, and saw he was looking paler than usual. "You okay?" I asked, trying not to let the least trace of laughter betray itself in my voice.

He opened and closed his mouth a couple of times, then nodded. "Yeah. Sure. It's just . . . There's so *much* of it!"

Now I did laugh, as did everyone else, even Molly. "Rain comes down a lot harder, and that doesn't seem to bother you," I pointed out.

Sean shrugged, starting to look sheepish. "Yeah, well, you didn't see me the first time it rained in Ireland after we got there."

"He was a mess," Molly told us, earning a glare from her brother. "I mean, all of us had to get used to it, but Sean—"

"Yeah, so I have a thing about stuff falling from the sky," he cut in. "Sue me. I'm getting over it. Mostly."

I put a hand on his sleeve, feeling guilty now for laughing, especially since he'd mentioned his near-phobia to me once before.

"Hey, it's okay. I guess it would take some getting used to after living your whole life where . . . well, stuff never *does* fall from the, um, sky." I still couldn't quite imagine living under a fake sky, even though I'd seen lots of pictures by now.

"Thanks." He put his hand over mine and I resisted the urge to pull away, even though I could feel Rigel's irritation radiating from Molly's other side. "I hope I can show it to you someday."

Now I did take my hand off his arm, but casually, not like I was jerking it away. "I hope so too," I said lightly. "Someday."

And I did. As long as "someday" was years away.

Or decades, Rigel added to my mental comment, with a touch of that all-too-familiar sadness.

I did my best to ignore it, determined to think positively. Everything *would* work out for the two of us, one way or another. Someday.

47

toachai (TO-uh-kay): *future; destiny*

The formal marked the start of winter break, which was both good and bad. Rigel and Sean and I didn't have to pretend at school for the next two weeks, plus I was spared Trina's endless barbs about my "fickleness." I was used to Trina being mean, but her sniping was a constant reminder that my compromise was hurting Rigel—which made *me* feel mean.

The downside was, now I only saw Rigel every couple of days, at the O'Garas' house, though it did mean more time for me to safely think about stuff I had to guard from him—like those Grentl aliens. Not that I really *wanted* to think about them, the idea was so terrifying.

Even so, Rigel sometimes sensed there was something I wasn't telling him. He pretended to accept it when I finally said, *Sorry, I can't. I would if I could,* but I knew it bothered him. I also knew he suspected it had to do with Sean, no matter how much I insisted it didn't.

Christmas Eve, the O'Garas had a small party and invited me, my aunt and uncle, and the Stuarts over, as well as the two Council members who had recently moved to Jewel, Breann and Malcolm.

Because my aunt and uncle were there, no Martian politics were discussed. That made it feel much more like a normal, festive occasion though, with my aunt there, Rigel and I couldn't hold hands like we usually did at the O'Garas.' Still, we were together, and given how close we'd recently come to never seeing each other again, that was good enough. Almost.

I hope we can get some real alone time soon, Rigel responded to that errant thought, reminding me just how attuned he was—and how careful I needed to be. *Maybe we can meet at the arboretum sometime this week?*

Let's make it happen, I thought back firmly. With our less frequent contact this week, I was missing him even more than I'd expected to.

Around nine-thirty, Aunt Theresa started making noises about how late it was getting. As if that was a signal, Mrs. O'Gara exchanged a significant look with Breann, then turned to my aunt.

"Theresa, I have a favor to ask of you. I saved it for tonight, hoping it might be a sort of Christmas present for Marsha."

"A favor?" Aunt Theresa was clearly surprised. So was I.

"Yes. We're planning to spend a month or two in Ireland this summer. Molly and Sean would very much like for Marsha to come along, and so would we. It would be a wonderful cultural experience for Marsha, as well. I've checked into study-abroad opportunities there, and I'm fairly certain she'll be able to qualify. Will you consider letting her apply? Something like this on her resume could greatly improve her chances of a college scholarship."

A jolt of alarm from Rigel mirrored my own.

Meanwhile, my aunt frowned, first at me, then at Mrs. O. "Ireland? For the summer? How much . . . that is, surely it would be very expensive?"

"Not at all!" Mrs. O'Gara assured her quickly. "We're staying with friends, and she would be able to stay with us. If her application is accepted, her travel expenses would be covered, as well. Your only responsibility would be to get her a passport."

Aunt Theresa looked at Uncle Louie, who, predictably, just shrugged. Getting no help there, she turned back to Mrs. O'Gara. "We'll have to discuss it, of course, but I suppose she can apply. *If* she's accepted to the program, we can work out the details then. I do appreciate you researching this opportunity for her."

In response to a glance from her mother, Molly jumped up. "Oh, thank you, Mrs. Truitt! I'll have a *much* better a time if M can come! We'll take super, super good care of her, I promise."

Rigel and I had been struggling to calm each other during the whole exchange. Was this yet another ploy to separate us?

I won't go without you! I promised him silently. Then, aloud, "Wow, that would be really cool! Ireland!" I hoped I'd injected a believable amount of enthusiasm into my voice.

"Yes," Mrs. O'Gara said, looking me directly in the eye. "Molly is very anxious to show you where she and Sean were born and grew up. I'm sure you'll find it . . . fascinating."

Realization hit me like a splash of cold water and it was all I could do to keep the smile on my face.

They weren't talking about Ireland at all.

"I'm . . . I'm sure I will," I stammered, shooting a half-terrified look at Rigel, wishing more than ever we could be holding hands right now. "Someday" was suddenly much, much sooner than expected!

I was stunned, outraged. But then excitement irresistibly bubbled up inside me. Because my compromise with the Council meant they *had* to let Rigel come along. Didn't it?

Mrs. O'Gara watched me shrewdly, possibly guessing my dilemma.

"Perhaps Rigel can apply, as well," she suggested to the Stuarts after only the slightest pause. "I'm sure Sean and Molly would enjoy that, given they're all becoming such good friends."

Sean's smile suddenly became a teensy bit less broad. "Um, yeah. That would be really great."

"We'll look into it," Dr. Stuart said so smoothly I could see she wasn't nearly as surprised as I'd been. Ninety percent of my alarm disappeared, replaced by eager anticipation—which Rigel reflected back to me.

"I can't wait," I said, no longer faking my enthusiasm at all.

"Well, that's just lovely," Mrs. O'Gara exclaimed, beaming around the room. "Now, why don't we all have some hot cocoa and sing a few Christmas carols?"

ABOUT BRENDA HIATT

Brenda Hiatt is the author of nearly twenty novels (so far), including traditional Regency romance, time travel romance, historical romance, and humorous mystery. She is as excited about her STARSTRUCK series as she's ever been about any of her books. In addition to writing, Brenda is passionate about embracing life to the fullest, to include scuba diving (she has over 60 dives to her credit), Taekwondo (where she recently achieved her 2nd degree black belt), hiking, traveling, and pursuing new experiences and skills.

Starcrossed is the second book in Brenda Hiatt's STARSTRUCK series. If you enjoyed reading it, she hopes you will consider leaving a review wherever you buy or talk about books. For the latest information about upcoming books in the STARSTRUCK series as well as Brenda's other books, please visit www.brendahiatt.com, where you can subscribe to her newsletter and connect with her on Facebook, Twitter or Tumblr.

Made in the USA
Lexington, KY
06 November 2015